WINGS OF STEELE
The Series

EPIC SCIENCE FICTION ACTION-ADVENTURE NOVELS

"I've read a lot, a whole lot, and this is the best of the best when it comes to science fiction. It is not just a fantasy thrown together but a well thought out, well written plot that covers more events, action and comedy than I could ever imagine. A word of warning, these books are addictive. I neglect a lot of other interests by getting so caught up in them that I find myself starting the first book and reading them again and again and again..." Bob. H.

"Ready or not, each book on this series just grabs you and drags you in, and this volume has not changed that. Jeff Burger is a talented author whose writing style puts you right into the action next to the character. A mix of factual places and events makes it eerily realistic. This series is a must-read for any sci fi or space opera fan." Cheri P.

"I seriously don't understand why this author hasn't been scooped up by a major publisher yet... This series is as good or better than much of the mainstream sci fi stuff out there. And these books are meaty! Easily enough material to be 2 novels each... I know it takes him a while to produce, but the wait is worth it! I'm looking forward to book 5." Joe B.

"This series goes so much further than sci fi... it's better described as sci fi-space opera-action adventure-alien spy thriller-murder mystery. And when you least expect it, it has humor too. The character interaction is wonderfully believable." Marilyn S.

"No spoilers here, but as a Mason, I can see symbolism and allegory woven throughout the series. It's quite good, and without revealing too much, I see it leading to a much bigger picture somewhere. A very subtle, da Vinci Code - in space. I can tell he's in it for the long game; I'm really interested to see if it's going where I think it is. Whether I'm right or not, it's a great ride and a blast to read!" David N.

"Jeff Burger blurs the line between fact and fiction and blends the two together so well, it feels organic, real. He does a tremendous job of painting chaos, discord, mistrust and confusion in this newest book. Anyone who has been in the military knows plans don't survive the first engagement and things seem to fall apart faster than a cheap Chinese toy. But to their credit, the characters adapt, overcome, persevere. And I was rooting for them every step of the way." Gunny

WINGS *of* STEELE
DARK COVER

A NOVEL BY
JEFFREY J. BURGER

Other books in the series...
Book 1 - WINGS of STEELE - Destination Unknown
Book 2 - WINGS of STEELE - Flight of Freedom
Book 3 - WINGS of STEELE - Revenge and Retribution

www.wingsofsteele.com

COPYRIGHT

First Print Edition November 2016

Published in the United States by Templar Press. Templar Press and the mounted Templar Knight colophon are registered trademarks and may not be reproduced.

TEMPLAR PRESS

Registered with the Library of Congress
ISBN-13: 978-0-9983408-0-7 (Templar Press)
ISBN-10: 0-9983408-0-4

Cover artwork, copyright © 2016 Jeffrey J. Burger
WINGS of STEELE logo, copyright © 2016 Jeffrey J. Burger
www.wingsofsteele.com

DEDICATION

I want to thank all my readers who have enjoyed the Wings of Steele Series of adventures and offered their support, enthusiasm, and interest in the continuation of the series. Please remember, as a self-published author, I thrive on your feedback and reviews.

To Fritz; I will miss you - your personality, your energy, your spirit. Everyone who met you fell in love with your charm and canine charisma. At 11 years old you left too soon and too quickly, leaving me totally unprepared for your departure from my life. I choose to believe dogs have souls, put on this Earth to guide worthy humans with your love, kindness and canine wisdom, destined to meet again.

May you rest comfortably in God's hands.

TABLE OF CONTENTS

PROLOGUE

THE WHITE HOUSE, WASHINGTON D.C. : *OVAL OFFICE*

Arms folded across his chest sitting with his feet up on the Resolute Desk, his mood rapidly darkening, the President of the United States watched the live television broadcast with the rest of the world. Which to his dismay, seemed to be *on every damned channel.* Wind whipped the rain against the windows of the Oval Office behind him, gentle flashes of light rolling through the clouds in the darkened sky, illuminating the silhouette of the Washington Monument in the distance.

Broken in frustration, the TV's remote control lay scattered in pieces across the surface of the desk. This was not just any desk... Created from timbers of the British Arctic Exploration ship, *H.M.S. Resolute*, the desk had been given as a gift from Queen Victoria to President Rutherford B. Hayes in 1880. The desk was an illustrative paradigm of British and American history dating back to its roots in 1850. Part of the expedition searching for the missing British explorer, Sir John Franklin in 1852, the ship Resolute was abandoned in 1854 when it became trapped in the shifting and growing Arctic ice. Recovered in 1855 by Captain James Buddington of the American whaling ship *George Henry*, the Resolute was returned to Queen Victoria in 1856.

Unfortunately, the man with his feet resting on the ornate hand-carved desk was unconcerned with its beauty, colorful history or significance. It wasn't that he was the first president to ever prop his feet up on the desk, no, it had been used by almost every president since Rutherford, save for Johnson, Nixon and Ford. But he was the first president who was so disconnected from American history, tradition, or culture, that in his eyes it was nothing more than an old piece of furniture. But then again, that's what one might expect from an illegal alien guilty of planetary subversion. And not just any alien, an *interstellar* criminal. A narcissist so self-centered, so callous, nothing mattered except his own agenda... his mission... something he never shared with anyone - except his Senior Adviser. Even his wife and children didn't know who, or what, he really was.

The President's Senior Adviser and Executive Press Secretary watched the broadcast with him from one of the pale yellow sofas near the center of the room. His Senior Adviser sipped her coffee and set the mug back down on the coffee table with a scrutinizing eye studying his reactions to the content of the news conference, "There's got to be something we can do. To stop the broadcast I mean..."

The President's eyes never left the screen, "Short of shutting down the entire power grid, no."

It wasn't a sarcastic or angry response, it was surprisingly matter-of-fact. It was obvious to her he was concentrating on the broadcast, listening for the unspoken, analyzing everything, thinking ahead. "That's not impossible, we *could* arrange that..." she observed.

He glanced over at her, the first time his eyes had left the screen since the broadcast began, a blank, expressionless, uncaring look on his face, "I never said *I couldn't*..." There seemed to be more he wanted to say but his concentration went back to the news conference. "It wouldn't change anything..." he grumbled.

"What's our exit strategy?" she probed.

The President glanced over at his Senior Adviser before shifting his gaze to his Executive Press Secretary. "Give us some privacy..." he said flatly.

The Press Secretary rose and nodded silently, gathering his notes and suit jacket draped across the arm of the couch before heading toward the door. He wasn't exactly sure what was going on in there and he was pretty certain he didn't want to know. Closing the door behind him, he nodded to the two Secret Service agents standing in the corridor outside the Oval Office. He hadn't been the Press Secretary for more than six months but he knew enough to know there was something highly secretive going on. And not knowing what it was, meant not having to worry about spilling the beans when he was feeding the press their nearly daily portion of official bullshit.

■ ■ ■

The President dropped his feet off the desk and stood up stretching his lanky frame, turning his back on the flat screen TV and his Senior Adviser, "I don't *have* an exit strategy..."

"You mean, *we*, don't you?" she snapped.

9

"Whatever," he grumbled, waving his hand dismissively. He moved to the window and watched the rain fall on the south lawn, his hands stuffed into his pockets.

She stood up and smoothed her tailored navy blue skirt, "Maybe you should have spent less time *vacationing* and more time concentrating on the job!" she replied sharply.

He spun around angrily, "Get off my back you shrew," he pointed at her. "Who knew these people would be so damned hard to motivate..."

"You underestimated them..."

"I didn't underestimate anything dammit, I followed the plan. If it's anyone's fault, it's theirs," he waved at the ceiling. "They're the ones who created the plan. And who expected the UFW to show up?" He thumbed at the broadcast on the flat screen, "This asshole Steele has screwed everything... The Council couldn't have warned us?"

"Oh stop whining," she waved, "and let's try to figure out how to get out of this mess."

The President leaned with both hands on the Resolute Desk and glared at her, "Have you *forgotten* you're talking to the *President of the United States?*"

She stood defiantly with her hands on her hips, "You've gotten far too attached to this role... And have *you* forgotten you're talking to a *superior...*"

"*SIR!*" The door of the Oval Office burst open from the corridor, a flood of Secret Service agents pouring into the room. "We have to go, Mr. President..."

The President straightened up, "What? Why? What's going on?"

"NORAD, sir. There's been a nuclear launch..." Two men rounded the desk another sealed the room from the corridor. A hidden door opened in a wall to reveal a narrow, dimly lit corridor, an agent holding it open motioning everyone inside.

"Renegade secure," announced one of the agents, talking into his sleeve. "Bonus, Dear Abby secure. Exit route; *Underground Railroad.*"

"Let's go Mr. President," said one of the agents guiding him towards the secret exit. "We don't have much time. You too, ma'am," he waved.

The President grabbed his suit jacket off of the back of his chair before he was escorted through the doorway and into the narrow corridor. "Who... what..."

"North Korea, sir. D.C. is the target."

"What about my girls? They're shopping..."

"The second detail has your family, sir. They will be taking a different exit and will meet up with us later."

"The football, who has the football?" asked the Senior Adviser.

An agent pointed the way as the corridor slanted downward and took a turn, "Meeting us at the train, ma'am."

"The V.P.?"

"Iowa, ma'am. He's secure."

"Can't we just shoot it down?" asked the President.

"NORAD said all our satellites are hobbled, 20th Space Control is basically blind."

"Dammit. How much time do we have?"

The agent checked his watch, "Twenty-five minutes. Strategic Air Command has launched assets..."

"I don't understand, wouldn't the Situation Room be safe?" The President allowed himself to be steered past an elevator, into another downward sloping corridor.

"Separation of assets, Mr. President. The COG System has been activated, we can't keep all our eggs in one basket."

"I'm going to pretend you didn't just refer to me as an egg..." frowned the President.

■ ■ ■

Taking an ancient elevator in a crisis, no matter how well maintained, is begging for trouble. The Secret Service opted for the ten flights of stairs to the lower level. That delivered them to the train platform over a hundred feet below the White House; the air damp and heavy, musty, smelling of earth and rock, some of the walls slick with moisture. A two-car train sat on one of two sets of tracks; silver, bullet-shaped at both ends so the engineer could drive in either direction, a tunnel heading in both directions disappearing into the darkness.

Two men in suits stood on the platform, one carrying a bulky leather satchel, the other the engineer who disappeared inside as soon as he saw the group approaching from the opening in the natural rock wall at the far end of the platform. The agent carrying the nuclear football glanced at his watch and waved them inside, "Hurry, hurry, we've only got about fifteen minutes."

The inside of the train was well appointed with comfortable loungers, and well equipped, like the rail version of Air Force One. As soon as the doors closed, the train began to move, the electric engines humming as it eased away from the platform. "Hello everyone, this is the engineer, please find a seat so I can bring her up to speed..."

The President chose a forward-facing chair and leaned back, "We're cutting this a little close, aren't we?"

The agent sitting in the chair beside his waved at the train around them, "She does nearly ninety at speed and we'll descend another hundred feet or so. We'll be about twenty miles out and under about two-hundred feet of concrete, rock, and earth, Mr. President. We'll be perfectly safe."

"How long..?"

"We'll be at the Greenbrier Hotel in about two hours. We may experience periods of communications blackout as we make the run, but the Greenbrier is fully equipped with a Situation Room, bunker and complete accommodations for over a thousand people..."

The President's Adviser cocked her head to one side, "I thought the Greenbrier was no longer in service..."

The lead Agent grimaced, "Some clown from the Washington Post wrote an article and blew the cover of the bunker in 1992. President H. W. Bush ordered it decommissioned shortly after that. In 2001, President G. W. Bush invested twenty million dollars and ordered it silently reactivated shortly after 9-11... It was ready for use by the end of 2002."

"But I thought they held tours through the bunker..." commented the Senior Adviser.

"They do," he replied, "but only a small portion of the bunker has ever been open to the public, it's immense. The rest of it has been updated. It's secure, stocked and ready for use; hidden in plain sight. G. W. took a gamble and it paid off."

Holding on to his communications console against the train's acceleration, the agent manning that station turned in his seat, "There's been another launch..."

"Who?" asked the President.

"Iran. They're targeting Israel."

"Hmm," grunted the President, looking neither surprised or disturbed, "Bibi's going to have to deal with it himself; we've got our own issues..."

The President's Senior Adviser indicated the leather satchel containing the nuclear football, "Is it time to consider North Korea's punishment?" Her lips and eyes held a hint of a smile to anyone who could read her face.

WINGS of STEELE – DARK COVER

CHAPTER ONE

AGERON PASS SYSTEM: DEEP BLACK, SCAVENGER TWO :
ONCE UPON A TIME

Cheriska Skye's *Kondor* wasn't a pretty ship with all its rust, wear, age and dents but it was purposeful. A salvage reclaimer was never built to be stylish, fast or particularly comfortable, it was built to do recovery and salvage work, sometimes in unfriendly territory. Extendable gantry arms, claws, heavy armor, it was an ungainly, clumsy looking beast of a craft... but it got the job done. Scavenger Two had served its previous owner reliably for many years before Cheriska won it in a high-stakes Ruge game... and now it served her; unlike her smaller, Scavenger One, which seemed to spend more time in the hanger eating up her spare parts resources than out in space making her money. She never did tell her clone sister, Cheriska Too, whether she had won the card game fair and square or not.

It wasn't that she was trying to keep it secret, it's just that Too had a somewhat different view on certain things, whereas Cheriska was, let's just say, morally flexible when it came to business and acquisitions. She never cheated an honest man, but a man trying to take advantage of her... or cheating at cards, well, he was open game. *Especially* if he tried to cheat at *her* game, on *her* home turf. That was just stupid.

Sitting in the Kondor's command chair, Cheriska reached to her left and backed the ship's throttle down, angling toward the marker on her navscreen of the abandoned party yacht. The Kondor's small bridge sat three crew members; captain, first officer and navigator, but for the run from Rikovik's Reef to Ageron Pass and back, it was hardly necessary. She reached over to the empty first officer's chair and turned one of the monitors toward her so she could watch the recovery cameras. There were no fancy holo-screens, either on the command chairs or a big view screen. Just cockpit glass and flat-screen monitors. It was simple but everything worked and that's what counted.

She keyed her comm, "Coming up on target, Mouse. You about ready?"

Mouse's seven-foot frame barely fit in the chair for the gantry crane command station. "Got it, Boss. Gantry on line, arm live..." came the voice over her headset.

"Hold on Mouse..." Cheriska zoomed in on her left screen, inspecting the damage on the yacht. "Eeew," she breathed.

"What's that?" came his voice in her headset again.

Cheriska's mind ran through a slew of possibilities and results. "Nothing, Mouse. Listen, stow the claw, we'll only crush this thing..."

"That'll make it easier to fit into the hold..." he joked.

"I don't want *scrap*, Mouse, I want *parts*."

"I'm looking at this thing, boss, I don't see parts, I see scrap. Let's just stuff it and go."

"Use the capture net, Mouse."

"Aww, I hate that damn thing..."

"*Net it,* Mouse."

His mic was open when he groaned in exasperation. "Alright, *fine*. Stowing the arm."

Cheriska knew how much he loved the claw; a giant robotic arm that could cut, chew, crush, dismember, hold and manipulate. A perfect man-toy, what's not to love? The net on the other hand, would gently capture the wreck and pull it against the hull of the Kondor like a cocoon, where it would stay until they got back to the hangar at Deep Black.

It took her over two months to get approval from the Syndicate to salvage the yacht; they were more than happy to leave it where it drifted. But truthfully it was a navigation nuisance. And since it had passed the time-frame for abandonment, she could have legally scooped it up at her leisure. But she had to live with the Syndicate on Rikovik's Reef, it was wisest not to step on anyone's toes... especially since the Syndicate weren't folks overly concerned whether something was legal or not.

"A little closer, Boss, I'm still out of range."

Cheriska acknowledged Mouse and crabbed the Kondor slowly parallel with the crippled yacht, watching the recovery screen over on the first officers seat. When the capture markers lit green she nudged the handle of the maneuvering jets to bring the ship to a stop, "Looks good, Mouse."

"Got it, Boss, firing net..."

From her place on the bridge, Cheriska could barely hear the air-propelled rockets as they launched from the Kondor's hull, towing the net as it unraveled from its spool. She watched on the monitor as Mouse steered the rockets around the wreck, wrapping the net around it.

"Got it snagged."

"Good, reel it in..." she replied over the comm.

■ ■ ■

With the yacht snugged in against the Kondor's hull, Cheriska gently spun the ship around and headed back toward the Genesis Gate for Rikovik's Reef, leaving the camera monitor on so she could keep an eye on her external cargo. Her headset chirped, "Say Boss, you've been up there for quite a while, you tired? You want me to fly for a spell?"

She thumbed the comm button on her flight stick, "No I'm fine, Mouse. Get some rest, I'll call you if I need a break." Her keypad pipped as she set the coordinates for Rikovik's Reef while the Kondor approached the gate, the swirling colors of the jump event reaching out toward her, lacy tendrils of energy dancing across her ship. Properly aligned to the gate, she released the controls and let the ship fly itself, stretching her arms and legs from her seat. She relaxed and let her head nestle back against the headrest. Her fingers tapped across her console, pulling up communications, selecting a broadcast frequency. "Scavenger Two - Scavenger Two..." she waited for an acknowledgment and tried again. "This is Scavenger Two..."

"Scavenger Two, this is Deep Black, go ahead."

"We're on our way back."

"Did you make the pickup?"

"Yep. All in one piece, we netted it..."

"I bet Mouse loved that..."

■ ■ ■

The seemingly endless, satiny, translucent silver lining of the jump tunnel made Cheriska's eyelids heavy, the only feel of motion a gentle ripple here and there or a muted and blurred star, passing outside the tunnel. With the ship's navigation computer doing its thing, linked to the auto-cruise system, there seemed no harm in closing her eyes for a minute. The engines droned on, a persistent rattle somewhere fading into grayness...

The warm touch on her bare hand raised her consciousness level, producing an image in her mind's eye of Mouse at her side on the bridge.

15

"Watcha need, Mouse..." she mumbled nearly incoherently, her eyes still closed, on the edge of REM sleep.

"You should probably wake now, young lady... We need to talk."

The unfamiliar voice was deep and mellow, producing a jolt of panic, shocking her awake as the realization came that someone was holding her hand. Plagued by the fog of sleep, her mind fought to get her bearings and make sense of her surroundings. The man sitting next to her in the dark gray cloak, a hood obscuring much of his face, held her hand. Realizing she was no longer dreaming, her fight-or-flight response attempted to launch her out of her command chair for fighting room as her hands simultaneously searched her body for her pulse pistol. The jarring result was her painfully bouncing against the loose straps of her flight harness, producing a labored grunt as she bounced back into her seat.

Panic took over and she clawed at the harness release, stringing together an impressive array of choice epithets so foul, it would make most salvage men blush. Successfully releasing herself from the straps, she launched herself free from her seat only to realize his hand still firmly gripped her wrist, her free hand searching frantically for the absent pulse pistol that was usually strapped to her waist.

"*Easy* child, you have nothing to fear..." His free hand reached forward, covering her hand as he gradually released his grip on her wrist, letting her arm slide free so they were hand in hand; where he kept her firmly but without force. "*Calm*... no fear... deep breath." She blinked mechanically, drawing in deeply, an energy of calm washing over her. "Now," he glanced at her console, "I fear you may have upset something, you may want to check it."

Cheriska shot a glance over her shoulder out through the Kondor's windshield, the errant ship approaching the shimmering silver lining of the jump tunnel. "Shit!" she exclaimed, pulling her hand free and diving into her command seat. Grabbing the flight controls, she wrestling the ship back on course. Satisfied, she reset the navigation and auto-cruise systems. "By the Gods, that was close..." she sighed. Snapping back to the present, she turned angrily toward her visitor, "Who are you and just how the hellion did you get on my ship? What are you doing on my bridge? What do you want? Why are you here..?"

"Voorlak..." he replied calmly, ignoring the avalanche of questions.

"What?" she blurted incredulously.

"Who I am... Voorlak."

She blinked hard and waved her arms expressively, "Is that supposed to mean something to me?"

The bridge door slid open with a squeak, disappearing into the bulkhead and Mouse strolled in carrying a large mug of coffee, "Though you might like this... Who were you talking to?"

Cheriska rotated her seat to accept the coffee, doing a quick check over her shoulder at the empty second officer's seat. "Uhh... You must be hearing things, big man."

Mouse glanced in the direction she had looked and only saw the camera monitor showing the yacht nestled in the net. He shrugged and shook his head, "Ok... let me know if you need a break." He turned and walked out the way he came, the door sliding closed again, leaving her alone with her thoughts. *Perhaps she had imagined the entire thing...*

"As I was saying..." continued Voorlak, reappearing in the seat.

Cheriska jumped in her command chair, nearly spilling the hot coffee, "Dammit," she hissed angrily, "what the hellion *are you?*"

"Let me tell you a little story," he began, a snifter of Diterian Brandy in his hand.

■ ■ ■

Cheriska Skye waved her hand, "Wait a minute, wait a minute, are we talking fairy tales or real life?"

Voorlak broke into a subtle smile, his brandy snifter paused in mid-air, "Excuse the embellishment my dear, but I find it puts a certain whimsy into a tale. Yes, this is a true story..." He sipped the warm, crimson liquid before continuing. "Many years ago there were two brothers..."

"How many years ago?"

"A lifetime ago..."

Cheriska eyed the old man, his features hidden in the shadows of his cloak. "Your lifetime or mine?"

Voorlak sighed, "Older than yours, considerably younger than mine. May I proceed?"

"Please," she nodded.

"The brothers; Leõn and Alfano, were born of the same parents, raised in the same household but could not have grown up more different from one another. Leõn was a strong natural leader; his vision was to help people in all walks of life. His brother, Alfano, was an industrious, self-centered young

17

man, more interested in fame and fortune than the welfare of others. And to the dismay of his parents, a depraved womanizer."

"What about Leõn?" asked Cheriska.

"A refined gentleman capable of great charity. To the absolute delight of his parents and grandparents, he became the antithesis of his brother, marrying a delightful young woman and having three wonderful children."

"How nice," commented Cheriska rather offhandedly. She sipped her coffee and glanced at her instruments, "But I don't see what it has to do with me."

"Presumptuous of you to think this story was about you..."

She looked at him sideways, annoyed. "Well I assumed since you're sitting on *my* bridge, appearing from who-knows-where, to tell *me* a story, that it just *might* have something to do with *me!* Otherwise what's the point?"

"You're quite right, of course," he smiled. "But I need to tell the story in its entirety for you to understand the significance..."

Cheriska rolled her eyes, "I suppose." *How long was this story? How much of this am I going to have to endure? Couldn't he just get to the point?*

"Patience my dear. It will all be clear by the end of the story..."

Using her best Ruge face, she tried not to react. *Did he just read my thoughts?*

Voorlak took a sip of the dark red liquid from his snifter. "I am quite sure we'll be finished before your hair turns gray..."

Cheriska's eyes widened, "Hey, stop that!" she pointed at him, "Get out of my mind."

"Evolutionary hazard, I'm afraid," he apologized. "May I continue?"

She closed her eyes for a moment and scratched her head, "Yes... just stay out of my head."

"I will do my best," he nodded. "Let's see, where was I..? Ah yes... When King Toberus passed the crown to Leõn, the oldest of his two sons, Prince Alfano was, to say the least, disquieted with the King's decision. Alfano felt he was better suited for the position and he set out to prove it. Unfortunately, he lacked the personal integrity... to be perfectly honest, he had the morals of a jackal. A jackal that had the reproductive urges of a rabbit."

"Sounds like he had tremendous potential." Cheriska raised an eyebrow and glanced at the Ancient sideways, "Sarcasm..."

"Yes, I understand," he replied. "In between Alfano's entrepreneurial efforts and his quest to make the new King Leõn look bad in their father's eyes, his rampant debauchery produced a daughter with one unfortunate woman and later, two sons with another. Being part of the royal family gave him undeserved legitimacy, allowing him to garner investors for his endeavors he would never have gotten otherwise. Terribly self-important and forever busy with his affairs of business and the flesh, he had no time or desire to devote to unwanted children, especially a female. Not that it was much better for his sons but at least he didn't kill their mother..."

Cheriska shot him a glance, "He killed the mother of his daughter?"

"Quite. As an unwed mother she had the audacity to ask for some support for her daughter and in a rage he killed her. Unfortunately, it was never proven and he went on with his life.

"Oh my... What happened to the daughter?"

"I'll get to that," he waved. "King Toberus who was still alive at the time, was rather relieved that the Peacekeepers couldn't produce enough evidence as it would have reflected badly on the royal family. But Toberus knew the truth, he wasn't a stupid man. As a result, he wrote an edict that prevented Alfano from ever holding a royal or governmental position."

"Ouch."

Voorlak sipped his brandy. "Yes. But of course, well deserved..."

"No argument there," agreed Cheriska, finding herself drawn into the story. "What happened to the sons?"

"The royal family, aware of their situation, took it upon themselves to make sure the boys had a good life and a good education. Both of them became pilots as adults. But I'm getting ahead of myself..."

"The daughter?"

Voorlak patted her hand, "Soon, soon... As the boys grew up with the children of the royal family, Alfano was busy building an industrial and mining empire. But he never forgot what King Toberus did and he forever held it against King Leõn after Toberus passed, because Leõn refused to rescind the edict. Alfano began funneling his substantial finances out of the economy and transferring them off-world to avoid taxation and did whatever he could to stunt the economic growth of the monarchy."

"Like what?" inquired Cheriska.

"Inciting unrest. Using his substantial financial standings, he influenced public opinion, competed with local businesses in a way to damage their profitability, and sapped the economy by importing illegal off-world foreigners to overtax the government. Using his influence, he managed to bribe a few select government officials and even one of King Leõn's core advisers. Once he accomplished that, he was able to influence the King's decisions."

"But why? For what purpose?" Cheriska up-ended her coffee mug and drained what was left.

"Revenge. Alfano wanted to destroy the royal family and take over..."

"By the Gods..." whispered Cheriska. "That's truly evil..."

"Not as evil as what he did to the weaker of his two sons. One was strong-willed, the other was a follower, more impressionable. It is unconfirmed, but it is believed he convinced this young man to murder two of the King's children to prevent an heir from being present. Remember these were children who all grew up together..."

"Despicable," breathed Cheriska, pulling on her lower lip. "Wait, I thought you said Leõn had *three* children."

Voorlak tilted his head, stroking his gray beard, "He did. But the oldest daughter had gone missing and was presumed dead. *Pirates*. Which was convenient and a perfect cover for the murder of the other two. I cannot fathom what torture it must have been for that young man to murder his childhood friends; a truly flawed individual with a fractured mind. Alfano had done some serious psychological damage to that young man."

Cheriska's mind was doing its best to put all the pieces together.

"No," joked Voorlak, "you are not the King's missing daughter."

It was only wishful thinking but it was on the tip of her mind. "You said you weren't going to do that..." she pointed.

"I didn't have to my dear, it was all over your face." Cheriska harrumphed and the old man continued, "Assaulted from many sides, the economy finally collapsed, the government was overrun, and the King and Queen were assassinated, never knowing the fate of their children, leaving the entire planet in chaos."

"Not much to take over, then," commented Cheriska.

"No there wasn't," admitted the Ancient. "But then again, Alfano never realized his dream. He never witnessed the culmination of his grand plan, having disappeared several years beforehand. Of course, once all the machinations were set in motion, much of it carried on by its own momentum..."

Cheriska's eyes went wide, "So it was all for nothing?"

"More or less. Although in the wisdom of the Universe, for every action there is a reaction and nothing is ever truly lost, but merely recycled. We are left to reflect on the past and remain vigilant to avoid repeating the ills and mistakes of those before us."

She shrugged, staring intently at him with one sparkling blue eye and one green eye. "OK, you lost me."

The old man's brandy snifter was suddenly full again, "You can take from something negative and make it positive. You want to avoid taking something positive and creating something negative..."

"Yeah, OK, that didn't help..."

"When Alfano disappeared, his money sat in limbo for some time before the financial institution had to account for the ownership or pay some rather massive penalties on it. The FreeRanger banks operate differently than those of the UFW..."

"Oh, I'm *well* aware of that," commented Cheriska with a look of distaste.

"So," continued Voorlak, "unable to locate Alfano, and confirm his existence, they began to seek out his next of kin..."

She watched him intently, hanging on every word. "His sons..."

"No, they were born *later*," corrected the old man. "*You* were the first born. And since your mother was dead, the money was to go to..."

Cheriska blinked, motionless, her mind trying to absorb and process that information. "That's not possible," she blurted, shaking her head. "My mother is still alive!"

"Rafaella is not your mother, child. She is your aunt; the sister of your mother. She rescued you from an orphanage on Darius a couple years after your mother's death. It took that long for her to find out and get to you."

"I was never in an orphanage..."

Voorlak bowed his head momentarily, "I'm afraid your memory of anything in your life before living with your aunt and uncle was cleared and rewritten with more pleasant events." He stroked his beard, "Rafaella felt the trauma of your mother's murder and abandonment at the orphanage was best buried."

"But, but, money... I've made my own *money*. I busted my ass for it," she replied defiantly.

"And there is no doubt you've done well for yourself..."

"But?"

Voorlak pulled at his beard, he knew he had to disclose everything. "But... you didn't do it alone."

"What do you *mean?*" she said angrily, her brow knitting.

"Cheriska Too has been a great partner..." he commented.

21

Cheriska nodded, her expression softening, "Well yes, of course. My sister has been wonderful. Mother had her cloned from me because my parents couldn't have any more children. We were rather well off and mother wanted me to have a sibling..."

"Cheriska Too handles your inventory, transactions, investments, banking and finances for all your businesses," offered the old man. "And you handle the personnel, product acquisitions and hands-on operations..."

"Yes..." she replied, curious as to where this was going.

"And you've never seen the statements, reports or accounts."

"I've never *had to...*" she frowned.

"What do you estimate as your holdings?"

Cheriska's eyes dropped to her instrument panel, not really seeing it, her mind trying to construct an educated evaluation. "Businesses, inventory and accounts..." She looked back up, "About fifty-million credits... When we started, mother and father gave us a couple million credits to start us out..."

Voorlak took a measured sip of his Diterian Brandy, the warm liquid slipping down his throat. He shook his head slowly, "No dear, your aunt and uncle are ordinary people; not poor, but certainly not rich enough to provide you with that kind of capitol for your ventures. The money is yours and always has been. You *started* with nearly fifty-million. Your mother released the remaining contents of the funds abandoned by Alfano, to start you out. It had been assembled into a trust for you by the bank. Your *current* financial standing exceeds three-hundred-million."

Cheriska looked at him blankly, seeing his mouth move, hearing the sound but not totally comprehending his words, *"What?"* she said flatly.

"More than three-hundred-million credits. Cheriska Too's creation was a condition required by the bank releasing the funds to your aunt and uncle, as a guardian ad litem loyal only to you, to protect you. Cheriska Too provided them with an agreed-upon stipend to assist them financially through your childhood with a lump sum payoff to sustain them when you left on your own as an adult..."

"Wait," waved Cheriska, "Too was created when I was about seven years old. How at that age, could she be my guardian?"

"Cheriska Too is a biodroid," he replied matter-of-factly. "Part you, part android programmed to protect your legal and financial interests. She acted like you, as a child, but she had the intellect and maturity of an adult. She needed to in order to be able to properly handle your affairs and representation. Biologically, she grew as you grew..."

22

Cheriska pulled up communications on her console, selecting a broadcast frequency. "Scavenger Two - Scavenger Two..." she called, activating a screen for a videolink.

Cheriska Too appeared on the screen, "Scavenger Two, this is Deep Black, go ahead."

"Too, what is our net worth?"

Cheriska Too didn't blink or react. "You've never asked that before, is everything alright?"

"Everything is fine."

Too nodded. "Of all our combined ventures?"

"Yes, Too. For everything. An exact amount if you know."

"Three-hundred-seventeen-million,   six-hundred-eighty-three-thousand. That of course reflects property and inventory values based on today's market rates," answered Cheriska Too without hesitation.

Cheriska found herself short of breath, having to inhale deeply as she sat back against her command chair, vaguely aware of Voorlak in her peripheral vision. "You didn't even have to look that up... how do you know that?"

"I recalculate our financial standing twice a day at open and close of the market because it varies. That figure was at opening of today's market."

Cheriska was feeling tunnel vision, "You are a biodroid?"

"Yes, of course."

Cheriska had already known, but the confirmation was like a slap in the face. "Why... Why... Why didn't you ever tell me?"

Cheriska Too shrugged, "You never asked, I assumed you knew. It was not my place to tell you, I thought mother had explained it. I'm sorry if it distresses you... I am still your clone-sister..."

CHAPTER TWO

TERRAN SYSTEM : UFW CARRIER CONQUEST

Chase Holt was barely aware of Karen's hand in his as they sat through the news conference on the Conquest's flight deck. The news conference, something else he was barely aware of. The rivet pattern on the steel floor in front of his feet blurred as his mind raced backwards, a week, two weeks, a month, two months; replaying history. He wondered if there was anything he could have changed, decisions that he could have made differently that would have impacted this outcome.

A couple months ago he was a man with a comfortable life, a career, a home. Penny; he hadn't thought about her for some time, *was she alive or dead?* He hoped that if she indeed survived, she would have a quiet, happy life ahead of her. Pam, Karen's roommate and best friend caught a bullet from the MIBs, her life senselessly snuffed out. Would it have been him if it wasn't her? Jesse... who was in many ways still just a kid; cut in half by a .50 cal sniper round. He deserved better than that. Chase was convinced that round was meant for him and some errant desert air currents played with the sniper's first attempt. Fate? Destiny? In retrospect, the poor bastard had no idea the shitstorm of hurt he'd released upon himself and his assault team...

Chase knew what he was dealing with; *survivors remorse.* Guilt. It was the same when he came back from the sandbox. In fact, it's why he went back. Twice. It was easier to deal with when surrounded by your own. Your brothers. After the third tour, he was just numb. But it got to a point where nothing mattered anymore; life, death, living day-to-day as a drone. He was burned out, he couldn't go back anymore.

Ultimately, he knew what it was and how to deal with it but that didn't make it any easier. Trying to make sense out of the organized chaos that was combat, whether you were an active participant or not, was pure folly. Trying to decipher the reasons for death or survival in the aftermath were just as futile... but that didn't stop him from trying. It was only natural, he knew that too. The only relief would come with distance, time, letting go. It never went away completely, no, those were the things that stayed with you for life, faded but indelible. He wasn't to a point yet where it didn't rest uneasily in his mind; he could push it off only if he was busy or occupied. But up here in space... *space...* that was not an easy concept... his mind had too much time to replay history, to feed on itself.

The only good that came out of this God-awful mess was Karen. His nearly imperceptible involuntary squeeze on her hand earned him a warm, loving glance that he was too lost in his thoughts to notice. She would know he was off in his own world and let him be. Karen turned out to be a lot tougher than he would have ever expected; resilient, accepting, flexible, adaptable. Her ability to cope with circumstances and go with the flow was remarkable. He wondered why *he* was having such a difficult time. Dan Murphy and Dancing Rain seemed to have accepted this all in stride as well. Hell, Dan was in his glory.

Chase mentally shook his head. Over a beer he told Dan Murphy he really wanted to see a UFO like the one Dan had seen on the beach near Steele's house and Dan had warned him to be careful what he wished for. Holt wanted to *see* one, not be *in* one, he reflected. Maybe it all came back to what he'd lost - everything - but that didn't seem to bother the others so much. His German Shepherd, Allie, nudged his free hand and he scratched her ears without breaking free of his internal conversation.

Steele seemed to be truly at home in his new surroundings, displaying a love for both, his natural born home *and* space with equal vigor...

His mind rewound an earlier conversation sitting in the Officers' Club; *Chase had cut into his steak, "So why did you come back here, Jack?"*

Steele looked up from his plate, "To check on my folks." He waved an empty fork, "we were in the neighborhood," he joked.

It was all so casual, all so normal for Jack. For all the times they'd discussed UFOs, NASA, aliens, conspiracies and space flight back in what he'd have to consider the *good old days*, Chase never really considered that some of what they were discussing was actually *real*. Now to find out that space was teeming with alien societies... that Earth was just a spec on a very big map to be visited or conquered... It was a lot to wrap one's head around. The whole aliens living on Earth thing was another one of those *holy shit* realizations. He admired the ease at which Steele had adapted to it all. And become an *Admiral?* What the hell was that? How the hell does that even happen..?

Steele accepted the drink from the waitress with a polite nod, turning back to Chase and Dan sitting across the table as she handed them their drinks.

He waited until she left. "Being in the right place at the right time," Jack said casually. "Timing is everything."

"Does being a smartass have anything to do with it?" prodded Dan Murphy, stirring his drink with a wry smile.

Steele shrugged with a grin, "It doesn't hurt."

Chase frowned, skeptical. "Seriously dude?" he countered.

"Look," said Steele leaning in, "maybe it was different for me, I kinda always knew this was out here. I felt it, dreamed about it all my life. It turns out I was right. You can call it luck, you can call it premonition, predestined fate..."

"What's your point?" motioned Chase.

"My point," replied Steele pointing his drink's swizzle stick in Chase's direction, "I had a head start. I won't lie, it was still a shock, sure, but I was more accepting of it. I didn't feel out of place. For me it was an exciting new adventure. Put the shock behind you, Chase. Get past it. Man, I can see you're fascinated - let that take over. Join the adventure." He leaned back, "Aren't you guys famous for saying, improvise, adapt, overcome?"

"That's the Marines," replied Chase with a smirk. "I was a Ranger, we say, Rangers lead the way!"

"Then fucking lead," encouraged Jack in a low tone.

"And do what, exactly?" gestured Chase, his open palms up. "Help me out here..."

"It's a big universe, buddy. Opportunities will present themselves in ways you cannot begin to fathom yet. You've got the stones and the brains, be alert enough to recognize them for what they are..."

"I'd rather go back home and have my old life back."

"Yeah, and I'd like to be twenty-one again and know what I know now," rebuffed Jack without missing a beat. He sipped his drink, "Ain't gonna happen my friend."

Steele had a genuine, honest way about him, with a command presence that imparted trust and seemed to cut through the bullshit without apology or malice. There was something about the ease in which he conducted himself, the way he treated people that prompted Dan to comment; *"Steele could piss on your head and you'd automatically think it was because your hair was on fire..."*

Then there was the other side; the guy you didn't want to cross. The one who would stroll through the gates of hell just to set your face on fire for having the lack of common sense or bad luck of fucking with him.

Chase *wanted* to adapt. He *wanted* to find a way to fit in and feel comfortable... he just couldn't picture what that was going to look like. At least not yet. He was used to being *that guy*. The guy with the answers and the plan, the backup plan and a handful of contingency plans. This didn't remotely fit *anything* he prepared for. Maybe it was denial of where Steele was really at all this time, or what Dan had seen and experienced, but suddenly finding one's self out in space wasn't on his chart of things to prepare for. In any event, he felt that whatever happened, he could count on Karen to be there with him.

He felt a squeeze on his hand that bought things rushing back in at him, the past fading into the background of voices and noise. A cacophony of sounds brought him mechanically to his feet even as his thoughts dropped away, surrounded by Dan, Rain, Kathy and officers of the Conquest...

One word stood out above the rest, "Did somebody say *nukes*?" he asked.

■ ■ ■

Vice Admiral Jack Steele stepped away from the podium and urgently waved Lisa to his side, turning his back on the audience and news cameras.

"Talk to me," she said, getting close.

Steele glanced around, "I need you to keep these people occupied. I don't care how you do it; maybe tell them about flying in a fighter, show them some flight videos of the systems we've been through. Or you could even take them to the galley and feed them. But don't release the satellites. We want to maintain control of the signals..."

"Won't we lose viewers?"

Steele pinched his lower lip for a moment, "Not if we have communications play an InterGal News broadcast until we get this handled and get back on the air..."

The holo-screen on Jack's eGo-H popped into existence floating above the unit that encircled his wrist. The *Tactical Engine Synthetic Service* animated character, TESS, appeared on screen. "Admiral," she began in a very human female voice, "the bridge is forwarding a communication from Red Flight Leader..." TESS's image shrunk and moved to one side, Commander Dar Sloan's face appearing from the cockpit of his Lancia fighter.

"Admiral, we've got incoming; two birds. I don't recognize them and there's no computer ident of any kind..."

"Where are they coming from, Commander?" asked Steele.

"The surface, sir. I was pretty sure I remember you saying your planet didn't have any spacecraft to speak of."

"NASA shuttles..." countered Jack, "but I thought the program was canceled."

Eavesdropping, Chase Holt trotted over from where he'd been standing. "The shuttle program *is* dead, Jack. They might be X-37B Spaceplanes, we saw two of them leave Area 51." He pointed at the holographic screen, "What do they look like?"

Steele grabbed the corner of the free-floating hologram and turned the screen toward Chase, as Commander Dar Sloane shared the target's profile provided by his fighter's computer. Chase nodded, "Yeah, that's an X-37B alright. They're unmanned but they're not *unarmed*. I don't think they could offer any real threat to your fighters though..."

Jack raised an eyebrow, "What kind of weapons do they have?"

"As far as we know, it's a smaller version of the lasers you guys destroyed on the ground. Templar Commandery's intel says it was developed to take out enemy satellites."

Steele raised an eyebrow, "I wonder if they're thinking of using them against those nukes..."

Chase shook his head, "No idea if they're capable of that or not..."

Jack went back to TESS's screen, "Commander, give them a wide berth but keep an eye on them. Keep us apprised."

"Aye, Admiral. Red Leader out." His face vanished and the screen closed on its own, disappearing.

Steele slapped his friend on the shoulder, "Chase, you're with me..." Heading to the elevators, Jack waved at Commander Derrik Brighton, the GIS, *Galactic Intelligence Service* agent whose real name was Colonel Durock Brithauz. He called him by the name he knew him best; *"Mr. Brighton..!"*

■ ■ ■

Side by side, Fritz and Allie trotted effortlessly to keep up with their human's long hurried strides, heading up the corridor toward the bridge of the Conquest. Vice Admiral Steele was absorbed in thought, torn between the press conference and the fact that the surface of Earth had taken that moment to erupt in random acts of highly destructive violence. He had to remind himself that the actions were likely diversions of the criminals they sought. Chaos meant time, time to disappear. "Mr. Brighton, these latest developments are seriously disturbing. Did you have any idea nuclear responses were likely?"

"Our intelligence... Well, these situations are rarely predictable Admiral..."

"I don't hear a *no* in there Mr. Brighton..."

"I'm sorry sir, these things are difficult to foresee..."

Steele raised an eyebrow in aggravation, "So this has never happened before?" He glanced at the Commander who was slow to answer. "Uh, huh," snorted Jack. "Again, not hearing a *no* in there. Y'know, a little warning might have been nice. A little heads-up on someone possibly pulling a nuclear trigger so we could have been prepared for it..."

Walking on opposite sides of the Admiral, Derrik shot Chase Holt a glance, hoping for some kind of diversion or break. Chase gave no indication of that, instead just listening to the conversation. Or verbal beating, if you will.

"Look, Admiral, these people have been in play for a long time, some for decades. Their plans have suddenly come to an abrupt end and they don't know what to do about it. They're desperate, they may be looking to misdirect our action so they can make an exit..."

Steele stopped abruptly in the corridor, the two German Shepherds trailing behind them nearly crashing into his legs, Chase Holt and Derrik Brighton stopping a few steps beyond him. "That's not what you said before we started this thing," Jack scowled. "I remember it very clearly, you said many of these people would go underground and hide... you never said *anything* about nuclear launches." He started walking again, "Dammit, this isn't some geeky socioeconomic science experiment," he waved angrily, "it's my *fucking home*. There's over seven billion people down there. Don't you think nuclear chaos and mass incineration of millions of people should have been something you should have mentioned..?"

"Honestly, Admiral, our intelligence indicated..."

"Fuck your intelligence, it was wrong. I expected better from you, mister. As a member of this task force and a member of *my crew*, I expected you to look out for *my* best interests. That includes information that you are privy to, that you think may or may not be applicable to our situation. I want your insight, your instincts, your experience, historical relevance and any other damn tidbit of information you can possibly think of. Do I make myself clear..?" He resumed his stride toward the bridge.

29

"It's my home too, Admiral," objected Commander Brighton, turning to keep up with the Admiral as he passed.

"No it's not, you don't have anything invested in that planet," commented Steele. He clenched his teeth, "We would have been better off sending down extraction teams..."

"Are we past that?" asked Chase, keeping pace.

"We are *well* past that, my Brother."

■ ■ ■

Steele knew he was demanding a lot of Commander Brighton, *Colonel Brithauz,* for information that the GIS was probably withholding, closely guarded. But at this point, Jack was not interested in playing their stupid *need to know* games, and he didn't give a shit if it put the Commander in a tight spot. Conflict of interest be damned, he wanted to know everything he needed to put an end to this insanity they had dubbed *Operation Magic Pawn* before his planet imploded. The Admiral snapped a return salute to the Marine at the entry to the bridge as he passed through the doors.

The bridge was a flurry of activity, all the stations full, the lights muted, extra personnel doubling up to coordinate information between the ships of the task force and the Conquest. Captain Anthony Ryan hazarded a quick salute, "Admiral."

After years of military service some habits die hard and Chase Holt saluted out of sheer reflex, shrugging it off with a sheepish look.

"Captain," replied Steele saluting back, ignoring his friend's faux pas. "Give me a sitrep."

"The missile fired by Iran had a very low trajectory, Admiral. It gave us no chance to mitigate its destruction with altitude. The warhead went live as soon as it entered Iranian airspace. We shot it down and the nuke detonated over open desert in Iraq, about fifty miles from the Jordanian border. Sensors indicate there were no population centers affected..."

"There may be fallout..." countered Steele. "What's closest to the detonation?"

"Ramadi in Iraq and Aman in Jordan, and they're well over a hundred miles away."

Steele nodded, "Continue."

Captain Ryan waved them over to the holographic chart table, the Earth suspended in detail, Green icons floating around it. "I have taken the liberty to spread the Task Force around the planet, assigning zones for best coverage. The ships are sharing real time sensor data..."

"North Korean warhead reaching its apex, Captain," called the tactical officer. "Its payload is active..."

"Is it clear of the atmosphere?" asked Steele.

"Yes, sir."

Captain Ryan pointed at the bridge's floor to ceiling holo-screen that wrapped around the room, a green diamond with notations to one side, a glittering speck in the center. "The Revenge is in position, she's locked on..." A quick streak of magenta triggered a brief but intense yellow-white flash that made Steele and everyone else on the bridge squint.

"Target eliminated," announced the tactical officer.

Steele let out a sigh of relief. *Maybe cooler heads...*

"Uh... Captain?"

"Go ahead Ensign," said Captain Ryan stepping back toward his command chair.

"Sir, we have a huge spark in activity..."

"What kind of activity?" interrupted Steele.

The tactical officer looked over his shoulder at the Captain and Admiral, "It looks like

launcher activity... lots of them..."

"Launch!" called an Electronics Warfare Officer at a sensor station. "Active launches! I have one, two, no three... make that five... Iran and North Korea again."

"Shoot them down," ordered Steele, *"now..!"* A proliferation of little red dots appeared on the holo-screen spreading across the globe, hundreds if not thousands. The United States, Russia, Europe, Great Britain, China, Israel. "What the *hell* is *that?"*

"Active launch systems sir," came the reply.

"What the hell could they hit without the GPS satellites?"

Chase leaned close, "It's called math, Jack. They have lists of targets with coordinates, fuel loads, travel times and flight paths all pre-calculated. GPS gives them pinpoint accuracy, within *feet*. These are nukes, they could be several miles off target and it wouldn't matter..."

"Good point..." acknowledged Jack, smoothing his mustache.

"Revenge and Westwind are firing... " indicated Captain Ryan, pointing at the big screen. Magenta streaks reached out from the ships, just icons on the screen, toward the planet below.

31

The communications officer turned in his seat, "Captain we have a heavily encrypted message coming from the surface..."

"Decrypt and report," ordered Captain Ryan.

"It may take a while sir, this isn't our code. I've never seen it before..."

Anthony Ryan spun his seat to face Jack, "Think there's someone else out here Admiral?"

"Mr. Smiley!" shouted Steele, "Get some extra birds out and *scrub this system!*"

"Aye, aye, sir!" Flight operations, mere feet away down a short flight of stairs at the rear of the bridge, made electronic communication slower than simply shouting. Commander of the Flight Group, Captain Paul Smiley, tapped the launch alarm putting the pilots and their fighters in motion, *"White and Yellow Flights, prepare to launch!"*

■ ■ ■

On the deck below, the launch horn sounded briefly as the pilots lingering near their fighters scrambled up the ladders to their cockpits, stunned news crews and visitors watching in awe from the forward area of the bay. The interlocking steel doors in front of the fighters sitting in their launch racks, were suddenly obscured by a translucent blue stasis fields winking to life. As soon as the stasis fields were stable the doors parted across the middle, hydraulic pumps thrumming, a toothy maw opening up to the darkness of space, the flicker of stars visible beyond the wavering blue veils.

The visitors stood open-mouthed, fascinated by the machinations. Just seconds before the lights above the doors winked green, Lisa Steele got to the podium mic, "Ladies and gentlemen, you might want to cover your ears..."

The launch-ready lights above the doors flashed green and the catapults fired, their sleds slamming to their stops, flinging White and Yellow Flights into the void. Almost immediately, the elevators in the center of the bay dropped out of sight, creating two huge holes in the floor, only to return moments later carrying fighters from the hangar deck to load the empty launch racks.

The launch doors closed, the stasis fields winked out and the visitors continued to stare in disbelief, watching the sudden activity all around the bay. Lisa tapped on the mic "Ladies and Gentlemen... you can uncover your ears now..."

■ ■ ■

"Targets destroyed, Capt... Waaait..." cautioned the tactical officer, interrupting himself.

"What?" asked Steele suspiciously, stepping toward the center of the bridge to survey the big screen. The *kachunk* and accompanying vibration of the launch racks as they slingshot the fighters into space, first from one side of the ship, then the other, preceded arcs of light that raced away from the Conquest like comets.

The Tactical Officer began marking icons on the big screen from his control panel, "Pre-launch indications across the globe..."

"How can you tell?" queried Steele.

"Thermal sensors and electronic surge sensors."

Steele pointed at the big screen, "All ships target and destroy any ICBM with engines on... get them in the silos before they're..."

"We have launches, Admiral..."

"...in the air," finished Steele. "Dammit. Shoot them down. Get them while they're low and slow..."

"Units firing..."

Even the guns of the Conquest were engaged, the ships main rail guns blasting away with a rumble and vibration Steele had never felt before; long, flaming steel alloy projectiles racing across the darkness down toward the planet below. The other ships in the fleet were newer ships with newer weapons and systems that were more graceful and reliable than the old noisy rail guns on the Conquest. What the rail guns lacked in targeting range and service life, due to their wearable components, they made up for in close quarters combat, dishing out brutal, hull-crushing, hammer-of-God penetrating power.

"We have launches all across the globe... United States, Russia, China, Great Britain, Israel... now Pakistan and India..."

Steele's mouth was suddenly dry, his stomach in knots. He was watching the end. "Shoot them all," he croaked. "Once we have the air clear, start killing the ones in the silos..."

"Even if they're not pre-launch?"

"Even if they're not pre-launch," he confirmed. "These morons can't be trusted with a match and a can of gasoline," he growled.

33

Chase Holt leaned in, "Jack, don't forget about subs and planes with nuke payloads..."

Steele rubbed his face, "Christ, I forgot all about *them...*" He swiped at TESS on his left wrist, "TESS; Lisa Steele..."

TESS's holo-screen popped into existence above his wrist, "Contacting Lisa Steele."

Lisa's face appeared in the holograph, "Go ahead Admiral."

"Lisa, there are few people from that group that might be helpful up here on the bridge..."

CHAPTER THREE

TERRAN SYSTEM : FREERANGER DESTROYER DD217

Having pulled back, concealed in the massive shadow of Saturn, FreeRanger destroyers DD217 and DD62 were closely monitoring the events on Earth with a remote sensor hidden in the asteroid belt beyond Mars near the dwarf planet, Ceres. Avoiding discovery by the roaming UFW fighter patrols scouring the system was critical if they were going to be of any use at all to the FreeRanger operatives on the blue and green planet. It wasn't the first time a man-made near extinction event was used as an exit strategy, though it was generally a last resort.

Commander T. B. Yafusco had never been fond of the highly controversial tactic that was neither approved nor condemned by the FreeRanger Council. Taking the neutral position of don't ask-don't tell, the Council maintained a level of innocence and plausible deniability of events where their freelance operatives were engaged. But by the same token, they realized a heavy liability existed if those operatives were captured by the UFW even if the agents didn't know their employers were actually the FreeRanger Economic Consortium. Shell corporations working under the guise of free enterprise isolated the Consortium to some extent, but discovery meant jeopardizing many of their legitimate contracts involving the UFW, which would certainly dissolve, creating heavy economic hardship for the FreeRanger network. Even legitimate companies used operatives like the ones currently on Earth, working hand-in hand with the Economic Consortium subsidiaries. It was business after all and profit was king.

But everyone knew what the UFW's super-secret GIS, *Galactic Intelligence Service,* was capable of... most operatives would crumble under their investigation and interrogation. Which meant getting them the hellion off the planet was imperative. Unfortunately, Commander Tibby Yafusco was fresh out of spare assault fleets to take on what the UFW had in place around the planet.

Tibby stopped pacing around his ready room and stared at the holo-chart, his hands on his hips, Commander Kindre Thurmer gazed at him from the screen of the monitor on his desk. His bridge officer and fiancee, Ensign

Grinah stood with her arms folded across her chest, leaning against the bulkhead, quietly monitoring the conversation, his first officer, Lieutenant Dash Zarnev sat casually on the sofa, his legs crossed at the knee.

Tibby leaned on the edge of the chart table with both hands, letting his head drop, stretching his neck muscles, "I am not sacrificing our ships for these people... because that's what it would be, *suicide*."

"Agreed, Tibby," nodded Kindre Thurmer. "It would be a waste... and nothing would change, the agents would still end up in the hands of the UFW."

"We wouldn't make it half way," added Dash, "much less make it out."

"What about after the *event?*" asked Grinah. "Think the fleet would go down for aid and recovery?"

Tibby shook his head without looking up, "No, not the heavies, they'd stay in orbit... And the fighters... we'd never get past them."

Dash Zarnev was reviewing the distress calls from the surface of the planet on an e-Pad sitting on his lap. "It's too bad, we'd only have to make a handful of stops..."

Tibby raised his head, "What? There's over two hundred operatives down there."

"Must be expendable," replied Dash. "The Council's list only sanctions rescue for about fifty of those names. Some may be paid conspirators."

"Some people will sell out their mothers for money," nodded Tibby.

"And then of course," added Kindre, "there are the ones who don't *want* to leave..."

"Like this guy here," continued Dash, tapping on the screen of his e-Pad, "Kim Jung-un... His Father was the original operative who died a few years ago. Says here; all contact was lost shortly after the father's death when the handler disappeared..."

Tibby straightened up, "Was his handler on the planet?"

"Yeah. Jang Sung-Taek. Data shows he was the uncle."

Tibby Yafusco shrugged and shook his head at the same time, "Sometimes these people get caught up in the lives they've built for themselves during these operations. If my memory serves me right, this operation has been running a long time. I'm sure it's been much longer than anticipated."

"Over a hundred years," confirmed Lieutenant Zarnev.

"Damn... That's a long time to be pouring resources into a project," commented Tibby.

"And we get to watch it conclude..." offered Grinah.

"Or turn to dust," countered Tibby.

"We're not done yet," announced Kindre Thurmer from the monitor, "I still have a call out to a few friends I haven't heard back from yet..."

The door to the bridge slid open with a hiss, disappearing into the bulkhead, an Ensign stepping into the doorway, "Someone pulled the trigger, Skipper. It's begun."

Tibby closed his eyes and inhaled deeply. "Thank you Mister, keep us apprised."

"Aye, sir." the door closed behind him as he stepped from the doorway.

"I don't look forward to this," said Commander Thurmer. She glanced over her shoulder at the big screen in her ready room on the DD62.

"Yeah," lamented Tibby, "I don't want to watch this, such a waste of a planet."

"And all those people..." whispered Grinah.

Feeding live data from the remote sensor to the holo-chart, they were able to watch the UFW ships maneuver around the planet, firing down at the missiles. Tibby reached into the hologram and pulled it closer, effectively zooming in the image for better detail.

"Think they'll be able to get them all?" asked Grinah.

Tibby shook his head, "I honestly don't know. Part of me hopes they can..."

"And the other part..?" asked his first officer.

"Well, we do need to get our people out..." He rubbed the back of his neck, "Though I really don't see how it'll help either way."

■ ■ ■

The alarm klaxon sounded a split second before plunging the ship into eerie red flashing light. "*Red Alert.* All hands to battle stations, *all hands to battle stations.* Captain to the bridge..!"

Launching himself off the sofa, Dash Zarnev nearly collided with his commander as Tibby raced past, heading for the bridge, Grinah close behind.

"Report!" shouted Yafusco sliding to a stop and dropping into his command chair.

"GOD event off the starboard bow, Commander."

A growing colorful electric mass of light and energy, swirled and undulated before exploding outward in a splash of neon, a ship spilling out into their space, cruising to a stop. "She's pinging FreeRanger, sir."

"DD62 is hailing sir..."

"On screen," waved Tibby. Hanging motionless just beyond Saturn's outer rings, the field of rocks and debris swept past on the left side of the screen as Kindre Thurmer's face appeared in a video square.

"The other ship is hailing as well..."

Tibby nodded silently and waved at the screen, a second video square appearing.

"Commander Yafusco," began Kindre Thurmer, "this is an old friend of mine..."

"Lieutenant Commander Aleese Portwin," saluted the woman. "This is the cutter, *Red Moon*, we are at your service."

"Ms. Portwin was in the academy the same time we were, Tibby. She was a year behind us."

T. B. Yafusco glanced down at his tactical screen then back up, "Ms. Portwin, it appears the Council assigned you a ship without any weapons systems on it... Why is that?"

"The Red Moon is a fast delivery and recovery ship, Commander. Speed and our GOD drive are our weapons."

Tibby glanced over at Grinah, recalling a fateful day not so long ago in Haruna Tier when the UFW caught their Captain's cruiser in an energy depleted state and literally blew the ship out from underneath their feet. It was a miracle they survived that encounter... many of their shipmates didn't; including their Captain.

Commander Yafusco rubbed his forehead with his fingertips in consternation, "Ms. Portwin..."

"*Lieutenant Commander* Portwin," she reminded him.

"Yes, of course... *Lieutenant Commander.* Look," he waved dismissively, "I don't know what kind of assignments or missions you've taken, but..."

Aleese Portwin raised her hand, "Let me stop you right there, Commander Yafusco, this is not our first extraction and it won't be our last. While I appreciate your concern, your condescending attitude is rather offensive."

"In case you haven't noticed," growled Tibby pointing in the direction of Earth, "there's a UFW Task Force out there..."

"I'm fully aware of the situation, Commander Yafusco..." Aleese said defiantly, her hands on her hips.

"What you may *not* be aware of," he interrupted, "is this may be the same Task Force that *laid waste* to our assault fleet in Velora Prime. I've been tracking them for months."

"During the hunt for the Freedom? Is the Freedom in this Task Force?"

Tibby shook his head, "I don't know. There is a ship that fits the Freedom's profile, but there's no way to be sure. It was never confirmed whether she survived or not..."

"We need to find out," urged Aleese Portwin, "the Council will want to know..."

"The Council no longer cares," countered Tibby. "They learned a very costly lesson in Velora Prime. The bounty has been rescinded." He waved off being sidetracked, "The *point is,* getting past this group blockading the planet has an extremely *low* probability of success. Getting annihilated has an extremely *high* probability..."

"Unless you have a GOD drive," countered Aleese Portwin.

"Yeah," waved Tibby dismissively, "we saw how well that worked out when they blew a battle cruiser out from under our feet. And for that jump-freighter we met up with in Zender's Trek." He glanced at Grinah, "Remember that one?"

She nodded in agreement, "Shot full of holes."

Lieutenant Commander Aleese Portwin waved both hands, "*Enough.* The Red Moon can GOD jump from here to the atmosphere above any set of coordinates and sit down, shields-up. Without armaments we have a much larger power cache, heavier shields, faster engines. If the assets are in place and ready for pickup, we will spend minimum time on the ground. My crew and I are aware of the risks... *and* the reward. The Council has offered quite a handsome bonus per body..."

"Alive I hope," offered Kindre Thurmer.

"Of course..."

"*Sir!*" Tibby's tactical officer turned in his seat, "Our remote sensor has been discovered by a UFW fighter patrol... *Aaand* it's gone. Sensor destroyed."

T. B. Yafusco winced, "Dammit." He looked up at the screen, "Forward the last known coordinates of all the UFW ships and flights to the Red Moon."

Aleese Portwin nodded, "Thank you, Commander... *Helm*, prepare for GOD jump."

■ ■ ■

The dark, relatively featureless shape of the Red Moon swung away from the DD217 and the DD62, the two destroyers hung motionless in Saturn's shadow, its outer rings sweeping past behind them.

Lieutenant Commander Aleese Portwin settled into her command chair, "Helm, take us to a safe distance to initiate GOD..."

"Aye, moving off..."

"Navigation?"

"Plotting course to our first stop Commander."

"Good." Aleese Portwin keyed her mic to the recovery deck, "Team ready?"

"JRT, *Jump Recovery Team,* ready Skipper," came the voice in her earpiece.

"Remember team, if they're not on the list, they don't board. No exceptions." Aleese released her mic button. "We don't get paid for excess baggage..." she breathed.

"Initiating GOD drive, Commander. Atmospheric control canards extended, bubble forming..."

"Shields?"

"Charged and standing by, Commander."

Aleese Portwin knew she didn't need to emphasize how crucial the shields were once they cleared the jump corona. This wasn't their first dance. "Initiate jump."

■ ■ ■

The air exploded over West Virginia's Jefferson National Forest, halfway between Eagle Rock and White Sulphur Springs, flattening trees in a mile circumference, creating instant thunderstorms which sprawled out in all directions, spawning violent tornadoes. The town of Covington, just a couple of miles north, was laid to waste, flattened by the onslaught of chaotic weather.

The Red Moon appeared from the storm, its dark shape racing away from the epicenter, arcing to the northwest. It descended as it crossed interstate I-64 and dropped out of the sudden torrents like a ghost, scattering people below in the parking lot, running from the alien object and spikes of lightning. Straddling the Greenbrier Hotel's front lawn, reaching across the parking lot and into the golf course, the Red Moon settled to the surface, crushing parked cars, splintering trees and destroying the golf course's pro shop.

Seated at his desk in the lobby, the man with the neatly-cropped salt and pepper hair on the phone with his wife, was the Concierge for the hotel. He stared out of the lobby windows in disbelief as people poured in through the entrance, "Honey, I think I'm going to have to call you back..." he hung up the phone without taking his eyes off the windows. *Once a Marine, always a Marine...* As he dug into his daily carry pack stashed under his desk, two security agents hustled past headed for the door, guns drawn. Pushing past his home-made lunch and locating what he was searching for, the Concierge withdrew a Glock 21 and two spare mags which he slipped into his pocket. Doing a quick press-check as he rose, he strode purposefully toward the commotion, dropping his gun hand, hiding it low and behind him. "What in the *Sam Hell* do we have here?" he wondered aloud. "These folks must be lost," he commented casually. "Sally, call the Sheriff..." he calmly instructed the desk clerk.

■ ■ ■

The President's Senior Adviser brushed her dark hair off her face with the back of her hand, her decidedly Arabic features spattered with blood, her dark eyes admiring her handiwork. "That's the last one..."

The President stepped gingerly over the body of the dead Secret Service agent at his feet on the floor of the train car, "Did we have to kill them all?"

"We?" she snorted derisively, "I don't remember you having a hand in any of this." She glanced around at the bloody carnage, the bodies of the agents scattered around. Their body armor offered no real resistance to her pulse-laser and she'd completely surprised them, shooting several in the back. Pointing at the nuclear football she fired the last pulse left in her pistol, effectively destroying the unit and preventing anyone tampering with their command orders. She tossed the pistol aside and searched the nearest corpse, recovering a Sig Sauer handgun. "Let's go," she hissed, shooting him a look of distaste. As far as she was concerned, his assignment was over; he was merely baggage at this point... She didn't like it, but maybe he still had some use – if nothing else it would save her from having to create a lengthy detailed report about why she didn't bring him back.

"What about my family?"

"They're not part of the mission," she replied matter-of-factly.

"But..."

She stopped mid-stride and turned, pointing the muzzle of the gun at his chest, "I'm only going to say this once, so listen carefully; they were window dressing, bought and paid for. They have no value. That greedy mooch caused more problems for us than she was worth, dragging those kids all over the planet. Stupid bitch didn't know the meaning of subtle or low profile... good riddance."

■ ■ ■

The Concierge watched the Greenbrier 's security agents engage the alien assault team, fire crisscrossing the front lawn and portions of the parking lot as the agents swung left along the parked cars for cover. Many of the rounds fired by the security agents did little or nothing, the alien armor deflecting much of it, producing an occasional stagger.

Two more of the Greenbrier 's security agents exited the building taking up positions behind the concrete pillars at the hotel's entrance, firing from concealment.

Hmm, more cannon fodder... The retired Marine stepped from behind one of the concrete pillars and moved right, stopping to line up his sights, one-handed, old-school, Camp Perry style. The Glock 21 jumped slightly, the .45 slug punching a hole through the visor of his first target fifty yards away, the alien assault trooper crumpling to the ground. *Every target has a weakness...* He sidestepped shots in his direction and began to walk forward, carefully taking shots, always at the visor. When his slide clacked open he thumbed the release, the empty magazine dropping to the grass, his free hand feeding in another with a positive slap. It was at that moment he realized he was hit, his hand slick with blood. He was unconcerned and unrattled; this was not his first rodeo.

Thumbing the slide release, he took aim and continued to fire, moving forward with purpose. He felt the hit in his gut and grit his teeth with a grunt, taking a painful step sideways, shooting the trooper in the face straight through his visor. He felt a hit in his back and it spun him...

"Allahu akbar!" screamed the President's Senior Adviser as she ran up behind the man in the Concierge's uniform.

She was so close the Marine swung his fist and connected solidly with her face, laying her out on her back, her nose broken, her face bloodied. When he saw the muzzle of her gun move there was no hesitation, just reflex. The Glock 21 vibrated in his hand and her head exploded across the grass. *"Aloha snackbar, bitch,"* he growled, turning back to the action. When the President ran past him toward the alien ship he barely took notice, only vaguely aware of his narrowing vision. Executing another magazine change, the Marine set his jaw against the pain and pushed forward, unwavering, determined to take advantage of the target rich environment.

■ ■ ■

The President placed his hand on the glass plate, the e-Pad scanning his hand, the Red Moon's officer passing a device over the back of the man's neck. The RFID implanted there gave up its information and serial number. "Identity confirmed," reported the officer into the comm. "Welcome aboard, agent Oroterra," he nodded.

Lieutenant Commander Aleese Portwin keyed her mic, "What about the other operative?"

"Dead, Commander."

"Dammit," she hissed. "Did we lose any team members?"

"Yes Ma'am. Five killed and four wounded."

Aleese Portwin felt the flush of anger race across her face. "What the hellion were they using?"

"Projectile weapons..."

"By the Gods," she groaned, pinching the bridge of her nose, "damn antiques... Helm, next stop."

"Aye, Commander, twenty-one minutes."

■ ■ ■

His left uniform pant leg and dress shoes red with blood, the Concierge turned over the closest body over with his foot, grunting from the pain. "Hmm, one of them aliens I suppose..." he commented, admiring his marksmanship, the visor splintered, the face of the man in the helmet unrecognizable.

One of the security agents appeared at his side, "Gunny, you're hit pretty good, why don't you sit down..."

The Glock 21 dangled in the Marine's right hand, his trigger finger resting on the frame, at the ready. He glanced up at the empty sky where the ship had disappeared, the rain having lightened considerably, the worst of the weather having moved on. "Damnedest thing I ever did see..." He took a deep breath and swayed where he stood, "Actually feels good..." he said blinking away the wetness. "Nah, I'll be OK," he waved, unaware that the security agent was supporting him around the waist.

A string of blue and red lights flickered along the main road and up the lengthy drive to the hotel, sirens wailing, "Sheriff's here, Gunny. Stand down."

"On time, just as always," remarked the Marine in the Concierge's uniform. "I'm being fucking sarcastic of course..."

"I get it, Gunny."

The Marine wobbled, "Y'know, I think I will have that seat, I'm feeling a little light-headed..."

"Semper Fi, Gunny."

CHAPTER FOUR

UFW CARRIER, CONQUEST : *THE SKY IS FALLING*

"Ladies and gentlemen, please return to your seats..!" With the television cameras rolling again, Ensign Lisa Steele stood at the podium and watched a pair of Space Marines escort a small group of key people her brother had requested, to the bridge of the Conquest.

"Ensign," called a newswoman from the front row, standing and adjusting her red blazer, "what is all that noise? What's going..?" The rail guns fired, cutting her off, their roar reverberating through the hull of the ship like a drum, the deck vibrating.

"What you're hearing is our rail guns. It appears the criminals on the e-RIPs you've been given," Lisa held up her *electronic Report In Progress* device, "have taken this opportunity to initiate a nuclear response to being captured..."

A wave of disruptive cross-talk swept across the audience...

"What does that mean?"

"What are we going to do?"

The sound of the rail guns momentarily silenced the group and Lisa jumped in before she could be talked over. "We are attempting to neutralize the threats in the most expedient way possible, while minimizing the risk to Earth's population. The military and intelligence people you saw leave your group may be able to assist us with that task..." She paused as the rail guns fired again and she looked into the cameras, "We ask that anyone who can still see or hear our broadcast seek shelter. Try to stay with us. We will do our best to keep you up to date..."

■ ■ ■

Standing in the center of the command deck, Captain Anthony Ryan had never had so many people on his bridge; with nearly three times its normal crew compliment it was utter chaos. Many stations were double-staffed to keep up with the activity along with the visitors from the planet's surface pitching in at tactical, communications and cyber-warfare. He understood

45

why the Admiral requested the presence of these extra bodies but he was more concerned with them getting in the way than actually having any useful participation.

"Captain, port-side guns are nearing overheat levels..."

Captain Ryan pursed his lips, "Mmm. Weapons; shut them down and let them cool. Alert the starboard turrets we're performing a combat roll." Ryan set his hand on the shoulder of the helmsman, "Combat roll, bring our starboard turrets to bear."

"Combat roll, aye."

"Admiral, comm coming in from White Flight..."

"On screen," acknowledged Steele.

A video square appeared, the colors muted and dull from the darkness of space, Lieutenant JG Nera Margareth's face showed, illuminated by her instruments, her eyes glowing eerily in the night vision image. "White Leader, sir; we've located and destroyed a passive remote sensor probe hidden in the asteroid belt beyond the fourth planet."

"Good job, Lieutenant." Steele glanced over at Captain Ryan, "Our hunch was right, we're not alone in the system..." He turned back to the screen, "Stay alert White Leader, resume your patrol." The Ketarian pilot saluted and the square winked out as the image on the main screen rolled, the blue and green planet trading sides on the panoramic screen before them.

With a minor pause in the firing order, the rail guns resumed their targeting and fired as the starboard turrets came into play.

"Captain, the Westwind just took a rail gun hit from the surface..."

Steele stepped forward, "Damage?"

"No Admiral, her shields held. It doesn't look intentional, probably a miss on a warhead."

"Who the hell has rail guns?" asked Jack, glancing in Chase's direction.

"The Navy," replied Chase. "But I didn't know they had any operational. Kind of like the lasers, they were in development and trial."

Steele stared at the big screen, mesmerized at the comet-like fireballs and multi-colored streaks of light crisscrossing the planet below, hot flashes of light punctuating the insanity. "Well they're in operation now..." he mumbled. *He felt numb, disconnected, helpless, angry... He wanted to do something to make it stop. Anything. But it was a runaway train of chaos with no conductor. Oh, to be Superman and fly around the world against its rotation and reverse time, or to have Rod Serling's magical time controlling stopwatch...* A sharp jab in the ribs brought the chaos rushing back in at him,

"Huh?" he blinked. Chase simply motioned with his eyes toward the tactical station, the tactical officer staring back at them.

"Admiral... the satellites have started shooting at each other..."

Steele's eyes widened, "Say what now?"

"Operation Blind Side," confirmed the US Air Force General standing at the tactical station. "It was a lead program to *Project Zenith* and *Project Ascension."* He motioned toward the big screen, "Which of course, you've already encountered. This mess must have initiated US Space Command's first-strike protocol."

"Can you stop it?"

The General shook his head, "No Admiral, we cannot. It was designed as a total space superiority protocol. Once initiated there is no pause, no turn-back. With the X-37B Ascension birds, our web of first-strike satellites will attempt to wipe out all opposing space borne hardware. Starting with opposing aggressor hardware."

"They have killer satellites too?"

"Yes, of course. But our technology is hardened, faster and more accurate. Our X-37Bs have surveyed every single piece of hardware up here. What they are, who owns them, their vulnerabilities, their flight paths, and their location at any given moment. Our equipment knows what to kill, how to kill it and when to kill it. Space Command will come out on top."

Steele ran his fingers though his hair in exasperation, "Strangely enough, General, I don't find that comforting."

An Electronic Warfare Officer turned briefly away from his communications station, *"Admiral,* data coming in from the Revenge; nuclear detonation in their sector, altitude two-hundred-twenty-five miles, several satellites destroyed..." The EWO quickly scanned the details and extrapolated additional results. "We have a growing debris field, moving in all directions; twenty-five percent falling to the surface, the rest staying in orbit. Collateral damage to additional units can be expected..."

"Christ," breathed the General, "we're going to have a chain-reaction cascade... *Our* first-strike system kills them - punches a hole through them and switches them off, not destroy them..." Looking stricken he rubbed his forehead, "This could be catastrophic."

"Best laid plans of mice and men, General," commented Steele sarcastically. "Looks like someone else didn't agree with your plan."

"Admiral, the Dark Star is reporting a distress call in their sector..."

"From where? Plot it on screen," commanded Steele. The declination plot and live image appeared as a large inset on the main screen. "Jesus, it's the International Space Station... Zoom in."

"Aye."

Jack instantly recognized the damage; the right PVA, *Photo Voltaic Array,* was broken and battered, most of the shining blue panels missing, the framework twisted, dangling, trailing debris behind it. It was still too far away to see if there was any damage to the modules but it was hard to believe they were undamaged considering what was visible. "Find their communications frequency..."

Admiral, their flight path is going to take them directly through the debris field..."

"How long?"

The EWO consulted the data on his screen, "Sixty-two minutes."

Jack turned over his shoulder, "Pappy!"

"Rescue shuttle, *got it!*" came the reply from flight control.

"We need a pilot who speaks English," called Steele.

"Maria?"

"Close enough..."

■ ■ ■

Her helmet already on, Maria trotted across the Conquest's flight deck, her boots clomping on the metal surface as she pulled her gloves on. She hazarded a glance to her left, "Are you really sure you want to do this? This is *not* for the faint of heart..."

Pulling on his own gloves as he clomped alongside her, Dan Murphy nodded inside his helmet, "I'm good. You need someone in the back who they'll understand, right?"

"OK, it's *your* stomach. Just remember you're going to be standing at an open doorway to space... You freak out and you're no good to anyone. And for the *love of God* don't puke inside your helmet," she warned.

"Yeah, I get that. I will have a tether, right?"

"Yes, it's on a retractable reel, you can go beyond the door. Just be forewarned, that first step is a doozy..."

Dan swallowed hard, "Swell."

"The thing to remember is that the shuttle has gravity; step beyond the door and that all changes. Just don't panic. You'll have another crewman to help you with equipment and recovery; Dooby, he's very good. I'd say let him handle the equipment, you handle the communications." Maria checked TESS's holo-screen hovering above her wrist, the unit itself under the sleeve of her suit. "Forty-seven minutes, we need to hustle. That station is going to sail through a field of debris at about twenty-thousand miles an hour."

"Good Lord, there won't be anything left of it..."

"No there won't. We have one chance to pull this off."

■ ■ ■

The best reason for using an opposite orbit to catch the oncoming space station was to save time. It was also the worst reason for using an opposite orbit... a closing speed greater than twenty-thousand miles an hour and having to come to a stop and reverse direction to match that twenty-thousand miles an hour. Having to fly through satellite debris to get to the station was another factor Maria wasn't too thrilled with either. So, she elected to chase it down from behind. It made for a much slimmer window for the rescue but it ultimately seemed much less dangerous. Not that it was going to be a cake walk, no, since the hit it took, the International Space Station's orbit was beginning to degrade and her attitude was beginning to wobble off her designed path.

The Conquest's Dragonfly rescue shuttles were different from the rather stubby craft on the Freedom; a long slender cockpit with a bubble canopy for enhanced visibility, the pilot in front, the electronics officer above and behind, a narrow walkway alongside to access the interior of the ship. Maria glanced up at the rear-view mirror mounted above her on a rib of the canopy, "Lieutenant, I'll need you to keep an eye on that debris. And I need you to watch for anything coming up from the surface."

"I got it, Skipper."

Dan was standing next to Myomerr's seat looking out through the canopy at the growing form of the space station ahead of them. Even at that distance, the damage was plainly visible. "Wooww..."

Myomerr glanced to her right and silently thumbed him to the back, the access door sliding closed behind him. From her controls she sealed the door, the cockpit pressurized independently from the rest of the interior which would be opened to space. She scrutinized the space station with a critical eye as they neared, "How many people did you say were up here?"

"Six astronauts..." replied Maria, angling for the universal docking hub.

"And they come up here *voluntarily?*"

"What are you saying? Are you saying there's something wrong with it..?"

"Well it's not exactly Blackmount Station," joked Myomerr. "Or even Resurrection Station for that matter..."

"Alright, that's enough," scolded Maria. "Considering we only learned to fly just a little over a hundred years ago, I don't think we're doing too bad..."

"Except for that mess down there," indicated Myomerr, waving at the planet below.

Maria made a face of distaste, "Yeah, well, figuring out more efficient ways of killing each other and winning wars always seems to take precedence over everything else... Besides, in case you've forgotten, we had some help."

"There is that, I suppose." With one eye on her screens Myomerr eyed the station as Maria matched the speed of the structure, sliding the Dragonfly under the shiny blue panels of the remaining PVA.

Maneuvering alongside the docking hatch, a safe distance away, Maria keyed her comm mic, "Dooby, can you use the arm to grab the truss above us? I think it will help us maintain position..."

"Copy, Skipper," came the reply in her helmet.

"We can't dock," offered Myomerr, stating the obvious, "how are they getting to us?"

"Space walk. They have EVAs, *Extravehicular Aids,* it's a personal maneuvering system."

■ ■ ■

Dooby activated the holographic control panel for the arm called the *Big Grip,* and slid his hand and arm into the hologram, taking direct control like an extension of himself, the arm's camera allowing him to see what he was doing on the holo-screen. "I need five feet up, Skipper." He watched the live image as he reached with the arm, "Easy, easy, hold there... got it!" He squeezed his hand and the Big Grip closed around the structure of the truss. "Big Grip, lock." he commanded before sliding his arm out of the hologram. He reached up and sealed his face-mask, making sure Dan Murphy did the same. "Depressurizing cabin, tethers secure, door open and ready to recover in thirty seconds."

"What's that groaning sound?" asked Dan.

Dooby looked at the Big Grips holo-panel, tapping on the flat surface at a digital stress meter in the yellow. "It's not really made for what we're using it for, it's showing some torque on the arm, we must be rotating or something..."

"We're on live comms with the station, let's get things rolling..." said Maria in their helmets. "Remember Dooby, talk to Dan, these folks won't understand you."

"Got it. Depressurization complete, door open, ready to receive."

Dan stood in the open doorway holding onto a grab rail and waved at the docking port window over a hundred feet away. "C'mon folks!"

There was momentary static in his helmet, "Thank you Rescue One. Two of our people exiting in sixty seconds. Over."

"Two? I thought you had six people..."

"That is affirmative, six people. Only two fit in the airlock at a time. Over"

Dooby palmed his facemask, "By the Gods, this is going to take forever. We don't have that kind of time."

"Any way to speed up the process over there?" asked Dan.

Static faded in and out. "It is a computerized station protocol that we cannot override. Over."

Dan Murphy anxiously watched as the hatch swung open and the first body floated out of the opening, gently powered by its EVA. "Understood. Please be as fast as you can."

Dooby got Dan's attention and indicated the Big Grip holo-panel, the arm's stress meter fluctuating from yellow to orange and back to yellow, "It's not going to be able to stand that for very long..."

Dan took a deep breath as he reached outward for the first of the astronauts nearing Rescue One, who was cautiously applying his jets to decelerate a pace that was already snail*esque*. Dan waved him closer, "For the love of *God*, don't *slow down!*" Hanging from the rail inside, he leaned out and grabbed at the astronaut's hand, connecting, using his leverage on the rail to yank him unceremoniously through the doorway. As soon as the astronaut crossed the threshold he crashed to the floor, his legs failing him, unprepared for the full weight of his suit and equipment.

"Mon dieu, gravity... how is zis so? You must tell me..." he exclaimed, in a thick French accent.

"Not the time, my friend," replied Dan Murphy, waving wildly at the next astronaut still twenty-five feet out. "Dooby, help him remove his EVA and secure him in a seat."

"You got it."

Dan planted himself in the center of the doorway, his arms wide, "Don't slow down keep coming, I got ya... land on your feet."

When she collided with him he stepped back and she dropped to the deck, landing considerably easier than the Frenchman. "Thank you," she said as Dan handed her off to Dooby.

Dan was trying to ignore the movement of the swaying PVA array, the blue panels glittering as they moved, the support truss twisting. The Big Grip's stress meter flashed red momentarily before falling to orange then back to yellow. "Dooby..."

"I know, I know. Keep going, don't stop."

■ ■ ■

Myomerr tapped Maria on the back of her helmet, we need shields... *now.*"

Maria looked out of the canopy to her right, watching two figures emerge from the docking hub. "I can't, we're open and recovering..."

"Then bring up the forward shields, hurry!"

Maria had the systems in standby, her fingers racing across the controls, the forward shields wavering momentarily as they materialized. "Shields..." The forward shield flared blue, becoming clear again. "Is that what you were worried about..?"

"No, it was bigger than..."

With a streak chasing it across the sky, a hot, mangled piece of an antenna array struck the shields hard enough to be felt as a vibration. "Shields seventy-five percent."

Maria checked her TESS. "What the hell was that? We should still have fourteen minutes left."

"I don't know," replied Myomerr, searching her scans and data. "Some of this stuff is too small to see or pick up on scans. It could be the fringes of the debris expanding, or..."

A dark shape and a flash of blue-green above them as PVA panels exploded, the array twisting, startled them both, the darkness of space momentarily filled with glitter before being swept away.

"Madre de dios!" exclaimed Maria. "We're out of time, we gotta go!" She keyed her comm as the forward shields flickered blue, deflecting little bits and particles, "It's *time to go* guys..."

There was an audible groan of protesting, anguished metal...

■ ■ ■

After seeing exploding PVA panels, Dan Murphy was done being nice or gentle; *it was like these people had all the time in the world.* He yanked the Russian through the door who landed clumsily on his feet, "Bozhe moi! You have gravity, how iz dat possible?"

"Yeah - yeah, gravity, we've already established that. It's a new invention," he added sarcastically, pushing him back toward Dooby. "To the back of the bus, Ivan."

"How do you know my name..?" asked the Russian, stumbling toward Dooby.

"It's on your suit, genius." Dan rolled his eyes, "Talkative lot, aren't they? The Israeli guy's the only one who hasn't said a word..."

"It's time to go guys..." came Maria's voice over the comm.

"We have two left out here..." replied Dan, returning to the door. The last two astronauts were in route from the docking hub when something the size of a bus, passed through the lab modules on the other side of the of the station, it's antenna array spinning off as the modules blew apart like soda cans, a cloud of air, sparks and debris lost, quickly swept away. He caught the electric flash out of the corner of his eye the same time as the collision alert in his helmet lit up, squawking at him, the Big Grip folding like a pretzel, simultaneously wrenching free from the mangled truss and tearing off of the shuttle, spinning past him. He was flung out of the door as Rescue One violently corkscrewed free.

Dan Murphy could feel and hear his shoulder pull free of its socket with a sickening crunch but his hand maintained its grip on the rail. Just barely. Hanging outside of the shuttle he was drawn in by his tether. *Dooby.* Good man. He could tell Maria was wrestling with the ship trying to maintain control and attitude to give them a chance to recover the last two astronauts from the station.

"Make it fast, we're playing roulette here..."

The station was beginning to tumble, throwing off pieces in all directions, its once impressive solar arrays shredded or folded in against themselves.

Dan stood in the doorway waving them in and without two hands had to stand back and let them come. "C'mon, *c'mon!*" He could see the astronaut's face through his visor, he was only a few feet out... In a dark flash he was gone. Like he had simply disappeared. Swept away by something at twenty-thousand miles an hour. Dan blinked expecting to still see him. But nothing.

A female voice filtered through static in his comm, *"Help me! My EVA is dead! Help me!"*

The same thing that had made Dan Murphy a good cop, and a good Mason, made him a good man - a good human being. He could not in good conscience leave someone alone in trouble... no matter what his fear told him was impossible. *I can't believe I'm even considering this...* With his injured left arm tucked against his body he crouched in the doorway and launched. "Catch me!" he screamed into his comm as he flew at her, his good arm open. They collided hard, spinning, tumbling, managing to stay together, her legs wrapped around one of his, her arms around him as he held on to her the best he could with one arm. The pain in his shoulder made him nauseous and on the verge of unconsciousness - he could hear Maria's voice in his head; *for the love of God don't puke inside your helmet.*

■ ■ ■

Maria started gently backing the shuttle away from the station as its wobble grew more grotesque, aware that the ship was neither secured nor sealed.

"Main debris field in thirty seconds," Myomerr reminded her.

Maria keyed her comm, *"Now or never Dooby!"*

"The tether is reeling in as fast as it can, Skipper!" came his reply.

Shuddering violently, the shuttle lurched to one side, rolling sharply, an image frozen in Maria's mind of a blackened satellite husk the size of a refrigerator. She fought with the unresponsive controls, her consoles lighting up with warning flashers, squawking alarms and a vibration in her flight stick that could not be ignored.

"We've lost the port engine!" called Myomerr.

"Yeah, I *get* that!" shouted Maria over the alarms.

"No, I mean it's *gone!* It took the engine off..!"

"I'm not as worried about the *engine*, as I am about *the fucking wing it was attached to!"*

■ ■ ■

Flung over the top of the shuttle like a YoYo on a string as Rescue One snap-rolled, Dan Murphy got a first-hand look at the mangled left wing and ribbons of fire coming from the slashes and gaping holes, a split second before he and the astronaut clinging to him slammed against the top of the hull before bouncing off. "Fire," he wheezed painfully, "we're on fire..."

"Hold on Murphy, hold on..." Dooby heaved on the tether line, taking over for the powerless winch. The Frenchman appeared at his side, pulling together, hand-over-hand.

The space station looked like it was falling away, shrinking, trailing bits and pieces of itself, a tail of atmosphere and smoke following behind.

■ ■ ■

"Ten seconds..." announced Myomerr. "Our only chance is to go under it."

Shutting down all the damaged systems, Maria keyed her mic on an open channel, Mayday, mayday, mayday... Rescue One is going down... repeat, we're going down."

"Conquest Control - Rescue One; what is your emergency?"

"We took a heavy strike, lost port flight systems and engine, fuel pressure zero, thrusters only, still open and recovering..."

"Cut your recovery, Rescue One, Make your exit with all due haste..."

Maria watched as the microdust of the leading edge washed past them, the forward shields deflecting much of it, larger pieces slashing past. "We live together or we die together," she grumbled. "I don't think we're going to make it, Lieutenant..."

"Skipper... skipper! Can you hear me? Can you hear me? We're sealed; go go go!"

Dooby's voice seemed to be connected directly to Maria's hand which slammed the throttle to the far stop, the thrusters firing up. "Full shields, Lieutenant!"

CHAPTER FIVE

EARTH - CHICAGO, ILLINOIS : *SANITY TAKES A HOLIDAY*

Ever since the air raid sirens started wailing, most of the city was quiet - in the activity sense... except for a few areas on the south side, where people were taking advantage of what looked to be the end of the world. Like a hot spark to straw, looting and rioting started as a glowing ember, quickly spreading, suddenly erupting into a full-blown conflagration of entire neighborhoods. Because - everyone needs a new flat screen TV, Doritos and a new pair of Nikes to greet the end of the world.

Chicago Police Sergeant, Bobby Fortuno maneuvered the heavy Crown Vic through nearly empty streets, the blue and red lights on his squad car flashing. The police siren seemed redundant, adding to the cacophony of the air raid sirens and he'd switched it off. "I wish they'd shut the damn things off... they're giving me a headache."

Sitting in the passenger seat, Patrolman Nick Osmanski checked the intersection as the cruiser rolled through against the light, wind-driven debris blowing across the street. "Clear." He looked up through the top of the windshield, "Looks like the clouds are breaking up... craziest weather I've ever seen..."

"Leaving as fast as it came in," commented Bobby. "Good riddance to it." He steered the Crown Vic around a fallen light pole. "I've never heard of a tornado in the city before, much less three of them..."

Nick pointed up the street, "Looks like Romano's Sub Shop is still open... the lights are on..."

With few people on the street and everything else closed, it struck him as odd and Bobby slowed the car, "Mmm, let's check on them, make sure everything's alright."

Nick retrieved his officer's cap and donned it as he popped his door, "Think they're going to call us for the south side?"

Bobby slid his cap off the dash, "No idea, Ski. Call us in..." He scanned the empty street, his hand resting on his sidearm. The stout red brick buildings were older in this neighborhood, built during the 30's and 40's - but well kept, apartments above, overlooking the stores at sidewalk level.

"We're logged," indicated Osmanski.

Having stopped at the curb before reaching the storefront, Sergeant Fortuno directed his partner to the closest corner of the restaurant, making his own way along the street side of the parked cars for concealment. "Watch the windows..." As he reached the end vehicle parked past the sub shop he made his way to the building, carefully peeking in through the glass store front. An old man sat alone on one of the stools at the lunch counter with a cup of coffee watching a television on the wall, a woman behind the glass deli cases doing busy work. The deli restaurant was empty of patrons and Bobby waved Nick in.

"Pop-Pop, Nanna, what are you doing here?" asked Bobby, taking off his hat as he entered.

The man turned on the rotating stool, "Hello boys..."

"People have to eat," said the old woman. "Are you hungry? Let me make you a sandwich," she said cheerily.

"I could eat," smiled Nick Osmanski.

"Ski can always eat," snarked Bobby Fortuno. "For me, I'll have a club sub," he pointed, "with the works."

The old man sipped his coffee, "We've been here more than sixty years, I've never heard of a tornado in the city..."

"Damnedest stuff *I've* ever seen," agreed Nick.

"How is it out there?" asked the old woman, spreading mayonnaise on the sub sandwich bun. "We haven't seen more than three or four people since the sirens started."

"Quiet," replied Bobby frowning. "Almost too quiet. There's rioting on the south side."

"We heard," said the old man pointing at the TV. "We got local news on the antenna – got tired of watching that space news stuff."

Bobby watched the screen, the sound turned down. "Regular broadcast, huh? Have they had any news from anywhere else?"

"A little here and there," commented the old woman. "Nothing good..."

"Washington was hit," offered the old man.

"D.C.?"

"D.C.," he nodded "They're estimating over two-hundred-thousand dead."

"From *weather..?*" frowned Nick.

"Nuke," replied the old man. "Nobody's sure whose it was. Not that it matters I suppose."

Bobby Fortuno suddenly felt light headed and reached out for the counter, "Oh my God..."

Nick grabbed his arm for support, "You OK, Sarge?"

"Tina..." he wiped at the sudden sweat on his forehead, "she was supposed to be going to visit a friend at Georgetown University."

"I thought your daughters were at Duke University?"

"They are... Tina had some time off..."

"What about Annie?"

"Annie was going surfing in Myrtle Beach with friends..."

"She's OK, Sergeant," reassured the old man, patting Bobby's hand.

"How could you know that?"

"Because you've been a good father, you've raised smart girls... she's probably not even there..."

Bobby Fortuno thought about the hundreds of times he'd bought his two girls into Romano's over the years for sandwiches, sodas, ice cream - the owners watched them grow up. They were like family.

"Thanks Pop-Pop," smiled Bobby weakly.

"You should call your girls," commented the old woman, "you'll feel better."

"No cell service, all the satellites are locked out," said Nick, holding up his useless cell phone.

"Papa," called the old woman, "give him the phone," she handed the store's cordless to her husband over the counter.

"Thank you Mama," he replied handing it to Bobby. "The land lines work..." He pointed at the clunky old style handset, "Pull the antenna up, the base is back in the kitchen..." he turned back and winked at his wife, the old woman replying with a knowing nod.

■ ■ ■

The weather was gorgeous for late spring but the surf, well, it wasn't doing much of anything; low undulating waves washing sedately upon the beach with a light breeze. The group of girls didn't seem to be too concerned, sitting on their towels, some in bathing suits, some in wet suits half-peeled down to enjoy the warmth of the sun, surf boards and sail boards laying scattered behind them in the sand.

"Anybody been watching the news?" asked a brunette, her hair in a ponytail.

"That would require going back inside. Why in the name of all that is this," replied a petite blonde, indicating the scenery around them with a wave, "would I want to do that?" There was a chorus of laughter from the group. "I've been freezing my ta-tas for months; it's a nice beach house but I'm not going back inside unless you all drag me in..."

"Sweetie," commented a tall redhead with freckles, "I could tuck your tiny ass under my arm and carry you in," she laughed.

"Where are you going to school?" interrupted the brunette, adjusting her ponytail

"University of Illinois..." replied the blonde.

"Aren't you from San Diego? Are you nuts?"

"Yeah, but you're at Georgetown, aren't you?"

"Well yeah," countered the brunette, "but winter there aint like winter in Chicago. Bbbrrrr," she shivered for effect producing another round of laughter.

"Bunch of lightweights," joked Annie, running her fingers through her short auburn hair, "Chicago's not that bad..."

"Say's the girl going to school in the warmest climate of us all," countered the redhead, rubbing sunblock on her arms.

"Well I did consider Florida..." grinned Annie.

The tiny blonde cocked her head, "Am I hearing a cell phone?"

"I thought the cell phones were down," offered the brunette digging in her beach bag. "It's not mine, I don't have a signal," she offered holding it up.

"I think it's *mine...*" Annie dug in her bag as it continued to ring, growing louder as she uncovered it. "It *is* mine." She held it in her hand and stared blankly at the screen, the icon showing no signal on her phone.

"Answer it, Annie."

"I don't have a signal either..."

"You've got *something... Answer* it!"

Annie answered cautiously, "Hellooo..?" Her eyes widened, *"Daddy?"*

"I'm so glad you're home, baby. Are you OK?"

"I'm fine daddy – but I'm not home, I'm in Myrtle Beach. I set my phone up for call forwarding before I left... But I thought the cell phones were down. *This is so weird..."*

"Yeah Annie it's weird. Annie, listen, where's your sister, did she go to D.C.?"

The stress in her father's normally calm demeanor was evident. "No dad, Tina's here with me; her friend from Georgetown decided to come here. Why? What's going on?"

"Oh thank God. Can I talk to her? I want to talk to her."

"You're freaking me out dad, what's going on? Are you alright? Is mom alright?"

"I'm fine baby. As far as I know your mom's OK too – I haven't talked to her..."

"OK, well, Tina went for a walk up the beach with a couple other girls," she glanced up and down the beach, "I don't see her, I'm not sure how long they'll be gone..."

"Keep an eye on the news Annie, stay out of the big cities..."

"Why? Dad..? *Dad..?*" She looked at the other girls who were all staring at her and listening intently. "We lost the connection..." she mumbled, staring at her phone, the no signal icon persisting. "He said we should watch the news..."

■ ■ ■

The owners of Romano's Sub Shop watched the Sergeant and his partner leave their restaurant, heading out into the empty neighborhood, the retreating clouds allowing streaks of late afternoon sunlight play across the buildings on the other side of the street.

"The sirens have stopped..." commented the old woman.

"Yes Mama, for now at least. But I don't think this is the last we'll hear them. It's bound to get worse."

"You're so negative, Papa..."

"Just being a realist, Mama. You know as well as I do these infiltrators are going to do their best to destroy this world."

"These poor people didn't even realize it was happening."

"It's a long con, Mama. What, going on a hundred years now? I think some of them woke up, but it's an uphill battle to get the willfully blind to see." The old man absentmindedly stirred his coffee, "The hardest part of being a *Watcher* has been doing nothing..."

"What we did for the Sergeant wasn't *nothing,*" argued his wife.

The old man shrugged, "Ach, a little thing. The Sergeant is one of the good ones. He deserved peace of mind, I am glad we could provide it for him. I hope his girls stay safe."

The old woman refilled her husband's coffee cup, "Do you think Watcher Control..."

He waved off her concern, "GIS has more important things to worry about than our comm usage or who we've been tracking."

CHAPTER SIX

WASHINGTON D.C. : *PRESIDENTIAL EMERGENCY OPERATIONS CENTER*

A planned security and operations meeting scheduled with the President and other members of the security council at the White House turned into a rather lengthy ordeal. But CIA Director of South American Operations, Stephen Miles, decided it was better than the alternative. He suspected his Washington office and most of its staff were incinerated in the blast. Of course, from the PEOC situated far below the White House, *or what might be left of the White House,* there was no way to tell yet what the extent of the damage to the capitol might be. Short of going topside, of course. And that would be a radioactive death sentence.

There were several crucial people missing from the gathering, made obvious by their absence, not the least of which was the President. Stephen Miles took the elbow of a Marine sentry, guiding him aside, away from the other attendees, "Have you seen the Director of National Security anywhere, Lance Corporal?" he asked quietly.

"No sir. I don't believe he made the meeting," answered the Marine just as discreetly.

"What about the NSA Director?"

The Lance Corporal shook his head, "No sir."

"Did you see the list of infiltrators when it was broadcast?"

"Yes sir. But I was not at liberty to view it in detail."

"I understand." Stephen Miles shifted his eyes about the room, "Now you will," he whispered, sliding a USB thumb drive into the Marine's hand. "Find a computer with a printer, it should be about twenty-five pages. Make ten copies and bring them to me. This is *national security,* son..."

"Yes sir."

Stephen gave him a friendly pat on the shoulder, "Good man. Go now."

■ ■ ■

A crafty little bit of code added to the file on the USB drive, put in motion a self-replicating message that emailed the printable list to any other computer it could reach in the PEOC network. With enough security clearance to access email databases and break free of the security protocols, it searched for outside access to other facilities tied into the system and sent itself there. It would eventually end up on NASA, Area 51, FBI, NSA, CIA, DOD, DOE, Pentagon and DARPA computers. That's when the real fun would start.

For his participation, although decidedly small, the Lance Corporal paid with his life. After a twenty-minute delay, Stephen searched for and found the Marine slumped over the keyboard of a computer in a small, darkened, unlocked office, a .22 caliber hole in his head behind his right ear, powder burns on his neck and collar.

"Son of a bitch," Stephen hissed, quietly locking the door behind him. *We have a mole.* With a pen light in his mouth, searching for clues, he found a paper jam in the shredder; ten pages of the list, with the bottom of the pages sticking out far enough to see the names. Whomever killed the Lance Corporal didn't have time to erase their visit. *Maybe they didn't have time to police their brass...* He dropped to his hands and knees to look for the spent shell casing from the bullet that ended the Marine's life. No luck.

The click of the door handle shot a spike of adrenalin up his spine and he stuffed the pen light into his suit pocked and drew his .40 caliber Sig Sauer P-226 as the door handle turned. *Did I remember to lock it? Did they see me come in here?* The handle rotated to the lock stop then back the other way, slowly, quietly, meeting resistance. He could see shadows under the door from the light in the corridor as the person moved away. Letting out a long, slow exhale, Stephen wondered if the code had executed successfully. He prayed it had. Nudging the mouse cleared the screen saver from the monitor as it winked back to awake mode... the code's gear and wing icon at the bottom right hand of the screen told him it had successfully done its job. A sudden thought hit him. Holstering his Glock, Stephen reached around the Corporal's body and pulled up the network screen finding he had access to fifteen printers scattered throughout the facility. A wry smile crossed his lips as he sent the file to all of them and ordered ten copies printed at each. *Someone's going to be very busy...*

Noticing the Marine's 9mm Beretta M-92 was missing from his holster, Stephen pulled the USB from the computer and slid it into his pocket, being careful to leave no evidence of his presence. *Great, now they have something bigger than a .22. Hopefully I can get my ass out of here without anyone seeing me...*

■ ■ ■

"Sir! What are you doing down in this area? This area is *restricted..."*

Stephen spun on his heel, trying to maintain his composure, "Ah, Sergeant, good to see you, I've gotten a little turned around, I'm looking for a restroom," he reached out and jiggled the handle of an office on the opposite side of the corridor.

"Sergeant Major," corrected the Marine. "You're not going to find it here, these are all offices. This area is restricted."

"Yes, you mentioned that," replied Stephen coolly. "I was hoping to find one with a private bathroom," he added rubbing his stomach. "A little bit of a bad lunch I'm afraid..."

The Marine scrutinized him momentarily before using a knife hand gesture to direct him in the opposite direction in a very regimented manner, "All the way at the end of this hall, turn left, half way down on your right."

"Thank you, Sergeant Major," said Stephen, turning away. *I bet this kid salutes the toilet after he takes a shit...*

"Sir..."

Stephen turned back apprehensively, "Yes?"

"Have you seen a Lance Corporal?"

Stephen shook his head nonchalantly, "Sorry, no."

The Marine turned sharply and marched in the opposite direction, mumbling. "I'm gonna kick his ass when I find him..."

Stephen headed back the way he came, *No you're not, Sergeant...*

■ ■ ■

"Signal up!" called an Air Force communications officer from the situation room. "We have a live drone feed!"

"Where's it coming from?!" shouted a four-star Air Force General, depositing his coffee cup on the nearest desk as he hustled toward the room, Stephen Miles close behind him.

"Andrews Air Force base, General."

"Andrews is still up, that's a good sign..."

"Altitude?" asked Stephen.

64

The communications officer pointed at the flat-screen TV, indicating the lines of information along the edges of the video feed. "Ten-thousand feet, and climbing. The MQ-9 Reaper has a ceiling of about fifty-thousand feet."

"That won't take it above the mushroom," countered Stephen.

"He's probably not trying to," replied the communications officer, "he's just going for operational altitude, about twenty-five-thousand feet..."

"I don't want to see the *cloud*, have him pan the camera below him," ordered the General.

"No direct communications yet, General, we're still rebooting and logging back into everything. Our stuff is shielded but the EMP from the blast still affected us... it must have been right on top of us." Stephen and the General exchanged worried glances as other staff and officers filled the room.

I have a hard line to Andrews," announced a Senior Airman, raising his hand. "Trying to get to flight control..." he added, cradling the phone receiver on his shoulder.

"Give me that," growled the General angrily, gruffly snatching the receiver from under the Airman's ear. "You listen here..."

"They were transferring me..." mumbled the Airman as the General shouted into the phone.

"This is General Burton... Hello? *Hello..?!"*

"Still transferring," commented the Senior Airman under his breath.

■ ■ ■

The situation room was standing room only, everyone watching the video feed from the drone, the Senior Airman back in control of the phone, directing the drone pilot, relaying the General's orders. Twenty minutes after the blast the detonation column had risen up into the mushroom cloud, the cloud spreading out, beginning its dissipation phase.

The epicenter of the blast was about a third of a mile across, featureless, black, smoking, the ground seemingly depressed, a stretch of Interstate 395 completely erased from existence. The blackened void was surrounded by a burning ring of near total destruction that extended outward, giving way to wind-blast destruction for miles in all directions, a black and gray landscape void of color.

"Mother Mary of God..." whispered someone.

"Sweet Jesus," muttered another.

"It hit east and a little south of us," observed Stephen.

"The Capitol Building is gone..." pointed an aide. "Library of Congress, Senate buildings... Smithsonian Air and Space is a loss..."

"Supreme Court is heavily damaged... Look, the Washington Monument is still standing!"

"My offices are gone," noted Stephen, his lips tight. "And the White House is nearly totally destroyed." He reflexively glanced upward.

"Smaller than I expected," commented the General. "Does Andrews have an estimate on the size?"

The Senior Airman looked back over his shoulder, "Fifteen to twenty kilotons. North Korean Taepodong 2, or a variant as the delivery vehicle..."

Standing behind Stephen, Vice Admiral Cooke shook his head in disgust, "Never thought I'd see the day..."

"That a short, certifiably insane, megalomaniac with a bad haircut pushed the button?" interrupted Stephen. "Personally, I'm surprised it didn't happen sooner considering his advanced level of crazy." He wanted to pace the floor but the room was packed, the conference table and chairs empty, everyone congregated near the communications consoles and video screens. "I need to get out of here, I have teams in the field I need to contact." His eyes swept the room, fully aware that somewhere in the facility was a murderer, likely an enemy alien sympathizer or traitor.

The General pointed at one of the screens that showed information from Strategic Air Command and NORAD, "One of our Minutemen made it through that dam screen up there; hit Pyongyang." He turned back to Stephen, "Fifteen times larger than that one out there," he indicated the live video feed from the drone, an evil smirk on his face. "Payback's a *bitch...*"

Stephen grabbed him by the elbow, "It's not a *competition*, General," he hissed. "We need to stop throwing these things around or you'd better get used to living underground for the next thousand years."

"It's *war* Mr. Miles - *damn right* it's a competition!"

Stephen reached back and tore a copy of *the list* out of the hands of an aide standing nearby, tossing it on the console in front of the General. "This isn't *war* General, this is *madness,* caused by the people on this list... and it needs to stop."

■ ■ ■

With the Dragonfly's remaining maneuvering and braking thrusters in a constant burn, Maria fought with the vibrating controls, the rescue shuttle flying about as good as a one-winged potato, waddling down through the atmosphere in a semi-controlled crash-dive. The tilted desert floor rushed up at her as she worked to keep the crippled craft upright on its glide path; if it rolled on its side there would be nothing left but a smoking crater and scattered pieces. "Route all shield power to the nose and belly."

"Aye, Skipper," replied Myomerr, making the adjustments.

"Hold on, everybody..!" Maria hauled back on the flight stick and applied full antigravity, the nose lifting slightly as the hull pancaked against the ground, bouncing upwards before slamming back down and skidding across the terrain, a cloud of sand and powder-fine dust exploding out in all directions. The deafening force of the initial impact bent the remaining wing down, the passing terrain tearing it off in a gut-wrenching scream of tortured metal and shattering composites, the hull banging and clattering along the ground for nearly a mile, groaning as it twisted and bent, half rolling as it came to rest in a depression in the desert, the nose crushing against a raised ridge of rock and sand.

A towering wall of dust and sand drifted slowly away from the jagged scar across the desert, about four miles east of Taybad, Iran, and four miles west of the Afghan border. A massive cloud of powder-like orange dust shrouded the alien craft, suspended in the air, drifting slowly across the parched terrain.

Myomerr shook off the stars in her vision, realizing her controls were dead and the door behind her, buckled to match the severely warped bulkhead. *That wasn't opening without a boron cutter.* "We've got smoke! Blowing the canopy..." she announced, grabbing and forcefully yanking the manual lever. The explosive bolts securing the canopy to the hull rippled off like a machine gun, the cracked bubble dropping loosely to one side. Ripping at the buckles of her flight harness, Myomerr cast them off and pushed upward on the bubble, rolling it off the cockpit, discarding it, letting it drop to the sand. "Let's go Skipper, get your ass up..."

■ ■ ■

The shuttle's waist door jammed partially open but it was enough for Dooby and Dan to get everyone out with a belly crawl. Free of their space suits, the astronauts wiggled out into the sunlight in little more than t-shirts

67

and shorts, Dan helping them from the outside as best he could one-handed, his injured arm in a makeshift sling. "C'mon," he urged, pulling the Russian free of the doorway, "we need to get clear, we're not sure where that smoke is coming from..."

Dooby half wiggled out, shoving an armful of pulse rifles into the sand,"Dan, take these, we might need them. I'll be right back..."

"Wait, Dooby, where are you going?"

"To find something to cover our guests, I'm guessing it'll get chilly real quick when the sun goes down."

"But the smoke..." objected Dan.

Dooby waved it off as he retreated back under the edge of the door, "I'll be fine, I'll be right back." With the emergency lighting failing, Dooby felt his way through the dimly lit interior, the tilted floor making it difficult to move around. He stumbled and fell over the heap of discarded space suits, cursing to himself. The moment the deck shifted beneath his feet, he knew he was in trouble, the slit of light under the waist door going dark.

"Dammit!" Dan Murphy put his shoulder against the shuttle's hull and pushed, his feet sliding in the powdery sand. "Dooby! *Dooby!*" He turned to the others, *"Help me...* Push! *Push!"* Even with them all working together, the hull remained unmoved, the bottom of the open door buried in the sand. "We can't leave him in there..!"

"I do not see what we can do, mon'ami," shrugged the Frenchman, "we have no tools."

"Dig," shot Dan, dropping to his knees, attempting to dig one-handed, moving the pulse rifles out of the way. "We have to get him out before he suffocates..."

The Russian bent down and lifted one of the carbines off the pile, examining it, "Perhaps we can use one of dese, da?"

"NOooo!" shouted Dan, leaping to his feet, grabbing the weapon's forward hand guard and pointing its muzzle to the sky. "You see that yellow pudding over there?" With a nod of his head he indicated a small but growing pool of thick, oily fluorescent yellow goo behind the shuttle. *"Fuel.* And the word *explosive* doesn't *begin* to adequately describe that stuff."

The Russian released the gun, "I am sorry, then I do not see how we can possibly..."

The explosion clanged loudly against the hull, making the entire group duck and cover, becoming fast friends with the sand at their feet...

■ ■ ■

Reclaiming control of the phone, General Burton ordered another round of Minuteman launches to strike high priority targets around the world. "If we've already hit something," he shouted into the receiver, "then choose another target, dammit!"

"This is *insane,* General..." insisted Stephen Miles. "This *has* to stop..."

"Harlan," called Vice Admiral Cooke, using the General's first name, "what the hell are you doing?" The Admiral brushed past Stephen, reaching out for the man he'd known for nearly two decades. *"Harlan..."*

"That's far enough, Robert," replied the General, turning to meet him, handing the phone receiver back to the Airman. He held a Beretta M-92 in his other hand, "What am I doing..? I'm doing my *job*. I'm eliminating our enemies..."

The Admiral waved off the noisy crosstalk in the room, *"Quiet!"* He calmly indicated the Beretta pointed in his direction. "Harlan, where did you get that?"

"It doesn't matter Robert... *we* don't matter. Nothing matters anymore." He waved at the crush of staff around the room, "Because we're not making it out of here. No one is." He pointed at the drone video feed, "We're under *that*. A *thousand* years of radioactivity."

"But..."

"What *matters*," interrupted the General, "is the *mission...*"

"What mission?" probed Stephen Miles, stepping forward. *"Whose* mission?" He pointed at the list of alien criminals still lying on the communications console, *"Their* mission?"

"Are you one of *them?*" asked Vice Admiral Cooke, coolly.

"No, I'm not on that list..."

"That's not what I asked you Harlan..."

"Something tells me he's not who you think he is, Admiral," interrupted Stephen. "It's why he doesn't know about the emergency evacuation tunnels or the train."

Vice Admiral Cooke hazarded a sideways glance at Stephen, "He's an imposter..." It wasn't so much a question as an educated guess.

"I believe so."

"Can you prove it?"

The Sergeant Major, Stephen had encountered in the corridor pushed through the crowd, his Beretta M-92 clear of its holster, hanging in his hand,

69

concealed at his side, the safety already off. "Sirs, I would like to ask the gentleman in the suit if he knows who might have killed my Lance Corporal... Since I encountered him outside the office where his body was found." The Sergeant Major's gun hand came up, pointing at Stephen, the crowd splitting to be free from the line of fire.

Years of work as a field agent and seasoning didn't fail Stephen who didn't even blink, his eyes turning away from the Sergeant to lock with the General. "You might want to ask the General that question, Sergeant Major, since he's holding the Lance Corporal's sidearm." His hand moved discreetly into his suit jacket, his hand on the butt of his Sig Sauer. "And I bet if we check the General's pockets we might even find the .22 caliber pen-gun he killed him with..."

"Put it down, Harlan," commanded the Admiral. "Or whoever you are."

The Sergeant Major's firearm transitioned smoothly to the General, "Sir, I'm going to have to ask you to put that down until we sort this out..." General Burton's eyes shifted nervously around the room, face by face. "Sir," insisted the Marine Sergeant, "please don't do anything foolish..."

Having clearly made a decision, the General straightened, stiffening up, bringing his heels together, his eyes straight forward, the muzzle of the Beretta swinging up under his chin. It happened so quickly no one had a chance to react. The muzzle blast liquified much of the tissue under the chin and a portion of the neck, the bullet exiting the top of his head and lodging in the ceiling, painting the ceiling, the big screen monitor, the Senior Airman and the communications console with blood and brain matter. His body went momentarily plank rigid before toppling backward like a tree, crashing into the wall behind him. Crumpled against the wall, his heart still pumping, his lungs struggling to breathe, he gurgled through the crater in his neck, his eyes rolling around, perhaps looking at the faces around him. There was no way to tell if he could actually see or comprehend what was happening. In another moment he was still, his eyes vacant, unmoving.

Searching the interior pockets of the General's uniform jacket, Stephen retrieved a .22 caliber pen-gun, opened the breach and extracted an empty bullet casing, sniffing it, "Fresh."

"But why?" asked the Admiral.

"We'll never know *now*," muttered Stephen, waving his hand in disgust at the bloody corpse.

"How did you know it was him?" asked the Sergeant Major.

Stephen indicated the printed alien criminal list on the console, "It was the way he said he wasn't on *that* list. It sounded specific, like he'd read it already. I'd asked the Corporal to make copies and there were some jammed in the shredder. Makes me think he killed the Corporal, altered the list and tried to shred the present copies. When I sent electronic copies to printers all over the facility he knew he wasn't on them."

"So you *knew* the Corporal was dead, you *were* in that office," confirmed the Marine Sergeant.

"Yeah, sorry about that, Sergeant Major," apologized Stephen. "I didn't know who I could trust..."

■ ■ ■

The Dragonfly's blown emergency hatch sailed over the heads of Dan and the astronauts, ringing like a bell as it hit the ground, rolling a few feet in the sand before dropping over with a thud, producing a puff of dust.

Dan looked up in time to deflect a flying emergency kit with his good arm, followed by a large, heavy, soft bag which he caught, knocking him to his rump. "*Hey*, what the hell..."

Surrounded by smoke, Dooby's head appeared in the emergency hatch opening, "Whoo, that's better," he breathed in. Lifting himself up through the hatch he leaned head-first from the top of the shuttle headed toward the ground. "A little help?"

Instinctively, hands reached up to meet him, "Let go, mon'ami, we have you."

While they were easing him to the ground, Dooby exhaled deeply, spitting in the sand, "I don't know what's burning, but it's *nasty*." He stood up and nonchalantly dusted himself off, "Had a heck of a time finding that damn hatch in the dark..."

"And we had no idea how to get you out." Dan handed Dooby the emergency evacuation kit, "We'd better get away from the ship, it's leaking thruster fuel all over the place," he motioned to the pool of gooey yellow slime pooling in the scar cut in the soil behind the shuttle.

"Don't worry about that," waved Dooby, "it needs a pretty intense ignition source."

"Like one of these?" asked Dan picking up a carbine.

"Ooh, yeah, that would do it."

71

Dan glanced at the Russian, "Good thing we didn't use one of these then..."

Dooby slung a carbine over his shoulder. "Let's get the flight crew and get to higher ground," he patted on the emergency evacuation kit, "I need to set up our comm beacon."

The group found Myomerr sitting in the sand, her back against the wreckage, head bowed, helmet laying near her, hands hanging over her knees.

"What's going on Merr?" asked Dooby, looking around, "where's the Skipper?"

The Ketarian raised her head, sobbing, her eyes filled with tears, the fine fur of her face wet. She thumbed up over her shoulder at the cockpit without speaking.

"Skipper?!" Dooby dumped the gear in his arms like it was radioactive. Jumping up, he caught the edge of the cockpit, pulled himself up and scrambled over the lip, disappearing.

Janine Luack, the American astronaut, was more stunned by the feline appearance of the Ketarian pilot, obviously a woman, than everything else she'd experienced so far. She knelt next to Dan who was speaking softly with her, only understanding his side of the conversation. *"How bad is she?"* He asked, holding her hand. The feline woman muttered something and shook her head, it didn't appear to be good news as he laid his hand on her shoulder, bowing his head.

■ ■ ■

Blinking away tears, Dooby eased Maria's helmet off and set it on the copilot's seat behind her. Her eyes closed, blood ran from her mouth and he eased her head back against the headrest. The nose of the shuttle was mangled upward and back, the flight controls jammed against her body, the dash crushed inward and folded downward against her legs and pelvis. Reaching up and underneath, he felt around, seeing with his fingers. Her legs and everything below her waist was pinned and completely crushed.

Dooby took her hand as he felt for a carotid pulse with his free hand. Closing his eyes he concentrated; it was there, but just barely. "I'm here Skipper, you're not alone," he whispered in her ear, squeezing her hand, kissing her on the side of her face. "You did a *wonderful job*, we're all safe." He paused to wipe his face on his shoulder. "Looks like you're up for a promotion today, Skipper; you're getting your permanent angel wings - *for exemplary performance in the face of insurmountable odds...*" He stroked the back of her hand with his thumb, and brushed matted hair away from her face with his free hand. "It's alright, you can let go now Maria, it's safe, the Gods will catch you... No pain. No worries... just complete freedom flying through the stars and the heavens..." There was an almost imperceptible squeeze on his hand, maybe just a spasm, but it felt intentional. Her goodbye. He searched for a pulse again but it was gone.

He stayed a while, holding her hand like that, sobbing. She was his favorite person in the universe. He never thought about acting on it, she was a level far above him in class, but he'd always had a secret love for her that went far beyond admiration. He carefully, almost reverently, peeled her squadron patch off of her flight suit and slipped it into his pocket, being careful not to fold it...

CHAPTER SEVEN

EARTH ORBIT, UFW CARRIER CONQUEST : *EYE OF THE STORM*

With his elbows on his desk in the dimly lit Admiral's office, Steele had his eyes closed, head in his hands, hoping his brains weren't somehow leaking out of his ears. The madness was staggering, the damage catastrophic. Casualty estimates were between ten and twenty million. He knew it was far too early to trust the accuracy of the estimates but even at the lowest level it was horrific. There was nothing more he could do on the bridge, Captain Ryan had it well under control so Jack retreated to his ready room, watching it all unfold had made him physically ill.

Fritz lay on the couch, his head on the armrest, watching over his human. Essentially he was a dog, but his CABL system, *Computer Assisted Biological Lifeform,* made him much more, and the significance of what was happening on the planet below was not lost on him. "It is bad?" he asked, annunciating slowly.

"Very bad," replied Jack without looking up.

"No more home?"

"No more home, buddy..."

"No more beach?"

As distressed as he was, that made Jack smile. He knew the German Shepherd's affinity for the water. "I'm sure the beach and the ocean are still there," he explained, "but it's not going to be safe to go there."

Fritz rested his chin back on the armrest of the sofa, looking deflated, "Hmph," he grumbled.

The door from the bridge swished open, disappearing into the bulkhead. Lisa walked into the room, stopping just inside the doorway as it closed behind her, plunging her into darkness. "What the hell," she stammered. "What are you, a bat?"

"What do you want," said Jack flatly.

"Seriously, can we turn on a light?" she demanded.

"What. Do. You. Want."

She rolled her eyes and shrugged, "We've completed the last broadcast and released the satellites like you asked..."

"Ordered," he corrected.

"What-*ever*. I'm not sure how much good it will do, there's not much left up here but junk."

"Have you seen the statistics?"

"Which ones?"

"The casualty list..."

Lisa felt a cold spike race up her back, "No..."

"Estimates range from ten million, to twenty million."

Her knees suddenly weak, Lisa moved over to the couch and plopped herself down, "Oh God..."

"Remind me again," Steele growled, "whose idea it was to go public and announce the list of infiltrators to the World..."

Lisa frowned, "The UFW's Galactic Intelligence Service. Commander Brighton, er, Major Brithauz, I mean... Why?"

For the first time since she'd entered, Jack lifted his head from his hands. "This is all their fault. *Operation Magic Pawn...*" he said with distaste, standing up. "Am I still the pawn..?"

"I'm not sure I follow you, Jack."

"If I succeed, they win. If the whole thing goes to hell in a hand-basket, they win."

"And who's winning what now?"

Steele strolled over to the holo-chart table, the map of the system winking on, filling the room with a soft glow. "What does the UFW have to gain with this operation..?" he asked introspectively, not expecting an answer. He put his hand into the three-dimensional holographic chart of the Terran system and grabbed the blue and green planet, pulling it closer until it was the size of a beach ball. He tapped on the holographic orb setting it into a slow rotation. "I feel like we're getting played. Do *you* feel like we're getting played?"

"I uh... I guess I really haven't had time to think about it," Lisa responded slowly, reflecting back. "Everything's happened so quickly since we've gotten back. There's been so much to do..." She looked down at the floor and back up at her brother, "What do you suppose they're after?"

"Same as any conquest. Resources. But there's so much here, I'm not sure what's the most valuable." He pinched his lips as he stared at the holographic globe, "I've been racking my brain for over an hour, I keep coming back to the same answer. *People.*"

"Slaves?"

Steele shook his head, "No, that would be something I'd expect from the Pirates... I'm thinking more sinister, more devious, maybe more sophisticated... Slaves are good for labor, servants, maybe breeding, but not much else. They require constant control and must be housed, cared for; that takes resources. But what's *better* than a slave..?"

Lisa shook her head, "I don't know, I think you lost me."

"Someone who thinks they owe you a debt of gratitude. Someone who will welcome you... Someone who will serve *willingly*. Who will work; create their own resources. Contribute. Even *fight* for you."

Lisa shook her head in disbelief, "So you're saying this whole thing has been a setup? That they're complicit with the FreeRangers?" Her eyes widened, "Ooo, or the agents are actually *UFW* and they're double-crossing them?"

Steele raised an eyebrow, "Hadn't thought of that last one..." He turned his back on the holo-table, leaning against it, arms folded, legs crossed at the ankle, "I'm thinking the UFW was being opportunistic. They knew the spies and infiltrators were here but didn't know what do about it... until *our* happy-assed little band of merry men stumbled into the picture..." He chewed on his lower lip. "When we lost the Freedom, it was perfect timing for them. They offer us a new ship... or a nice big juicy *task force*. Like a dumbass," he waved, "I take the task force." He refolded his arms. "I forgot the *KISS* principal..."

"Keep It Simple Stupid?"

He tapped the tip of his nose and pointed at her, "Exactly. I let my ego get in the way of a clear decision."

"To be fair, Jack, maybe that's why Admiral Higdenberger wanted an immediate decision. He didn't want you thinking about it too long. He..."

"Suckered me in," added Steele, finishing her sentence.

"I was *going* to say, took advantage of your sense of integrity," corrected Lisa.

"That's a nice way of saying he suckered me." Jack ran his hands through his hair, "Man, I got played... Hard."

Lisa stood up, the glow of the holo-table allowing her to see well enough to cross the room and grab a bottle of water from the mini-fridge. "Are you *sure* you're not just overthinking this whole thing? Allowing your imagination to run away with you?"

Steele shook his head, "I don't know. I don't think so. I remember Captain Gantarro telling us how unique we were... how much we were needed, our way of thinking, our clever warrior tactics..." He flung his hands wide, "*Dammit!* It goes back *way* farther than I thought..."

"But, how could it? The UFW didn't know you back then... You guys were just a consequence of a random accident. Weren't you?"

"Maybe yes, maybe no," countered Jack. "There were quite a few *accidents* that brought it all together... I don't get the feeling that it was all that random, *or* all that accidental. I don't know if I told you this, but we all had tracking chips in our necks; me, Brian, Mike and Pappy, Maria... we were all prior abductees. *Holy crap,*" he slapped his forehead, "could they have been planning this for decades?" Suddenly, everything from their initial disappearance until now came into question. Was the arrival of Captain Kidd and his pirates planned? A test? Or was that one of the few happy accidents in an otherwise complete plan?

Lisa pointed her capped water bottle at her brother, "Hold on, Jack, you need to calm down. I think you're getting way ahead of yourself. I think it's a real stretch to tie this all together. If this was a plan, there would have to be a less complicated way to do this..."

Jack wagged his finger at her, "What happens when a house burns down? Where do the roaches go?"

Lisa cocked her head, "What? I dunno, the next house?"

"Exactly," he replied. "Willfully. We are the cockroaches..."

"Ew."

"And the UFW is the next house," continued Jack. "But they didn't want to burn it down completely; they couldn't handle seven billion refugees. But what about a few hundred thousand? A few million? New laborers, scientists, engineers, farmers... *warriors?*"

Lisa contemplated that for a second, touching the water bottle to her chin. "So they sent an entire *task force* of fire trucks to keep the house from burning down completely," she said slowly, seeing his rationale. "Oh, man..." she groaned. "And they couldn't let you go down in teams to pick up the infiltrators one by one; it would take too long." She tapped absentmindedly on the cap of her bottle, "What do you suppose they would have done if you had chosen a replacement ship instead of the task force?"

Steele shrugged, "I don't know. For something this big they must've had an alternate plan. I suppose the end result may have been the same."

"Then you can't shoulder this, it wasn't your doing..."

"Yeah, but I just *hate* getting played," he growled through gritted teeth.

"Have you discussed this with anyone else?"

"No, it's just all coming together in my head now."

Lisa sipped her water, "Swell, I get to be the first rider on the insanity train..." she mumbled.

"What's that?"

She waved it off, "Nothing. You know, you *could* be wrong."

Steele turned back to the slowly spinning holographic planet, "That would actually be a relief. But there are too many coincidences to all of this..."

"And there are few coincidences in life," she sighed, repeating one of her brother's idioms.

Jack's TESS chimed, the holographic window popping up, hovering above his wrist, "Incoming message from flight control, Admiral."

"Connect, TESS."

Her animated face swept to one side, becoming a postage stamp on the screen's side panel as Captain Paul Smiley appeared in the main frame. "Admiral, we have a bird down..."

"Who? Where?" shot Jack.

"Maria's rescue run went sideways. They went to ground to duck under the satellite cascade. With all the targets we lost tracking during their descent. There's no emergency ping..."

"Wouldn't that be automatic, Paul?"

"Maybe not if they hit hard. I don't like saying it, hell, I don't like thinking it, but it could have been catastrophic."

"Any idea of the area they went down? Can we initiate a search?"

"Jack, I love Maria dearly, you know that. But with all this crap falling down through the atmosphere, I don't like the idea of sending any of our boys down for a look. I have a rescue and crew ready to go and birds for escort but we really ought to wait till things calm down..."

Jack rubbed his forehead and sighed, "I get it. Any luck on that UFO bouncing all around the planet?"

"The only thing we know for sure is she's got a FreeRanger ident beacon. The silhouette and characteristics don't produce anything from the UFW database. The Dark Star got a pretty good look-down on her; the only thing we can tell is, she doesn't appear to have any armaments on her..."

"That's gutsy," commented Steele.

"Or just plain stupid," countered Paul.

"You think she's picking up operatives?"

"I'd bet on it, Jack..."

"Can we get a shot on her?"

"Wasn't a priority, Jack. Our gunners had their hands full."

Jack nodded, pursing his lips, "If the opportunity comes up, whoever has eyes on her should take the shot..."

■ ■ ■

The FreeRanger cutter, Red Moon, dropped down through the weather and swept in under the clouds over Ramenskoye Airport, following the winding Moskva River as it pointed them northwest into the city. A spring snow swirled and blew, randomly hiding and revealing vision below them; the fresh green trees, brown and gray rooftops nothing more than smears of color. On the helmsman's monitors, animated 3D mapping overlaid a live video feed. "Nice weather," he remarked sarcastically.

Lieutenant Commander Aleese Portwin glanced casually at the big screen before checking her chronometer, "Time to coordinates?"

"Sixty seconds to Red Square, ma'am."

"Good, right on time. I hope our pickup doesn't keep us waiting." She switched channels on her comm console, "Recovery deck, is your team ready?"

"Recovery Team ready, Skipper..."

"Fine. One minute to LZ, stand by." Aleese Portwin pulled up her tactical screen. "*Hey*, I'm seeing atmospheric craft vectoring in on us... were you planning on telling me?"

"Yes ma'am," replied the tactical officer, "I'm watching them. They're about seven minutes out, we should be clear by then..."

"*I* want to know these things when *you* know these things, understand?"

"Yes ma'am. My apologies, I am doing a ninety degree up sweep with the sensors for atmospheric entries."

Aleese nodded her approval, "We don't want to get hit by any debris. Carry on..."

"Approaching LZ, Commander..."

"Very good, helm. Take us in. Shields?"

"Aye, descending. Upper shields at maximum, flank shields down for boarding."

On her command chair, the Commander pulled up a screen with a live video feed of the starboard side boarding area. "Extend gear..."

"Extending gear... Down and locked."

79

■ ■ ■

Long, dark, subterranean tunnels linked all the buildings inside the Kremlin walls; the Grand Kremlin Palace, the Arsenal, the Presidium, the Auditorium and even the various cathedrals of which there were several. Some of the network of elaborate passageways were service ways and old steam tunnels. Some, near the cathedrals, were catacombs dating back to the 14th and 15th centuries. And yet, a few others were purpose-built for secretive movement of special members of the Kremlin and their families. That's not to say the KGB hadn't had cause to use the tunnels a time or two... Or more. Not that they'd admit it, of course. Their headquarters in the Lubyanka building was nothing more than a convenient five-minute drive from the Kremlin. But no one was talking.

The rumor was that there was more than one tunnel that ran down beyond the Kremlin's south wall, ending in a secret room under Kremlevskaya Street, bordering the Moskva River. A room with a pool... That was connected to the river. People who went into that room were never seen again, at least not alive. Dubbed *The Bathhouse,* your visit there meant appearing somewhere along the banks of the Moskva as a floater. Days later, weeks, or even months depending on the winter thaw. During the KGB heyday in the 1960s through the 1980s meant in the winter months *The Bathhouse* got a lot less use, lest it create a logjam of sorts during the spring thaw.

Even after the *closure* of the KGB in 1991, bodies still continued to appear in the river, reminding the citizens *The Bathhouse* still operated and the secret police were still at work, lurking in the shadows. Anyone who knew for sure, also knew to keep their mouth shut; *or else.*

Only one secret tunnel reached beyond the walls of the Kremlin that allowed safe passage; St. Basil's Cathedral in Red Square. A century newer than the Kremlin's Cathedral of the Archangel, St. Basil's colorful, ornate and detailed 16th century architecture housed an elaborate museum of the churches.

The Kremlin custodian was a thin, spry man in his late sixties, and he had known the President for decades, working alongside him in the KGB. He walked with a limp from an injury during service that did nothing to slow him down. "This is the last one, Mr. President," he commented, turning the old steel key in the ancient lock, the mechanism squeaking as he turned the key. "We must hurry if you are to make it on time."

"You have been a good friend Alexi, you are to be rewarded for your service," replied the President.

"My service to you has been reward enough..."

"Nonsense," countered the President, "you will need something to retire on..."

The group made their way through the sub-basement of St. Basil's Cathedral, the catacombs having been cleared and sanitized for the storage of the museum's overflow of artifacts. Reaching the stairs, the President sent the girls on ahead and he paused on the landing with Alexi. "This should keep you well..." he continued, handing him a piece of paper. "You will know what to do..."

Alexi followed the President up the stairs as he stuffed the folded paper into his pocket, "I fear money may have little value in this new world..."

"*Gold* always has uses, my friend," smiled the President. "And the guns will allow you to keep it..."

■ ■ ■

"I don't like this Papa, I want to go back to Paris," complained Yekaterina, walking down the steps of St. Basil's Cathedral, her high heels clicking on the stone steps.

"And I want to go back to Holland," added Mariya. "Where's Jorrit?"

"Jorrit did not make it," replied the President. "And you were forcibly deported from Holland. Remember, da?" He nudged his wife, a former Olympic athlete thirty years his junior, "Hurry Alina."

"Why is mama not coming?" inquired Yekaterina.

"Because she is *not*," he fired back angrily. "Now *hurry up!*"

The swirling snow whipped around them, blowing across the cobblestones of Red Square, the massive area devoid of people. A long, dark shape lay ahead, mostly featureless to the uninitiated, an opening in its side, two men standing on either side of a short ramp.

"Papa, what is that?" asked Mariya.

"A ship. Keep going."

"I don't want to go, I want to stay..." she said fearfully.

The howl of air raid sirens wailed mournfully, first one then another and another. All around them, all across the city. The president glanced up at the sky seeing nothing but the swirling white and put his hand on her shoulder

81

from behind, moving her forward. "There may be nothing *left* to stay for... But you will like where we are going," he urged, "much nicer than Paris."

"New York?"

"Like New York and Paris combined," he lied, pushing her past the crew members and up the boarding ramp, Alina in tow. Out of the dampness and sharp wind, he shook the snow off of his open overcoat, moving the girls to one side. He greeted the Red Moon's officer with a salute and without words, the officer held out an e-Pad. The President placed his hand on the glass surface, initiating a scan. "Welcome to Moscow," he blustered casually, "you enjoy our lovely weather, da?"

Stone-faced, the Red Moon's officer didn't respond, passing a device over the back of the Russian President's neck, the implanted RFID confirming his identity and serial number. "Welcome aboard, agent Putin," he nodded. "I'm sorry, who are these people?" he pointed in the direction of the three women.

"My wife, Alina and my daughters; Yekaterina and Mariya," Putin indicated with a wave.

"Katerina..." corrected his daughter.

"Family is not part of the extraction protocol..." began the officer matter of factly, as if he simply regarded them as luggage.

Before the man could finish his thought, the President's hand dipped inside his coat, producing a Tokarev pistol, pressing the muzzle under the officer's chin. "Maybe we change that protocol, da?"

The officer swallowed nervously, "None of the other agents were allowed..."

"To *hell* with other agents" growled Vladimir Putin, no longer a president, just a father. "I will make clear for you; those sirens? Not music... missiles are coming. If we go, we live. If we sit, we die." With a click, he pulled the hammer back on the Tokarev, "But *you* die first."

The officer backed away, "Identity confirmed," he reported into the comm. "Close us up," he waved at the crew.

■ ■ ■

"Atmospheric craft closing fast!"

Aleese Portwin glanced at the status for the recovery deck, "Speed it up Ensign, we are out of time!"

"Identity confirmed," came the reply over the comm.

The indicators on the Commander's panel for the hull winked to *secure*, "Launch! Get us off the ground!" she shouted.

"Launching, Commander..." The ship sprung free of the surface as the helmsman cranked down on the antigravity actuator, swinging the ship to a new heading, the Red Moon's tail chopping one of the minarets off of St. Basil's Cathedral like it was made of balsa wood, the blue and white structure exploding and crashing to the ground in pieces.

"Atmospheric craft identified as MiG-29M..." announced the tactical officer.

"How many?"

"A four ship formation, Skipper. We *are* targeted."

"Hellllm?"

"GOD drive on line, prepared to initiate at speed..."

Aleese Portwin watched the speed sensors climb, "Shields down. Initiate GOD..."

"The MiG-29s are *firing!*"

"Fire countermeasures! Fire countermeasures!"

"Firing decoys..." announced the tactical officer, her fingers tapping across her glass control panel. Miniature torpedoes emerged from launch tubes along the spine of the ship, jetting up and away, corkscrewing across the sky filled with an assortment of jammers and false signals to lure enemy missiles off target. "Decoys away and functioning."

"Initiating GOD; bubble at ten percent..."

The science officer pointed at the holo-screen, *"Space debris!"* Angry flaming streaks of destroyed hardware, trailing molten metal, dropped through the clouds and swirling snow, passing all around the ship.

A heavy metallic *whang* vibrated through the hull as a satellite frame crushed itself against the armor of the Red Moon's upper hull, bouncing off. "That's going to leave a mark," mumbled the Commander, wincing.

"GOD bubble unaffected. Forty percent."

Aleese was on the edge of her seat, watching the GOD drive readout; sixty percent, seventy percent... "Go, go, go..." she whispered to herself. A flaming hunk of twisted metal the size of a small car shot past the nose of the Red Moon and she recoiled out of reflex, sucking her breath sharply. *Eighty percent...* Colorful tendrils of energy covered the hull, reaching around her nose, the holo-screen changing colors, the clouds and snow barely visible through the swirling color, the jump corona fully formed in front of them.

A flash of intense light, deafening thunder and the ensuing violent shudder flung the Commander to the floor, alarm klaxons screaming with a myriad of warning chimes ringing across the bridge, the Red Moon rolling to her starboard side. "Report..." she said weakly, bringing herself to her knees, clutching onto her console for stability.

"Direct hit, our starboard atmospheric canard has been destroyed."

Aleese Portwin glanced up at the screen, relieved to see the silky lining of the transition tunnel. "Well that puts an end to further recoveries," she groaned, pulling herself to her feet, "the rest of those folks are on their own." She dropped herself into her command chair, her ego as bruised as her knees. "Alter jump course to our exit coordinates. And let's stop this roll..."

"Aye, alternating coordinates to the dark side of Saturn..." the navigator entered the new destination.

"Damn space junk," grumbled the Commander. "Tactical, what the hellion hit us?"

"Sensors recorded fire from orbit. I believe it was a rail gun charge. We were very lucky, multiple rounds bracketed all around us..."

CHAPTER EIGHT

TAYBAD, IRAN : *FROM THE FRYING PAN INTO THE FIRE*

"Dooooby!"

Dooby's head popped up over the edge of the shuttle's cockpit looking down over the side, "She's dead, Dan..." he lamented, tears in his eyes.

"I sympathize, Doob," replied Dan Murphy, pained. "And not to be disrespectful, but her worries are over now, ours are just beginning..." He motioned over the rise in terrain that had finally stopped the shuttle, "We don't have time to morn buddy, we have company. And I don't think they're the friendly type."

"I'll be down in a minute," called Dooby, disappearing from view.

"I need your ass down here *now!*" commanded Dan Murphy. "You need to set up that beacon and we need to secure a defense!" One-handed he grabbed Myomerr by her flight suit and yanked her to her feet, "Pity-party is over Missy, it's time to fight."

Her demeanor changing in the blink of an eye, the Ketarian pilot viciously sweeping his hand away, leaning forward and baring her sharp feline teeth with a snarl, *"Never* touch me again..."

"That's the spirit," smiled Dan, not missing a beat. "Hold on to that anger, we're going to need it..." He bent down and scooped a carbine off the pile, handing it to Myomerr, "We need your head in the game..."

Her eyes narrowed, *"Game?"*

"Focus. I need you *focused.* I assume you know how this works?" he asked, tapping on the rifle in her hands.

"I am familiar," she replied.

"Good, then maybe you can give a quick lesson to our friends here?" he motioned toward the astronauts.

"They will not understand me, Murphy," she reminded him.

He patted her on the shoulder, "I have faith in you to make them understand..."

Her expression darkened, staring at his hand, her lip curling enough to raise the hair on the back of his neck.

"Right, you have issues I see. You might want to see someone about that," he commented, snatching a carbine off the ground for himself, pointing the weapon's muzzle up at the hill, "We need to be up there..."

Without speaking she gathered the remaining carbines, turned and headed for the astronauts watching the desert from higher ground.

Dan Murphy blinked away the image of her fangs in his mind's eye, "Doo..."

Dooby dropped to the ground beside him, cutting him off, a small bag slung over his shoulder. He snatched up his carbine and emergency kit from its position next to the shuttle's hull, "OK let's go." He glanced around at the landscape as they headed for the rest of the group, "Can't say I like your planet much." He kicked at the ground as they walked, acrid dust billowing around his boots.

"We're not in the best of neighborhoods," remarked Dan. "In fact we're probably in one of the biggest armpits on the planet. Where I come from it's lush and green..."

"You know where we're at?" interrupted Dooby.

"Educated guess? We're in the Middle East somewhere; Iraq, Iran, Afghanistan... something like that."

"I don't know what that means," interjected Dooby, his eyebrows raised.

"It ain't good," countered Dan, his nose wrinkled. "Chase was right..."

"About what?"

"It has a very peculiar smell..."

"You mean it *stinks*," offered Dooby.

"Like camel shit, piss, armpits and ass..." nodded Dan, remembering conversations with Chase about the particulars. "Aww, what the hell is this?" he grumbled upon reaching the top of the crest. A haphazard series of ridges, trenches and dirt roads wove a broken maze, stretching a half mile to the road, about a thousand feet wide. "Looks like it was built by a bunch of fucking crack addicts..." He crouched next to the others, peering over the top towards the road.

"They stopped out there," pointed the Israeli astronaut, peering through the sights on his carbine, adjusting the magnification.

"Technicals," nodded Dan. "That's what they call those armed pickup trucks," he informed Dooby. "They don't look like rebels though... they look like regular military."

"There's a man on the back of both vehicles," observed Myomerr, "but the men that got out have moved up the road toward us, they are in the far ditch along the road."

"I see them." Dan's eyes narrowed, looking west, a plume of dust followed a convoy of vehicles in their direction, coming from a low, sprawling town of drab buildings. "Dooby, get that thing working and get us out of here. *Quick.*" Laying on his stomach, Murphy adjusted his sights one-handed, focusing on the first pickup sitting in the road; a green, white and red flag with a red symbol in the center, fluttering slowly in the stale desert breeze. "Iran. Man, it just keeps getting better..."

■ ■ ■

Steele paged through the action reports, only half seeing, half interested, his mind divided in a multitude of ways. Lisa stood at the holo-chart her back to her brother, researching the independent station at Nelson's Point. "Looks like they've got a pretty good reputation..." she commented as she turned toward him, her voice trailing off. *"Jack..."* she croaked, little more than a whisper, staring at the spot on the sofa next to the sleeping Shepherd.

Steele looked up from the e-Pad in his hand, realizing his sister wasn't looking at him and followed her gaze to the sofa. A semi-transparent figure sat next to Fritz, looking down at him, petting him gently. It silently leaned over, encircling him with ethereal arms, giving him a tender embrace. The Shepherd lifted his head, leaning into the hug, looking up adoringly as the form rose to its feet, becoming more corporeal.

"Maria," breathed Jack, dumbfounded.

She looked back at Lisa and smiled, her eyes moving to Jack, momentarily locking eyes with him before striding purposefully for the bridge door, dissolving and disappearing mere feet from the door's surface.

Jack let out a low breath, not realizing he'd been holding it in. A sudden chill raced through him and he shuddered.

"She came to say goodbye" said Fritz, annunciating slowly. "She was not sad."

"And she said; *help them,*" added Lisa.

Jack rose from his chair, "I heard that too... how did she do that? Is she... is she *dead?*"

"That's what I felt..." Lisa nodded, her hand over her mouth in astonishment.

87

"Dammit. Me too... Damn, damn, *damn,*" he groaned, his voice cracking. One step toward the door and he paused, looking back at Lisa, "We all saw that, right?"

■ ■ ■

Standing in the flight tower, Captain Paul Smiley scratched his forehead, "Along the Iran – Afghan border..?"

Steele nodded, "Yeah. Don't ask me how I know, I just know..." He wrung his hands in thought, "And something about the number thirty-six. Not sure what that means."

Paul shrugged, "Hey, you're the Admiral. But you do realize that's a huge area to cover..."

"I'm aware of that; I'm hoping we get lucky."

"It *has* quieted down out there..." noted Paul, rubbing his chin. "An armed shuttle and a four bird escort work for you?"

Jack nodded, "Add the Zulu with the advanced sensor magnapod."

"Will do."

"As soon as you can. Maybe some Marines in case they need..."

"Wouldn't send a shuttle to Indian territory without them," interjected Paul. Still facing Jack, Paul reached back and tapped a control officer, motioning to the deck. "They'll be out the door in under five, Admiral."

■ ■ ■

"Mr. Murphy," whispered Janine Luack, "I think you're really going to need both arms... *We* need you to have both arms."

He looked up from his sights, "Oh, so you're an astronaut *and* a doctor?" he asked sarcastically.

"Well, *yes.*"

"Oh... The MD kind or the PHD kind?" added Dan suspiciously.

"Both, actually. We need to get your shoulder back in."

"We don't have any..."

Janine grabbed him by his good hand, "We don't need anything. Follow me," she coaxed, sliding down the ridge in the tan work jumpsuit Dooby had salvaged from the shuttle. "It's a simple manipulation..."

"Easy for you to say," quipped Dan, "Your shoulder doesn't hurt like hell. How can you be sure it's not broken?"

"That's the Axillary Nerve, it's pinched. It happens quite commonly in an anterior dislocation. Once we get it back in place the pain should subside some – though it will still be sore for several days. Maybe a couple of weeks."

"I'm more concerned about the next several hours..."

"I understand," she replied, taking control of his arm. "Just sit still, this shouldn't hurt... much."

"Much?"

"There are three steps..." she continued, ignoring his objection. *"Relax."* She spoke out loud as she moved his arm, so he knew the steps, watching his face, "Abduction..." she moved his arm away from his body, elbow bent. "Extension..." she gently extended his arm forward. "External rotation..." she slowly rotated his arm by the wrist and elbow. "There." She guided his arm back down. "See if you can move it on your own."

"I *did* feel a pop," he noted, gingerly testing it.

"Don't go to full extension if you can avoid it; keep it closer to your body if you can..."

"Murrrrphy!"

Dan launched himself up the ridge, favoring his left arm, keeping it semi-tucked, digging in with his right hand to scramble to the top. He dropped down next to Dooby, peering over the crest. "That's a *tank...*" he whispered in astonishment.

"Two tanks," pointed the Russian astronaut. "T-72s"

"And two trucks of men..." moaned Dan, watching them spread out, running across the pale yellow terrain. The Tanks had taken up positions on either side of the divided highway, their main guns pointed at the ridge formation.

"This is not a defensible position," announced the Russian. "They can easily go around us on either side, it is like an island."

"Yeah, I can see that," lamented Dan. "I wasn't expecting *tanks*." He turned to Dooby, "You got that beacon running?"

Dooby held up broken parts, "No..."

"Oh, *fuck me,*" grumbled Dan. "How did it..." he waved off the question, "doesn't matter. We need a new plan."

"The tanks are slow," said the Israeli, we can easily avoid them down in-between the ridges. The tanks are valuable, they won't risk them. They won't bring them in where they're vulnerable..."

"We don't have anything that can hurt a tank..." he glanced over at Dooby, "do we?" Dooby shook his head, no.

"They don't know that," replied the Israeli. "They'll use the men, the men are expendable. As long as we stay inside the outer ridges..."

"It occurs to me," began Dan, "that this looks like either a fighting position or a training area. In which case, they probably know it better than we do..."

"We are out of options," announced the Russian, slithering over the top of the ridge to the other side, now inside the maze formation.

■ ■ ■

It was difficult to determine which vehicle it was coming from, but an Iranian broadcast drifted across the terrain from a loudspeaker, the soldiers holding their scattered positions, some as concealed as possible, some standing boldly in the open. The announcer spoke fair English, heavily flavored with his own language, "You have violated sovereign Iranian airspace and sovereign Iranian territory. You will surrender yourselves and equipment, or suffer the wrath of the almighty Mohammed... allahu akbar."

"Allahu akbar," chanted the soldiers in response.

"If the infidels surrender immediately, you will be given medical attention and treated fairly..."

From his position the Frenchman turned to Dan, "We are doctors, scientists and astronauts... we are no threat to them. Surely we can reason with them. Non?"

"Nyet," countered Ivan. "Murphy, you cannot possibly..."

Dan waved the Russian off, "Not even thinking about it, Ivan." He turned to Dooby, "Any luck with that thing?"

Dooby was struggling with the various parts of the emergency beacon trying to create a working unit. "Not yet. But I think I can..."

"OK, keep working on it... but keep an eye on your flank; if they get around us we're in deep trouble."

"We are already in deep trouble, mon'ami. We have, how you say; jumped from the skillet into the fire..."

"Frying pan," corrected Dan.

"Excusez-moi?"

"Never mind," waved Dan, adjusting his carbine's sight, watching the first truck.

90

■ ■ ■

Lieutenant JG, Nera Margareth switched her sensors over to magnetic as they skimmed over the desert, looking down out the side of the cockpit perspex from her Cyclone. "Not much down there but sand..."

Commander Dar Sloane adjusted the sensor sweep spread on the Zulu's sensor magnapod hanging from the ship's belly. "You're supposed to be watching the sky, Lieutenant," he admonished.

Lieutenant Torn Dado, caught movement well inside his sensor sweep, "White Two, I've got two flights of four, ten o'clock. They're coming off the deck, climbing to our altitude..." A schematic appeared in another screen as the targeting computer locked on to the lead craft and researched Earth's military database for a definition of the target. "First group of four identified as Dassault Mirage F1s..." He selected the lead aircraft of the second flight, "Second flight identified as Saeqeh-80 Thunderbolts... Wait, hold on. We've got another flight lifting off..." He adjusted his targeting computer, "Third flight identified as Northrop F-5 Tiger IIs. Looks like they've got a little of everything..."

Dar Sloane dropped the Zulu lower, the shuttle following him down, separating his search and rescue flight from the four Cyclone fighters. "You know what to do, White Leader, keep them away from us..."

"I know my job, Commander," she snapped.

■ ■ ■

"This is Colonel Kabir ali Kahn of the Royal Iranian Air Force, you have entered sovereign Iranian airspace. Leave our airspace *immediately*, or you will be shot down!" Equipped with both MICA AAM and MICA Magic IR AAM missiles, the Colonel called up his Mirage F1's weapon stores, selecting the superior infra-red imaging MICA Magic. But he would have to wait until they got within the missile's 50-mile range to fire. The Colonel had no idea what his target was, it defied his computer's attempts at identification, throwing an *unidentified* warning on the radar screen.

Despite his repeated efforts at radio contact, his commands went unanswered and the enemy craft did not deviate from their flight path; part of the group dropping below the other, defying his final commands. Blaming the accumulated results, or lack thereof on the aircraft, the Colonel cursed its

91

computer system, electronics, radio, the French builders who created it and the ground crew who maintained it in a lengthy diatribe of Arabic furor. Nudging the throttle forward, he ignited his afterburners, keying his mic, *"Enough!* They have been warned. *No* more talk. The infidels must *die* for their cursed insolence. Allahu akbar."

"Allahu akbar," came the response in his helmet.

■ ■ ■

Ensign Fidos leaned left and visually scanned the desert passing below his Dragonfly shuttle, "I see a lot of nothing down there..." He glanced up in the mirror mounted to the canopy rib at his EWO in the rear seat, "Do you see *anything* Jarosh?"

The electronics officer shook his head inside his helmet, "Lots of sand... *Woah! Launch!* We have a *launch!"* Warning lights flashed, alarms chirped and Flight Officer Jarosh tracked a missile on-screen coming up from the surface of the desert. *"Break right!"* he grunted as Fidos instinctively threw the shuttle in a right-hand corkscrew. He initiated countermeasures and ports on the Dragonfly's hull popped self-propelled decoys into the atmosphere, blinding and confusing the Iranian Sayyad-2 SAM. *"Second launch!"* called Jarosh, triggering a second volley of self-propelled decoys which left the shuttle's hull as Fidos threw the Dragonfly around, sincerely hoping everyone in back was securely strapped into their seats.

"Rescue Two to Zulu One..! Rescue Two to Zulu One!"

"Keep your shirt on, Rescue Two," grunted Dar Sloane, nosing the Zulu over and bumping the throttle. A snarling sandstorm followed the Zulu across the desert as the chin turret's gun pipper settled on the target, the twin argon pulse lasers coming to life with a squeeze of his finger, intense slashes of purple lancing toward the target, the guns producing a unique alternating sound; *zink-zunk, zink-zunk, zink-zunk,...*

A third Sayyad-2 was leaving the launcher as the Zulu's argon lasers cut through the launch vehicle and missile rack, a fierce fireball cratering the desert and glassing the sand around it, lifting the Zulu on a heat and concussion wave as it passed through its center. A river of fire, smoke and debris followed the alien craft as it exited the far side of the maelstrom, its shields shrugging it off, letting it rain down on the desert below.

A winding dry desert wadi erupted in anti-aircraft fire, from a ZU-23-2 nestled in low brush, its twin barrels pumping out 23mm rounds at a combined 800 rounds per minute. Dar Sloane jinked the Zulu as they flashed past, rounds splashing on the shields, clattering on the armor.

"Projectiles decelerated. No damage skipper."

"Somebody kill that thing," Dar ordered calmly.

"Got it boss..." The gunner in the stern turret tracked the AA gun as it retreated in his targeting reticule. A short squeeze and it disappeared in a flash, white-hot parts flung outward, its own rounds cooking off, smoky little bursts flowering in midair like fireworks.

Dar cranked on the antigravity as another ZU-23-2 appeared on his threat assessment screen, his HUD marking its location on a hill off the nose of the Zulu. The stream of 23mm rounds passed underneath the hull, deflected away by the shields before he punched the throttle. Hard. Thundering over the gun at Mach 10, it blew apart from the compression, flattening the crew and crushing the equipment truck, sending it rolling across the desert rocks like a crumpled tin can. "Talk to me Fidos..."

■ ■ ■

Ensign Torn Dado's threat indicator squawked as infra-red painted his Cyclone, "I've got a picture taker..." He reached forward and lifted the safety covers, flipping the toggles, arming his weapons, the Cyclone's gun generators spinning up momentarily to top off the charge for its strontium laser auto-cannons. The active targeting screen automatically identified the target who had electronically engaged his Cyclone. "Lead Mirage F1... they're one-hundred miles and closing."

"You've got the lead, Tornado?" asked Nera Margareth. "Good. That's the guy who keeps running his mouth... OK, lock them up boys and girls, random targets; shake them up." She blinked at her targeting screen, choosing the lead Saeqeh-80 Thunderbolt of the second flight. With her index finger hovering over the trigger and her other hand on the throttle, she broke into a wry little smile, her feline fangs showing, "Straight through on my command... Fire!" She squeezed the trigger and magenta streaks slashed across the sky, her strontium laser auto-cannons thrumming a short burst from under the chin of her fighter. "Boost!"

■ ■ ■

Colonel Kabir ali Kahn saw the first bolt of hot magenta pass his cockpit on the right, and in an infinitesimally short nano-second, his mind registered stunned amazement, curiosity, fear, loathing, and finally, recognition of the danger that was so overwhelmingly alien to him he attempted to evade in panic. His core so flooded with adrenalin, time slowed, and with horror he actually saw the second bolt coming as it tore through his left wing, shearing it off like a hot knife through butter. His reflex was to reach for the ejection handle to evacuate his stricken aircraft but his hand had barely released the flight stick when the third bolt passed over the cockpit shearing off the tail, the fourth punching through the F1's nose, passing through the cockpit and exiting out through the engine, instantly incinerating him and turning his multimillion-dollar fighter into flaming, molten confetti as it exploded at Mach 1, an oblong fireball splashing angrily across the sky.

The Colonel's wing man, Lieutenant Fadel Mohammed, saw the four-round burst of magenta light incinerate his flight leader's fighter and out of his peripheral vision, the fourth aircraft in his formation came apart in the blink of an eye, disappearing in ribbons of fire, smoke and pieces fluttering lazily Earthward. He was not about to wait for the hand of the devil to strike him from the sky, forcing the nose of his Mirage F1 down with a grunt, hammering the throttle to the far stop, pulling his aircraft into as tight a turn as he could maintain consciousness through. He headed out across the desert in the opposite direction. *"Allahu akbar. Allahu akbar. Allahu akbar..."* he chattered, panic overriding all of his other senses.

▩ ▩ ▩

"Hammerhead *right*, in three... two... one... *Execute,"* commanded Nera Margareth.

Along with the other members of White Flight, Ensign Torn Dado pulled his throttle back past the zero mark, firing breaking thrusters, simultaneously rotating the antigravity collective to maintain altitude and kicking the right rudder pedal hard, his Cyclone sliding flatly in a right-hand arc, driven by maneuvering thrusters, the nose coming smartly around, facing back the way he had come.

Overshooting the Iranian flights by ten miles at about Mach 6, White Flight accelerated again to pursue the flights that had panicked into wholesale retreat, having lost five fighters on the first pass to an enemy they were unprepared to meet.

Nera Margareth looked out and down at the five pillars of smoke reaching into the sky, the pale desert scorched where the remains of the fighters had hit the surface. "Back it down, the rest of them are running..."

Torn Dado's voice cut in on her comm, "Were letting them go?"

"As much as I'd like to chase them all down, Tornado, it's not what we're here for," she countered. Nera adjusted her comm frequency, "White Flight to Zulu One – Status?"

■ ■ ■

Perhaps; *suck my dick you dirty fucking goat-humpers,* was not the desired answer when the Iranians demanded surrender. But in Dan Murphy's defense, he wasn't current on proper protocol when dealing with hostile foreign forces. *Screw it!* He'd never been terribly fond of political correctness anyway.

Thunderclaps and the crashing rumble of sonic booms rolled across the desert, mixed with sharp explosions, marked by fire in the distant sky, angry, dirty black ribbons drifting against the blue, and columns of smoke rising from the ground. Dan would have liked to take a better look, but he was too busy trying to not get shot, ducking behind the ridge as AK-47 fire rippled across the sand on the other side of the berm that concealed him. *"Dooobyyy!"*

"Sorry, Dan!" came Dooby's voice somewhere from his left, "I can't shoot and work on this thing... and shooting is more critical at this juncture!"

"So who's telling you *not* to shoot? Can you fix that piece of junk *or not?!"*

"I don't have a lot of hope for it, no."

"That's just great," grumbled Dan through clenched teeth. He peered over the top of the ridge through his carbine's sights, "I forgot my own advice..."

"What's that?" asked Janine Luack, crouched at his side.

"Never volunteer." He squeezed off two shots at the lead truck parked in the center of the divided highway, the carbine whistling. Crimson streaks punched through the fender and into the engine, fire blowing out underneath the front of the truck on the other side with a muffled boom. "Hmmph," he grunted, " I was hoping for more than..." The troop truck lifted off the ground in a cloud of dust and flying parts, the heavy *whump* reaching him a moment later, as the flaming hulk thudded back to the ground heavily, the sound of protesting metal as it crushed itself against the ground delayed by

95

the distance. "Well *that's* a little better," he mumbled, ducking back down, AK-47 rounds sailing over him with a snapping *zing*. "Keep moving around, people! " shouted Dan, rolling to his right and pushing Janine Luack ahead of him.

"They're coming in through the main entrance!" called Ivan, picking targets carefully, squeezing off single shots from the pulse carbine. He ducked back to cover as return fire swung in his direction.

12.7mm machine gun rounds passed through the ridge of the berm just a few feet from Dooby, the crest disappearing in clouds of sand and rock as they chewed through his cover, sending him rolling down the slope to safety, scrambling in Dan's direction. "What the hellion was *that?*"

"A *Dushka,*" yelled Ivan. "Russian made DshKM; *Degtyaryov-Shpagina.* A heavy machine gun. He's on the back of one of the technicals..."

"Can you hit it?"

"Not from this angle..." the Russian ventured a look over the top of his cover, "Avi, can you hit it?"

"No," shouted the Israeli. "But I can see the tanks moving back, that's not good..."

Dan raised an eyebrow, "Why?"

"They are moving back for a firing solution on our position!"

There was a low whistle which made them all shrink reflexively; the top of a ridge forward of their position exploding in a giant geyser of sand and fire, shaking the ground underneath them, a cloud of dust and sand carried by the stale desert breeze raining down on them.

Indicating the direction the fire came from, the Frenchman motioned over the ridge to the East, "I think our troubles, they get worse..."

"More tanks!" shouted Avi.

"Tanks on *both* sides..? Where the hell are all these things coming from?" growled Dan.

Myomerr motioned toward the center of the maze, "The troops are pulling back!"

"Then let's give them a little parting gift," commented Dooby, opening the soft bag he'd been carrying around from the Dragonfly, retrieving a small glass cylinder about five inches long with metal ends, a shimmering blue-green substance swirling inside.

"What's that?" asked Dan, sliding up next to him, hoping for a grenade or something equally as devastating.

"A liquid bio-plasma system fuse," he said, seeing disappointment in Dan's face. "Inert unless you expose it to atmosphere..." he smiled wryly, whacking the metal end on a rock. He checked the glass cylinder, shaking his head before striking it again. Satisfied with the crack he had created in the tube he cocked his arm back and threw it in the direction of the entrance like a quarterback throwing for the end zone. "They're under pressure," he grunted, ducking down, pulling on Dan's sleeve to get him below the ridge.

A dull *whump* that could be felt to the core, accompanied an intense blue flash reaching out in a sphere, incinerated everything it touched; turning sand to glass, men to ash and metal to slag. Dan peered over the crest of the berm watching a lone survivor drag himself across the smoking sand, nearly naked, his legs gone below mid-thigh, meat cauterized with his bare femurs protruding from blackened stumps, most of his clothing flash-ignited off his body.

"Good. *God...*"

"They're attempting to flank around the outside..!" snarled Myomerr.

A chorus of blasts split the air, a stereo of low whistles screaming in from the left and right, prompting the group to retreat as far to the bottom between the ridges as they could get, the high explosive rounds from the tanks shaking the earth, sizable craters appearing in the outer berms on both sides of the maze.

Dan scrambled back to the top, followed by Dooby and Janine Luack, "Is everybody *OK?*"

"They're trying to breach the walls," called Ivan, "if they do, we are finished."

Closest to the outer wall of the maze on the right flank, the Frenchman, covered in dirt and sand, managed to claw his way to the top of his berm, staggering along its ridge, his eyes glazed over, blood running from his ears, dragging his carbine loosely by the barrel.

"Phillipe, get down from there!" screamed Janine Luack. "Phillipe! Get down! *Phillipe..!*"

Dan pulled her down by the arm, "He can't hear us..."

Dropping her carbine, Myomerr sprang up from cover and sprinted across the top of the berm; a blur running along its ridge, AK-47 rounds whizzing past all around her. The Frenchman staggered and stumbled, his body twitching, bullets passing through him before one struck something solid, pitching him backward out of sight.

Myomerr dove after him, sliding with him to the bottom between the berms, eight feet below the top of the ridges. Rising to one knee, she crouched over him looking at the blood splashed across his jumpsuit, trying to access his injuries. "My friend gave her life to save you. You are not *allowed* to die..." Hearing the roar of the tanks' cannons, she threw herself over the Frenchman and covered her ears with her hands. The concussion of the high explosive rounds on the outside of the maze bounced her bodily off the ground and covered the defenseless pair with nearly a foot of sand and rocks, stunning her into semi-consciousness.

Pressing herself into a kneeling position, it took Myomerr a moment to get her bearings and regain her senses, her ears ringing, her head buzzing. But the hereditary huntress in her had not lost her sense of smell... she knew he was there before he realized what he was seeing.

■ ■ ■

The figure rose out of the sand, its back to the Iranian soldier, a head of hair like a lion's mane, wild platinum and gray striped fur. When the figure turned to look at him, dressed in a dark-gray flight suit of some kind, the Iranian soldier froze, stunned to see a human tigress with bared fangs snarling at him, steely platinum-gray eyes staring through him, unblinking. It didn't immediately register as real in his mind, it was beyond his meager comprehension. Not truly *wanting* to look away, knowing he *shouldn't* look away, he hazarded a glance over his shoulder for support from someone, *anyone,* in his squad. When he looked back, he'd realized his mistake, but it was too late for him. In a low-ready position, he tried to raise the muzzle of his AK-47, but the sling over his shoulder slowed his response and she was almost on him at a full run, arms outstretched, claws extended, teeth bared, emitting a bone-chilling, gut-wrenching snarl. She caught the fore-grip of his rifle, her nails digging into the wood, redirecting the barrel and passed him shoulder-to-shoulder, yanking and turning him around as she ran up the berm perpendicular to the ground, then down, spinning on her feet and using her momentum, swinging him, slamming him face-first into the opposite berm with bone-crushing force. Torn from his grasp, she pulled the rifle behind his back and choked him with the sling, her knee between his shoulder blades for leverage, wrenching the rifle violently, breaking his neck.

■ ■ ■

Freeing the sling from the body, Myomerr had yet to figure out how the primitive weapon worked when a second soldier appeared, yelling for support. Holding the rifle by the barrel, she launched herself, using the weapon like a baseball bat, connecting with his jaw in a home-run swing, the heavy wood stock destroying bone in a sickening crunch, spraying blood and flying teeth. He stumbled backwards and fell on his back, unconscious, his own AK-47 flung wide.

Retreating back to where Phillipe lay, Myomerr fumbled clumsily with the rifle. Frustration overtaking reason, she grabbed it by the barrel and flung it overhand with both hands at the approaching footfalls, the rifle cartwheeling through the air end-over-end like an axe. Its weight dropped it to the ground too soon and the Iranian soldier coming to the call of his fallen squad mate kicked it harmlessly aside. Roaring with her teeth bared as she tore at the hybrid 1911 charged particle blaster holstered in her chest rig, she knew it was going to come down to who shot first.

Unsure of what manner of human deviltry he was witnessing, the soldier took a step back, his confidence shaken after seeing the nearly faceless soldier on the ground. Hesitation in combat is deadly. The moment her 1911 cleared its holster, two more soldiers appeared and she knew the tables had turned against her. But Ketarians aren't known for surrendering – in fact, there wasn't even a word for it in their vocabulary, though they understood the concept. Flattening against a minor depression in the wall of the berm, she sighted one-handed as the 1911 vibrated with each squeeze of her finger; *pom, pom, pom...*

Her hearing returned in a rush of sounds; the bark and metallic clacking of the AK-47s, the sound of her own particle blaster, the AK rounds whizzing past her... and the whistle of a laser carbine on full auto, a cloud of magenta streaks coming from high and behind her. In a blink it was quiet again, the soldiers cut to pieces by laser fire and charged particle projectiles. The respite was sure to be temporary and short-lived.

"Get your ass up here!" shouted Dan Murphy, peering over the ridge behind her, ejecting his carbine's power cartridge into the dirt and slapping in a fresh one.

The Ketarian turned and sprinted, holstering her handgun on the run, detouring halfway up the side-berm on the way, scooping up Phillipe's carbine from where he'd dropped it. She dove over the ridge past Dan and

99

they both slid to the bottom together on the other side. There was no time for thank you's or discussion, they were in danger of being overrun.

"Phillipe?"

"Dead..."

Scrambling up the next berm, Dan looked back over his shoulder in the direction of the fight, seeing new arrivals, *"Dooby! We have more company! Make some noise!"*

Dooby smacked another bio-plasma system fuse on the rock next to his knee, *"Going out..!"*

■ ■ ■

"Skipper, our sensors are picking up a series of small plasma emissions."

Commander Dar Sloane shot his EWO a glance. "Where?"

"Bearing two-fifty-eight."

Dar keyed his mic, "Zulu One to Rescue Two; you seeing any plasma traces, Fidos?"

"Affirmative, Commander. Just picked one up at about thirty miles off our port side."

"Vector us in," Dar ordered his EWO.

"Aye. Come to a heading of two-forty-one..."

The Commander keyed his mic, "All birds come to a heading of two-forty-one. Weapons hot; choose your targets carefully, we have friendlies down there somewhere. Rescue Two, drop back a bit."

Nera Margareth lead White Flight through a high yo-yo, pulling up, rolling and turning back, dropping from altitude to the new heading at a five-hundred feet, ahead of Zulu One and Rescue Two. She glanced down at the pale sand passing below them, a dark stripe ahead, cutting across it at an angle. "You heard the Commander, no mistakes."

Flipping scan frequency from IR to pulse magnetic, Torn Dado caught the two helicopters as they skimmed the desert ahead. "White Two... I've got two craft called; *AH-1 SeaCobra* - described as combat rotary craft, on an intersecting course. Altitude, two-hundred feet, and below two-hundred miles an hour. No other details available..."

"Copy that, White Two," replied Nera Margareth. "Approaching coordinates, we'll do an assessment pass first... Eyes open, people."

■ ■ ■

The Israeli looked a Myomerr over his shoulder, "Where is Philippe?"

"Dead," replied the Ketarian without looking up, checking the level of charge in the carbine she was holding.

"We need to go get him!" urged Janine Luack.

Myomerr looked up, her head tilted to one side, "But he is *dead*."

"We can't just leave him out there..."

Myomerr's feline ears twitched, rotating in agitation, "I am afraid I do not understand your obsession in risking a live body for a dead one..."

Ivan could hear them before he could see them, *"Helicopters!"* he croaked, his voice hoarse from yelling and the blistering heat and sand.

Dan caught the sun's reflection off the cockpit canopies coming from the west, "Over there," he pointed. Skinny bodies..."

AirCobras," offered Ivan.

"SeaCobras," corrected Avi, "Iran has SeaCobras..."

Dan looked confused, his eyes flicking from Ivan to Avi and back again, "I thought only the U.S. had Cobra gunships."

The Israeli shook his head, "Back in the 1970's when America was friendly with Iran, and the Shah was still in power, Iran was allowed to purchase American equipment..."

"Then we're screwed," groaned Dan.

"Three barrel 20 mm XM197 cannon, Aim 9M Sidewinder missiles and either AGM114 Hellfire missiles, or 70mm Hydra rocket pods..." offered Avi.

"Gee thanks," sighed Dan, "that makes me feel better..."

"It does?"

Exasperated, Dan Murphy blinked slow with a sigh, "Nooo, I'm being sarcastic."

Myomerr watched the troops withdraw from the maze in a hurry. "There they go again."

Fountains of sand danced across the desert surface just outside the maze walking toward them at an alarming rate, 20mm explosive rounds from the XM197 chin turret thumping the ground, leaving little smoking craters.

"Down! *Everybody down!*"

Huddled all together at the bottom of the trench, they were either going to survive together or die together. The 20mm rounds thumped the outside of the berm, sand raining down upon the group, accompanied by an ear-splitting bone-shaking explosion that pushed down on their bodies and

101

squeezed the air from their lungs, sucking the oxygen away, leaving them gasping. *Rockets, it had to be rockets...*

The Earth bounced them off the ground like rag dolls as the left berm collapsed in on them, the ridge above them exploding, accompanied by the sound of screaming metal, crushing glass and flying debris, smoke and fire.

Numb, dazed and with ears ringing, it was a fight to claw and scramble free of the avalanche of sand and rock, crawling and stumbling over one another. There was no telling how much time had passed, whether they had been unconscious or not... Crawling on all fours, Dan wasn't sure if the metallic *clom, clom, clom,* sound of hoof-beats was his heartbeat inside his head or something else. He could feel it through his hands as well... He staggered to his feet, "Is everyone alright?!" He knew he was talking loud, but he could barely hear himself, his senses reeling.

Thunder split the sky and he ducked out of reflex, a heavy wave of compressed air pushing down on him, threatening to drive him back to his knees. The world around them, out of sight from their vantage point, sounded like all-out war; artillery strikes specked with small arms fire.

Heavy clouds of smoke drifted over the top of the ridges, blotting out most of the cloudless sky and it was a tempting thought to just hide where they were and wait it out. But waiting to get overrun or captured was not an option. Like it or not they were going to have to fight. Whether they would survive or not was anybody's guess.

Dan Murphy cleared the sand and grit off his carbine by banging on the side of it, looking at the faces around him, "Are we ready..?"

A dark metallic shape dropped down through the smoke, sliding down the face of the berm like a surfer riding a wave, a cascade of sand and gravel following it to the bottom with a heavy teeth-rattling thud, *"Aah Woo!"*

Janine Luack screamed in terror when the heavily armored figure dropped into the trench ahead of them, looking like a six-and-a-half foot tank with legs, staring at them through a faceless gold visor.

"We'd prefer you stay put," said Marine Warrant Officer, Dale Alaroot with a wave of an armored hand, his voice metallic through the suit's speakers.

Dan had swiveled to face the armored figure, the muzzle of his carbine following suit, "We who?" he asked suspiciously. Standing closest to him, Janine was on the verge of apoplexy, her eyes threatening to leave her head.

"Warrant Officer, Dale Alaroot," replied Dale reaching out with an armored hand, index finger extended, gently guiding the muzzle of Dan's carbine in a safer direction.

"UFW Space Marines," called another heavily armored Marine, dropping into the trench behind them with a dust-raising thud. "3rd Battalion, 347th Platoon..."

"Where did you come from? How many of you..."

"They're off the Conquest," interrupted Myomerr."

"There's four of us," answered Dale, "we have a Dragonfly standing by to pick you up, but we have to secure the zone first."

Dan raised an eyebrow, "Four? They have tanks and over fifty men..."

The Marine smiled inside his helmet, invisible to the others, *"Heh-heh-heh,"* he chortled, "not for long..."

"The helicopters..."

Dale Alaroot reached past Dan and tapped on the bent gun barrel of a SeaCobra's chin turret, sticking out of the berm behind him, "Oh, you don't have to worry about them. As it turns out, they're pretty fragile little fellas. Fell right out of the sky when White Flight passed over them on their recon run. They were only doing about 2500; but I guess these guys couldn't handle the shock wave."

The second Marine tapped on his helmet, "WO, White Flight is reporting all armored targets are neutralized... Zulu One is remaining on station, White Flight returning to CAP."

"Rescue Two?"

"Headed for the LZ."

"We need to get going then. Have Rusty and Dagger police up enemy targets and cover us while we extract these folks," waved Dale.

"Aye, aye, WO." He turned and made his way back up the berm, "Rusty, Dagger, this is Tin Man..."

Dale turned back to Dan, "Are we missing someone?"

"We lost one of the astronauts on the other side of that berm there..." pointed Dan.

"And Maria didn't make it," added Myomerr quietly, tears in her eyes.

Having consistently held it at the ready, the muzzle of Dale Alaroot's light machine gun dropped downward, pointing at the ground. He reached up with his free hand and touched the visor control on his helmet, the gold ballistic glass hissing as the seal released, sliding up and disappearing into a slot in the headgear, his face becoming visible in the opening. "Ahhhh, geez," he winced in anguish. "How..?"

Myomerr took a deep breath, "She was pinned in the crash. She was... crushed."

■ ■ ■

Commander Dar Sloane crabbed the Zulu gunship sideways across the highway, holding on station near the maze, high enough to look down inside but low enough to be a difficult target for anything airborne. "Zulu One - White One; status?"

"White One is back on top, angels ten. We've got you covered Zulu One. Get it done and let's get out of here."

"Copy that. Rescue Two, make the pickup."

"Copy, Rescue Two inbound."

Dar Sloane caught the line of dust rising from the road coming from Taybad and taking gun control from the EWO, swung the nose turret in that direction, the targeting pipper following his eye. He squeezed the trigger and the Mercury Gatling growled, cutting a wide trench across the highway, the road simply disappearing in a cloud of gravel dirt and concrete dust. "That ought to hold them for a while..."

■ ■ ■

"Watch the right, Rusty, watch the right... they're flanking..."

"I see him Dagger."

"Watch it! Watch it! He's got one of those RPGs. Remember what it did to Corporal Dunnom..."

"I know! Dammit I'm stuck in another dead end..!"

"Dagger to Zulu One, we're pinned here!"

Dar Sloane leaned the stick over, the horizon tilting as the Zulu slid sideways, the nose coming around as he kicked the rudder pedals, firing maneuvering jets. "Zulu One has targets... engaging." Infra-red allowed him to see the enemy troops through the smoke and confusion, outlining the Marines on the ground with green halos provided by their suits, an ID for each Marine, tagging each outline.

"Danger close, Zulu One, danger close!"

"Head down Rusty. Fire out..." Dar Sloane squeezed the trigger and the Mercury Gatling growled, following his eye in a line, cutting through the group of Iranian soldiers concealed around the corner from the Marine, their silhouettes turning into splashes of fading heat as they disintegrated.

"No movement," announced the EWO, "you got 'em all Skipper."

Dar Sloane keyed his mic, "Zulu One - Clear. Repeat, clear. Ground units pull back to LZ..."

CHAPTER NINE

UFW CARRIER CONQUEST : *THE TIMES THEY ARE A CHANGIN'*

Studying a live zoom of the planet below, Steele looked up from the holo-chart in the Admiral's office, "Come..."

Captain Paul Smiley stepped through the door as it slid into the bulkhead, saluting casually. He walked without speaking to the chart table, standing across from Jack. "Rescue Two has lifted off; they're all headed back..."

Steele didn't look up from the chart, staring blindly through the image. "Did we lose any birds?"

"No..." Paul fidgeted, staring down, avoiding eye contact, lest he lose his composure. "Ahmm," he cleared his throat nervously. "We um... We... We lost Maria."

Steele straightened up and took a deep breath and let it out slowly, "Yeah. I know."

"You *know?*" asked Paul incredulously.

"Yeah."

"How?"

Jack rubbed his forehead, "Remember when I told you where they went down, but I said don't ask me how I know?"

"Yeah..."

"She told me. Well, *us* actually – me, Fritz and Lisa."

Paul raised one eyebrow, "What," he said, deadpan.

Jack pointed at the sofa where Fritz was sitting like a human, his right foreleg on its arm, "She sat right there, where Fritz is sitting now. She hugged him."

"She came to say goodbye," annunciated Fritz.

Paul's eyes shifted from Jack to Fritz and back again. "You're serious."

"Completely."

"You realize how this sounds, right?"

Steele smirked, "And the reason I didn't share it with you earlier – we didn't have time for a debate."

" And Lisa saw this too?"

Jack casually folded his arms, "Yep."

"Holy crap." Paul was pinching his mouth with his hand, "But how did you know where we should search?"

"It wasn't so much that she *said* something," recalled Jack. "It was more of an image. Like an area of a map or something."

Paul shook his head in disbelief, "Well you were right. They were halfway between Taybad and the Afghan border on Highway 36. Iranian military units stationed five miles in either direction. If we hadn't known where to look, they wouldn't have made it; they were surrounded."

Steele was chewing on the inside of his cheek trying to stay on task and not think about Maria's loss. "What did we do about the Dragonfly?"

"Destroyed," replied Paul. "But not before they cut Maria from the wreckage. Her remains and the remains of the French astronaut are returning on Rescue Two."

"Thank you," exhaled Steele, relieved he would get a chance to say goodbye to the woman who had been a big part of their lives for the past three and a half years. He swallowed the aching lump in his throat, "I'm going to miss her..."

"Me too," croaked Paul. "I'm still trying to wrap my head around her loss... She deserves a citation for bravery..."

"Absolutely. Look into whatever is appropriate."

"I wonder how Commander Brighton is going to take the news..."

Jack's moth skewed sideways with distaste, "Not really sure I give a crap."

"Look," began Paul, "I know you're not exactly in the Derrik Brighton fan club..."

"An understatement..."

"Buuut," continued Paul, "he and Maria were pretty tight. You can't discount the fact that they were emotionally and physically involved."

Steele rubbed his temples, "I think you're giving that lying, sack-of-shit too much credit for having a heart... I trust him about as far as I can throw him. And that's not something I want to say about an Ancient Knights Templar."

"I remember when you had similar sentiments about Maria," countered Paul.

"Yeah. Well. That was different."

The door from the bridge chimed a moment before it slid open with a hiss, a lanky communications officer standing in the doorway, "Sorry to disturb you sirs, but we have a new arrival to the task force. It just jumped to us from the Elyse Core gate and is falling into formation now..."

"What is it?"

"The UFW655, a new type of fast cargo, Admiral. Never seen one before." He pointed at Steele's communication's screen, "Her Skipper is hailing on a secure frequency, asked for you directly."

Steele nodded, "Send it."

Jack shrugged, exchanging a curious glance with Paul as he dropped into his seat, Paul standing silently off to one side, out of the camera's angle. Steele typed in his pass code and a blue UFW screen flashed before showing a line profile of the other ship as the connection initiated. The form was bulky like a cargo ship but sleeker, smoother, more elegant. The fact that she had a GOD drive, jumping across the system from the gate to the Task Force was a surprise; he wasn't aware of any UFW jump-capable cargo vessels. "Hm," he grunted, "It's called a *Quasar*..."

"Kind of an over-impressive name for a cargo ship, isn't it?" commented Paul.

Steele touched his lips with his index finger signaling Paul to remain silent as the screen flashed to picture; the connection complete. Steele stiffened visibly, *"Fleet Admiral Higdenberger!"* he saluted. "I wasn't expecting *you.*"

"Of course not, Mr. Steele," replied Higdenberger. "Why would you?" The question was rhetorical and the Admiral continued; "Meet me on your flight deck in fifteen minutes, Mr. Steele; I'll be shuttling over." The comm winked out, back to the blue UFW screen.

"I don't like the sound of that," commented Paul Smiley.

"You and me, both," replied Jack. "But maybe it's for the best..."

"Huh?"

"The Fleet Admiral and I have a few things to discuss..."

"Jaaack," cautioned Paul.

"This whole *Operation Magic Pawn* fiasco..."

"Don't do it, Jack..."

Steele's jaw set, "I don't like being played, Paul. This whole thing; *everything*," he waved at the holo-chart, "it was all a setup. A plan." Jack called up his TESS, "Lisa Steele..."

Lisa's face appeared on his screen, *"Yes Admiral?"*

"Meet me on the flight deck. Ten minutes."

"We flying?"

"No, we're meeting Fleet Admiral Higdenberger." Steele swiped the screen and it ended the connection, the holographic screen disappearing. The little voice in his head was shouting all sorts of warnings to what he was thinking. He pushed it out of his mind.

"This isn't a good idea, Jack. In fact, it's a really *bad* idea."

"I know, Paul. Walk with me, we need to discuss a few things..."

Fritz launched himself off the sofa to catch up to the two men as they passed from the office out onto the bridge.

■ ■ ■

Jack and Lisa Steele stood on the flight deck watching the Admiral's shuttle taxi to a stop, directed by a deck hand using comms and hand signals to communicate with the pilot. Fritz sat at Jack's right hand, leaning against his leg.

"I hope you know what you're doing, big brother," commented Lisa.

"Funny, Paul said the very same thing."

"Well he's not wrong, you know..." lamented Lisa.

"I can handle this."

"Be *nice*," she urged. "For the love of *God*, be diplomatic."

"When am I not?"

Lisa shot her brother a look of utter disbelief, "Seriously? Are you *kidding* me?" She shook her head, "You're about as diplomatic as a hand grenade..."

The shuttle settled to the deck, squatting, an armored panel in the side popping outward, tracking up and over the hull, the interior hatch already open. Two Space Marines exited first, stepping to the deck, bracketing the entry. A Lieutenant Commander stepped to the deck a heavy bag slung over his shoulder, saluting, "Permission to come aboard."

"Permission granted, Lieutenant Commander" responded Steele with a salute.

Fleet Admiral Warn Higdenberger appeared in the hatchway, stepping down to the deck with a briefcase sized valise, saluting casually without waiting for a response. "Lieutenant Commander, issue the announcement."

"Aye, Admiral." The Commander flipped open the cover of his e-Pad and busied himself with electronic files.

Having returned the salute, Steele stepped forward anticipating a handshake. Getting no indication of that gesture he resisted the urge to extend his hand. "Welcome aboard the Conquest, Fleet Admiral. To what do we owe this visit?"

The Admiral exchanged looks with the Lieutenant Commander, getting a subtle nod in return. "You are relieved of command, Mr. Steele..."

Steele's eyes widened in surprise, *"Excuse me?"*

"You are relieved of your command duties, Mr. Steele." repeated Higdenberger calmly.

"What the hell for?!" shot Jack. He felt Lisa's boot kick against his and waved her off. "No, I want an answer! I *deserve* an answer."

"In my office, Mr. Steele."

"Your office?" he scowled.

"You remember the one - it used to be *your* office," commented Higdenberger, walking passed the stunned Steele, Lieutenant Commander in tow.

■ ■ ■

"TASK FORCE LANCER: To all ships - effective immediately; Vice Admiral Jack Steele is relieved of fleet command; further communications are prohibited. Fleet Admiral Warn Higdenberger has assumed task force command for the duration. All ships are to maintain current assigned operational status until review and further notice. That is all."

"Whaat?!" Brian Carter smacked his knees on the console of his command chair when he jumped to his feet, "Son of a bi..." the rest turned into an unintelligible grumble as he rubbed his smarting knees. "What was that crap?" he snarled, nodding at the comm screen. "I don't get it, what the hell is going on here?" He limped toward his ready room, flexing his knees. "Mr. Ragnaar, you have the bridge."

Brian took a deep breath and stared at TESS's holo-screen, contemplating the ramifications. Her animated face staring back at him, awaiting his command. *Screw it.* "TESS, Jack Steele."

"Connecting with Admiral Steele," she replied. The usual strings of digital code scrolled past underneath TESS's image but her image did not give way to a comm screen, her expression reflecting concern.

"What's going on TESS?"

"I am having difficulty connecting with Admiral Steele, Commander Carter."

"Is he out of range, or is his TESS off?" inquired Brian.

110

"No, Commander. I can see his TESS in the network... it appears I am being blocked from connecting."

"Is there any way around that?"

"I will try an emergency response ping..." Her face turned momentarily to a profile and Brian could imagine her unseen hands working a keyboard or console. "No," she turned back to face him, "that has been blocked as well."

Brian ran his fingers through his hair in frustration, "Well what the hell do I do now..." he mumbled aloud.

TESS's holo-screen remained floating midair in front of him, "Might I suggest, Ensign Steele?"

"Ahh, *good idea,*" nodded Brian, "she ought to know what's going on. Connect to Lisa Steele."

"Connecting to Ensign Steele." Again, the strings of digital code scrolled past underneath TESS's image but her image did not give way to a comm screen.

"Aww, *c'mon!*" ranted Brian. "Really?"

"Her TESS is connected, Commander. She is simply not responding." Her expression changed, "Wait... incoming." *NOT NOW* appeared on the screen below TESS's image.

Brian pointed at the text on his screen, "What the hell does that mean?"

"I believe it means; *not at this time...*"

Brian waved his arms in frustration, "Yeah, I know what it means, but what does it *mean?*"

"I fail to see the difference in your distinction, Commander."

Remembering he was attempting to converse with a literal computer who had no reference to emotion, intuition or interpretation outside the boundaries of literal meaning, he ditched his line of thought. "Connect to Pappy..."

"I have no *Pappy* within the TESS network."

Eyes closed, Brian Carter took a deep breath, exhaling slowly. "Captain Paul Smiley."

"Connecting..."

Paul Smiley's face appeared almost instantly, *"Brian..."*

"Pappy, what the hell is going on over there? I can't get Jack, I can't get Lisa..."

Pappy shook his head, "Don't even try. Jack's been cut off, you'll only get yourself in hot water."

"What about Lisa?"

"They're all in a meeting in the Admiral's office..."

"All *who?*"

"Higdenberger, his aide - some Lieutenant Commander..."

"*Fleet Admiral* Higdenberger? He's actually *here?*"

"Came in on the UFW655. He's in a meeting with Jack, Lisa, Derrik Brighton..."

"*Durock Brithauz...*" muttered Brian with distaste. "What *happened?*"

"Paul's face looked away from the screen momentarily, apparently making sure he was alone. "Jack's a little hot under the collar, he feels we got duped by the UFW on this whole thing... that they were taking advantage of us or something."

"I could see that pissing him off..."

"Yeah, well," continued Pappy, "When the UFW655 jumped in and first contact was a secure comm with Higdenberger, Jack was in fight mode..."

"Aww shit," groaned Brian, "what'd he do?"

Pappy rubbed his forehead, "My boys on the deck said Lisa had him on a pretty tight leash, he looked calm. As soon as Higdenberger stepped off the shuttle he dropped the bomb, Jack barely had time to greet him..."

Brian's eyes narrowed, "What the hell..."

"It's obvious." countered Paul. "It was pre-planned."

"But why?"

Paul looked around again, "I don't know. Maybe Jack was right..."

"Man, I don't like this."

"Me neither. Just keep it together, brother." He looked over his shoulder then back, "I gotta go, Rescue Two is on final approach. You heard about Maria?"

Brian sighed, "Yeah. Kinda breaks my heart after all we've been through together... after all *she'd* been through."

Paul nodded, "Tell me about it. Ok, listen, I'll get back to you as soon as I know more... I'm out." The video frame flickered and winked out, leaving Brian with more questions than answers.

▪ ▪ ▪

"That's *absurd!*" scolded Fleet Admiral Higdenberger in the ready room's muted light, waggling his finger in Jack's direction. "That is probably the most ridiculous thing I've ever heard come out of your mouth, Mr. Steele. The thought that we would welcome this type of outcome," he waved at the

112

hologram of Earth floating over the holo-chart, "is ludicrous." Sitting in the chair behind the desk, he steepled his hands in contemplation, "Though given the circumstances and how the chain of events played out, I suppose I can see how you might have come to that conclusion - *no matter how flawed it is,*" he swept his hands wide in exasperation.

Lisa sat mute next to her brother and Commander Derrik Brighton sat in a chair across from them in his official position as Colonel Durock Brithauz; GIS spy. It didn't have the same ring as, James Bond, 007, but his sudden smug and cool demeanor annoyed Jack. Steele redirected his gaze, "With all due respect, Admiral, you can't expect me to believe..."

"Mr. Steele, I can assure you," interrupted Higdenberger, "the UFW is not in the business of conquering worlds, we are in the business of creating allies. In my many years of service, I have personally been involved in nearly a dozen operations to recruit planets into the Federation, and every one has had unique and different problems that arise - including violence. But *nothing* on this scale. *Never* have I had an operation go so entirely off course as this." His posture changed, leaning forward, his hands on the desk laying palms-up and open, "It pains me greatly that this has occurred... I consider any loss of innocent life, tragic." He shot Derrik Brighton an angry glance, "Our intelligence is usually quite good, but when it falters, it has the potential for disaster. It is *why*, Mr. Steele, we sent *you*..."

"Excuse me?" Jack responded incredulously. "I'm not sure I follow your reasoning there..."

Higdenberger pursed his lips, "You had an invested interest, to do whatever you could to protect your fellow Earthers. We knew you wouldn't overlook any measure to do whatever was needed to avert global disaster. And for as bad as it looks right now, I can guarantee the results would have been far less favorable than they are at this moment had we sent someone else..."

Steele angrily indicated the holo-chart, "You call this *favorable..?"*

"Admiral Steele," ventured Derrik Brighton rising from his chair, "we..."

Steele pointed, flashing him a furious glare, "Don't you *even...*"

"Gentlemen, *gentlemen,"* urged Higdenberger, raising his hands. "Please," he waved at Brighton's seat, "sit down." He redirected his gaze at Steele, "Jack, your task force did a tremendous job under staggering pressure; I expected nothing less should things go wrong..."

"And it did," countered Jack.

"Yes. But to your credit, and the credit of the men and women of your entire task force, you saved countless lives and disrupted one of the largest covert enemy operations I have personally ever seen."

"Like Veloria?" queried Jack.

"Veloria was amateurish compared to this; though it was a UFW failure to recognize the severity of the situation. Unfortunately, we're spread pretty thin – both militarily and in the intelligence gathering sense. It's a big Universe out there and predicting where their interests or targets are, is... well, highly difficult to predict. The positive *here*, is that your planet and its people will recover. They will be stronger than before, and you will have brought them the benefits of space travel, science and commerce that they may never have survived long enough to attain..."

"But you knew this was going on *here*..." injected Lisa. When all eyes shifted to her, she thought maybe it would have been wiser to stay silent. "Why would you have waited so long to act?"

"That is true, young lady," nodded the Admiral, "but there is something to be said about monitoring an operation to farm intelligence from it, and that's exactly what we were doing in this case. It was a matter of timing. And it's one of the reasons we had the names of so many of the implants and their Earther accomplices." He steepled his fingers, his elbows on the desk, "These operatives prey on people afflicted with greed and avarice, turning them against their own; for fame, fortune, power or political gain. Some societies are more susceptible to it than others. We find that those races that are most competitive, are the most vulnerable because of their personal drive." He opened his hands, "Your strength is also your weakness..."

"Well thank you for pointing that out, sir..." Steele said sarcastically. He sat back, folding his arms defensively, crossing his legs at the knee. "And while this is all very... *informative*, it doesn't explain your arrival here. On a transport, no less... Or my removal from command."

Fleet Admiral Higdenberger leaned back in his chair, a wry smile creeping across his face, "You know what I like about you Mr. Steele?"

"I'm a smartass?"

Higdenberger's face reflected a mixture of surprise and confusion, "I am not familiar with that term..."

"I am an irreverent ass?" clarified Steele.

The Fleet Admiral nodded approvingly, "Smartass, I will remember that one. Yes, I suppose a little. But you are unafraid to speak your mind and you do what needs to be done. You are a man of action... I suspect you are not the only one of your people with such character."

Steele pursed his lips, wondering where this was going, "No, I'm not."

"There are thousands..?"

"Hundreds of thousands," corrected Jack, his arms still folded. "Maybe millions. But how is that relevant?"

Higdenberger's wry smile was back. "It means your strengths far outweigh your weaknesses. And that your world will make a fine ally for the UFW."

"But they have not accepted..."

Higdenberger nodded, "*Yet*. I am confident they will. They have everything to gain and very little to lose." He waved toward Derrik Brighton, "But I digress, I have not answered your other questions, "Colonel Brithauz, if you please."

Derrik Brighton moved over to the holo-chart and laid a wafer the size of an American quarter on the surface of the table, the planet disappearing, giving way to a table-sized three-dimensional wire-frame schematic of the Fleet Admiral's UFW655, a holographic control panel appearing on the table's surface. Higdenberger rose purposefully and strolled over to the table, waving his hand at the ship, "Mr. Steele, meet your new ship, the UFW655..."

Jack rose to his feet, scowling, "You took away my task force to give me a fffff..." he squared his jaw and bit his tongue before continuing, "a damn *transport ship?!*" He ran his hand through his hair in frustration and exasperation, "You can't be *serious!* What the hell am I supposed to do with *that* thing?!" Higdenberger was grinning like an idiot and Jack failed to see what was so amusing.

"Oh it is much more than a transport ship, Mr. Steele..." His fingers tapped the keys of the holographic control panel, the ship becoming solid, its skin and outer hull visible. "The UFW655 is brand new and currently one of a kind. The size of a cruiser, she is loaded with surprises; like a GOD drive, two P-57 light assault fighters, a photo-reactive skin, an advanced electronics warfare suite and enough firepower to rival some cruisers..."

Jack waved at the holographic image, "What are you talking about..." he said deadpan, "I don't see a weapon on her anywhere..."

"Appearances can be deceiving, Mr. Steele," commented Higdenberger, tapping on the holographic control panel. The image animated, sections of the hull opening, turrets swinging into action, a main turret at the top and

115

one at the bottom; one simply rising up the other dropping down out of the hull.

Her curiosity getting the better of her, Lisa stood up and walked over to the table for a closer look moving around to the other side, "Are those missile racks?" she pointed.

Higdenberger shook his head, "Small, high-speed torpedoes. It was determined that encounters with this ship would likely be much closer than a military engagement. In that space, a high-speed torpedo, slower than missiles but much-much faster than conventional torpedoes, would be devastatingly effective."

It's a Q-Ship," muttered Jack, reaching into the hologram and turning it. "The fighters go in here?" he pointed at door markings on the belly.

"That's right."

"What's a Q-Ship?" asked Lisa.

"I am curious as well," said Higdenberger.

"During World War One and Two," began Jack, "The Allied losses to German U-Boat attacks on supply columns was terrible. And the Allied navies were spread so thin they couldn't provide enough escorts. The Allies came up with the idea of merchant supply ships armed with hidden weaponry. The U-Boats would surface to engage what they thought was a helpless supply ship at short range and the Q-Ships would open up and sink them. It was pretty effective."

"Except the UFW655 is not for hunting Mr. Steele," countered the Fleet Admiral. "Her capabilities must be kept secret and only used defensively as a last resort... Her job, *your job,* is subterfuge and espionage." He tapped the holographic controls, the ship's weapons hiding again, "Your new assignment," he motioned to the image, is *Operation Dark Cover.*

CHAPTER TEN

TERRAN SYSTEM – UFW655 : *COLD SHOULDER*

Considering he'd lost the Conquest's Fleet Operations office to Higdenberger, Steele commandeered Captain Ryan's ready room... for the time being.

Steele hadn't realized the secure long-distance conversations he'd conducted with Fleet Admiral Higdenberger concerning deep cover operations, was going to show up and bite him in the ass over a year later. They had discussed ideas, tactics, targets, methodology... he didn't recall ever volunteering for anything. But maybe he'd been too convincing. *Dammit to hell.* Higdenberger had given him forty-eight hours to make ready and shove off on the UFW655 – which also needed a new name for the fake registry. His mind was still working on that. There was only a small handful of people who knew the story behind Steele's loss of command; thankfully Pappy, Mike and Brian were in the loop.

"I thought Maria's service was very nice," commented Lisa from the sofa.

Jack looked up from the UFW655 manuals he was reviewing. "Yeah, it was. I understand it will take the casket about three months to reach the sun."

"What are they going to do with the astronaut's remains?"

"Send him back down to his family I suppose. All the astronauts will be going back home in a day or two. I'm sure NASA will have a ton of questions for them..."

There was a moment of silence and Lisa struggled with the question in her mind - whether to bring it up or not. "So... do you believe him?"

Jack looked up from his studies, his brow furrowed, "Who?"

"The Fleet Admiral. Everything he said... or, *didn't* say."

"Yes. And no. It's not that I don't trust him..."

"But you don't trust him," injected Lisa, flatly, finishing her brother's thought.

"Yeah. I don't. I want to... but I get the feeling that there's too much that he's leaving out."

"Does it worry you?"

Steele bit his lip and sighed deeply, "Yeah. To some extent. I can't tell yet whether what I don't know is minutiae, or monumental. I want to believe it's just unimportant details."

"What's your gut tell you?"

Jack shrugged, "My little voice has been quiet so far."

With that, silence had returned and he went back to his studies. After a brief interlude, Lisa looked up from her TESS's screen, "Hey, did you hear they tracked the pirates out of the system?"

"No," frowned Jack, "how did you find out?"

"Higdenberger has given me access to intel as a liaison. Two destroyers ran and took the gate to Alpha Centauri. The third GOD jumped, they're not sure to where."

Steele's brow furrowed, considering the escape. "Hmm... Wait, backtrack - what's his Lieutenant Commander doing? I thought *he* was liaison."

"Don't know," she shrugged.

Jack smiled, "Son-of-a... he knows you're going to tell me, he's giving me an information pipeline for the task force."

"Well he *did* say this arrangement was temporary. That you'd get Lancer back..."

"I don't know. Somehow in the back of my mind I keep thinking that will never happen..."

"The little voice?"

Jack shook his head, "More like a nightmare.."

The door chimed and Lisa checked her schedule, "Your first appointment. You sure you want to do this? You *do* hate spies..."

There was no one on Higdenberger's *hand-picked* crew on the UFW655 that Jack knew. He needed a few select people he could trust and the Fleet Admiral had given him no objections. "Enter."

Mercedes Huang sauntered into the room as the door slid into the bulkhead. Her straight, shoulder length, blue-black hair, caramel skin and almond-shaped eyes gave her a certain feline quality, though nothing like the Ketarians of course. "Admiral. Ensign," she acknowledged, nodding at each in turn. She moved smoothly, sitting at the opposite end of the sofa from Lisa. If she noticed Lisa's eye-roll, she gave no indication of it.

"I trust you are feeling better? Healing well?" asked Jack.

"Yes. Thank you. And you?" she indicated his leg.

"Doing well," he nodded. He paused for a moment, abstractly considering her beauty before deciding to be direct, "It has occurred to me that there may, or *may not be,* a position left for you to fill back on Earth. And," he continued, not allowing her to respond, "that even if there was, your skills and experience might be far more valuable to humanity *out here.* With us. Hunting the people who did that..." he thumbed over at the planet hovering above the holo-table.

"Do you plan to capture them and bring them to justice?" she asked.

"No. No... I plan to hunt them down like the sub-human filth they are and kill them wherever we find them..."

"I'm not an assassin," she replied coolly.

"Neither am I. But, these heinous cretins tried to execute an extinction level event on our humanity, simply to escape capture. A level of evil that defies description. I don't expect they will offer us an alternative."

"I see your point. But what if you manage to capture one alive?"

"Then it will be up to you to extract whatever information you can, in any manner you can. Being a deep cover CIA operative, I suspect you have those skills..."

"I do."

"Good. Then we work to repeat that success."

"I see. And once you've eliminated them all?"

"I can't say for sure we'll catch up with them all, but there is much more to this mission than just the operatives. I can't tell you more until I am assured you're committed. Suffice it to say, I expect we'll be putting your skills to the test."

"I understand," she nodded. "Why me?" She saw the sudden pained expression cross Steele's face, "Ahh, the loss of Ms. Arroyo."

"I need someone I can trust," he replied. "You risked your life to save mine, that tells me there's something in you that's inherently good. I trust my instincts - they're usually pretty spot-on and I get the sense that I can trust you. I believe we may have some things in common."

"I appreciate the offer and I'm honored by your trust," she mused, examining her hands. "I think I can safely say," she began, looking back up, "that I have nothing else pressing at the moment. You can count me in."

■ ■ ■

Chase Holt cut another slice of his steak, the tender meat, pink in the center, "Why me, Jack? Seriously, what could I possibly add?" Dan Murphy watched the conversation, sipping a beer.

"Your security and electronics background is sure to be helpful..."

Chase made a face of skepticism, stabbing the slice of meat with his fork, mopping some gravy off his plate, "Doubtful. I don't know squat about this technology."

"I'm not saying there isn't a learning curve..."

Chase nearly spit the meat out of his mouth when he laughed at the absurdity, *"Learning curve?* C'mon Jack, be serious..." He stared down at his plate as he chewed, "Besides..."

"Your prior life is gone, buddy," replied Jack, as gently as possible. "You have Allie, Karen and all of us..."

Chase dropped his fork on his plate and leaned back in the booth, his arms folded across his chest, "You really know how to ruin a guy's appetite, you know that?"

"You know that's not my intention, don't be a drama queen."

"I went out of my way to help your folks..." scowled Chase.

"I haven't forgotten. I appreciate everything you've done. And we are going to do everything we can to make your folks comfortable. Dan is staying here on the Conquest. I have secured permission for him to go with the landing party. If your family needs anything he'll make sure they get it. If they want to leave, he'll get them out..."

"Veloria?"

Jack nodded, "Yes, Veloria. I will make sure they're taken care of."

Chase rubbed his face with his hands, "And Karen?"

"She'll be safe, you know that. They'll all be waiting for us when we get to Veloria. You can leave Allie here with her if you want..."

Chase shook his head vigorously, "No, no... Allie stays with me."

Steele nodded, "Fair enough - just a suggestion. But I need you with me; I need a Brother I can trust at my back."

"Alright, alright... don't beg," gestured Chase, picking his fork and knife back up. "But you still owe me..."

Jack nodded with a smile, "Yes I do."

■ ■ ■

His goodbyes complete and last minute details checked off, Jack Steele, about to assume his new identity as Jax Mercury, waited on the flight deck with his sister.

Lisa Steele stood next to her brother with her hands on her hips watching the deck crew load the shuttle from the UFW655, the flight bay of the Conquest a flurry of perpetual motion.

"I can't believe you convinced Brian to let go of Ragnaar..."

Jack shrugged, "Well I kinda figured if we're going to try to blend in with Pirates and FreeRangers, it might be helpful to actually have at least *one actual Pirate* in the crew. It took a little convincing but he eventually saw it my way."

"How hard did you have to twist his arm?" she prodded. "You didn't have to break it, did you?"

"Not quite," smirked Jack, "but it was close."

"Who else did you take?"

"I wanted another pilot. The two on the 655 look alright, but they're still green. I pulled Torn Dado..."

"Tornado's a good pilot," agreed Lisa, "not as good as me, but..."

"Nothing doing," countered Jack. "You're staying here - it's safer."

"Unless Lieutenant Margareth kills me..."

"You can stop worrying about Nera Margareth, you're out of fighter rotations," countered Jack. "You're heading back to the Revenge; you're the only experienced Reaper pilot left, since Maria..." his voice trailed off.

Lisa nudged the conversation past its awkward pause, "Draza Mac still my back seater?"

"Yep. And if you're lucky, you might get some time on the bridge."

"Oh, that's sweet! Say, did you ever come up with a name for the 655?"

"Yeah, *Perseus.*"

Lisa's brow furrowed, "The name sounds familiar but I can't place it..."

"In Greek mythology, Perseus was the first recorded hero - his adventures were legendary; defeating monsters and demons... His exploits provided the framework for the founding myths of the *Twelve Olympians* - the major gods of the Greek pantheon. He was the hero who beheaded Medusa, and in another adventure killed the sea monster Cetus, sent by Poseidon. That little victory won him the hand of Andromeda in marriage. *Aaand,* he was the only one to have tamed and flown Pegasus."

Lisa's eyes narrowed, "Your ring," she pointed at his hand, "and the logo you used on the Freedom..."

"That's right."

Her lips pursed in thought, "*Interesting...*"

Jack glanced at his sister out of the corner of his eye, "Were you able to take care of that little project I gave you?"

"The old eGo units? Yeah."

"Think anyone will notice?"

Lisa shook her head, "I don't think so. When the Supply Chief heard the request was coming from you, he pulled them off the inventory list and marked the log entries as destroyed and recycled. No questions asked. I've got most of them distributed already..."

"Mom and dad?"

"Dad's got one – I reminded him to keep it concealed. The key visitors you listed got theirs before we shuttled them back down."

Jack raised an eyebrow, "And the rest of the units?"

"Will be going down to the GIS Watchers that Derrik Brighton provided a list of. He seemed rather pleased that there was something he could do for you..."

"He's trying to get back into my good graces..."

"Is it working?"

Steele smirked "I'll let *him* think so..."

Marine Warrant Officer Dale Alaroot strode up and snapped a salute, "Admiral."

Jack returned the salute before extending his hand, "Dale..."

"Sir, I just wanted to say, I think what they're doing to you is a *complete* mistake; one they're going to regret. It was a pleasure serving with you."

"Thank you, Dale. But it's not as bad as it looks; everything is going to work out, you'll see..."

"Of course, sir." Dale went from handshake back to salute, turning on his heel and returning to the line of Marines standing at parade rest.

"He seems more than just a *little* upset," commented Lisa quietly.

"Yeah, I noticed that..." Steele rubbed his chin, "We've had a chance to get to know one another. I like Dale, he's a good man and a good Marine. He's taking this too personally..."

"Want me to have a word with him?"

Jack eyed his sister, "What would you say?"

"I don't know yet..."

"Because you can't tell him much. This is all very secret."

Lisa chewed the inside of her cheek, "I know. But he's always had your back, even when you didn't know he was doing it. I'm just worried he might... I don't know, do something impulsive?"

Jack took a deep breath and held it for a moment, contemplating. "Alright," he sighed, "but only if it becomes apparent that you have to. And keep it to a minimum."

"Got it."

Jack checked the device on his wrist that replaced his UFW military TESS. The device was the most advanced available on the civilian market and had been upgraded to meet UFW standards while looking no different than any other MOBIUS unit in circulation. MOBIUS - *Mobile Optical Bio Information User System.* MOBI for short. The character driven software was in some respects similar to TESS, but Jack quickly recognized he was going to miss *his* TESS. There was something about her unique character and style.

"Not as nice as your TESS..." commented Lisa, watching her brother flip to an updated schedule screen. He just grunted a confirmation. "Don't worry," she continued, "your TESS is in hibernation, you'll get her back."

"Even after the improvements, I don't like the software as much," he grumbled. "Guess I'll have to live with it for now."

A grizzled old deckhand strolled over, his ham-sized hand extended, "Admiral,"

"Chief," acknowledged Jack, shaking the man's hand, "what's the good word?"

The man's weathered face crinkled around his eyes and mouth as he smiled, "*Retirement.* We probably won't be seeing each other again; I've only got about a month left."

Jack smiled warmly, "Good for you! Going to spend some time with the wife and kids, Chief?"

"And grandbabies," he grinned widely. He thumbed over his shoulder at the shuttle, "All loaded and everyone aboard; they're just waiting on you, sir."

"Thank you Chief..."

The Chief leaned closer, "Not that it's any of my business, mind you; but something tells me there's a lot more to all of this than meets the eye," the old man whispered. He looked around like he was checking for eavesdroppers, "I don't know where you're going or what you're doing, but keep your head on a swivel, Mister, try not to get it shot off..." He winked, tossed a loose salute, turned on his heel and headed toward a passing equipment trolley that slowed to pick him up.

"Well that was..."

123

"Interesting?" offered Jack.

"I was going to say *colorful*," replied Lisa.

"ATTEN-*shun!* Fleet Officer on deck!" The unified metallic clomp as the line of over fifty Marines snapped to attention, their boots stomping on the flight deck, echoed in the bay, all other motion coming to a stop. For a moment there was silence except for the thrum of the ship's engines. "SA-*lute!*"

Halfway to the shuttle, Steele stopped, turned to the center of the bay, the heels of his civilian dress boots snapping together as he came to attention. It was then that he realized how big his audience was, including the officers in the flight tower looking down on the deck. He snapped a salute, holding it for a moment, bringing his hand down slowly, deliberately, "CARRY *on!"* he bellowed.

■ ■ ■

When the shuttle's hatch popped open with a hiss, a rush of warm air entered the cabin and for a moment Jack detected a new-car smell. It struck him funny and he cracked a crooked smile as the hatch cleared the opening, folding up over the hull. He was relieved to see a mostly unpopulated bay - save for a few deckhands and a tall man about his size with closely cut salt and pepper hair and gray eyes. The man stepped forward, and extended his hand, "Captain Vastyque. Welcome aboard the UFW655, Admiral Steele." The meaning was friendly, the tone was not.

"Jax Mercury," Jack corrected him. "Let's never make that mistake again."

"Of course, sir." He looked over the group exiting the shuttle, including the two German Shepherds. "Mr. *Mercury*, might I inquire, what are those?" he indicated the two animals.

"Ah," nodded Jack, pointing , "that is Fritz and that is Allie. They are *dogs*. Animal companions..."

"I see..."

"Problem?"

Captain Vastyque shook his head, "Just a little... *unusual*," he replied, choosing his words carefully.

"This is the rest of my team;" continued Jack, ignoring the Captain's discomfort. "Derrik Brighton - my intelligence officer. Ragnaar - navigator and pirate expert. Mercedes Huang - tactical advisor. Chase Holt - securities specialist, and Torn Dado - combat pilot."

"We do have two fine fighter pilots..."

"Yes, I'm aware of that," replied Jack. "I reviewed their files. But it never hurts to have extra people."

"Of course..." agreed the Captain. As the group walked the bay - headed for the elevators, Steele took in as much as he could; the layout, the sterile cleanliness of everything, the pressed and crisp crew members. It was all so... new. *Too perfect.* "I assume," began the Captain, "you'll want to get straight to the ready room?"

"That's right," replied Steele.

"Fine. I will have the crew tend to your things and get your people assigned quarters."

"Good, good. I want everyone in the ready room for a briefing in thirty minutes," Jack announced over his shoulder as they walked. "Except you, Tornado. I want you to meet with the other pilots and get to know them a bit. Have them show you around, take a look at the fighters and get familiar with them. I will expect you to report back to me on your findings."

"Aye, sir," replied the pilot.

"I want you checked out and familiar with the birds before we leave the system. I need to put in some stick time as well..."

"That's highly irregular, Admiral," interrupted the Captain.

Steele stopped dead in his tracks and glared at the Captain, everyone behind having to come to an emergency stop of sorts to avoid collision. "Mr. Vastyque," he said slowly, "are you new here?"

"Sir?"

"Did you just acquire your rank yesterday?"

"No sir."

Steele raised one eyebrow, "What is my *name?*"

The Captain stiffened, "Jax Mercury. Sir."

"Say it *again.*"

"Jax Mercury."

"You *do* understand our mission, don't you?"

"I do..."

"Then I don't need to explain to you the dangers of failing to maintain character at *all* times." The Captain looked like he was about to speak and Jack cut him off, "I will make this abundantly clear, do not *ever* make the mistake of calling me by anything other than Jax Mercury again. Or you *will be* relieved of command. Permanently." Steele started walking again, passing the Captain, "Have you ever commanded a ship with pilots before?"

"No, sir."

"Then I or Ensign Dado will handle flight operations."

"One of my pilots outranks your Ensign..."

"Captain, I feel we may be getting off on the wrong foot here..."

Captain Vastyque's brow furrowed in confusion, "I'm not sure I understand."

"You are pissing me off," explained Steele, "and that's not where you want to be. I will explain myself one *last* time; you have two pilots. Both unproven. I had nearly one-hundred-fifty. And Mr. Dado was a shining star in that group, of *many* shining stars. The training and experience he's been exposed to, far outweighs anything your pilots have encountered. So, you will excuse me if I defer to his talent and experience over your people. Don't fight me on this."

■ ■ ■

The UFW655's bridge was sharp and spotless, the crew trim and their uniforms perfectly pressed. Steele paused there, flanked by Fritz and Allie, Chase Holt on her other side.

The Captain stepped past to his command chair, "Set course for Alpha Centauri, prepare for GOD jump..."

"Belay that order," interrupted Steele, stepping forward. "Cruising only, best speed."

"But..."

Steele shot the Captain a *shut the hell up*, look. "GOD jumps will make us stand out," he announced to the bridge, "we need to blend in. Jumps will be for emergency or extenuating circumstances."

The crew did not respond, waiting for orders from their Captain. "There are two types of *best speed*, Mr. Mercury; a common transport's best speed, and the 655's best speed."

"I am aware of that Captain. When I say *best speed,* that's what I mean."

The Captain motioned toward the helmsman and navigator, "You heard the man, best speed."

"Best speed, aye."

Steele indicated the entire bridge with a sweep of his hand, "And have the entire crew change into the civilian clothes they were issued, including their civvy rank markers. All UFW uniforms and insignias are to be incinerated and ejected before we reach the gate. No UFW keepsakes or mementos, everything gets spaced." Steele didn't wait for an answer, turning and heading for the ready room. "Oh and Captain," he paused looking back, "I'll need to see the Chief Engineer and his senior team in my office."

"Now sir?"

"Now, Mr. Vastyque."

■ ■ ■

Steele shrugged off his leather flight jacket and dropped it across the arm of the sofa, heading for the mini-fridge. Chase Holt did the same, the two German Shepherds roaming around the suite inspecting everything within reach. "Little warm in here," commented Chase.

"Computer, three degrees cooler," announced Jack. He pulled two water bottles from the fridge at the bar and tossed one to Chase.

"Weren't you a little hard on him?"

Jack shrugged, "You've been in the military, you tell me. Was I unfair?"

Chase paused to open his bottle, "I guess not. He did seem rather... resistant."

"He's defensive," countered Jack. "This is his ship and he doesn't want to be told what to do on it. He resents us being here."

"Kinda like you and the Fleet Admiral?"

Steele nodded, "Yeah, kinda like that. Except I'm not going to take away the Captain's ship."

"Unless you *have* to," added Chase.

"I certainly hope he doesn't press me that far..."

The door chimed and slid smoothly open, the ship's Chief Engineer and three other officers filed in, followed by the Captain. Steele wasn't surprised, though he hadn't asked for the Captain's attendance, he had inserted himself into the meeting without apology. Steele ignored it. He also ignored the fact that they were still all in UFW uniforms.

"Gentlemen," said Steele, stepping over to the holo-chart, "I have something I'd like you to take a look at." He slid a data wafer from his pocket and laid it on the surface of the holo-chart table. The table awoke with the contact, showing a three-dimensional hologram of the Terran System, flickering as it read the data wafer before switching to a view of the UFW655's propulsion systems, controls, schematics and operational statistics. Jack reached forward as the engineers huddled around the information and flipped through a series of pages. "Do you understand all of what you're seeing here?"

The Chief Engineer was engrossed in the data, "Yes, this is quite interesting..."

"Can you make the updates?" asked Steele.

"Yes, I..."

"Wait a minute," objected the Captain, attempting to intervene, "what possible updates could you possibly be suggesting? This is a *brand new ship. One of a kind. No one* knows more about her engineering than this man right there," he indicated the Chief Engineer.

Steele imposed himself between the engineering team and the Captain.

"If these calculations are correct," muttered the Chief, "well, this is just fascinating..." The three engineering officers were chatting quietly pointing out different bits of information to one another, ignoring the conversation behind them.

His back to the men huddled around the table, Steele was in a stare-down with the Captain, "Chief, does it make sense to you? Can you make the adjustments?"

The Captain's lips were mashed thin, his jaw tight, "How could you possibly make improvements to a system you've never seen before..."

"Chief?" reminded Steele.

"Well it looks like he's rewritten a good deal of the manual, we'll have to study all the notes..."

"Chief," spat the Captain, "you will do no such thing! I..."

"If this all bears out," continued the Chief, paging furiously through the materials, "we can get at least another five percent out of the engines, shields and GOD systems. Maybe as high as eight percent!"

"Chief!" barked the Captain, on the verge of totally losing his composure.

"The engineers turned, facing Steele's back, "Mr. Mercury, who did you say rewrote these materials?"

"I didn't. But it was my Chief Engineer of Development, Hecken Noer."

The Chief's eyes widened, "The one who redesigned the cruiser frame for the refit to Freedom Class Carriers?"

Steele was still nearly nose to nose with the Captain. "That's the one, Chief..."

"I've seen his work, he's damn brilliant!"

"How long do you think it will take your team to work out the adjustments?"

The Chief glanced at his team, "A minimum of two full days. It shouldn't take longer than five. I'll want to stress-test each step to be sure there are no mistakes. It can be delicate work."

"Of course," agreed Steele. "Get it done, then."

"Aye, sir." The engineering team hustled past the faceoff, headed for the door to the bridge.

"One more thing, Chief... Civvies."

"Aye, sir."

In retrospect, Jack was a little concerned that maybe he was *enjoying* antagonizing the Captain, and wanted to give the man the benefit of the doubt; but his rancorous attitude was making it very difficult. Recalling the step off the shuttle to the deck, there it was - a wall of attitude. Jack had picked it up immediately but had chosen to ignore it. Maybe to his detriment, it had only gotten worse. And it needed to stop, he was becoming concerned that maybe the Captain couldn't be trusted. *Had it gone that far?* His little voice was telling him those concerns were valid.

"Chase, give us a minute?"

"Sure, no sweat." Chase Holt turned for the door, patting his leg, Allie trotting along at his side. Fritz climbed up on the sofa and plopped down at the armrest, eyeing the conversation.

Steele waited till the door slid closed before turning away and moving over to the desk to break the faceoff, picking up his water. "What's your deal, mister?"

"Permission to speak freely..."

It wasn't a question so much as a demand, but it's what Jack wanted right now - answers. "Sure."

"I don't like you..."

"Pfffttt," snorted Steele, "try telling me something I *don't* know. Like *why*." The Captain looked like he wanted to say something but was fighting to put it into words. "Let me help you," started Jack, sitting on the corner of the desk. "The Fleet Admiral builds you a cool new ship. Then he orders you to shuttle him around on it. After which he reveals a secret mission without telling you the secrets. Then this guy just strolls onto your ship, brings his own people, whom you haven't met, for a mission you don't know enough about, and starts making plans and giving orders to your crew without even consulting you. He reprimands you on protocol, takes over your office and

129

starts making changes without considering your input." Steele crossed his arms, "Does that about sum it up? Did I leave anything out?"

"No, that pretty much covers it."

"Well suck it up. Believe me when I say I don't care. I'm not here to be nice, or diplomatic, or even considerate. I have a job to do and so do you. This very thing happened to me a couple days ago, but instead of having to *share* my ship, I *lost* my ship. *And* my task force. For *this* tub. No offense, it's a nice ship and all, but it's not an Oijin squadron-class carrier." He waved his hand for emphasis, "And yes, I'm well aware that the Conquest is a century old. I will reiterate, I don't care. It's a *squadron-class carrier.* So, let's get this straight; I'm not *taking* your ship, I do not *want* your ship. But for this assignment, I *need* your ship." He rubbed his forehead, "Look Captain, you don't want me here and I don't want to be here, but we're going to have to deal with it. We don't have to be friends, you don't have to like me, you don't have to agree with my decisions, but this friction ends here and now. Or you're gone. I can and will relieve you of duty if I can't rely on you."

The Captain folded his arms in defiance, "And just who do you think you'd replace me with? I walked her hull for weeks while she was being built, nobody knows her better than I do. Except the Chief."

"Well honestly, if you want to put it in those terms, it sounds like as long as I keep the Chief on, I'm good to go. I could replace you with anyone who knows the crew; for instance, your second in command. I'm sure he wouldn't mind a bump in position."

The Captain smirked, "You mean Lieutenant Commander Reegan? One of my hand-picked crew? A long-time friend?"

Steele thought back to his encounters with the insane Admiral Pottsdorn and wondered how much different this circumstance was to that one. Were there similarities? Maybe a few, he conceded. But he had been protecting his ship and crew from a madman and that's where it differed wildly. "Let's take a different tack, Skipper; what's your end-game here; I share all the mission secrets with you? Or maybe my people and I just leave? Go back to where we came from? Or maybe you just want to be in control of the whole show..." Jack pointed at him, "None of those things will happen. This will end one of two ways; with you, or without you. You work with me, or I ship you back to Higdenberger with a note pinned to your shirt that says; *does not play well with others. And* anybody else on this ship that has a problem." Jack watched a change of expression momentarily wash across his face.

"Oh, you didn't think I would relieve you and let you stay on this ship, did you? So you could undermine me, cause problems? Nah. Off you'd go, *buh-bye.*" Steele folded his arms, "So what's it going to be, Mr. Vastyque? Are you in, or are you out..?"

Vastyque stood his ground, arms folded, mirroring Jack's posture, "I have no intention of taking orders from the likes of *you*. A *caveman* from a non-spacer planet who tricked and wormed his way into command. I've dedicated my life to the UFW, it took me twenty years to get where I'm at. You," he indicated Jack, "you haven't earned the privilege. You don't belong out here, Steele..."

"Your funeral, Mr. Vastyque," shrugged Steele. "We're done here. Pack yourself up and *get off my ship...*"

■ ■ ■

"Lieutenant Commander Reegan," greeted Steele from behind the desk. "Please, sit," he motioned to a chair. "Let me ask you, Commander, do you have any idea what our mission is?"

"No, sir. I don't."

"What are your opinions about working with me and my team?"

The Commander looked introspective, answering carefully, "Well sir, other than Mr. Holt and his dog, I really haven't met any of your team, so I really don't feel I have enough information to make a judgment. But I imagine, since this was arranged by Fleet Admiral Higdenberger, it should be quite interesting."

Ahh, a clean slate. Steele nodded, "Good... Commander have you ever skippered a ship?"

"Yes sir. My last post; the UFW721, an armed fleet service ship. Three years."

"Think you can handle *this* ship and her crew?"

"I do all the time, sir, I..."

"As her skipper," interrupted Steele.

Commander Reegan's eyes widened, "Yes... I... Wh - what happened to Captain Vastyque?"

"The Captain is leaving us, Mr. Reegan. *Irreconcilable differences.*"

CHAPTER ELEVEN

ALPHA CENTAURI SYSTEM - THE PERSEUS : *OPERATION DARK COVER*

The holo-screen of Jack Steele's MOBIUS flickered before appearing over his wrist on his way down to engineering to meet with the Chief and his team. "Incoming from the bridge, Mr. Mercury."

"Connect, MOBI." He grabbed the screen and placed it at a more appropriate height so he didn't have to hold his arm up, the screen hovering in front of him as he walked, Fritz pacing alongside him.

MOBI's dark-haired, pixie-like face disappeared as the communications officer appeared, " "Secure comm connection coming in from Task Force Lancer. I believe it may be the Fleet Admiral."

Steele's mouth skewed sideways, "Yeah, I'm sure it is. Has our shuttle gotten back from Lancer?"

"Yes, sir. The transfer is complete, the shuttle has docked."

"Time to the gate entrance?"

"Thirty-five minutes, Mr. Mercury."

"Noted. Go ahead and send the comm to my MOBI."

"Aye, sending," his face disappeared, replaced by the Conquest's logo. "Mr Steele..." said a familiar voice, the audio preceding the video. "Do you want to explain this?"

"Admiral, Higdenberger, so good to hear from you, sir," replied Steele fighting a nervous smirk, the Admiral's face finally appearing on the holo-screen. "You have a question?"

"Damn right I have a question! What the hellion is Vastyque doing here, and what the hellion is *irreconcilable differences* supposed to mean?"

"Technically, sir that's two questions..."

"Steele!" bellowed the Admiral, red-faced.

"Easy Admiral, don't go blowing a gasket. Vastyque has a severe attitude problem and..."

"You have a severe attitude problem, Steele!" interrupted Higdenberger. "I would think the two of you would get along famously; you're two of a kind."

"That's the problem, sir," replied Jack more seriously. "The moment we stepped off the shuttle there was hostility. He fought me on everything, defied my orders and generated a tremendous amount of friction. It got worse quickly and I honestly didn't see the situation improving. As a last effort to find some common ground I had a private discussion with the Captain hoping we could build some mutual guidelines but he was adamantly contradictory."

"You gave him opportunities to cooperate..."

"As many as I could sir. I wanted to be fair, but there was a lot of resentment to me and my team being here. It wasn't going to be conducive to a successful mission."

His eyes down, Higdenberger looked contemplative, " Hmm, he waited months for that ship. Emotionally invested; maybe too much so. We can't have that kind of acrimony. Not on a mission of this type." He looked back up at the screen, "I suppose you did the right thing... Who did you replace him with?"

"His second, Lieutenant Commander Reegan."

Higdenberger nodded in approval, "Don't know him personally but he has a solid record. He's close with Vastyque, any sense that he'll offer any resistance?"

"No, Admiral."

"Good. So, what is this *irreconcilable differences* nonsense supposed to mean?"

Steele sidestepped a couple of crew members passing him in the corridor, "You told me Vastyque was a personal choice of yours; I had to assume he was in other circumstances a good officer. We couldn't get along but I didn't want official charges to damage his career. I thought I'd leave it up to your discretion to manipulate the paperwork how you see fit."

His lips pinched tight, the Admiral nodded his appreciation, "Generous. Thank you for that, Mr. Steele. I will inform Mr. Vastyque of your good will, *and* his luck. Carry on, Conquest out."

The screen flickered before disappearing, allowing Jack a much-needed deep breath and cleansing exhale.

■ ■ ■

It took more than one shift rotation for everyone to get the swap complete, but it was good to see that the crew had all made the change to civilian clothes. Some a little more flamboyant than others... but that was fine, it was considerably less UFW now. At least in appearances. Next it would be Ragnaar's turn to school the crew on how to act like a pirate. Steele was looking forward to *that* class.

It was going to take a little adjustment to get used to the new style of rank markings, they were so much different than the military symbols he'd become accustomed to. Being the *owner*, and not *of the crew*, he was one of the few people on the ship without any markings on his clothes... but he was still going to have to memorize them all; nothing would give him away faster than failing to properly identify ranks while attempting to mix-in somewhere.

"Thirty seconds to gate exit, Mr. Mercury," noted Lieutenant Commander Reegan from the command chair.

"Gun crews?"

"At stations, sir."

The silvery lining of the transition tunnel seemed to end abruptly ahead, a black circle at the end, a light dusting of color drifting across its middle. Standing next to Jack Steele, Chase Holt leaned on the railing at the back of the bridge overlooking the command pit three steps below them, the glow of the different stations the only light on the bridge. "So... we're in a *worm hole?*"

"Something like that. We're in a tunnel between two gates, which are, for description's sake, stable worm hole generators. Think of it as a garden hose. We are about to exit this end..."

"It just spits us out here?"

Jack nodded, "Pretty much."

"That opening doesn't look big enough..." pointed Chase.

"Perspective," commented Jack. "The opening is about ten miles wide."

Chase Holt watched in wonderment as long, thin, strings of iridescent color reached out from the center of the gate toward the ship, swirling around, dancing. "Dude what the hell is that?"

"Just watch," whispered Jack. "Watch and be amazed..." The colors intensified as the lightning storm of color and liquid electricity danced and swirled around the hull.

"Entering the corona..." announced the navigator.

Chase Holt was unaware his mouth was open, his eyes riveted on the big screen as the color became a solid swirling, multicolored mass. "Whoa," he breathed. The center opened up, dark and full of stars, a planet to the right.

The kaleidoscope burst outwards, prompting a sharp inhale from Chase. In a moment it was gone, they were through - and he released his breath, "It's like being born," he whispered.

"I suppose it is," agreed Jack. "Never thought of it like that. But everyone has a different reaction to it the first time."

"I could watch that over and over..."

"It doesn't get old," remarked Jack. "And each one is a little different - no two are ever the same. Never fails to give me goosebumps."

"So where are we, now?"

Jack waved at the big screen, "Welcome to Alpha Centauri, Brother."

Chase had yet to look away from the image that wrapped nearly two-thirds of the way around the bridge, "Hard to fit my head around this... Are there any people out here?"

"How about it, Mr. Reegan?" prompted Jack. "Any habitable planets here?"

"Yes sir. Layetone; I believe your people call it Alpha Centauri Bb. Equatorial diameter is 8,346 miles; a little bigger than your Earth. Her orbit lasts 698 standard days and her solar day is 25.5 hours. Her gravity is 1.11 g, with an oxygen rich atmosphere. Her inhabitants have yet to leave the surface."

Then let's give her a wide berth, Mr. Reegan; we don't want to frighten the natives if anyone is watching the skies."

"Already calculated in, sir," advised the navigator.

Steele leaned on the rail to look over the Commander's shoulder, "Any sign of those two Pirate destroyers our flights encountered in the Terran System?"

"There's a faint energy wake, but not much left of it. They have a good seventy-two hour jump on us. But what's left of the trail points us right to the multi-gate for Barnard's Star and Wolf 359."

"Which one takes us to Nelson's Point?"

Commander Reegan turned his chair to face Steele, "We would need to pass through Wolf 359. Why Nelson's Point, sir?"

"The ship they were escorting took a rail-gun hit from the Conquest. Tactical showed it damaged their atmospheric control surfaces. My best assessment is they're heading to Nelson's Point to affect some repairs; they made a rather hasty exit. It's the closest place we know of that has suitable facilities. I'm guessing the destroyers will be meeting it there."

Commander Reegan cocked his head quizzically to one side, "Why not jump straight into Nelson's Point? We could easily reach it from here."

"No undue attention," replied Jack. "Besides, if they're unlucky enough to have any mechanical failures in route, I don't want to bypass them and possibly miss them. And I don't expect that any repairs they need are going to happen overnight. We'll catch them."

Reegan rotated his seat back toward the front, "Very good, sir. Tactical, activate the ARC system as we pass Layetone."

"Aye, Skipper. The *Automatic Reflective Camouflage* system is on line and standing by."

■ ■ ■

Steele pulled on his flight gloves as he walked around the P-57 light assault fighter sitting on a marked area of the deck. There were two, nearly wingtip to wingtip, their landing skids nestled into indentations on the deck. "So, considering we're facing a bulkhead, tell me how we get these things out of here..." He tugged on a missile mounted on the wingtip, making sure it was secure.

Checking his own fighter, Ensign Torn Dado pulled his helmet on, "Each floor panel rotates 180° on the center line." he explained, flipping his hands over, palms up. "The sections the skids are on, are magnetized. Once the deck section hits 180° the magnets reverse and pop us free from the surface."

"We'll be upside down..."

Torn Dado nodded inside his helmet, "That's right, relative to the ship of course."

"And recovery?"

The Ensign thumbed over his shoulder at the landing bay doors, "One at a time through the main door, then right back here. You good with your checklist, sir?"

Jack's expression registered satisfaction, "I'm good, Mr. Dado. Let's saddle up."

Odd expression, Lisa Steele had used it too. So thankfully, Torn didn't have to ask for an explanation again. These Earthers had some strange colloquialisms that didn't seem to translate well. In retrospect, they translated – literally, but they didn't make any sense until you fully understood the explanation. The Ensign shrugged it off as he climbed up into the P-57's slender cockpit. His Lancia seemed rather spacious in comparison.

The P-57 was a long, thin, windswept looking fighter, with sharp graceful lines and rather short forward angled wings and nose canards. Armed with a gun under the nose and one in each wingroot, she sported two missiles on each wingtip and room for two capital ship attack missiles called Hellraisers on the sides of her rounded belly. While they were stocked in the armory of the Perseus, the P-57's were fitted with long-range sensor pods instead.

"How are you doing over there, sir?"

Steele looked to his right, the ladder of Torn Dado's fighter folding into its hull as its canopy slid closed. Jack felt the pat on his left shoulder before his crew chief disappeared down the ladder. "Good to go, Mr. Dado." He pulled the canopy handle and it slid forward from behind, *thunking* softly as the seals met, the air system automatically kicking on. Accustomed to heavier fighters, it was a bit disconcerting to have so little armor. Granted it was a highly advanced light composite, and the shields were reinforced, but there was something to be said for the peace of mind that heavy duty ablative armor provided.

All pre-launch systems up and running, Steele adjusted the size of one of his holographic HUDs, moving it into a more favorable position, giving the individual in the small control office a thumbs-up.

Over the nose of his P-57, Steele's view of the ship's bulkhead rotated, giving way to the light-flecked darkness of space, the magnets reversing polarity, pushing the fighter away, giving him the sensation he had been dumped out of a basket and was free-falling from the Perseus. He reached forward and punched the ignition, rewarded by a low chorus of thumps as the three engines lit. Steele keyed his mic, "Perseus, Mercury is clear."

"Dado is clear."

"Perseus, copy. Have a good flight gentlemen."

"Come to our patrol heading, Mr. Dado." Steele pointed the P-57 without rolling it upright, because of course, once he was away from the ship it didn't seem to matter; upright was relative to *his* point of view. He nudged the throttle to about one-quarter power, streaking away from the Perseus.

"Aye, Mr. Mercury. Coming up on your starboard wing..."

Jack checked on Torn Dado as he scanned the system spread around them; the brighter star, Alpha Centauri A on the left, Alpha Centauri B on the right and the red dwarf, Proxima Centauri barely visible ahead, glowing weakly. *Damn, this is a big system...* Checking his navigation screen, he selected the gate to Wolf 359 as a waypoint and adjusted his heading, his wingman sticking in tight formation.

As much a checkout ride as a patrol, the two pilots threw the fighters around to get a feel for them, quickly realizing the fighters were savagely more maneuverable than what they had become accustomed to. "Holy crap," muttered Steele on open mic, "these things are insanely twitchy..."

The comm in Steele's helmet crackled momentarily, *"Mr. ... Mercury,"* said a deep voice, pausing to be sure he used the proper protocol. *"Lieutenant Loech Braskus. You are flying heavy-handed. It is common when new to the 57. If you look to the left, low, just forward and above your throttle quadrant, you'll see a small digital readout called ODS. Do you see it?"*

Steele located it, just where the Lieutenant described. "I see it. The digital reads one-hundred."

"Good. That is the Operational Dampening System. There is a small jog roller underneath the readout that will allow you to adjust the 57's control response. I suggest setting it at sixty. As you become accustomed to the 57's characteristics, you can make further adjustments to your liking..."

"Where do you usually set it for yourself?" inquired Steele, adjusting the setting, watching the digital readout count downward.

"We fly them at one-hundred. But we learned on the 57s, we have never flown anything else..."

Steele keyed his mic, "Thank you, Mr. Braskus. Stick around in case we have any other questions..." He looked out over his right wingtip at Torn Dado's P-57, "Did you catch all that, Mr. Dado?"

"Every bit, sir."

Jack had to use his fingertips to fly the thing at seventy percent, seriously doubting he would get any closer to one-hundred percent no matter how much he practiced. It was a neat little fighter – actually pretty, it's lines graceful, but what an unpredictable little wench if you man-handled it. In retrospect, he supposed transitioning from actual aircraft to the fighters he'd become used to, was a little like this. But that seemed a lifetime ago. Then again he'd spent so much time in them that they'd become second nature. Perhaps it would be the same in this case. Though he was going to need more stick time to accomplish that. A *lot* more. If he was forced to fight in the P-57 now, he would probably be in dire straits, reverting to heavy-handed reflex. Maybe there was something to be said for not being able to fly it in a straight line... he'd be hard to hit.

■ ■ ■

Jack leaned back and relaxed in the seat of the P-57, the canopy sliding back, bringing with it a wash of tepid air from the bay. His muscles ached from his body fighting against itself, tensely refrained from overreacting and over-controlling.

"Everything OK, Mr. Mercury?"

Steele turned to his left, his helmet rolling against the headrest; Torn Dado's face peering at him from outside the open cockpit, obviously standing on the fighter's ladder. "How far were you able to adjust your ODS to, Torn?"

"I was flying at about eighty-five. I wasn't comfortable with that, but I could manage. I dialed it down to about sixty on landing approach though... How about you?"

Steele pulled off his gloves, "I couldn't get past seventy. Had it set at fifty for our approach."

Torn Dado reached in and helped Steele unfasten his helmet and unplug his umbilical cords and cables, "It'll take some practice, that's for sure. We'll get it..."

Jack flexed his arms and fingers as he unfastened his harness, "I feel drained. The kind of drained you feel after a dogfight..."

"A *what?*"

"Flight combat," clarified Jack. "I'll explain it later," he waved, knowing Torn Dado didn't understand the Earth reference. "I don't think I ever want to fly one of these things again..." He handed the Ensign his helmet as he pulled on the windshield frame to stand up, "That was an exercise in frustration."

"If I may say so," said Torn, stepping down to the deck, "you don't seem like the giving up type, sir."

"I'm not. But a famous man once said; *A man's got to know his limitations*. I'm thinking he was right."

As Steele stepped to the deck, his MOBIUS flickered before its holo-screen appeared over his wrist, "Incoming from the bridge, Mr. Mercury."

He moved the screen to free-float in front of him, "Connect, MOBI."

Lieutenant Commander Reegan's face appeared on the screen, "How was your flight Mr. Mercury?"

Steele wobbled his open, free hand in view of the screen, "Meh, I've had better."

"Problem with the 57s?"

Steele's mouth skewed crookedly in distaste, "Problem with what I've become conditioned to."

Reegan nodded, "Personally I've never flown one, but I understand the 57 can be a cruel teacher."

"They weren't wrong," replied Jack.

"Not to change the subject, sir, but your sensor pods showed a great deal of nothing out there and we're clear of the planet, Layetone. With two normal suns and a red dwarf, this is a rather large system. It might be worthwhile to make an in-system jump to save some time."

"Are we still tracking the energy wakes of those destroyers?"

"Yes sir, the trail is a little clearer here, we are gaining on them. That being said, they are far enough ahead that they've left the system. They are most likely somewhere in Wolf 359 already."

"Alright Mr. Reegan, let's make a jump. I'll be up in 5 minutes, I'm interested to see how a GOD jump feels."

"You may be disappointed, Mr. Mercury, it's truly no different than a gate jump except that we are the epicenter and corona instead of the gate..."

"Aww," groaned Jack, "don't ruin it for me, Mr. Reegan."

"He's right you know," said a deep voice behind him. Steele turned around as the holo-screen dissolved; a thinly built man in a leather flight jacket standing next to Torn Dado leaned casually on the wingtip of the closest P-57.

"Mr. Mercury," began Torn Dado, "Lieutenant Loech Braskus." he waved at the thin man who was a good head shorter than Steele.

The Lieutenant had a sharp, angular face, short-cropped hair that looked like strands of shiny copper wire and the most disturbing orange-amber eyes. They almost appeared to glow and Steele had to force himself not to stare. "Good to meet you Mr. Braskus," he nodded, shaking the man's hand. For a slightly built man his grip was nearly vice-like.

Braskus shoved his hands into his jacket pockets, shrugging, "Don't worry about your first flight sir, the 57 grows on you..."

The three men turned and started walking across the deck toward the elevators. "How long have you been flying them?" Asked Jack.

"Fourteen months," replied Braskus. "My wingman is a few months behind me, but we both finished near the top of our classes." He ventured a glance at Steele, "You're a big guy, did you feel comfortable in her cockpit?"

"Not entirely..."

"What have you been flying? If you don't mind me asking."

"Cyclones, Lancias, Warthogs, occasionally a Zulu..."

Braskus smiled, "Warthog – wow, that's an oldie. And the Zulu, by the Gods, that thing's a hammer, eh? All *great* hardware. But where they are designed to go head-to-head, trade blows and slug it out; the P-57 is a scalpel. She's not too bad to learn on if she's the first and only thing you've ever flown. But truthfully, you're going to have a tough time considering the experience level you're coming from."

"I can see that..."

"And, no insult intended, but you're not exactly built for her either..."

Steele raised an eyebrow, "Meaning?"

"Sir, physically, you're a big guy..."

"I guess that's a matter of perspective, have you met Mr. Ragnaar?"

"The giant? Yeah, what do you feed someone that size?"

Jack smirked, "Pretty much whatever he wants..."

Braskus shrugged it off, not recognizing the humor. "What I'm saying is, most 57 jockeys you'll meet are *my* size."

Jack nodded his understanding, "I get you."

"But if you really want to learn the 57, I'll be more than happy to work with either of you..."

CHAPTER TWELVE

WOLF 359 SYSTEM - THE PERSEUS : *OPERATION DARK COVER*

As Lieutenant Commander Reegan predicted, a GOD jump held little difference from a gate jump. Though there was something to be said about creating your own gate - that made the whole thing more impressive in its own right. Jumping from their present location to the gate into Wolf 359, the twelve-hour trip was uneventful. To anyone in the system, it would have looked like they entered through the gate from Alpha Centauri like any other normal ship.

Wolf 359 was a dreary place, the star itself a red dwarf, the darkness of space there bathed in an eerie reddish glow, its weak light reflected off the dust drifting in the system, resembling the ground fog in some old black and white Dracula movie. At an estimated 9% of the Terran Sun's mass, the red dwarf put out about .01% of its light.

Jack's eyes searched the bridge's main screen, "Any planets out there, Mr. Reegan?"

"No, Mr. Mercury. Nothing larger than a drifting planetoid in this system."

"The place gives me the creeps."

"If you mean it gives one the feeling of being rather inhospitable and dangerous, then I agree."

"That's exactly what I mean. Let's get a probe out there."

Reegan's fingers pipped across his control surfaces, pulling up a probe command screen and setting its parameters. A dark-gray garbage-can sized object fired from a port in the nose of the Perseus, propelled across the darkness, a soft blue glow its engine's only signature. "Recoverable probe away. She'll come back to us before she runs out of fuel."

"Go with your instincts," advised Steele, "if your gut tells you something doesn't look or feel right, pay attention to it."

"Understood."

Steele turned on his heel and headed for the door off the bridge, "Call me if you need me."

■ ■ ■

With the *team* assembled, Steele stood behind the high-backed leather chair at the head of the briefing room and leaned on the headrest, his arms draped casually over one another.

Chase Holt leaned back in his chair interlocking his fingers and stretching his arms above him, "So what's the plan... *man?*"

Jack ignored his attempt at levity. "Let's cover what we know so far. Mr. Ragnaar?"

Ragnaar called up a file on his MOBIUS, sending it to the big screen behind Jack; the technical sheet and layout for a FreeRanger destroyer appearing. "Both of the destroyers are Miro Class. An older but still solid design; fast, and maneuverable. No room for a GOD drive... unless someone has come up with a way to shrink them. The Perseus can outrun them, and outgun them. Two might be a problem though - especially in the hands of capable commanders."

"Any fighters?"

"No, we have an advantage there."

Steele turned to Torn Dado, "How good are our pilots?"

"Sir, I've seen their transcripts, scores and training videos... I'd have to say pretty remarkable – even by Captain Smiley's standards. They're certainly better than you or I in those things, and we're both considered exceptional in what we fly."

"Wait a minute," interrupted Mercedes Huang, her leather jacket creaking as she leaned forward. "Are you considering an outright assault? I thought this was supposed to be a covert operation?"

"It is covert, Mercy," replied Jack. "We're just covering what we know here. If something goes wrong, *because we all know how well plans hold up under adversity,* and we have to slug it out, I want to know what our likelihood of success is. It's not our first choice... it's just an option." He pointed at Derrik Brighton, "Anything on the third ship?"

Derrik swiped his MOBIUS sending a file to the screen behind Jack, a technical image with limited statistics. "She's a new design, nothing in the UFW or GIS database. What data we have is what we've gathered from our encounter. She's frigate sized, considerably smaller than a destroyer. We saw no indications of armaments of any kind and it appears she is specifically designed for fast rescue missions. Which would mean less armor to save weight and improve atmospheric maneuverability. She likely has upgraded

143

shield systems and quicker GOD jump generation because of reduced mass and overall size."

Steele pinched his lower lip in thought, "Think she can outrun us?"

"Possibly. But she should be easy enough to stop with a few well-placed hits."

"Then we'd have to board her..." Steele rubbed his chin, "How many Marines do we have?"

"Twenty-seven," responded Chase, raising his hand. Jack arched an inquisitive eyebrow, prompting Chase to lower his hand out of embarrassment. "Ah-um, two squads of twelve each, two squad leaders and one CO."

"Combat experience?"

"Mixed. But very capable. I don't think you have any worries there."

"What kind of equipment are they using?" asked Jack. "Is it UFW military?"

"Professional; mercenary and contractor grade," replied Chase. "Looked like good hardware and gear... I was told they were allowed to pick what they wanted, so they chose the best available..."

"Y'know," began Steele, "it seems a bit remiss that we're not getting input directly from some key people." He pointed at Torn Dado, "Tornado, get the Skipper and his command staff down here, the pilots, the Marine CO and his squad leaders."

"Aye, sir."

■ ■ ■

The meeting covered a myriad of scenarios, responses, tactics, what ifs, and possible resolutions – both good and bad. They could never cover everything, there were simply too many variables or outcomes. Some things just had to be done live, on the fly. There would probably be just as many reactionary decisions as planned ones. But Steele knew; *"If you fail to plan, you plan to fail." ~Winston Churchill.*

In Jack's view it went fairly well. And for the first time since they left Earth's orbit, the command officers knew the whole story and the mission at hand. The time for need-to-know had arrived. Understanding what was at stake, the complexities and the risks, their mindset reflected the focus of the mission; the previous difficulties between Steele and Captain Vastyque filed away as ancient history.

Interrupting their closing conversations, the lighting dropped to flashing amber a second before the alarm gong rang.

"All hands on deck! All hands on deck! Skipper to the bridge! Command staff to the bridge..!"

"Something spooked him," commented Steele jumping to his feet. He pointed at Lieutenant Braskus and his wingman, "You guys suit up, just in case..."

■ ■ ■

An inset video of the derelict ship on the big screen greeted Steele and the command staff on their arrival to the bridge of the Perseus. A marker on the plotting screen displayed the location in the distance, the ship invisible, unmagnified. Whatever it may have been previously, was unidentifiable and heavily damaged, a dead, burned-out carcass.

"The drone picked her up on its return route," announced the tactical officer, vacating the command seat for Commander Reegan.

"What is she?" asked the Commander dropping into his seat.

"A bulk hauler. Well at least she *was*... "

"Why did you call for a yellow?" asked Jack.

"She has a power signature, sir," replied the tactical officer, returning to his station.

Reegan examined the readings and stats on one of his command screens. "I don't see anything showing life..."

"Not from here, Skipper," replied the tactical officer. "The drone picked it up on its return pass."

"Could be residual power, I suppose," commented Reegan. "She doesn't look like she's been out here long..."

"It is more likely an observation beacon hidden in her wreckage," advised Ragnaar, replacing the current navigator. "It is a common pirate tactic for monitoring a sector."

"Then we should destroy it?" asked the tactical officer.

"That would be ill-advised," replied Ragnaar. "Any action we take other than passing it by would inform whomever is monitoring it, that we are more than we appear to be. And, they are often booby-trapped, so I would recommend a safe distance."

Steele was examining the image on the main screen and it bothered him that there was something missing that he couldn't quite put his finger on.

145

"Looks weird," mumbled Chase, "like a car crash without the mess..."

"That's it!" snapped Steele. "There's no debris field... she was *moved* here!"

Chase scratched his forehead, "Why?"

"Because there's nowhere else out here to hide anything."

"We don't want to leave it out here to spy on traffic..." commented Reegan, looking over his shoulder.

"Astrometrics," announced Jack, "Enter it into UFW military charts for destruction, but *do not* enter it into the public AllStar charts. We don't want anyone else knowing we made note of it."

"Aye, sir."

It would have been nice to jump across the system to the gate to Nelson's Point... Wolf 359 was such an empty, depressing system. But, they were being watched... "Stand us down from yellow, Mr. Reegan."

■ ■ ■

Pillows stacked behind her, TESS' holo-screen free-floating at eye level, Lisa stretched out on her bed, the familiar hum of the Revenge welcoming her back to more comfortable quarters. It wasn't that the Conquest was all that bad, but realistically, the ship was a century old... Her quarters there had the overall ambiance of an industrial tin can. And beyond the sterile odor of cleaner, you could almost smell the decades of men and women who had bunked there. The Revenge was fresh and new, the only scent in her quarters was her own, the style simple but modern and clean. Elbowing her pillows, she leaned back as her TESS connected to Jack's MOBIUS using the ship's long range secure comm signal. "Hello big brother."

Jack looked tired. "What's up kiddo?"

"Thought I'd check in and see how things were going..."

He shrugged loosely, "They're going."

Lisa frowned, "That good, huh?"

He yawned heavily, leaning back in his chair, "I'm bored out of my skull. There's not a whole lot for me to do. It's not like the Freedom or the Conquest - you get bored, you hang out on the flight deck for a while..."

"Perpetual motion," she nodded.

He rubbed his eyes, "I feel like a third wheel. I can't even fly the fighters..."

"Why not?"

"So completely different than what we're used to... I..." he shook his head in dismay, "I can't control the damn thing. It's like trying to fly a hummingbird with a jet engine stuck up its ass."

In rather unladylike fashion, Lisa snorted before laughing, "Oh my God, you mean there's something you *can't* do?" With one eyebrow raised he glared silently back at her. "OK, OK," she waved, "can't you just put in some seat time and practice?"

"It's not that simple. We don't have a simulator and we have to really look and act like a commercial ship, so we have to stay all buttoned up."

"Mmm," she nodded appreciatively. "Sucks. Sooo, how close are you to catching up with the destroyers?"

"We're in the transition tunnel between Wolf 359 and Nelson's Point. We'll hit the exit gate in about twenty-four hours. Then about a day across the system to the station. That's where we expect to catch up with them."

"You guys have a plan?"

"There are few options," Jack admitted. "But it's likely we're going have to call our plays on the fly." He ran his fingers through his hair, wanting to change the subject, "How's it going there?"

"Well I'm back on the Revenge, but the Admiral has been keeping me in the loop and he video-brief's the ship captains daily. Brian lets me listen-in off-screen."

"Good. Is Brian letting you sit in the second seat at all?"

"Some, but there's not a lot to do right now..."

"Learn the systems," urged Jack. "You'll be glad you did. Study up on everything you can get your hands on. Maria was his normal second, or Ragnaar, so he's short on command staff."

"He's still got Raulya though..." she countered.

"Yes, and she's a very good officer but he needs to keep her at tactical, that where she shines." He looked momentarily pensive, "What's happening down on the surface?"

Lisa tried to keep her face expressionless, she wasn't sure if she pulled it off or not. "You sure you want to know?"

He took a deep breath, "Yeah..." he said slowly, concern washing over his face.

She tried to keep her feelings and emotions in check, for his sake. "It's a mess. Pretty much everywhere. The nukes have stopped, but there have been a few dirty bombs. Lots of ground fighting..."

"Ground fighting? Where?" he interrupted.

"Sections of Europe are a shambles. A lot of those refugees from the Middle East..."

"Yeah, I knew *that* was going to happen," he sighed.

Her face pinched in distress, "They're fighting all over Europe, Great Britain, some in Canada... and our unsecured southern border has allowed thousands to pour in unchecked..."

Jack closed his eyes, "How bad are the States?"

She shrugged, "The U.S. has an armed populace. We're not in as bad a position as, say, Great Britain. But it's still not good. The power grid has taken some major hits; millions of people are without power. But I think that's a universal problem all over the world. The National Guard was called up but they're spread pretty thin considering how many were deployed. Oath Keeper militias have sprung up all over the country and are managing in many areas to maintain order, even engaging in firefights with insurgents. They've been pretty successful so far."

"Any military movement?"

"Israel bombed the crap out of Iran, took out their nuclear facilities. But it looks like most countries have withdrawn militarily to some extent to help with civilian recovery. Surprisingly enough, Russia has been the light of reason in the Middle East, pounding the hell out of the jihadists over there."

"What about China?" asked Jack.

"Staying out of things. Pretty quiet," replied Lisa.

"Makes me wonder what they're up to; not sure I trust them."

Lisa smirked crookedly, "Nobody trusts anybody right now. But I'm sure, knowing that we're up here has something to do with them behaving themselves."

"Do we have a government?"

Lisa nodded, "The Speaker of the House was sworn in yesterday as the President; everyone above him was either killed or is missing and presumed dead. The survivors of the house and senate have been moved to a secure location for protection. Command staff has been dispersed to key locations."

"Jesus..." Jack pinched his lower lip, "Probably Cheyenne Mountain... most secure place I can think of."

"Not to change the subject or anything," waved Lisa, "I know we've been busy and you've had a lot on your mind, but have you talked to Alité lately?"

"Sure, a few... days ago..." he said slowly. Jack's eyes narrowed as his mind tracked backwards, "A week or so..." he nodded, convinced.

"That was almost six weeks ago," interrupted Lisa.

"Nooo..." he mumbled in disbelief, his expression blank.

"*Yeeaaah,*" she countered.

"Aww *craaap...*"

CHAPTER THIRTEEN

VELORA PRIME, VELORIA, AIR & SPACE PORT : *REBIRTH*

Alité Galaýa Steele, Queen of Veloria stood at the fourth-floor windows of the ASP main-terminal in the executive conference room, staring blankly, unseeing, recent history playing back in her mind's eye of the court she had held in this very room. Of the traitors and infiltrators prosecuted there. Of the sentences for the guilty. Death. Most were guilty. Those lacking unified proof to condemn, were micro-chipped and banished from Veloria for life, entered into the UFW's criminal database, their history to follow them like a dark cloud wherever they ventured in the Universe.

The executions were grisly and terrifying; the guilty slowly lowered naked into an open laser meat processor. Passing through a fine laser grid, slicing them vertically like potatoes through a french-fry maker, horizontal lasers swept back and forth, cutting off one inch bits, their remains dropping into a tank below like little charred cubes as the machine ate them alive. There was little bloodletting as the lasers cauterized each cut; no early escape from the horror by bleeding to death. No, they felt every agonizing moment of their demise. Their horrified screams left no doubt to the levels of excruciating hell they suffered for their crimes. The Queen had ordered all banished micro-chipped criminals to witness the executions so they would know what fate awaited them if they returned. And to serve as a witness to warn all those across the Universe who might intend to do Veloria harm in the future; it would not be tolerated.

Against Alité's initial instincts, she allowed Prime Minister Nitram Marconus to convince her it was unnecessary to expose the good citizens of Veloria to the horror of the executions. Rumors and leaked tidbits would suffice. She knew the fate was cruel, exceedingly so... but she felt the punishment matched the crime of slavery and planetary subversion. And the death of her entire family. They had been responsible for hundreds of thousands of lives lost. It would not, *could not* stand. She was determined that it would never happen again, she would be a smarter, wiser leader, learning from the mistakes of the past.

Standing elegantly in a feminine but functional pale gold suit, hands on hips, Alité's vision and awareness crept back in, forcing the historical playback to dissolve and drift away.

A light rain fell from the mottled overcast sky, deepening the green of the fields and valley beyond the runways. She took a cleansing breath as she studied the lines of the Freedom Class carrier sitting on the pad just beyond the tower, its shiny, wet, deep-gray hull boldly marked with the crest of the Royal Velorian Navy. The first of five, ordered from the UFW as part of the negotiations for mining rights in Mine 01 on the third continent, now named Alexandria. The *Wronin* had arrived the night before last with a skeleton crew who would stay as long as necessary to familiarize and train a Velorian crew before returning to the UFW Naval Yards on Tanzia.

A line of four Warthog fighters playing follow the leader, taxied out past the stern of the Wronin, heading for the far runway, a blue glow under their landing feet.

Having never seen the Freedom except in the darkness of space, Alité wondered if the Wronin looked exactly like the Freedom. That part of history, little more than a year past, seemed so long ago. She looked at the shapes of the city in the distance, merely shadowy columns in the rain, knowing some of those buildings were finally becoming habitable again. The four fighters slashed past in the grayness, extending out over the farm fields, disappearing from view.

Breaking her train of thought, she turned away from the windows when the door to the room opened, an armed Peacekeeper allowing a casually-dressed figure in dusty khaki clothing and wide-brimmed hat to pass. "Hat," was all he said to the visitor, prompting the man to uncover his head.

"My Queen," he smiled warmly.

Alité beamed at the scruffy old face as he walked towards her. She spread her arms wide for an embrace, *"Professor Edgars!* So good of you to come... It's been too long!"

"Please, just Walt." He held his hand out, stalling her, "Fresh from the Wilderness, my dear, dust and all. Your suit will never forgive..."

"Nonsense, Walt," she scolded, grabbing him in a tight embrace, dust blooming off his clothes. "So good to see you. I've missed you..." She held him at arm's length examining him. "The Wilderness agrees with you, you look fit."

"And you look stunning - as *always* my dear..." He awkwardly indicated the transferred dust on her clothes, reaching to brush it off and hesitating,

151

"You've got some, ah, there..." he waved his hand without really touching her.

"Oh stop," she cajoled, brushing the dust off her blouse and jacket. "Quit worrying about it." She put her arm around his shoulder, turned and guided him to the windows overlooking the runways. "Look..."

"Oh my," he breathed, "she looks bloody new."

"She is," replied Alité. "She came in the night before last." She watched his profile, he was studying it closely. "She's called the Wronin... She needs a Captain, Walt..."

Walt Edgars was half listening, half admiring, when he noticed her staring at him out of the corner of his eye. "What... *Who me?* You can't be seri..."

Alité held her hand out palm up and opened her fingers, a set of shiny gold Captain's pips in her hand, "She needs a Captain, Walt," she repeated.

He glanced down at the pips, up at the ship and back at her face, "But, I..."

"Take them Walt. The Wronin is yours."

"There must be someone else you'd rather..."

"No one. You are the most qualified man on the planet. You'll feel right at home, she's just like the Freedom..."

"Fat lot of good I did her," he grumbled.

"Stop right there, *mister*," she rebutted. "I'll not have one of the finest officers I've ever met, disparaging himself," she frowned. Her face softened, "Walt. I *need* you..."

He picked the pieces of gold up out of her hand and rolled them around in his palm, contemplating their meaning, a smile slowly creeping across his face, "I never could say no to you, could I?"

"No. And I hoped you wouldn't start now," she smiled back, brushing dust off his beard.

■ ■ ■

Lieutenant Commander Walrick stepped past the Peacekeeper who held the door open for him, entering the same room in which he'd said goodbye to Vice Admiral Steele a year ago. He hadn't been in that room since and his stomach was filled with butterflies of uncertainty. He'd had little contact with the Queen during that time but had diligently done his job, day in, day out, recruiting pilots and training them in the aging Warthogs, constructing a skilled cohesive unit he felt Captain Paul Smiley would be proud of. Even

152

with the addition of a handful of UFW Cyclones, he still had more than twice as many pilots as fighters to fly. But that didn't bother him much, he managed to stay positive.

Pausing at the corner of the table, he came to attention, holding a salute, the Queen with her back to him, occupied with something out the window. He cleared his throat, "Your Majesty?" he prompted.

She turned smoothly, gracefully, "Mr. Walrick," she smiled, "so good to see you." She returned his salute, allowing him to rest. "Please, sit," she motioned to a chair, sitting at the table as well. "Have you seen our new addition?"

"Yes, your Highness. It is a beautiful sight... a long time since we've had a ship of our own flying Velorian colors..." He watched her toy with a small box under her hands.

"There's much more than just the ship, Mr. Walrick... She is fully packed. I understand she carried enough parts and electronics to rebuild and upgrade your Warthogs to the advanced D model..."

"The D model requires new engines," he interrupted. "Pardon me for interrupting..."

She merely smiled, "Engines, electronics, weapons... And I'm told, ten brand new flight simulators."

He smiled weakly, "That's wonderful. And I don't mean to complain, *really*, but what we really need is additional craft. We have..."

Her eyes danced, "Oh, we have that too. Twelve, P6 Raiders and twenty-four Cyclones – the new model."

His eyes widened, "That would be the V2..."

"If you say so," she nodded. "Here's the catch; twenty-four fighters have to stay on the Wronin, the rest are for the base. You can choose how you want to distribute them... But before you make that decision," she slid the box she'd been toying with in front of him, the top open, "know that I want *you* on the Wronin as her CAG."

He looked down at the Commander's markers in the box, "I am *honored...*"

"Who is your second in command?"

"Lieutenant Garith T'Posh," Walrick replied mechanically, dumping the gold markers into his hand.

"Now known as Lieutenant *Commander* Garith T'Posh," she added. "Give him your pips, he will be taking over base flight operations. You will set up a curriculum for him to follow for training new candidates, and he will follow it to the letter. Or else."

"It's already in place," he replied, "he's a *very* good instructor."

"Good, it's done then... Create a roster of pilots for the base and the Wronin. List the flight inventory for each and arrange to move the equipment as you see fit. When that is complete, report to Captain Edgars on the Wronin."

Walrick's eyes widened, "The Professor is *back?*"

"As of today, Commander..."

■ ■ ■

Alité had felt tiny standing under the monolithic hull of the *Wronin* waiting for the massive freight elevator to be offloaded. Mechanical transports stacked with crates and equipment departed, floating on a blue-green light of their antigravity drives, heading toward the hangars. On her ride up into the belly on the now-empty lift, she felt like she was being swallowed into a great maw. The nose of a dark blue-gray P6 Spectre waiting to be loaded onto the elevator came into view, its wingtips folded upward. It was evident to her that Commander Walrick had wasted no time issuing his equipment dispersion orders.

"Your Majesty..?"

Standing on the Wronin's mostly empty bridge, flanked by her Prime Minister and a few other officers, Alité snapped back into the conversation, "Yes," she replied automatically, her hand on the headrest of the command chair, picturing her husband there. "It's all so *very* familiar..."

The ship's UFW Commander continued his presentation on the changes and upgrades the Wronin enjoyed over the original design of the cruiser Ynosa. "The Freedom Class Carrier you see here is more akin to an actual carrier than a cruiser, but shares the best of both worlds..." he droned on.

Prime Minister Nitram Marconus leaned close, whispering in her ear, "Are you alright Princess?"

"Yes Boney," she whispered back, patting his hand discretely, blinking away the wetness that had welled in her eyes, "many memories..."

"I'm sorry," he responded quietly, "bad memories? Maybe we should go."

The corner of her mouth curled a bit, "No, I'm fine. The good outweighs the bad. I choose to remember the good... the victories."

The TESS wrapped around her wrist chimed, "Incoming communication from the ASP tower, your Majesty."

She glanced at the curved glass image of TESS' face on the device, preferring the discreet screen over the holo-screen. "I'm in a meeting TESS..."

"I am told it is a secure signal from your husband, *the King...*"

"By the *Gods,* TESS, put it through immediately!" Without excusing herself Alité ducked through the automatic door at the back of the bridge into the Captain's ready room. It swished open smoothly, closing behind her, leaving her alone in silence. She switched to the holo-screen as the video shifted, Jack Steele's face appearing before her. "My husband..." she sighed, her eyes welling up again.

"Howdy Slim," Steele joked, tipping an invisible hat. "You're a sight for sore eyes..." Her head tilted, her eyes quizzical. "I miss seeing your face," he explained.

She smiled warmly, "I miss you as well, my King. How are things on Terra?" She sat on the sofa and placed the holo-screen at eye level.

"Earth is, well, a complete mess... They tell me it could have been much worse... "

"What happened? How bad *is* it?" she asked. She could see the shift in his expression, it showed in his eyes.

"Escaping agents started a nuclear war to cover their escape. Casualty estimates were incomplete, but they were between ten and twenty million. There is scatted catastrophic damage. It could get much worse before it's all over."

"By the *Gods!* But worse? How?"

"There is a fanatical religious faction, an ideology really, that has taken advantage of the chaos, to create *more* chaos. They take particular delight in murder and mayhem."

"They sound truly evil..."

Jack sighed, "Oh they are. No doubt about that. And they've infiltrated nearly every country on the planet under the guise of refugees."

"I am sooo sorry, darling. I know our resources are low, but is there anything Veloria can do?"

"We may have refugees of our own..."

Her eyes brightened. "Your parents?"

"Yes, there's nothing left here for mom and dad. Maybe we can find something..."

155

"Bring them!" she interrupted. "They will want for nothing. I promise you that."

"There will be others," he added. "From all walks of life. Looking for a fresh start, looking for adventure..."

"We will welcome anyone who wants to work toward a future here on Veloria, you know that. I will work with Boney to create some kind of program to assist them when they arrive. How many do you think there will be?"

Steele's eyes narrowed, "Hard to tell. Probably only a couple hundred right now. But that could turn into thousands. Maybe eventually millions..."

Alité's eyes widened, "Oh my. Then I must speak with Boney immediately. When do you expect you will be arriving home with them?"

Jack rubbed the back of his neck, "Yeah, about that. I don't know... the task force may get back before we do."

She raised an eyebrow, moving closer to the screen, "What aren't you telling me, Jack? What's going on? And why aren't you in uniform?"

Jack glanced down at his clothes, "Oh yeah, well, um..." his mouth twisted nervously sideways, chewing on the inside of his lip. "That's the thing, see, I can't tell you..."

"Where are you?" she asked suspiciously, rising from her seat.

He chewed the other side now, "I can't tell you that either."

"You are my *husband,*" she said beginning to pace the office, the screen free-floating in front of her. "Why can't you tell me?"

"I'm under direct orders of Fleet Admiral Higdenberger. It's *top secret.*"

"Oh for the love of the Gods," she snapped sharply, "I'm your *wife,* a *Queen.* And you are my *King...!*"

"I'm sorry, sweetheart," pleaded Jack. "Really. But that doesn't override top secret orders... I've probably told you too much already."

"Maybe I'll have to contact the Madame Directorate's office then..." threatened Alité.

"You will not!" snapped Jack. "As your husband... *as your King,* I forbid it!" As it flew out of his mouth he regretted having said it, a chill racing up his back, knowing full well she was not someone who could be forbade anything. "Speaking about this to *anyone* could risk lives. *Our* lives. *My* life."

Her expression softened, "You are right of course. I apologize."

Really? He wasn't sure what concerned him more, the fact that he had forbade her from doing something - or that she had seemingly capitulated.

Actual compliance might be a wholly different matter. The entire thing was to say the least, a little disconcerting. He would have to replay that in his head later to see what might have caused this unusual success. "Thank you." It was all he could think of to say. Through her pacing, Jack was able to see several different angles of the office. "Are you on a ship?"

"That's *top secret,*" she countered a little sarcastically.

"Ooookayy," he sighed, not knowing where to go from there.

She smiled, satisfied with annoying him. "Doesn't it look familiar?"

"I guess it does," he nodded, squinting to see details.

"It's a brand new refit Freedom Class," she waved. "It's one of five new ships we negotiated with the UFW for mining rights for one of our mines. Two of these, two brand new destroyers and a brand new jump frigate."

"Fully loaded?"

"Yes. And lots of extras, like new fighters for the ASP."

"How are you going to crew them? The ships I mean."

"You let me worry about that," she countered. "You just do whatever your job is over there," she said circling her finger at him, "and get yourself home."

The bridge door behind Alité swished open, a well-groomed uniformed figure stepping into the room, saluting, "Captain Walt Edgars reporting for duty, your Majesty."

Jack's eyes widened in surprise, "Walt is back..?!"

CHAPTER FOURTEEN

WASINGTON D.C. : PRESIDENTIAL EMERGENCY OPERATIONS CENTER

More than one-hundred feet beneath the blackened crater that claimed the nation's iconic symbol of leadership and strength, the IT and communications specialists working diligently, managed to reconnect the PEOC to the rest of the military and intelligence communications grid using outdated but still functional secure hard lines.

Surrounded by other military officers including Stephen Miles, Admiral Robert Cooke saluted the video screen in the communications control room, "Mr. President..."

The former Speaker of the House, now President, returned the salute, "Good to see you General, I'd thought we lost you all. How are you and your folks holding up?"

Admiral Cooked glanced left and right at the faces around him, "Still here, sir."

The President scanned the faces around the Admiral, "Secretary of Defense?"

"MIA, sir."

"Chairman of the Joint Chiefs of Staff?"

Admiral Cooke glanced down, his lips pressed and back up again, "Took his own life, Mr. President."

The president looked saddened, "He was one of *them?*"

"That's what we suspect, sir."

"That makes you Chairman of the Joint Chiefs of Staff, Admiral." His eyes shifted to Stephen Miles, "CIA..." it was a cross between a question and a confirmation.

"Yes, Mr. President."

"I believe you are the highest ranking member surviving?"

"I believe so, sir. The Director and Deputy Director never made the bunker."

The President momentarily bowed his head, his face pinched in grim consternation, "Then you have just become the Director." He rubbed his jaw, "I fear this isn't over yet. I fear in our weakened state we will be a target..."

"What's it like out there?" asked the Admiral, "Across the country?"

"Large swatches of the country are without power and will be for some time... People are scared and desperate..."

"It's been slow for us to reconnect, sir," interrupted Stephen, "we've had to rely on hard lines, we can't reach any of the satellites..."

"There are few satellites remaining, gentlemen. Information is and will continue to be, slow." He glanced up momentarily, "Unless our friends up there see fit to do something about that."

"Not sure if they are a help or a hindrance at this point," ventured Stephen Miles.

"Well, I can confirm there would be little left on this planet had they not intervened. Their efforts removed hundreds of missiles from play..."

"No offense Mr. President," commented Stephen glancing upwards, "But they didn't get them all."

"You're right," replied the President, "they didn't. But we don't know if that was by bad luck or design. Hopefully we will know more soon. Groups of people from all over the world that had the privilege of meeting them and attending their news casts live, have been returned to Earth. There is a group here, as a matter of fact, being debriefed as we speak."

The Admiral resisted the urge to ask where that might be, he suspected the President was somewhere deep in Cheyenne Mountain. "In the meantime, Mr. President, I recommend we pull our assets back from hot zones, bring them closer to home where we will be better positioned to protect the States."

"As long as we don't leave our men on the ground unsupported somewhere, Admiral," agreed the President. "And if we have any assets in port, activate them - let's get them out where they're less vulnerable."

"Yes sir."

"And I recommend we close all our borders," added Stephen. "We can't control what we can't see."

"I agree," nodded the President. "We've already grounded all commercial air flights. Primarily because traffic control would be spotty at best but also because we don't have the organizational power to control it either in the air or on the ground."

"It will also be easier for military controllers to watch the skies without the clutter," added the Admiral.

"Of course," nodded the President. "Robert," he said after a long pause, "I'm sorry but you and your people are stuck there for a while. Is there anything you need? I believe the tracks are clear, we can get you supplies. We will move you when things stabilize some..."

"I'll have the staff make up a list and we'll get back to you."

The President saluted, "Good luck Admiral..."

■ ■ ■

Five miles straight west of Des Moines Iowa was a small, quaint town called Adel, with a population just north of four-thousand people. Its outskirts had large plots, deep green lawns, rolling hills, even greener fields and wide open spaces - something midway between farmland and suburb. What the suburbs used to be before urban sprawl overran them and turned them into the next cramped neighborhoods surrounded by malls and parking lots. After living shipboard for a year, it all seemed impossibly foreign to Lisa Steele. It was beautiful, peaceful to be sure, but the thought of not having something like the Reaper strapped to her backside seemed rather, well, *ordinary*. Mundane. Watching-the-grass-grow *boring*. But nonetheless, a piece of her missed it. Not that it had ever been *her* life, mind you, but it was a place she had visited many times. No, her life had mostly been the concrete, steel and glass towers of Chicago. The traffic clogged streets and the noisy crowds. *God, that seemed a decade ago... was it really just a year ago?*

Lisa was busy watching the rolling green terrain pass underneath the Reaper, looking for familiar landmarks, "Anything on the scopes, DM?" It all looked so much different from above.

Sitting directly behind and slightly above her, Marine Sergeant Draza Mac shook his head inside his helmet, "Not a damn thing, Skipper."

"That's almost creepy," commented Lisa, switching and looking out the other side of the Reaper's cockpit. "To not see *anything* in the sky..."

"Well to be fair, they *have* been informed the Conquest would be running missions to the surface..." He adjusted his sensors, "Ah, see there, we just got a radar ping. Military no doubt."

Lisa checked her screen, "Think they saw us?"

160

"Not likely, the ARC system will probably defeat their primitive system. We disappeared as soon as you slowed down." He smirked, "Now your entry, as spectacular as it was, probably lit up their system like a searchlight."

"Too fast?" she mused, watching the landscape.

"Yeah well, entering atmosphere at Mach 10 has a tendency to do that."

"That's why I came down over Lake Michigan..."

"Heh," he snorted, "doesn't matter where you came down, we were visible with the naked eye at that speed. What did you say was that big city we passed over?"

"Chicago. It's where I grew up..." her voice trailed off, spotting the Raccoon River just beyond Des Moines, running along the edge of Adel, ahead.

"Big place. Hope we didn't break every window in the city..." he joked.

"C'mon," she countered, "I was down to Mach 1 when we passed over."

"Mach 2, and we were only at five-thousand feet."

"Oh." She spotted the golf course just north of Adel along the river, "There it is..." She swung the nose in a slow arc and coasting on antigravity, descended gently, silently, save for the low crackling growl of the system that kept the Reaper floating in the air. Drifting over the empty golf course toward a stand of trees separating the fairways, she dropped the landing gear and set it for auto-level.

Draza Mac announced the height as they descended, allowing Lisa to concentrate on fitting the Reaper into the trees, focused on the fighter's faint outline, the ARC system showing a minor distortion around the edges. "Three... two... one... aaand we're down."

Lisa went through her check-list shutting everything down except the ARC system. She pulled the canopy release and the seal hissed as it broke free of the frame, motoring back, the pungent smell of cut grass, damp leaves and pine trees flooding in. It was heavenly and she drew it in as she unbuckled and disconnected her umbilical cables. She pulled the ladder release and it dropped out of the hull and extended toward the ground.

"So who are we going to see?" asked Draza Mac.

Standing in her seat and pulling off her helmet, Lisa turned to face him, "I'm going to see family on my dad's side - *you're* staying here to watch the ship."

"Aww," he grumbled, "can I at least get out and stretch my legs?"

"Just don't go anywhere. If anyone see's you, you're going to be hard to explain..." Heck, she would be hard to explain in her flight suit. Somewhere in the trees above them, birds sang, twittering back and forth, a flutter of color and movement here and there. In that moment, right there, the world seemed normal and it gave her a sense of hope. A hope that maybe they, humans, the people of this planet, could pull life back together and get things right.

There had been very little movement in the neighborhood or even in Adel for that matter, so she hoped she wouldn't encounter any of Kirk and Tisha's neighbors. Stepping off the ladder she opened an access panel on the Reaper's fuselage, retrieving a small courier bag from within, slinging it over her shoulder. She considered removing her hybrid 1911 and shoulder rig, but shifting the courier bag to that side to hide it, decided to keep it on. "I've got my comm in my ear..."

"How long will you be gone?"

Lisa shrugged "Thirty - forty minutes." She tapped her earpiece, "We'll stay in touch."

■ ■ ■

The houses were on a rise that ran along the edge of the golf course and Lisa had gotten the Reaper closer to the house than she had originally thought; a little over three-hundred feet away. It felt odd checking the fairway in both directions looking for golfers before crossing in the open. *Who would be playing golf during a national emergency, anyway?* She still felt exposed, most of the houses with large windows and sliding glass doors with patios and decks facing the golf course. She wondered if it was wiser to walk casually, or hustle. She really had no choice, her legs nervously hustling her along against her will to be less conspicuous.

Passing into the landscaping that bordered the fairway below the houses, she felt a little less exposed. Reaching the third house, she climbed the slope, wondering if she should jump the rail on the deck or go to the front door. Not wanting to be exposed to the street, she climbed over the deck rail and headed for the sliding glass doors at the back of the house. Her senses were buzzing with nervous energy. *Were they even home?* It appeared the house had electricity while some of the others appeared dark - it was difficult to be sure in the daylight.

"How are you doing boss?"

Draza Mac's voice in her ear made her jump. "Ssshhh," she hissed, a spike of adrenaline zipping up her back.

"Sorry," he whispered.

Peering into the house through the sliding glass door she rapped gently at first then a little harder, her gloved hands deadening the sound.

"Just stand real still there... what do you want, eh?"

Lisa froze, her peripheral vision shifting as she moved just her eyes, a figure standing to her right, the barrel of a gun pointed at her. "I..." she had a sudden urge to pee. "I..." she turned her head ever so slightly, the muzzle-break of an AR-15 coming into focus inches from her face. Heart pounding, her mind blank - overrun with adrenalin, her brain was washed in white static. "I..." She fought to focus her mind and it took effort, her wide eyes stumbling across the figure dressed in jeans, loafers and long sleeve shirt. Her brain refused to make sense of the face - overwhelmed with the shape of the rifle, her eyes finally locking in on the notched collar of a Clergyman. *"Kirk?"* she squeaked dryly.

The rifle dropped away, "Lisa?" Her cousin, Pastor Kirk Jonas reached past her and tugged on the door handle, the sliding glass easing open on its track. He ushered her inside, "I didn't recognize you in that..." he gestured toward her black flight suit, "whatever that is. What in Heaven's name are you doing here?" He slid the door closed and laid the rifle on the kitchen table, *"Tisha!"* His wife appeared from the next room, tentatively at first. "Tish, look who it is!"

Tisha paused in the archway, her head tilted to one side, "Lisa? My word, what are you doing here? How did you even get here?" She moved over to where Lisa stood and gave her a hug.

■ ■ ■

The AR-15 propped up in a corner like a mere broom, they sat around the kitchen table; Lisa with a soda in hand, her cousins drinking coffee. Lisa set the can on the table, her hands not steady yet. Kirk and Tisha's Golden Retriever lay on the floor, his chin on his feet watching the conversation.

"Sorry about that," began Kirk, "there have been some break-ins and looting. Mostly in Des Moines, but the Sheriff warned it could get just as bad here."

"The police department called everyone in, the boys are both working extra hours," added Tisha. "The Sheriff out here is very pro self-reliance - he recommended people stay armed."

"Good advice," replied Lisa, taking a deep draw on her soda.

"We saw you and your brother on the news broadcasts before the signal disappeared," said Kirk, staring into his cup. He looked back up, "It's hard to wrap one's head around the state of the World... and the whole alien thing." His head tilted as he half smiled, "It's almost a letdown that aliens aren't little green men..."

"Well, there *are* some like that," confirmed Lisa. "That's another story..."

"I'm sorry, I have to interrupt," said Tisha, cutting in. "Not to be rude, but how did you get here? And," she gestured toward Lisa's flight suit, "What on Earth are you wearing? Sweetie, it looks like some kind of futuristic space suit or something..."

"It *is* a space suit," Kirk nodded knowingly. "Isn't it..."

Lisa smiled, "Yeah, I'm a pilot." The extraordinary circumstances of her life came rushing back in, filling her with a sense of accomplishment and duty. "I fly a specialized fighter interceptor. It's hidden in the trees out on the golf course." Kirk rose to his feet. "You won't be able to see it," countered Lisa, "it's... *camouflaged*." He stared out at the golf course, his eyes searching. "You *might* be able to see it if you're standing right in front of it *and* you know what to look for," added Lisa. "But not from here."

Kirk felt a tremendous curiosity, tempered with a measure of skepticism. "I'd like to see it. Would you show us?"

"Wait Kirk," Tisha stalled, "we haven't given her a chance to tell us why she's here." She turned to Lisa, "Why, Sweetie? Are your parents alright?"

"Mom and dad are fine, Trish. They're up on the ship now. They're leaving with us. You guys and your family are the only part of our family left on Earth..."

Tisha paled, "They're leaving? Where are they - you going?"

"A planet called Veloria about eight to ten months from here. It's a beautiful place... Jack's wife is the Queen there..."

"Of the entire planet?" shot Kirk.

Lisa nodded, "Yep. They had a similar experience there as we have here, though not as bad. They are rebuilding now. My understanding is the infiltrators have been eradicated..."

"Are you asking us to leave?" asked Tisha.

Lisa nodded again, "Yeah, if you want. It got real bad here for mom and dad. We had to pull them out - they were in a lot of danger."

"What kind?"

"The government kind," replied Lisa. "We were worried you might experience the same thing. We also thought, with all that's going on here, it will certainly get worse before it gets better and you might want the chance to get out before it turns to chaos. Anarchy is a real possibility..."

Kirk shook his head grimly, "No. I can't abandon my parishioners like that. They will need us more than ever now. It's a pretty tight-knit community; blue collar people that know the value of working together and protecting one another. And the boys - their sense of duty? They would never leave..."

"Neither would Leena or her husband," added Tisha.

Lisa pursed her lips in disappointment, "There's room for all of you..."

In resignation, Kirk stuffed his hands in his pockets and shook his head, "Nope, can't do it. These people will need me. Will need the word of God. I can't deprive them of that. I will not run from adversity."

Kirk was a strong-willed man with a rare dedication to service and she knew he wouldn't change his mind. She smiled, "You could think of it as bringing the word of God to a whole new world..."

"Heh heh," he chuckled, smiling back. "Nice try."

Lisa picked up the courier bag she had set beside her on the floor, laying it on the table and opening it up. Digging inside she pulled out and slid an eGo across the table to Kirk and one to Tisha. "Then we want you to have these... It's a communication device. They don't ever need batteries; they charge and run off the electrical energy field your body creates." She walked them through the setup so the units would pair with them, and left enough units for the rest of the family.

"At full charge, it can sit on standby mode in a drawer for a month before it needs to be worn again. I suggest you keep them on and keep them concealed..."

"How are they any different than cell phones?" asked Tisha.

"They don't need cell towers or satellites. They can communicate with each other anywhere on the planet and into space across most of this solar system..."

"*This* little thing?" exclaimed Kirk, adjusting it on his wrist.

"TESS," called Lisa, the holo-screen popping up through her suit, hovering above her wrist.

165

TESS appeared on screen, "Yes Ensign?"

Lisa adjusted the size of the screen and turned it so Kirk and Tisha could see it, "Lieutenant Commander Brian Carter."

"Connecting..." her face dropped off to the sidebar.

Brian appeared, sitting in the command chair of the Revenge, "Carter, go ahead, Ensign."

"Just a communications demonstration Commander. We will probably do one more."

"No problem." He nodded to Kirk and Tisha, who were staring at him wide-eyed, "Folks," he acknowledged politely. The screen went blank, TESS moving back to the center of the picture. Lisa tapped the corner and it dissolved. She pointed to the eGos on the table, "Yours are not holographic..."

"Where, where was he?" stammered Kirk.

"On the bridge of the Revenge. In orbit."

"Oh heavens..." muttered Tisha.

"You can ask TESS to connect or look it up in the directory and choose it. I pre-programmed them for you."

"Jack's contact is in here," commented Kirk scrolling through the directory, "but the listing is red. Why?"

"His unit is currently offline," replied Lisa. "He is on a special assignment and cannot be reached. Any one in green can be reached. If they do not answer immediately they may be temporarily unavailable – like in a meeting or something. But they will be notified that you attempted contact." Lisa put the additional units in the bag and slid it to the center of the table, "I'm going to leave these with you. One recommendation, use them sparingly for now. Emergencies. Keep the communications short. I will contact you after the alliance treaty is signed and communications can be more open."

"Treaty?"

Lisa folded her arms comfortably, leaning back, "The intended outcome is that Earth will become a member of the United Federation of Worlds. As a whole, there is a lot to be gained; technology, health and medical advancements, space travel, advanced communications..."

■ ■ ■

The sun dropping low, the trees cast long shadows across the fairways, the spring air chilling with dusk, a few early crickets clicking and singing as Kirk and Tisha walked Lisa across the golf course to the Reaper.

"Will we always be able to reach you?" asked Tisha.

"Once we get a comm satellite or station in place up there, it won't matter where we are in the universe. There will be a slight delay sometimes but still pretty amazing."

"Fascinating," mumbled Kirk, shifting the AR-15 slung over his shoulder while staring down at the screen of the device wrapped around his wrist.

"How long will you, they, *the aliens,* be up there?" asked Tisha, stumbling through her thoughts.

"That information's above my pay grade, I'm afraid," shrugged Lisa.

Kirk reached out and touched her shoulder as they walked, "How many people can you take?"

"Why? How many do you have?"

"What are you thinking, honey?" interrupted Tisha.

Kirk combined a shake of his head with a shrug, "I don't know, Tish, just wondering I guess." Happily married for over thirty years, Tisha knew when her husband's mind was running through ideas. She also knew that probing would be of no use - when he was ready to discuss it, she would be his sounding board. She let it go.

Lisa stopped and faced them, "Look for what it's worth, well, I'm just going to put this out there; whether it's just the two of you, or two-hundred of you, we'll find a way to make it happen."

"How would..."

"You're going to have to trust me on this; I can make it happen. That task force up there is *Jack's* task force. And not only is he a Vice Admiral, he is also a King... Those people are devoted to him. They will get it done."

"A King?"

"His wife had him coronated before he left Veloria in case something happened to her, her people would still have a leader."

Kirk rubbed his forehead, "Does that make you a..."

"It makes me his sister," interrupted Lisa, her mouth grinning crookedly. "That's it." She turned and headed for the Reaper, the two of them in tow. "If you talk to him, don't mention you know that; he doesn't really like to discuss it."

"Why not?" asked Tisha.

"He just doesn't..."

Lisa's earpiece chirped, *"Is that you, boss? I hear voices coming this way."*

Lisa touched her comm button, "Yeah, it's me, Mac. Go ahead and warm her up."

"Copy that."

"What was that?"

"That was my REO, he's my back-seater..."

The shadows had lengthened and deepened, covering the Reaper completely, the sunlight quickly fading, making it nearly impossible for Lisa to see the outline of the fighter even though she knew what to look for. She paused at the edge of the trees with her cousins standing with her. "Mac, I can't see a damn thing, kill the ARC, will you? I don't feel like walking into the wingtip."

Draza Mac waved from the cockpit, visible from his shoulders up, "Got it, boss, ARC off..."

Eyes wide, Kirk and Tisha stared at the figure floating in mid-air, "How..."

The Dark ship slowly materialized from thin air as the sensors and emitters drained their power, the fighter slowly solidifying into something visually complete. "Guys, this is the Reaper. And that," she pointed to Mac as he stood up in the back half of the cockpit, "is Marine Sergeant Draza Mac, my friend and REO."

Mac waved, "Hi folks."

Pale and wide-eyed, Tisha teetered on her feet and Kirk held her steady, "*You* understand him?" he asked, glancing in Lisa's direction.

Giving a; *holy crap, I totally forgot,* wave of her hand, Lisa fished a temporary translation disc out of one of her flight-suit pockets. Leaving the peel-off backing intact, she held it against Kirk's neck with her gloved index finger. "Say something again, Mac."

"Sure, boss - what do you want me to say?"

Kirks eyes narrowed, reaching up and pulling the disc from under her finger examining the nickle-sized flexible wafer. "What the heck? How does it do that?"

Lisa shook her head, "No idea how it works. That's a temporary translator that goes in our survival kit. You can keep it, I have more. Just peel off the backing and stick it on your neck behind your ear..."

Kirk realized her hair must be hiding it, "You're wearing one?"

"I have a permanent one *under* the skin," she tapped her neck, "right here."

Still standing, Draza Mac pulled his helmet on, "We really ought to be going, Skipper, we're going to light up the night sky like a comet..."

Lisa hugged her cousins. "Tell everybody I said hi. Mom and dad send their best..."

They watched her climb the ladder into the dark, angular fighter with the strange, twin upside down tails on the bottom of her fuselage. Helmet on, settled in, Lisa activated the antigravity system, the Reaper becoming buoyant, lifting off the ground on a strange blue glow.

An electric crackling hum made their mouths water as they retreated, giving Lisa room to maneuver the Reaper out of her hiding spot. She leaned out of the open cockpit to see the wingtips and clearance. Floating on ten inches of antigravity pressure the craft swung effortlessly around, crossing the green of the fairway without making so much as a mark on the grass. She waved to them as the canopy moved forward, locking closed with an audible *ka-chick*. They could see the two figures inside the cockpit bathed in the glow of their instruments as the craft rose straight up, the hum and light of the antigravity intensifying.

A deep thump they could both feel to their core, accompanied the lighting of the twin engines as the fighter drifted away. A quick waggle of the wings and it moved off, the glow of the antigravity disappearing as the fighter streaked across the evening sky. It disappeared over the trees with a rolling thunder of a sonic boom, reappearing again a moment later as it shot straight upward, a brilliant trail of light pushing it upward, thunder clapping as it suddenly accelerated and nearly instantly, disappeared.

"Reverend Jonas..!"

Startled, Kirk jumped, as did Tisha. *"George!"* grunted Kirk, "For crying out loud, you scared the heck outta me!"

"Sorry Reverend, Miss Tisha," he tipped his ball cap. "Looking at the lights? I saw them too."

"We were just taking a walk when we saw them..." Kirk said slowly, wondering how much the neighbor had seen.

George Hebert adjusted his hat, "Must be one of them alien things..."

"What makes you say that, George?"

"Well I don't think *we* have anything that can do that... And I don't expect the Ruskies or the Chinese do either."

169

■ ■ ■

The red and blue strobes on the roof of the police cruiser reflected off the darkened buildings on both sides of the street as the car ahead pulled slowly to the curb. Sergeant Bobby Fortuno eased the Crown Victoria in behind it, adjusting the spotlight to hit the mirror on the car's door, blinding the driver's rearward view. "Remember Ski, I just want to run wants and warrants on these guys, I'm not interested in anything else..."

"Got it." Officer Nick Omanski called the license plate number into dispatch as he exited the car on the passenger side. "Hold on Sarge..."

The four occupants sat motionless as Fortuno moved up to the rear fender, laying his hand on the back of the car, leaving his hand and fingerprints on the surface. Omanski stood at the front fender of the police cruiser, at an angle that allowed him to watch the passenger and back seat occupants, his hand on his sidearm.

Seeing the motion in the back seat, Omanski flicked on his flashlight, simultaneously drawing his firearm, a rifle barrel visible in the brilliant halo of the light in his hand, *"Gun! Gun! Gun!"*

Fortuno jumped away and back, the driver stomping on the accelerator, the tires squealing as it sped away, tire smoke and bits of gravel flying out across the asphalt. Omanski re-holstered his Glock as he leapt back towards the cruiser, "Dammit..."

Bobby Fortuno dashed back to the open driver's door, swinging into the driver's seat, "Which one?"

"Back seat, passenger side, looked like a rifle..."

The Sergeant threw it into gear and planted his foot into the pedal, "You sure?"

"Looked like an AK-47 to me..." he cocked his head and turned up the volume on his radio, the dispatcher chattering in the earpiece in his ear. "Car's stolen, Sarge."

"If he's got an AK, that's the least of our worries. Call it..."

"2047 to dispatch; he rabbited, we're in pursuit. Occupied four times, at least one is armed, believed to be an AK-47 - requesting additional units..."

Fortuno muscled the cruiser around debris in the streets from burned-out buildings and demolished cars, most of the street lights out. Relaying information to dispatch to guide other units. Nick Omanski called out the streets and direction on the radio as they gained on the stolen vehicle. "He's going south on Cottage Grove..."

Fortuno stood on the brakes and steered into the corner, the cruiser's tires wailing as the big car slid. He planted his foot back into the accelerator, the tail lights of the stolen car farther away than they should be... "How'd he do tha..."

The windshield shattered, a concrete cinderblock punching halfway through, showering the interior with nuggets of glass and dust. Bobby Fortuno stomped on the brakes, the cruiser's tires screaming as the car skidded to a stop on an angle in the middle of the street. The front of the cruiser was taking hammer blows, jagged holes appearing in the hood, fenders and windshield. The mirror on the passenger door exploded, leaving just a stump and the door glass blew in like horizontal hail.

Trying to hide below the dash, Bobby threw the car in reverse and buried his foot in the accelerator as both front tires blew apart, the steering wheel yanking on his hands. The engine raced as the rear tires spun, pouring smoke, hopping on the pavement, trying to drag the heavy cruiser clear of the carnage.

Omanski was sideways in his seat, as low as he could get, glad for the armor in the doors as he screamed into his mic, *"10-99! 10-99! Officer needs assistance! Shots fired! Shots fired! 2047 - we've been ambushed, we're under attack... 75th and Cottage Grove!"*

The cruiser's tortured engine let go like a grenade, blowing the mangled hood upright, clouds of smoke and steam billowing, dribbles of flame running out and below the car from a ruptured fuel line, the electric fuel pump still trying to feed the dead engine. Bobby threw the driver's door open and rolled out onto the pavement, crawling toward the rear of the car, Omanski crawling out behind him over the console and computer. "I'm not getting anyone on the radio, Sarge!"

"Keep trying!" Behind the rear axle and most of the car, Bobby pushed Nick Omanski around behind him so he could get back to the interior and unlock the shotguns in the rack. A Molotov cocktail with a flaming tail sailed over the top of the car and smashed behind them in the middle of the street, a tower of fire erupting and spreading out. Rounds skipped off the pavement, zinging past, another thumped the top of the car shattering the light bar as he lay across the driver's seat fighting with locking mechanism of the shotgun rack.

Nick moved to the far corner of the cruiser, positioning himself behind the rear wheel and axle, gun drawn, peaking low around the corner of the fender, letting loose with a barrage of fire at the figures in the shadows, focusing on

171

the muzzle flashes. A Mossberg 500 slid across the asphalt under the car coming to rest against his foot and he ducked to holster his Glock and scoop it up, racking a round into the chamber.

A shotgun of his own with a small pouch full of rounds slung over his shoulder, Bobby Fortuno racked a round, firing through the car's missing windows staying low and behind the rear wheel as best he could. The fuel fire was spreading under the car. "We gotta move Nick..." shouted Bobby, his ears ringing.

Nick pointed to a dark gangway between a couple of store fronts thirty feet away and Bobby nodded. Seeing a figure maneuvering around the parked cars along the curb, Bobby peered under the cruiser firing a round through the flames, the double-ought Buck bouncing off the pavement and taking the assailant's feet off above the ankle. Pulling extra rounds out of his pouch, he thumbed them through the Mossberg's loading port into the magazine tube, ignoring the man's screams.

Nick pitched backward, sprawling out on the pavement, his shotgun clattering to the ground behind him. "Nick! *Nick get up!*" Bobby grabbed his mic, *"10-53, officer down, officer down!"* There was nothing but dead air.

Bobby caught an attacker taking advantage of his downed partner, swiftly advancing on the sidewalk to the exposed flank, not expecting Bobby to be there. "Fuck you," snarled Bobby, the Mossberg roaring. At that range, all eight of the steel double-ought Buck hit the thug square in the chest, taking him off his feet. Fortuno couldn't hear the feet running to his right, he only saw the blur as he attempted to swing the barrel of his shotgun. He went down like he'd been hit by a linebacker, a strong-arm across his chest.

The round-faced black man leaned into his line of vision, pulling him upright by his tactical vest, one-handed. "Don't be shootin' me boss..." The big man snatched up Nick's shotgun and lay it across his body as he began to scoop him up. "We gotta get you outta here, or dey gonna kill you fo sure." Half off the ground he maneuvered the shotgun in his right hand underneath Nick's knees, pointing outward. He nodded to the gangway,"You go firs', I cover you, den you cover me. Got it?" Bobby nodded. "Go..."

Bobby bolted and the big man stood up cradling Nick in his arms, the shotgun on its side. He used the weight of Nick's legs to rack the Mossberg's pump, shooting as he moved to the gangway. Bobby fired from the cover of the building until the big man passed behind him, then ducked out of view, the police cruiser engulfed in flames, a pyre of black smoke rising into the night sky.

"Try to keep up," called the big man in a forced whisper, jogging with Nick in his arms. "Dey gonna try to follow us."

Bobby reloaded his shotgun as he trotted behind them, constantly checking behind him. "Where are we going?"

"Jus' keep up..."

They ran for three blocks between houses and through yards, finally cutting across a side street on an angle and passing between houses again, only to stop at the side door of a garage that faced an alley. The big man managed to turn the knob and pushed the door open with the toe of his boot, leading Bobby inside, the interior pitch dark. He felt the man brush against him and heard a wooden *thunk* behind him.

"We OK fo' now boss, but we gotta stay quiet." A lamp sitting on an end table came on, illuminating the interior of the garage; old but clean furniture laid out neatly, a television, bed, sofa and refrigerator in a kitchenette off in one corner. Plywood covered the windows.

"You live here?" asked Bobby, noticing the horizontal 4x4 timber used as a bracer bar that secured the side door.

"Ain't much. But it's comfy..." He knelt over Nick where he had laid him on the floor and unbuttoned his shirt, "Don't see no blood. That's a good sign."

Bobby set the shotgun against the wall and dropped to a knee next to the big man, who he realized had to be six-foot four, and in the neighborhood of three-hundred pounds. His khaki pants were worn but clean, his t-shirt had seen better days, his arms cluttered with tattoos that were difficult to see against his dark skin. But the Eagle, Globe and Anchor was clear enough. "Marine Corps?"

"Oorah, Sergeant."

"That's Nick, I'm Bobby."

"Denny."

The two men worked to remove Omanski's ballistic vest without moving him more than they had to, "What you did out there..."

"Weren't no big thang," grimaced Denny looking at the softball sized bruise over Omanski's heart. He checked for a pulse on the carotid. "At's a bad hit, boss. Bad spot. He needs a Doc..."

"What the hell did he get hit with?"

Denny flopped the ballistic panel over and pulled on the mangled slug imbedded in the puckered material with his fingernail, ".357 maybe. He dropped the panel and stood up moving to the refrigerator, opening the freezer door. "Never seen a .38 or 9 leave a bruise like dat." He retrieved a frozen gel pack, mushing it up and wrapping it in a dish towel. "He ain't got a lot of time if he got sumpin' tore up in dere." He stepped back over to Nick and gently laid the cold pack over the bruise.

Bobby Fortuno tried his radio again, "2047... 2047 to dispatch." He tried several times with no response, alternately trying Nick's radio with the same results. "Dammit. You wouldn't have a land line, would you?"

Nope."

"A car, so I can get us out of here?"

"No," he whispered, bringing his finger to his lips, "sssshhh..." He reached over and turned off the lamp on the end table, leaving them in pitch darkness again. Running feet and urgent voices passed between the garages, stopping in the alley just beyond the overhead door, arguing and swearing for some time, before finally splitting up and moving off. "Think you stuck here fo' a while, boss. Dey ain't givin' up..." Denny reached over in the dark, snapping the light back on again. "Dem boys jus' plain evil. Causin' all sorts of trouble since de end of da World started. Course, dey always been bad, not one of 'em ever been any good. Animals. Robbin', beatin', stealin'..." Denny lifted the gel pack off of Nick, "Don't want it too cold... swellin's gone down some..."

Bobby Fortuno realized his hands were shaking, his body too, the monumental adrenalin dump falling away, his body reacting to the loss like a junky going through detox. He felt weak, nauseous.

Denny studied him for a moment, "You been hit?"

He looked at his arms and hands, "I don't think so..."

Denny stood up grabbing Bobby by his tactical vest and lifting him to his feet, turned him around to examine him. "I don't see nothin', must be adrenalin crash..." He moved him over to the old sofa, continuing to hold him upright before sitting him down. The big man moved over to the refrigerator, retrieving a cold soda and a chocolate candy bar. "Here, you need some sugar... helps take the edge off." He popped the top of the soda and handed it to Fortuno, "First gunfight?" He set the candy bar on the arm of the sofa before returning to Nick on the floor.

"Yeah..." Bobby sipped the soda, its chill shocking him into focus. "Think I killed that guy on the sidewalk?" His face was a mixture of anguish and steady resolve.

"It'd be my guess. Ain't nothin' he didn't deserve though." He was examining Nick, finding a goose-egg on the back of his head from the fall he took. "Dat explains why he's still out..." He slid the cold gel pack under his head. "Dat dude you took out under da car was a neat trick."

"How much did you see?"

"I was on da sidewalk. Ducked between da buildings when da shootin' started. It was an ambush, plain and simple. You was set up. I couldn't do nothin till dat last dude went down."

"I'm glad you did."

"Ain't no big thang, boss. Right thing to do is all."

"Why did you knock me down?"

"I was hollerin' at you, but you both was tunneled... If you turned at the wrong time you would'a shot me. I hadta' be fast."

"I guess it was a good thing you weren't one of them," replied Bobby, sipping the soda again.

"Wasn't your time yet, boss. Da man upstairs has a different plan fo' you." He glanced down at Omanski, "Not sure 'bout this boy yet."

Static in his ear made Fortuno start, quickly turning down his volume and adjusting the radio's squelch.

Nick Omanski's eyes popped open, his hand drunkenly pulling at the wire to his earpiece. "Oowww..." he drawled. Attempting to focus on the roof of the garage, the dark rafters didn't make sense to him," What the he..." he groaned. When Denny's face appeared in his field of vision he felt a spark of panic, Bobby Fortuno's face appearing a second later.

"How you doing, Ski?"

"Suurge," he drawled, recognizing Bobby. "Who's on my chest?" His eyes rolled around like loose marbles.

"You got hit, Nick," replied Bobby. "But you're going to be OK, your vest caught it."

"Don't feel like it," he panted. "I can't hardly breathe..." He mumbled and Bobby leaned in to listen.

"What'd he say?" asked Denny.

"Something about an elephant. And a sledgehammer. Or an elephant with a sledgehammer, I'm not sure."

"He might have a broke rib or two," commented Denny.

"Whozat?" mumbled Nick.

"His name is Denny. He's the reason we're still alive. We're hiding out here in his place..."

"No backup?"

"Radio system is down again, Nick."

175

"How many weeks now? Third time today," he breathed. "They really need to get that fixed... somebody could get hurt..."

CHAPTER FIFTEEN

NELSON'S POINT SYSTEM - THE PERSEUS : *OPERATION DARK COVER*

The cargo hold of the Perseus wasn't full by any stretch of the imagination, but, it was stocked with high quality goods. Courtesy of the UFW. Something to bargain with, something to sell or trade, something that didn't make them look like they were just entering the business. Liquor, and lots of it.

Sitting on plastic and carbon-fiber crates, Jack Steele and Chase Holt were comparing notes on their MOBIUS devices, holo-screens floating in front of them, their two dogs running and playing around them.

Chase Holt gazed up over the top of his display at Fritz, watching him rough-house with Allie, "Y'know, it's really remarkable what your guy did for him," he nodded in the dog's direction. "The guy must be a genius."

Jack glanced up and back at his screen again, "Genius would be an understatement for Hecken Noer. Though I'm not sure there's a better description for him..."

"He looks completely normal again."

Steele was scanning through the inventory rolls, "He's definitely an artist... He built my eye too."

"Wait, what?" Chase shot him a sideways glance, "You have a fake eye?"

Jack turned to look at him, "The left one. And to be accurate, it's not fake, it's mechanical. In fact, it's far superior to my real eye."

"Uhhh..." Chase shifted from one eye to the other, "I can't tell the difference."

Jack produced an exaggerated Cheshire cat imitation, "But I can. There's a targeting system, a HUD, a zoom, and it focuses and responds faster than a real eye. Part of it, I suppose, is the CABL system tied to my brain that drives it. It seems to keep improving itself. My original replacement looked a lot like Fritz's eye before his new one..."

"That's... wow, amazing. I would have thought they would, I don't know, clone you an eye or something..."

"Steele nodded, "They have that ability, but for both, me *and* Fritz, the damage went beyond the eye. There was brain damage behind the eye. So, no way to do a genetic implant. It had to be mechanical with hardware and software to implant it and drive it."

Chase looked quizzical, "Does it need... *batteries?*"

Steele smirked, "No, it actually powers off the body's natural electrical field."

"That's pretty freaky."

"It's pretty awesome, is what it is," corrected Jack. "Fritz had major brain damage, almost half of his skull was destroyed. A large portion of his brain is a CABL system..."

"That's why he can talk?"

"Yeah. He's a lot more than a just a dog now. He thinks and processes information more like we do."

"That's incredible. I guess replacing his fur was actually simple compared to the technological aspect..."

"Being a perfectionist," explained Jack, "Hecken Noer studied Fritz's hair follicles and skin to duplicate it with a biological 3D printer. The hair is biologically real, embedded in a semi-biological, rubberized skin-like material. Then they just bonded it to his metal skull plates..."

"Whoa."

Fritz, followed by Allie, trotted over and standing on his hind legs put his paw on Jack's knee, staring at him with matching eyes the color of melted chocolate. He dropped a well-worn thoroughly wet tennis ball in his human's lap. "Eww," frowned Jack, "dog slobber." He picked it up with his fingertips and tossed it across the hold, the ball bouncing off crates and down an aisle, pursued by the two German Shepherds. "No idea what I'm going to do when he wears out that tennis ball..."

"I'm sure we'll find something," commented Chase. "Earth can't have the only toy balls in the universe." He paused mid-scroll on his screen and turned, with a curious look on his face, "Do they have sports out here? Baseball? Football? Basketball..?"

Jack paused as well, looking back at his friend in the same curious manner, "You know, I never thought to ask. I haven't a clue..."

"There's got to be something, right?"

"I don't know..." Steele's eyes glazed for a moment, looking through his holo-screen. "You'd think so..."

"God I hope so..."

178

"You hope so, what? Asked Ragnaar, walking into the conversation.

"Sports."

"Sports?"

"You know," added Chase, "games of sport. Teams competing?"

Ragnaar's blank stare was disturbing, "Oh, that sucks," mumbled Chase.

"There you go," offered Jack with a wave to Chase, "You can invent the UFL..."

"UFL?"

"The Universal Football League. You'll be famous. You'll be idolized and worshiped. Rich beyond your wildest imagination - you've just stumbled upon the future you were looking for."

"Huh," grunted Chase, contemplating the possibilities.

"Sir?" reminded Ragnaar.

"Right." Steele turned his holo-screen for Ragnaar to see, "What do you think are our best options for offering here in Nelson's Point?"

Scrolling on the screen, Ragnaar's brow furrowed, wrinkling the tribal style tattoo that covered half of his face. "Most of these will be in demand... Oh," he pointed, "you can't offer *that*."

"Why not?"

"Because that comes from a Federation distillery with a tax production stamp. See the little icons in this column? Anything with that icon originates from a Federation territory distillery."

"So?"

"So, you offer that to a FreeRanger or neutral territory facility and they're liable to think you can't be trusted. They're going to wonder how you got it. Only a licensed dealer can get it and licensed dealers don't sell to non-Federation facilities - they'd lose their license." Ragnaar pointed to an entry on the inventory list, "Diterian Brandy for instance, would *never* be sold outside Fed Territory."

Jack's eyes widened, "Diterian? Damn I must have missed that..." he scanned the screen. "Hmm. Five cases... *yoink*," he gestured, marking them to be moved to his quarters.

"You're taking them all?" asked Chase.

"Drink of the Gods, my friend. Not for sale. This is the good stuff - never tasted anything like it and it's staying with us." Jack nodded, "You'll see."

Chase wrinkled his nose, "I hope so, because I can't drink the stuff they pass off as beer out here... I just *can't*. It's disgusting."

Ragnaar frowned, "What's wrong with our ale?"

179

"It tastes like..."

"It's fine," interrupted Jack. "We're just used to drinking our beer cold and it doesn't taste the same the way you drink it out here...

"But we *like* it warm..."

"No biggie..." offered Jack, "just a difference in personal taste." He stood up and patted the big man on the shoulder, turning him away, "Listen Ragnaar, thanks for coming down and helping me out with this, I really appreciate it. Valuable insight, it really helps me decide how I'm going to approach this..."

The former pirate nodded sullenly and headed off to the lift to return to the bridge, venturing a curious glance over his shoulder. Steele waited until he was sure Ragnaar was out of earshot. "For the love of God," he hissed at Chase, "don't ever insult his beer again."

"Geez, all I said was..."

"Yeah I know, just don't go there," Jack interrupted. "I've learned he's very sensitive about it."

"Why does he take it so personally?"

Steele shrugged, "Hell if I know. But he drinks the stuff by the drum." Chase lifted an eyebrow in disbelief. "OK," waved Jack, "I'm exaggerating. But just a little."

Chase's voice was in a forced whisper, "So he's a drunk?"

"No. Actually I've never even seen him the least bit tipsy," countered Jack. "He must have been weaned on the stuff or something - drinks it like water."

The broadcast comm pinged once, *"Mr. Mercury to the bridge - Mr. Mercury to the bridge please..."*

■ ■ ■

A blue station marker appeared on the big screen, "Nelson's Point station in optical range, Skipper."

"On screen," commanded Steele, striding through the bridge doors; Chase Holt and the two German Shepherds as part of his entourage.

"Aye, on screen."

"Magnify please."

The image of the station zoomed in; distance calculations, size, dimensions and specifications appearing alongside it. The general shape of the station was that of a barbell standing vertically, the center shaft spherical midway between the two discs. The top of the shaft above the upper disc had a slightly flattened orb, the very bottom, pointed with an assortment of delicate antennas and sensor probes protruding from the station's lower hull. Docking structures stuck out from the upper and lower discs like spokes reaching out from a hub, a half dozen or so ships moored in various places, room for at least a dozen more.

"We have a problem..."

"What is it Mr. Ragnaar?"

"There are no ships docked at the station matching the destroyer profiles that we've been following."

Steele ran his fingers through his hair, "Dammit. Tactical, anything in the system?"

The tactical officer turned, his seat rotating with him, "Nothing matching their profiles within sensor reach."

Steele rubbed the stubble on his jawline, "Any energy wakes? Anything we can track?"

"Yes sir, it is a relatively busy hub. There are four gates, trackable ion trails to all of them. I have a Pellucidar transport at the edges of our sensors here..." a marker winked into existence on the left side of the big screen. "And he is headed out of system."

"Can we determine if our destroyers are in the mix out there somewhere?"

The tactical officer shook his head, "I'm afraid not."

"Well shit." His head down eyes closed, Steele's mind was trying to come up with solutions. "Doesn't this just suck."

"Mister..." Ragnaar's mind stumbled over the right address, "*Mercury*. I believe the *jump ship* is docked on the upper level."

Jack's head snapped up, his eyes locked on the zoomed inset of the station, "Show me." A red outline appeared as a halo around a ship docked on the upper level on the opposite side of the station, partly obscured. "Are you sure that's her?"

"She matches the profile, and she is moored at a repair dock. It's the best I can do from this angle and distance, she is shut down and her ident beacon is off."

"It's a pretty reasonable assumption," agreed Jack. "It definitely warrants a look. Skipper, take us in."

181

■ ■ ■

"Skipper, we're being hailed."

Lieutenant Commander Reegan motioned toward the big screen, "On screen."

A pleasant looking woman dressed in a suit, her hair pulled back, appeared as an inset on the big screen, *"Welcome to Nelson's Point Trade Hub. I am traffic coordinator Maydena, can I be of assistance?"*

Reegan rose from his command chair, "I am Reegan, captain of the Perseus. We would like clearance to dock..."

"Wonderful. And might I say, what a beautiful ship. Is she new?" Maydena smiled politely.

"Thank you, yes."

"Will your ship be requiring any service or maintenance? We have wonderful repair technicians."

"No ma'am, the Perseus is ship-shape."

"Wonderful. I'm assigning you to berth L-7, just follow the on-screen holo-markers. At the final marker follow the on-screen prompts, the docking master will contact you and secure your vessel. Have a wonderful stay here at Nelson's Point Trade Hub." The communications square unceremoniously winked out, a series of directions and taxiing markers appearing on screen to an open spoke off the lower hub.

Steele frowned, considering the interaction, "She seemed... rather mechanical?" It was the best way he could think to describe it.

"'Yeah," nodded Reegan, "definitely an AI."

"Android? She looked pretty human."

Reegan glanced at Steele, "Some are pretty remarkable. She probably only exists from the waist up, though. Never leaves that console."

"They need to expand her vocabulary a little..."

Reegan smirked, "Why? I thought she was *wonderful...*"

■ ■ ■

The group paused at the end of the L-7 corridor where it connected to the station's lower hub, their conversation anonymous in a cacophony of voices and sounds from the busy mall. Steele checked the proximity of passers-by, "Does everybody understand their assignments?" A round of nods and the group split up, the station's layout on their MOBIUS devices. "Stay connected," he called, tapping on the device wrapped around his wrist as they all disappeared into the crowd. He studied the direction where Chase Holt, Mercedes Huang, Fritz and Allie had melted into the crowd.

"Ready Mr. Mercury?" asked Ragnaar.

Steele looked pensive for a moment before his expression lightened, "Sure. Let's go."

The station's central bank of elevators served the entire station for patrons and visitors, available at all levels. The outer banks of elevators were for station business, offering a view outside the station through heavy glass walls. Ragnaar and Steele stepped into the elevator car, looking out over the ships moored on the spokes reaching away from the hub. They looked down on the Perseus moored at L-7 as it dropped away, the elevator ascending over a hundred levels up into the sphere midway up the shaft of the station. It was the only place where the outside view disappeared.

Steel felt slightly weightless as the elevator slowed, his footing quickly returning as the car reached the station's business level, the doors opening into an office complex rivaling any modern skyscraper.

One of the two women sitting behind the illuminated glass and chrome reception desk rose from her seat, "Can I help you?"

"We're here to see the station's product buyer," offered Ragnaar.

"What category?"

Steele raised a questioning eyebrow.

"What type of products are you selling?" she clarified, her aqua eyes sparkling.

"Liquor."

"That would be Druando. Follow me..." Her stiletto heels clicked on the marble floor as she led the way.

■ ■ ■

Chase Holt and Mercedes Huang had the two German Shepherds in the corner of the express elevator to protect them from the crush of people in the car. A non-stop to the upper hub, it would save considerable time. "What level did you say it was?" whispered Chase.

"U-11," she whispered back.

He nodded his response and watched the levels tick away as they flew past the residential and administration stops - nearly two-hundred levels. The

183

acceleration was so gradual Chase barely noticed it. But when the car slowed as they approached the upper hub, he reached out to steady himself against the wall of the elevator car. A soft verbal *"wheee"* coming from the riders around them as the car came to a halt. The doors opened, spilling them out into the trade mall on its lower floor, leaving the foursome alone in the car as the doors closed back up.

■ ■ ■

Preferring to work alone, Derrik Brighton stepped off the elevator at the seven-level *Summit Night Club* in the sphere at the top of the station's structure. Dressed in a fine navy-blue Zandurian suit with gold braid on the cuffs and collar, spoke money and status to anyone who had the slightest notion about style and class. The loss of Maria still weighing on his heart made it a conscious effort to do what he was about to do. But he was a professional and a job needed to be done. *Sorry love.*

With a keen eye, he studied the people around him as he walked through the first level of the club. Taking a quick glance upward at the flashing lights he realized he was under a dance floor. A *glass* dance floor. "Well *that's* an interesting perspective."

"Did you say something?"

Derrik turned to his left, a stunning woman with flowing auburn hair, an elegant red dress and amber eyes studied him, a cocktail perched delicately in her hand. "I'm sorry, did I say that out loud?"

"You did," she affirmed with a wry smile.

"I should probably be more careful about that..."

"You never know who could be listening," she mused, whispering.

"Why..." he smiled, "who is listening?"

"The walls have ears," she whispered. Then she laughed at her own joke, the sound falling on Derrik's ears like the ringing of fine crystal. He laughed with her, eyeing her curiously. She looked up at the people dancing above them, "Makes me grateful to be wearing my most beautiful underthings..."

"I cannot imagine you wearing anything that wasn't worthy of your stunning beauty..." he offered.

"Oh, you'd be surprised," she joked, "there are always *those* days."

"The maid's day off," he smirked.

"Exactly." She motioned toward him, "And you?"

"Silk. But you know men," he shrugged, "our things are more utilitarian than fancy..."

She reached out and touched the sleeve of his jacket, feeling the material, "Somehow I don't see anything about you as being ordinary..." She tilted her head back and drained what little was left of her cocktail. She hooked her arm out, bent at the elbow silently requesting an escort, "Buy me a drink?"

"Of course," Derrik hooked his arm in hers, guiding her towards the bar, his eyes scanning the crowd.

"So what brings you here?"

"I have a shipping business," he replied. "We're making a delivery. And you?" Derrik selected two drinks on the electronic menu, his eyes flicking around the room.

"Just passing through." She set her empty cocktail glass down on the bar. "So do you travel with all of your deliveries?"

"Heaven's no," he shook his head. "I have several ships. I travel a little with each from time to time. It gets me out of my office... with a bonus; it keeps my crews on their toes."

She nodded, "Smart. But shouldn't you be with your shipment then? To keep your crew on its toes?"

He handed her a fresh cocktail and sipped his own, 'This is the *getting me out of my office* part," he smiled. He was beginning to realize their conversation had swung from hyperbole and innuendo to more of a gentle probing and he wondered what she was searching for. While *he* searched the faces around them for an indication of who might be the captain or crew of the wounded jump ship.

"You keep doing that..."

"What?"

"Scanning the crowd. Like you're looking for someone... Am I not interesting enough?" she asked, somewhat indignant.

Derrik wasn't sure if it was mock or real indignation but he didn't miss a beat, laying his hand on her forearm and turning on the charm, "Darling, you are the most ravishing creature in the room. I could not hope to find anyone to compare..."

"But..." she prompted.

"But I'm also hoping to spot a friend of mine," he lied. "He's the captain of that ship down on U-11."

"Ooh, the damaged one?" she asked, suddenly becoming more interested.

"That's the one. You know it?"

185

She sipped her cocktail, "I've seen it." She lay her hand atop his and leaned in playfully, "I bet there's an *exciting* story to all that damage..." her eyes sparkled, "what do you suppose it might be?"

Derrik shook his head, mirroring her posture by leaning in, "I have no idea, I haven't spoken to him and I haven't seen the damage myself..."

"It looked like damage from a fight," she interrupted excitedly. "Do you think it was pirates?"

"It's possible I suppose. Though I don't think there are any pirates in this sector. At least *we* hadn't seen any..."

She leaned back again, her tone more serious, "And where did you say you had come from?"

Derrik straightened up, "I didn't."

"Hmm," she snorted, scrutinizing his face. "No, you didn't. I don't think you're going to find your friend... *the captain.*" She watched the reaction in his face, it was almost imperceptible but it was there if you knew what to look for. And she did. *Hmm, he's pretty good.*

"How would you know that..?" he asked, curiosity peaked but cautious.

She set her empty cocktail glass on the bar and reached to the neckline of her dress, which plunged precipitously in loose draping folds. Upturning the silky material, she revealed the command pips of a Lieutenant Commander pinned to her dress. "Lieutenant Commander Aleese Portwin. Skipper of the Red Moon. That is *my* ship," she hissed, leaning in seductively almost body to body, "And that is a *Needler* you're feeling against your thigh..." she whispered. "Now I don't know who you are, and I really don't care. But for whatever reason, you've found me. The question of the day is, what the hellion do you want? And it better be a *good answer* if you want to ever walk on two legs again."

Derrik could feel her breath on his cheek, warm and soft, her perfume filling his nostrils - diametrically opposed from what she appeared to be and what she actually was. She was right, the Needler was a wicked little one-shot derringer-sized weapon with a harpoon-like projectile. The harpoon, split down the shaft in three even slices was slightly corkscrewed, the three sections connected by micro-thin, braided tungsten-carbide cables. It could gut a man, the wire cutting through his spine like a saw. In this case, it would likely cut off his leg straight through the femur bone.

Derrik knew the Needler was relatively silent but the result of her pulling the trigger would be bloody and he was relatively sure, full of someone screaming. It would not be without its theater, impossible to ignore and she would know that. With steely nerve he studied her eyes, "You wouldn't ruin a man's best suit, would you..?"

CHAPTER SIXTEEN

RIKOVIK'S REEF SYSTEM : DEEP BLACK - *RUNNING AWAY FROM HOME*

Deep Black, the largest parts supplier and salvage warehouse of Rikovik's Reef, was dwarfed by its secret warehouse a level below their publicly accessible facility. The single largest room on the entire planetoid, the warehouse which doubled as a hangar stretched over twelve-hundred feet long and nine-hundred feet wide. One chiseled stone wall was fitted with enormous bay doors opening to space.

The level was stocked with small to medium spacecraft of all types in various conditions; some intact, some parted out, only separated by natural stone pillars scattered throughout the massive space. A boxy, two-hundred foot, salvage and service runner sat facing one of the largest bay doors, the overhead lights in that section lit. Most of the rest of the bay was dark.

Cheriska Sky dropped the loaded duffel bag at the open door of the squatting Vulture, Deep Black's *Scavenger One*. "Mouse, did Tinker get *everything* squared away on this thing?"

The big man stood off to one side with his hands in his pockets looking helpless. "Yes ma'am. Tink said he covered everything; electronics, hull, propulsion..." he had withdrawn his hands to tick them off on his fingers. "Fuel delivery, control systems..."

"OK - OK," she waved, "I get it." She paused, her hands on her hips staring at him, "Stop sulking - you make that face you look like an abandoned puppy. You're not going and that's that." He harrumphed, looking sullen. "So," she continued, "what *did* he find?"

"He called Gizmo," Mouse replied, stuffing his hands back in his pockets. "It was a software issue. Gizmo says the last firmware update corrupted the system."

"How did we end up with a parts-eating monster, then?"

Mouse shrugged big shoulders, "He said the corruption was running some of the systems at the wrong amperages. It burned stuff up. He wiped the system and did a completely new software install off GalNet and everything seems to be back to normal. Tink ran tests and all the power levels are where they're supposed to be now."

Cheriska pulled her puff stick from her back pocket and drew in, letting out a cloud of aromatic smoke. "Last time that thing had a software update was by the warranty technician. *Jerkoff!* Have Cheriska Too call the dealer, I want compensation for all the crap this put us through... You still have the list of all the parts we put into this thing since then, right?"

"Yes ma'am."

"Good," she pointed at him, "make sure Too has that handy when she chews them a new one." She took another puff, "So what do we owe Mr. Gizmo for his assistance?"

"A tank of fuel for his runabout and dinner for two at the CherriPit - he said he has a date."

Cheriska shuddered, making a face of distaste, "Ew, who would date that man..." She waved it off, "Never mind, I don't want to know." She headed back to her office to grab another duffel bag.

Mouse scrunched his face, following her, "So, um... where are you going?"

"It's probably best that you don't know."

"Unhhhh," he groaned, rubbing his face, "So, how long will you be gone?"

"Don't know..."

"So why are you taking the Vulture, why don't you take the yacht?"

"Because nobody wants to hijack a salvage rig, there's nothing of any great value. Besides, I might run across some choice part picks along the way." She wove her way around crates stacked in the aisle.

"So is this a salvage picking trip, then?" he followed behind her like a puppy.

"Not telling youuu..." she replied musically.

Awww, *come on!*"

Cheriska Too met her sister at the office doorway, "What's his problem?" she indicated Mouse with a tilt of her head.

"He wants to know where I'm going."

Cheriska Too pointed at Mouse, "You don't need to know, so stop asking."

He stuffed his hands in his pockets and pouted.

"Again with the face?" commented Cheriska.

Cheriska Too shook her head at Mouse, "Pitiful. Just pitiful."

189

■ ■ ■

Despite being smaller than its cousin, the Kondor - Deep Black's Scavenger Two, the Vulture, was considerably more comfortable with a more spacious bridge, much newer technology, more automation and nicer accommodations. With almost a third of its bulk dedicated to engines, the Vulture was faster and stronger than the Kondor. *As long as they could keep it running.* Hopefully with Gizmo's software updates Cheriska would have a trouble-free trip.

Her cargo and bags stored, she dropped herself into the Vulture's command chair, half of the ship's systems already up and running, awaiting main engine startup. Running through the preflight checklist, Cheriska checked the atmosphere quality, hull seal integrity, and power levels. The stasis field in front of the ship flickered, stabilized and became a solid blue sheet of wavering static, the bay doors on the other side of it parting vertically down the middle. Stars glittered beyond the electric haze of the stasis field.

Cheriska reached to her left console, toggling the landing gear to extend for takeoff, lifting the hull from its squat to a standing position for more clearance. The antigravity active, she rotated the collective on the throttle grip, the two-hundred foot hull lifting off the deck. "Deep Black - Scavenger One is ready to depart..." The doors reached the outer stops, the signal light over the door winking from red to green.

"Copy, Scavenger One. Your path is clear. Have a good trip, sister... stay in touch."

Cheriska smiled, half nervous, half excited for this new adventure. "Will do, sister. I'll try to bring you back something interesting." She nudged the thruster throttle, the Vulture easing out through the stasis field into open space, a freighter off to her right lining up in the traffic lane for the main harbor bay of Rikovik's Reef.

"Scavenger One, you are clear."

"Copy, Deep Black... And do try to keep Mouse out of trouble." Cheriska toggled off the antigravity, toggling in the landing gear and listened to the hum of hydraulics as they withdrew into the hull and locked in place. Indicator lights on the left console winked out. Lifting the security covers on the main engine ignition switches, she held the toggles up, the engines firing up, a *whoosh* reverberating through the hull as they ignited, dropping to a low rumble. She released the toggles and the covers snapped back down into place. *Whelp, here we go...* She eased the throttles and swung the Vulture in an arc, pointing the nose toward the gate to the Gedhepp System.

Traveling alone was far from ideal, in fact it was downright dangerous, but there were plenty of scavengers out there who did it. Some people found solace in the solitude. Not for Cheriska so much, she was a social person – and with a clone twin, even when you were alone you never really felt alone. But this was going to be different - she wondered how far that ethereal connection with Too would reach. They could pretty much feel each other anywhere on the Reef. And even across deep space on short parts or salvage runs. But this, *this...* they were going to be star systems apart. Sure, they could still video comm, but would the *connection* still be there?

■ ■ ■

The Captain of the FreeRanger destroyer, DD229, was a thin man with grayish skin and blue-black hair, his pale gray eyes as lifeless as his pallor. *"Ms. Skye, what brings you out this way on this fine day?"* he flirted.

Cheriska smiled sweetly at his image on the video comm, "Heading out to visit family, Mr. Pimm." It was not a total untruth.

"I see you have your Vulture running again. I hope she proves to be more reliable than in the past?"

Cheriska nodded, "Got all the problems sorted out, thank you."

"Hoping to do a little part picking along the way?" he inquired.

"One can hope," she replied. "If I don't pick, you folks don't have parts," she reminded him with a waggle of her finger.

"And thank you for finding those sensor pods for us, by the way."

"You're welcome, Mr. Pimm. And *thank you* for paying your invoice so promptly." He nodded and waved, their niceties complete, the video square winking out. Needing a little something stronger to wash the distaste out of her mouth, she spiked her tea with a splash from a little silver flask she kept on her belt. *I need to do something to find a better quality of men out here...* She sipped her tea, the liquor successfully washing away the mental *ick* she felt.

She thought back a few months; the name he had given was Jax Mercury. He had left a veritable wake of death and destruction behind him as he literally blew through the Reef. But the stories she'd heard led her to believe he'd done it for noble reasons. And anyone who could kick the Syndicate in the teeth and get away with it was alright in her book. Someone worth knowing. She'd searched through the wreckage of the yacht when they got it back to Deep Black in hopes of finding something, anything that might tell her who he really was, but there was nothing. She had to believe he was still alive - despite the lack of any trace of him or the women he pulled away from the Syndicate. Perhaps if Voorlak ever showed up again he might have some answers...

Pulsating in front of the Vulture, the gate's tendrils of light and color swirled, reaching out to dance across the hull. Next system, Gedhepp. The first of many on her trek to Velora Prime. She hoped the old man was right. She hoped this wasn't all a big mistake, a cruel joke. She'd have to track him down and kill him if it was...

■ ■ ■

Cheriska Too sat in her office staring at the empty comm screen, deep in thought. The thought of being separated from her sister for so long bothered her, they had never spent more than a few days apart. Ever. Her job was to look after her sister, protect her... Too knew it was more for her sister's legal and financial issues but still, it didn't sit right with her. She would have gone with Cheriska without hesitation, but *someone* had to run the business... and closing it temporarily was clearly out of the question. The Vulture had only recently been fixed and Too was not convinced that their mechanic, Tink and hired electro-wizard, Gizmo, had been able to rid the ship of all its gremlins. In her mind, one short test drive around the system wasn't enough to prove its reliability. But her sister insisted. "Mouse... *Mouse!"*

"What, *whaaat?!"* he mocked her, running to the office doorway leaning in around the corner. "What..." he said flatly.

"Pack a bag Mouse. Have Tink pack one too. And make sure the Kondor is ready to go; fuel, food supplies, whatever else she might need."

Mouse grinned, "Got it! Where are we going..?" He was hoping they were going to follow Cheriska, he really wanted to know where she was going. Not knowing was killing him.

"Nowhere."

"Huh?" His face dropped. "But..."

"If that Vulture starts crapping itself again," she pointed at him, "you and Tink will be out the door the moment her call comes in. Got it?"

"Yeah..." he sighed, disappointed.

"I don't want her waiting around because we're unprepared."

192

"Yes ma'am."

CHAPTER SEVENTEEN

NELSON'S POINT STATION : *OVERKILL*

Mooring spoke U-11 attached to the upper hub in an outer ring, a section of the station dedicated to repair and service which was a great deal less glamorous and considerably more utilitarian than the rest. It wasn't seedy per se, but a good deal more worn, cluttered, and industrial in appearance - including the dirt and grime that's associated with that function.

Chase Holt and Mercedes Huang followed Fritz and Allie as they traveled the poorly lit corridor, out of sight of the main mall and all of its visitors. Chase glanced down at his MOBIUS, checking the station map, "He seems to know where he's going, we're headed the right way."

Mercedes shook her head, "I know this is all real," she whispered, "because I keep pinching myself to be sure, but this all just seems too surreal. I feel like I'm in a damn movie or something."

"I'm with you there, sister," replied Chase, his voice hushed. They passed two men in work overalls standing against a wall talking. He waited until they were out of earshot before continuing, "If you had told me a few months ago I'd be doing this... here... I would have assumed you'd escaped from a rubber room somewhere. This is insane."

"We just passed U-10 back there, U-11 must be next..."

Unlike the lower hub, the upper hub's spokes were separated into two levels, service and maintenance access on the bottom and crew or visitor access on the top. As they neared the stairs to U-11 Fritz stopped dead in his tracks, Allie halting next to him. The Shepherd looked back over his shoulder at Chase and Mercedes, "Trouble," he growled, before slinking around the base of the stairs toward the service access.

"Uh oh..."Chase snapped his fingers and Allie returned to his side as he moved to follow Fritz, his hand dipping inside his jacket to the grip of his hybrid 1911.

"Hold on," urged Mercedes, snagging him by the sleeve of his leather jacket. "This is *not* the mission. *Stay on mission!"* she hissed.

"We don't know that until we investigate," he replied in a hushed tone. He moved to follow Fritz who had paused, waiting for them.

"Dammit, Holt..."

"Objection noted," he whispered motioning for Fritz to move on with a nod.

Clearing the solid base of the stairwell, Fritz launched, his legs scrambling on the metal floor like a cartoon character on takeoff. Teeth bared he snarled as he disappeared from sight. Chase leaned into a sprint, Allie already accelerating ahead, Mercedes Huang attempting to catch up while checking behind them. Chase cleared the corner just in time to see Fritz in mid-flight, three-feet off the floor, grab the first of two men by the shoulder, his teeth sinking in, swinging him around and off his feet, the duo tumbling to the floor, the man with his pants down around his ankles screaming in pain and surprise.

Allie tackled the second man, hovering on his knees over a supine woman on the floor, her multicolored dress pulled up over her head. Allie missed a solid grab, tearing the man's shirt off his body, over-running him and sliding to a stop beyond him. Chase was right behind her, on the man as he tried to right himself, who folded under a crushing right hook from Chase, laying him out on the floor with one shot. He spun to address the second man who was fighting a losing battle with a very angry forty-two tooth buzzsaw. Fritz's face was covered in the man's blood as he released and reattached himself on any limb swung in his direction.

Mercedes pulled the semi-conscious woman free of the melee, covering her body back up with her clothing, watching the amazing speed of Fritz as he mauled the first attacker.

"Fritz, *leave!*" called Chase. Fritz released and backed up, the exhausted man dropping over on his side in a pool of blood, the floor spattered and smeared from the struggle. Both of his arms had been ravaged, one hand crushed, his calf punctured, his pants shredded and one shoe missing. "Geez, dog, you don't play around..." Chase grabbed the man by the foot and dragged him over against the wall under the stairs with the other man who was still unconscious. "Well, shit..." grumbled Holt, straightening up, examining the mess.

"I told you not to get involved," reminded Mercedes.

"Yeah, yeah," he waved. "I'm not going to ignore a girl getting raped by a couple rabid little punks like *this.*" He punctuated his point by kicking the closest one in the groin, watching him curl into a ball in agony. *"Bitch."*

"You know we have to eliminate them," whispered Mercedes.

Holt dropped to a knee, "What? No... I'm not *executing* them..."

195

"They jeopardize the mission."

"What about *her?*" asked Chase nodding to the girl who was barely cognizant.

"We leave her, she's drugged. I don't think she's even aware of what's going on." She touched his hand, "There's a lot riding on this, we can't risk them telling anyone..."

Chase was staring at the floor, "I don't like this..." Killing non-combatants was against his training and good conscience - and these two were done.

She moved in a crouch over to the two prostate men, "Neither do I." She tore the second man's shredded shirt all the way off and tossed it back at Chase, "Here, clean Fritz up the best you can..." The standard-issue Space Marine survival knife slid cleanly out of the sheath that was tucked into her boot.

"Wait," pleaded the shirtless man as his eyes rolled around, trying to focus as he came-to. Mercedes didn't reply or even acknowledge him, placing her knee and weight on the side of his head, forcing the knife blade between the C1 and occipital bone at the base of his skull, producing a juicy bone-scraping sound accompanied a grunt from him as she severed his brain stem. The blade made a sucking sound as she yanked it out, blood pouring onto the floor. The other man, regaining consciousness was wedged behind his friend against the wall and tried unsuccessfully to retreat, fighting back with bloody arms and a broken hand. She viciously pounced on him, shoving the nine-inch blade up into his throat above his larynx, a spray of blood as he gurgled, trying to breathe as she drove the knife to the hilt. She wrenched it sideways, cutting the right carotid artery, a spurt of blood spraying across the legs and feet of his deceased friend. She yanked hard, the blade resisting at first, pulling free with a sickening slurp. He lay there, gurgling, his eyes searching, his body shuddering, finally falling quiet, vacant eyes staring at nothing.

"This is all your fault," she pointed the bloody knife at Chase, her hands dripping.

He unapologetically held the shirt out to her, "Here..."

■ ■ ■

Sitting the unconscious girl on the stairs to the upper access of U-11, leaning her against the outer wall, her clutch bag under her head, she looked rather peaceful. Unaware of her previous predicament. "She looks alright," offered Chase approvingly.

"She'll be fine. Let's go before someone comes along," urged Mercedes. "I hope nobody finds *dumb* and *dumber* down there..." She scanned the corridor behind them as they climbed the stairs.

■ ■ ■

Jack and Ragnaar sat in the buyer's office for Nelson's Point Station; a sleek, stark, white, chrome and glass room with a broad floor plan and windows overlooking the docking spokes a hundred levels below them. The buyer's secretary deposited a tray of drinks on the glass coffee table and left the three men to serve themselves.

"Help yourself," said the buyer, pulling up a holo-screen from a tablet on his side of the table. "Let's see what you have for us..." The man's black suit, shirt and tie was in severe contrast to his surroundings.

Steele sat back in his chair, casually crossing his legs at the knee, sipping the soda-like beverage, studying the buyer who was reviewing the offerings from the Perseus. *He likes to be the focal point. Desperately wants to stand out. He's overcompensating...*

"I can easily purchase your entire inventory," the man commented arrogantly, not looking up from his review. "Hmm, most of your prices are reasonable..."

Ragnaar frowned at the word *most*, and Steele shook his head nearly imperceptibly hoping the Lieutenant would not voice his objection. "Well then, let's make a deal," volunteered Jack.

"You do seem to have some... *irregular* stock, Mr. Mercury."

Ragnaar shot Jack a quick *I told you so* look which Steele chose to ignore. "How so?"

"Well I'm seeing some Fed stamps in your inventory. I don't get the sense you're a licensed Fed dealer... Are you?"

"No, we're not. We sometimes acquire items in... *unconventional* ways."

"I see..."

"We have friends in some trade hubs that help us in locating these... *specialties.*"

The buyer leaned back in his chair and touched his fingertips to his lips, "I suppose we could buy these from you... not something we see too often."

Steele shrugged, "Or not. No pressure; if you don't feel comfortable, don't buy those items. We won't hold it against you, we *will* find other buyers."

The buyer waved off the thought, not wanting to lose out on the opportunity for superior product at a bargain price. "No need for that, I think we can come to an agreeable price."

Steele nodded, "Wonderful."

The buyer waved casually, "The Diterian Brandy for instance..."

Jack's eyes widened, "I'm sorry, that is private stock, it was supposed to be removed from the inventory listing..."

"Don't be so hasty," countered the buyer. "I would be willing to offer, say, three-hundred per bottle."

Illustrating his years of pirate experience and his negotiating skills, Ragnaar calmly adjusted his position, leaning forward, "I believe you've left a zero off your offer."

The buyer pulled back like someone had taken a swing at him, "Three-thousand per bottle? That's *absurd!*"

"What's *absurd*," growled Ragnaar, "is that you insult us with the paltry offer of three-hundred!" He stood up, addressing Jack, "I believe, Mr. Mercury, he does not appreciate our offerings and we should take our inventory elsewhere..."

"Wait, *wait,*" waved the buyer on the edge of his seat. "Let's not be hasty... one-thousand..."

"Two-thousand."

"Two-thousand," mumbled the buyer, somewhat uncertain.

Ragnaar's posture softened some, confident in driving his deal home, "Two-thousand on the Diterian stock, one-thousand on all our other premium Fed-stamped stock and a five percent raise in all our other stock. Final deal or we find another buyer."

"Fine, *fine*," nodded the buyer reluctantly. "You drive a hard bargain..."

"It's worth every credit and you know it," replied Ragnaar, satisfied, returning to his seat.

The buyer rose from his chair, "Excuse me, I will have my assistant prepare a purchasing contract."

As the buyer walked toward his office foyer, Jack silently motioned to the time on his MOBIUS, tapping on the screen. Ragnaar replied with a shake of his head and a shrug of his shoulders.

■ ■ ■

Half way down the service spoke of U-11, Chase dropped to a knee next to Fritz, the dog's tennis ball in his hand. "You know what you need to do, right?"

Fritz nodded with a snort, "Yes."

"You sure you can find it?"

Fritz sighed heavily, "Yes."

Mercedes Huang shrunk to a crouch next to Chase, "Are we sure this is going to work?"

Chase gave her a sideways glance, "A little late to be asking that question."

"I just meant..."

"You do realize his brain is half-computer, right? When we hacked into the station's repair and service network, we were able to locate the ship's schematics on their database. All those plans are in his head... like a road map."

"OK, OK..." she said quietly.

"Ball," Fritz reminded them.

Chase gave the Shepherd a pat, "Alright kid, it's up to you... keep Allie safe." He chucked the heavier-than-normal tennis ball down the corridor, being careful not to actually throw it airborne, keeping it on the floor. The two German Shepherds dashed after it, flashing past the open boarding tube connected to the Red Moon's hull. Chase and Mercedes pulled back out of sight, hiding behind a power station mounted to the floor of the U-11 service spoke.

"Hey, did you see that?" asked the mechanic talking to a sentry stationed at the mouth of the boarding tube.

"What?"

"I don't know," said the mechanic stepping out into the U-11 corridor. "Something ran past. Something short..."

Curious, the sentry stepped out behind him, looking left and right, "I didn't see anything. What did it look like?"

"Not sure. I thought I saw two of them..."

Fritz appeared from their right, running full out, the fuzzy yellow tennis ball clutched in his mouth, Allie in hot pursuit, weaving their way past equipment and parts stacked near the boarding entrance. The mechanic jumped back with a shout of surprise as Fritz shot past him, turned hard and raced up the tube towards the ship, Allie close behind, the stunned sentry standing mute in disbelief. *"Hey!"* he shouted ineffectually, after-the-fact. "What the *hellion* was that?"

"I don't know... But don't just stand there!" urged the mechanic pointing up the tube towards the ship.

"I'm not supposed to leave my post!"

"A little late for that... *Go!"* pointed the mechanic.

Keying the mic on his earpiece, the sentry sprinted up the tube, "Sentry One, we have two, um, *animals* aboard."

"Sentry One, did you say animals..?"

■ ■ ■

Shooting past the two crewmen was easy and Fritz brushed against the wall of the boarding tube as he turned in, giving him something to push against without having to slow too much. Being taller and faster, he did a quick check over his shoulder, careful not to pull too far ahead of Allie. The CABL system had improved his strength, speed and agility; not to mention the capability of his artificial eye which allowed him to see far beyond his God-given abilities. Having studied the Red Moon's schematics and service information, now stored in his CABL module, the information played back in front of him like a road map on a HUD.

Entering the ship, Fritz's HUD directed him to the left toward the stern of the ship. He slid on the relatively smooth floor covering and dug in with his nails for traction, scrambling some to maintain his footing. He slowed to allow Allie to catch up before accelerating down the first corridor at a gallop. Leaning left and right like slalom skiers, the two Shepherds weaved past a few startled crew members as they raced past. With most of the Red Moon's crew on liberty aboard the station during repairs, foot traffic was light.

A ship-wide announcement alert chimed over the comm, *"All security teams; we seem to have animals loose aboard ship. Apprehend but use due caution..."*

■ ■ ■

Derrik Brighton watched Aleese Portwin's eyes, a look of grim determination on her face, tiny beads of sweat forming on her brow. Derrik eased the muzzle of the Needler off his leg with his index finger before

200

covering it with his hand and gently turning it out of her grip. He leaned in close as he tucked it into his jacket pocket, "If you're wondering why you couldn't seem to pull the trigger, it's called *Nepatolin*. It's a nerve agent. A little slight of hand, a little drop or two in your drink..." He watched the concern in her eyes, "Don't worry, its effects are temporary; but you're going to feel *very* drunk *very* soon." He looked around the club; no one seemed to be paying any attention to them, the music covering their conversation. "We need to get you somewhere quiet," he added, helping her to her feet.

Halfway across the entry lobby towards the elevators, Aleese Portwin's knees buckled and Derrik scooped her up, cradling her in his arms, "Up you go..." Her eyes rolled lazily.

"Is she alright?" asked someone in passing.

"Oh she's fine," he replied casually, continuing towards the elevators. "She's never been much of a drinker."

■ ■ ■

Ensign Tug Widdish was not much of a dancer but he was having fun. The liquor was tasty, the music was great and the crew needed to let off some pressure; the run over Terra having been highly stressful. He was watching his feet as he danced, trying to keep up with the steps he'd been taught when he caught a glimpse of something on the lower level through the glass floor and stopped cold, other dancers bumping into him.

"Hey Tug, what gives?"

He pointed at the floor, "Isn't that Commander Portwin?"

"Those are called feet," his crew mate replied sarcastically.

"No, no..." Tug spread his arms out, moving dancers aside, creating a larger window on the floor, attempting to follow the people below, "Who is that guy?"

"I don't know, he doesn't look familiar..." He elbowed Tug playfully, "Maybe the Skipper is going to get her some..."

"She *fell!*"

"Ah, he scooped her right up..." commented his crew mate with a nod of appreciation. "Nice move..."

Tug was pressed against the glass wall at the edge of the club looking down at the entry lobby towards the elevators, slapping the glass to get her attention, "Commander! Look up! *Look up!*" He turned to make his way across the dance floor toward the exit, "Something's wrong, we have to get down there!"

"Hold on Tug," said the other man grabbing him by the sleeve, "If she's just drunk and you ruin her little romantic escapade, she's going to have your head..."

Tug pulled free, heading for the exit, "And if she's *really* in trouble?"

"Hellion," muttered his crew mate, turning to follow him, "I hope I don't regret this..."

■ ■ ■

Fritz paused at the intersecting corridors checking for foot traffic, finding it increasingly difficult to evade the security teams running around the ship. So far he and Allie had been successful in giving them the slip.

He could hear the hustling footfalls approaching from behind them and dashed across the intersection, Allie close at his side. The schematic on his HUD said the first door was a private quarter and he stood on his hind legs and pawed the door switch, the door sliding open. They ducked inside and the door slid closed behind them, the security team passing outside a moment later.

"Well hello there," smiled the woman stretched out on her bunk. "Aren't you the handsome couple..." She pulled off her headphones and propped herself up on one elbow, "What are you, and where did you come from..?" Fritz cocked his head to one side and his tail swayed slowly, hearing the music from the woman's headphones - she hadn't heard the alert announcement. He stood up and pawed the door switch and quickly slipped out. "Come back and see me again," she called, pulling her headphones back on.

The duo shot past the elevators and headed for the stairs to descend four levels to engineering. So far there had been no sign of the VIP passengers that were supposed to be aboard the ship... maybe they were somewhere on the station like so much of the crew.

Coming from Florida where most houses have few stairs, Allie was not accustomed to dealing with them and heading down was the most difficult part. Fritz paced her, keeping her between him and the wall to give her some sense of support.

■ ■ ■

Mercedes Huang tapped on the face of her MOBIUS, her nails clicking quietly on its surface, indicating the time. Chase nodded, staring at a holo-screen floating above his own MOBIUS, "I know, I know..." His eyes followed a green dot moving through the ship's 3D floor-plan.

Mercedes suddenly wrapped her arms around him in an embrace and pressed her lips against his in a passionate kiss, pinning him against the power station anchored to the floor. It happened so fast and with such intensity he had no chance to react or object.

Laden with tools, the two mechanics simply laughed as they walked past toward the boarding tube for the Red Moon.

"What the hell," muttered Chase, easing her off, rubbing the new bruise in his back from the electrical conduit running along the wall.

"You're welcome," she replied, checking their surroundings. "So, where are they?" She pointed at his MOBIUS.

"Port stairwell, heading down to engineering..."

"This is taking way too long," she hissed.

"Calm down, he *has* to make his deposit..."

■ ■ ■

Mid-step, Fritz froze, pinning Allie against the stairwell wall as a two-man maintenance team entered through a doorway directly below them. Absorbed in their conversation, they turned away and continued down the stairs in the opposite direction, prompting an exhale from the Shepherd who was unaware he'd been holding his breath.

Pausing at the landing, Fritz peered out through the open bulkhead doorway, the corridor clear in both directions. His HUD told him engineering was to the right down at the end of the corridor. The blast doors separating the critical section from the rest of the ship stood wide open for the maintenance and repair teams working on the various ship's systems.

"Here they are! They're headed to engineering!"

At a full gallop, Fritz checked over his shoulder, a security officer emerging from an intersecting corridor behind them, another man rounding the corner behind the first at a full run.

"We got them!"

Fritz's head whipped back around, two men in work suits having appeared in the open entry to engineering, crouched, their arms open wide. Fritz hit the brakes, his butt dropping to the floor, his front legs locked, sliding on the floor, his rear end slipping out underneath him, dropping him to the floor on his side, feet out, kicking wildly. He hit the legs of the man on the left and took him out like a bowling pin, the crash forcing the tennis ball out of his mouth, shooting it across the floor. Behind and to his right, Allie bared her teeth and leapt, the man on the right ducking as she sailed past him in the gap, over the man on the floor, landing on Fritz, the two of them tumbling and sliding across the floor in a heap.

Scrambling to untangle from Allie and get to his feet, Fritz was more concerned about his tennis ball than the crewmen converging on him from all sides.

■ ■ ■

Trying to be as nonchalant as possible, Derrik Brighton waited patiently for an elevator, Lieutenant Commander Aleese Portwin draped across his arms. Another couple standing nearby tried not to stare, looking rather uncomfortable.

"I'mb gonna killd you, you know..." mumbled the woman draped limply across his arms.

"Hush my love..." Derrik elbowed the elevator call button again, smiling sheepishly, "She means for letting her get drunk. She doesn't handle alcohol well... It's our honeymoon you know." The couple nodded sympathetically, smiling weakly. He saw trouble coming before he could hear their calls, two men on the far side of the lobby rotunda running towards the elevators. *Hurry up.* He said nothing and elbowed the elevator call button yet again. *Was one of them a boyfriend? Husband? Crewmates?* None of those choices were favorable. If he was lucky he could explain it away and prevent a confrontation. Killing someone in public was an absolute worst case scenario he wanted to avoid, but he didn't want to have to give up his capture. He turned away not wanting to acknowledge them, able to see their reflection in the elevator door.

"Commander! Commander..!" The other couple turned to see who was calling, the two men waving as they ran, *"Wait! Stop!"*

Oh bloody hell... Derrik poked the call button repeatedly with his index finger, his hand sticking out from underneath Aleese Portwin's limp form.

"I'ma futing ki you..." she burbled.

204

"Shut up or I'll give you another dose," he hissed. A chime announced an arriving elevator as the doors opened one car over. He made it past the opening doors before the crowd of new club-goers poured out, putting their mass in-between him and the men; slipping in as the last person exited. Delayed by the outpouring of bodies, the men attempted to shove their way through the crowd. Derrik pushed the floor and close-door button, "Sorry lads..."

■ ■ ■

Side-by-side, Fritz and Allie whirled, snarling at the group of men surrounding them, a security officer drawing his sidearm, "To hellion with this..."

A machinist mate lunged at the security officer, successfully grabbing his forearm and steering it away, "Have you lost your mind?" He waved at their surroundings, "Computers, energy banks, ion drive systems..?" Fritz launched through the gap, Allie right behind him as hands grabbed for them, their reactions delayed by the visage of getting bitten.

Spotting his worn, fuzzy yellow target, Fritz deviated, diving under a console to snatch it before running along the length of the starboard main drive, the men behind in a losing footrace to keep up. Scrambling up a metal stairway, the Shepherds reached a network of inspection catwalks above the entire engineering section of the ship. Allie looked down through the open mesh which gave her great pause, her canine eyes unable to provide her enough detail. She smelled it, pawed it and tested her footing before tentatively venturing after her companion as someone climbed the stairs behind her. Feeling more confident, she dashed ahead to catch up.

Fritz peered down into an opening in the catwalk, a ladder reaching downward, the tennis ball invisible, hidden somewhere below... *uh oh.*

"Ok we got them now! They have no place to go..."

Fritz's attention snapped back up, a man cautiously approaching on the narrow catwalk ahead of him, some kind of metal tool in his hand. He was holding it like a club but the German Shepherd's keen nose could smell the man's fear. Allie's butt at his shoulder and her guttural growl told him the situation was similar behind them. Displaying his teeth, Fritz snarled, lunging, his pearly canines clacking together, taking advantage of the mechanic's apprehension, forcing him to stumble backwards out of reach.

"Now what?" called the mechanic, barely maintaining his footing, trying to gather his composure and muster his courage.

"You have five pounds of steel in your hand," replied someone from below, *"for the love of the Gods, grow a pair and hit him!"*

Testosterone was thick in the room but Fritz could tell it wasn't from the mechanic. Not allowing him to recover, the Shepherd lunged again, driving the man backward, ducking an awkward defensive swing, creating a gap between him and Allie. "Allie, *hup!*" he barked. *"HUP!"* She ducked under the catwalk rail and dropped the six feet to the surface of the control console, the glass surface activating and cracking under the weight of her impact. Doubling back from the way they came, she ran across multiple consoles toward the exit, her feet creating music as she scrambled across the glass surfaces before diving to the floor at a run.

Stunned, the crew members on the deck stood motionless; as first one, then the other of the two animals dropped from the catwalk above them and raced across the computer consoles heading for the exit. Fast as lightning, they were nearly halfway to the door before anyone could shake themselves free of their amazement.

■ ■ ■

"Where the hell are you guys?" Jack's expression spoke volumes and Chase was not sure if he had an acceptable answer, moving the video screen to the right of the 3D map so he could view both.

"He's dropped the package in engineering, though it's not clear where in engineering, *exactly.*"

"I don't care *where*," snapped Jack. "What's taking so long?"

"It's... complicated," replied Chase uneasily, sensing Mercedes giving him the evil eye.

"Dammit, then *un*-complicate it! How soon before event trigger?"

"About five minutes..."

"What?! Crap, get them the hell out of there and get your asses back to the Perseus. *Now!"*

"Chase..?" Chase waved Mercedes off, wanting, *needing* to finish his conversation with Jack and get him off the comm. *"Chase..."*

"Just a *second,"* he hissed.

"Chase!" she punched him in the arm for punctuation. He closed the comm and looked back at her, her eyes locked on something outside the

206

window of the U-11 spoke. He followed her eyes, a halo of color swirling around the middle of the Red Moon, tendrils of electricity reaching out and dancing around the hull of the ship as the plasmic ball of energy grew. "What is *that..?*"

A chill raced up his back and a spike of adrenalin hit him like a bolt of electricity as he realized the aurora was reaching through the walls of the spoke and growing in the corridor. "Holy *shit,* the GOD drive has been activated..."

"Is that bad?"

"It sure as hell ain't good."

■ ■ ■

Facing the prospect that Nelson's Reach security teams might be looking for him and Ms. Portwin, Derrik Brighton made an unscheduled stop on a lodging level. Looking much like any other hotel, the corridor was lined with doors in both directions. The third one he rang offered no response and he slid his card into the passkey slot, an attached decoder the size of an American nickle, hacking the door lock. It took less than ten seconds and it pinged a tone, the light turning green, the door sliding open. He pocketed the card and entering cautiously at first, unceremoniously dumped Aleese Portwin's limp form on the bed when he realized the room was clear. His arms ached and he flexed them with a wince, stretching.

Doing a quick check of the closet he found only men's clothes. *It would have to do. First things first...* He removed and flipped his suit jacket inside out, stripped off his pants and flipped them inside out as well. Re-dressing, his Zandurian suit had gone from navy-blue to silver-gray in sixty seconds. Adjusting his collar, he checked his image in the mirror; *well done.* He glanced over at Aleese, "Sorry lovey, the red dress has to go..."

"Toush me an I cut dur balds off..." she mumbled.

He began unfastening her dress, handling her firmly, stripping it off none too gently, "While I appreciate your sentiment darling, I'm afraid I'm not after your goodie bits... Although I must offer my compliments, *good show.*"

"Fug off..."

He wiped her mouth with the hem of her discarded dress, "Do try not to drool dear, it tends to ruin the illusion..."

Dressing her in a man's suit, even too large for her, was far more difficult than stripping off the dress - like trying to feed a limp noodle into a straw;

albeit a large straw. It took a while but finally complete, he let her drop back onto the bed. With four pairs of socks, the men's shoes finally stayed on her much smaller feet, "Eh, no matter," he waved dismissively, "you won't be walking anyway..." Calling up the screen of his MOBIUS he called the Perseus.

■ ■ ■

Chase and Mercedes ran towards the security officer standing at the boarding ramp of the Red Moon, *"Sir!"* called Chase. "Have you seen two dogs come by this way? They seem to have gotten away from us..."

He regarded them suspiciously, "Those two hairy animals," he held his hand out, "about this high?"

"Yes, that's it! Have you seen them?"

"They ran aboard; our people have been chasing those vicious things all over the ship! Where the hellion have *you* been?"

"Looking for them." Chase glanced over the man's shoulder at the growing jump bubble, "We are terribly sorry if they have been any trouble, we can get them - they're OK, right? You haven't hurt them?"

"Not yet, but they've tried to bite several members of our crew..."

"Let us help you get them off the ship," urged Chase, "before anyone gets hurt..."

The sentry regarded them carefully, it was against protocol but after a moment of deliberation he agreed. *"Fine.* Follow me..." he turned and trotted up the gangway toward the ship. "I don't know why anyone would own such dangerous animals..."

Alarm klaxons sounded throughout the ship, the lights flashing amber, the sentry tromping to a stop just inside the corridor past the airlock, "What the hellion..?"

"GOD drive..." shouted a crewman running past, toward the stern of the ship.

"What?"

The Shepherds appeared down the corridor, shooting past the crewman running in the opposite direction, splitting as they passed him on either side at a full gallop. The Red Moon's sentry suddenly put the puzzle pieces together, realizing the connection between the event and the animals, reaching for his sidearm.

Chase deflected the blade in Mercedes hand as he grabbed the man by the head and bounced him off the frame of the airlock with a *whang*, knocking him unconscious and letting him drop to the deck in a heap. "C'mon!" he waved at the dogs, shoving Mercedes toward the airlock and open exit. "You and that knife," he grumbled, urging her through the airlock and down the ramp, "Go, *go!*"

The Shepherds cleared the boarding tube in a flash, turning to head toward the exit of the U-11 spoke. *"Run!"* roared Chase, guiding Mercedes by the elbow. She leaned into a run, pulling ahead as he looked back; the electric plasma filling U-11 behind them. Chase's MOBIUS screen popped into view, counting down from ten...

■ ■ ■

"Shut it down! Shut it down!" The overload alarm klaxon screeched, the lights flashing red as the engineers of the Red Moon attempted to undo the chaos the animals had created by running across the engine, power and GOD drive, control consoles.

"I can't just shut it down, the consoles are cracked, they're not responding!"

"Route the controls to another console, if we don't bleed off the excess power she'll burn down!"

No one knew what the result would be if a GOD drive actually initiated with a ship at standstill, much less without destination coordinates. "I've got her holding at sixty percent, how long can she handle that?"

"Not long, her natural power curve programming is to reach one-hundred percent for jump..."

"Look what I found," said a mechanic climbing down from the catwalk. He held out a fuzzy yellow orb, "I found it in the inspection drop for the energy ramp, what do you suppose it is?"

"I'm a *little busy* here... Who the hellion *cares?"*

"One of the dogs was carrying it..."

Conversation stopped abruptly when it split in half, automatically separating with an audible *pop*, producing a one-inch gap between the halves. Overlapping silver mesh flower petals mechanically swung out one-by-one creating a saucer, a small red counter ticking downward; five... four... three...

"Ruuun!"

■ ■ ■

Heart pounding, Chase slammed his hand on the emergency button as they passed out of the U-11 airlock into the station, the massive interior door slamming shut, the locking mechanism latching noisily into place. Running down the stairs he realized the girl they left there was gone but they didn't stop, sprinting toward the mall. He glanced at the readout on his MOBIUS as it reached zero, producing a digital message; *EMP Event Triggered.* The lights around them flickered before going dark, bulbs exploding, showering the floor and walls with glass and sparks.

They tromped to a stop and froze in the darkness. Chase could see the Red Moon through the observation windows, the glow of the jump bubble casting swirling, colored light across the interior walls. "I have a bad feeling about..." The bubble swelled in an instant and he looked away, pulling Mercedes against him to shield their eyes as they instinctively dropped to their knees, an audible static crackle followed by a vicious snap that momentarily lit the interior like daylight. His hair stood up and he could feel Mercy's hair flow across his face.

And then it was over.

Cautiously he opened his eyes and they separated, her black, silken hair, still sticking out wildly, both dogs looking like balls of fluff. Emergency lights flickered on, yellow warning lights flashing throughout the maintenance area.

Moving to a window, they stared in disbelief. The center half of the Red Moon and most of U-11 was simply *gone.* No debris, no burn marks, no explosive damage, just... *gone.* The back quarter of the Red Moon and the portion of the U-11 spoke it was moored to, floated free, drifting slowly away. The bow section was still moored in place, the stub of the spoke still attached to the station.

Mercedes tried to blink away the image, "What happened? *Chase?* "

"I-I'm not sure... Maybe the EMP triggered the GOD drive?"

■ ■ ■

Steele paced on the bridge of the Perseus. "What the hell happened?"

Lieutenant Commander Reegan watched the Admiral pace. "Sir, comms to our people are still out, the EMP had a larger effect that we expected. Our sensors indicate that for some reason the Red Moon was running tests on her GOD drive..."

Steele ran his fingers through his hair in exasperation, "Live? Moored at a station? That doesn't make any sense... Who does that?"

"Obviously, we don't know the details yet. But it appears the EMP may have triggered the drive to runaway unchecked and it initiated an incomplete jump."

"How bad was it?"

Standing next to his command chair, Reegan pulled up a report on his second screen, "Our people situated at the observation platform in the mall, say the Red Moon has been all but completely destroyed."

"Dammit, that wasn't the plan... I just wanted to disable their systems quietly, delay their departure... Have we heard anything from our teams?"

"Mr. Brighton requested assistance escorting a target back to the Perseus, we sent a two-man team to rendezvous with him and escort him back..."

"And the team assigned to the Red Moon?"

"Nothing yet. Would you like me to check with station security? Maybe they have security cams of our people..."

"No, no, no..." grumbled Steele shaking his head, "we don't want to tell them who to look for. That would incriminate us *and* our team." He turned to the officer at science, "We were able to get in to their service database, can we get into the security system? View their cam feeds?"

"No sir, their security system had much better protocols. If we tried, they would see us coming."

CHAPTER EIGHTEEN

NELSON'S POINT STATION : *RECOVERY*

Chase, Mercedes and the German Shepherds hid under the darkened stairwell of U-13 as the security and service teams ran past, heading to U-11. "We need to get out of here," whispered Mercedes.

"Ya think?" he hissed, leaning out of the shadows just far enough to look up and down the corridor, the men disappearing from view. "I just don't know if we're better off mixing in with the people in the mall or moving around back here in the service corridors."

"Less cameras back here but if we're seen we stick out like a sore thumb." She tapped on her MOBIUS with no response, "Still dead."

"The EMP toasted them... or maybe the GOD jump. Who *knows* what *that* does."

"Then why didn't it effect him?" she indicated Fritz. "Doesn't he have one of those computer things in his head?"

"Yeah, he does, but the power source is his own body so it's not truly electromechanical... and my understanding is the structure is similar to a Faraday Cage." He stroked the top of the dog's head, "Are you OK buddy?"

"Fine." Fritz shifted his weight gingerly, holding up his paw, "Feet hurt."

Chase nodded, "I know buddy, it's from all the glass. I think we got it all out but you have cuts..." He wiped his hand on his pant leg, "You're still bleeding too."

Mercedes was kneeling next to Allie, "Her wrist is swollen, I think it's sprained. They're not going to be able to walk very well."

"I can carry Fritz, think you can carry Allie?"

"I think so, but..."

"We're going to stand out like a sore thumb," he interrupted. "I know. But I'm at a loss for any other ideas. And I really need to find something to wrap his feet; at least the front one, that one's the worst."

"I don't understand it," whispered Mercedes, her mind breaking away from the topic at hand. "Why did the EMP go off at all? We were supposed to trigger it manually when we were clear..."

"Don't know. Don't much care at this point," replied Chase. "We have other things to worry about. Like the blood trail from their feet," he nodded at the floor. "Anybody sees that we're screwed. We gotta move." He scooped up Fritz and stood. "Grab Allie and let's move. I want to find a better spot for you three while I take a look around the mall and see if I can come up with any ideas. Or a discreet way to contact the Perseus."

■ ■ ■

Derrik Brighton glanced up at the video panel on the wall when the door chime rang, two men standing outside in the corridor. One man he recognized, the other was unfamiliar to him. Hand on the laser pistol inside his jacket he opened the door from the control on the video panel. "Ensign..."

"Commander."

The door closed behind them and Derrik indicated the other man, "Who's this?"

"I brought the ship's barber instead of just a pair of scissors."

"Well done, Ensign." He waved the barber toward the unconscious woman on the bed, "She needs to look like a man..."

"Seems a shame, cutting off all that beautiful hair..."

"What would be a shame," countered Derrik, "is getting caught after we've gotten this far. Cut it off."

"Who is she?" asked the Ensign, leaning against a tall dresser, watching the barber start his work.

"Skipper of the Red Moon."

The Ensign's eyes widened, "Well you hit the jackpot right there, didn't you?" He motioned toward the bed, "What'd you put her out with?"

"Nepatolin. It's a nerve agent. She's not really out, she just doesn't have gross muscle control. It affects the major muscle groups." He lowered his voice, "She can still see and hear everything, so watch what you say."

"Hmm," nodded the Ensign appreciatively, "interesting."

Derrik turned to the barber, "How's it coming?"

"Five, maybe ten minutes."

"It doesn't have to be perfect for God's sake..." bemoaned Derrik.

"But it has to be believable; don't rush me."

"How..." Derrik leaned in and dropped his voice, "how are the other teams doing? Any luck?"

The Ensign cleared his throat, keeping his voice a whisper, "Something went wrong up on U-11; they're reporting an in-place GOD jump..."

"What? *They who?* Who's reporting?"

"Station administration. We have a team of spotters on the observation deck that are confirming the event. Half of the ship disappeared along with a portion of the mooring spoke. And we've lost contact with the team. Mr. Mercury is going crazy."

Knowing who was on the team, Derrik chewed the inside of his cheek, "I'll bet..."

■ ■ ■

Despite the power being out in a section closest to U-11, the mall was fairly busy and seemed to be mostly business as usual. Though Chase was noticing more security officers than they had seen earlier in the day. Maybe it was just his imagination. Just the same, he avoided eye contact and kept his distance, trying his best to blend in with the crowd. Being on a main floor, there were several levels above him, rings and partial floors, a network of walkways, bridges and ramps to reach the scores of shops and restaurants. The levels repeated themselves above and below over and over, hundreds of retail businesses, eateries, theaters, clubs and casinos. He made note of his level and the stores near the doors he had emerged from; it would be easy to get turned around.

In the center of the mall floor a man and a woman played simultaneously on something resembling two grand pianos molded together, though the sound was more akin to a full orchestra. As mesmerizing as it was, he forced himself to break away. He needed a variety of things and finding them in this maze was not going to be an easy task.

■ ■ ■

After a short absence, Steele walked back onto the bridge of the Perseus, "Update."

Lieutenant Commander Reegan swung in his seat, "Our team from the observation deck has sent video of the event, we're reviewing it now. Mr. Brighton and his assistants are on the move with the *package*, they should deliver in about ten minutes; we're tracking their progress. The product delivery to the station is nearly complete, the fund transfer has already been delivered."

Steele raised an eyebrow, "Delivered?"

"Cold, hard, gold credits."

"Cash... I wasn't expecting that."

"Benefit of being freelance," volunteered Ragnaar. "Cash means off the books. Which means no taxes. Good for everybody."

Jack nodded pensively, "What about..."

"Nothing yet," countered Reegan. "I've got three people scrubbing the video from the observers to see if there are any clues."

Steele took and released a deep cleansing breath. Which didn't seem to relieve the anxiety he was feeling as he'd hoped. He wanted to do something. Anything. His nervous energy was nearly overwhelming. *Jumping jacks... I need to do jumping jacks. Mmm yeah, they'll think I'm nuts...* "I'm going to stretch my legs. Keep me apprised."

Lieutenant Commander Reegan waited until the bridge door close before he spoke, "He's wound awful tight."

"You have no idea," remarked Ragnaar, moving closer. "He treats his people like family," he said quietly. "And the dog... he's killed for that dog before. That man, Chase Holt, is his brother..."

"Brother? I understand he has a sister on the Revenge, I didn't know he had a brother..."

"Fraternally. Brother *Templars.*"

Reegan dropped into his seat, "As in the *Ancient Celestial Order of the Knights Templar?!*"

Ragnaar leaned in to keep his voice low, "The Terran version of the Order, yes."

"I didn't know they still existed."

"They do, and they walk among us..." whispered the big man.

■ ■ ■

Chase couldn't shake the feeling he was being watched. Followed. But he couldn't pinpoint the source of the nagging sensation. And he didn't want to blatantly look for the source of his suspicions and give himself away. He had to slyly look in mirrors, or casually look beyond objects he was inspecting. He had to avoid risking bold or obvious scrutiny. But the source, if there truly was one, eluded his observations, limited as they were.

He strolled into the next store, open in the front like a stall in a bazaar and walked straight back past the inventory, staring at the glass cabinets behind the counter. He squinted at the glass, suddenly aware of the older man staring at him with large eyes and pale gray-blue skin from behind that counter.

"Is there something you wanted to see?" he asked, sliding the glass door open, ruining Chase's rearward view.

Without a word, Chase's expression reflected disappointment, "Ah-oh... no, I'm sorry..."

"Perhaps you are watching that woman who seems to be rather interested in you?" asked the shopkeeper, sliding the glass cabinet door closed again.

"Woman?"

"Over your left shoulder. Short dark hair, rather average looking, drab clothes, keeps checking her MOBIUS and looking through the holodisplay in your direction." He pulled some items out of the counter cabinet and spread them out for Chase to examine, one eye regarding Chase, the other looking past him.

Chase found that ability a little disturbing and tried to ignore it, glancing up at the glass cabinet, "I've not been able to spot her..."

"I'm not surprised, she is *remarkably* unremarkable. My guess is she's an undercover security agent for the station." His hands hidden between them, he motioned toward Chase's pants, "Could it have something to do with the bloody hand print on your pants? Or perhaps it's just that you're a messy eater - some kind of sauce?"

Holt felt compelled to tell him the truth, "No, it's blood..."

"Hmm, a bloody hand print but no signs of injury to your hands. How interesting," he smirked slyly.

"Maybe *you* are the detective," retorted Chase uneasily.

The man's head tilted curiously, "Perhaps in a previous life. No, I am simply a purveyor of trinkets and baubles with a keen eye." He ceremoniously swapped out the things on the counter for something else, making a show of it. "And I know a man in trouble when I see one."

That last statement raised the hair on the back of Holt's neck. If a store proprietor could nail him like that, what chance did he have of getting his entire team back to the Perseus?

"I can see you're a man with a lot on his mind." The storekeeper pushed a button under the counter and a section swung outward creating an opening, "Come, come, I have something to show you," he waved. Chase passed in and the counter swung closed behind him, the owner motioning to his assistant to keep an eye on the store. "I am sure you will find something in the warehouse to your liking," he announced loudly, leading the way, an apprehensive Chase Holt following cautiously. "You can be safe in the knowledge you have nothing to fear from your conductor or anything that lies herein..." hinted the old man.

"What did you just say?"

"Follow me." The man took him by the arm, guiding him gently back to a stock room that dwarfed the store itself.

Chase glanced down at his hand, the gold that encircled his finger of his left hand, a seal showing two Knights riding tandem on one horse, "You saw my ring."

"Indeed I did, *my Brother.*"

Holt's eyes widened, *"You..?"*

"Oh, I have not yet reached the Ancient Celestial Order of the Knights Templar," he shrugged, "but *I am* a Brother..." He pulled on a gold chain hanging from his vest pocket, withdrawing a fob shaped like an ornate gold sphere about an inch in diameter. He laid it in Chase's palm. "Have you ever seen one of these?" He unfastened a three-fingered clasp and the orb rolled open, the hinged segments shaped like little pyramids, their rounded backs laying against his hand. The connected, open segments formed the shape of a cross and each face of each pyramid was delicately engraved with different tools and symbols of Masonry. "This has been in my family over five centuries, handed down through the generations. I received it from my father the day I was raised to a Celestial Mason, like he received it from his father and so on."

Chase examined the engravings, "It's gorgeous. Such detail..." He rolled it up and handed it back, "The oldest one I've ever seen was about two-hundred years old. If I remember correctly, the oldest one I'd heard of on my planet was about three-hundred-fifty years old..."

"Oh they've been around much longer than that. Probably as long as Masonry; hundreds of thousands of years..."

Chase felt dumbstruck. *"Whaaat..?"*

The holo-screen on the old man's MOBIUS popped into view with a chirp, hovering above his wrist, the store's cameras focusing on the undercover security agent that had grown impatient and entered the store. "I fear this conversation will have to wait for another time..." he said, disappointment in his voice. "We need to change your appearance..." He grabbed a pair of new pants, a shirt and a jacket, handing them to Chase, "Here, these will fit you." He motioned toward the back of the stock room, "We're going out this way..."

"Wait," stalled Chase, "I'm not alone."

"But you came in alone..."

"I know, I was looking for a way to get my partner and two dogs back to our ship on spoke L-7."

"Dogs?"

"Animals," clarified Chase displaying size with his hands, "about this big."

"Oh, that *is* unfortunate," lamented the shopkeeper. "Not much chance of disguising *them*. And where might they be?"

Chase was hesitant, it was a huge risk, but he didn't see any other options... it was time to go *all in*.

■ ■ ■

"Who the hell is this guy?"

"This is the *Holy Grail* of captures, sir..." Derrik motioned to the two men shouldering the limp form of a man between them, "Holding cell two."

"Who is he, Mr. Brighton?" asked Steele, watching the Ensign and ship's barber tote the man down the corridor, feet dragging loosely.

"She," corrected Derrik. "Aleese Portwin, Skipper of the Red Moon, our little jump ship up on U-11."

"Well, that's where it *used* to be..." commented Jack, grimly.

"Yeah, I heard," winced Derrik. "Any word from Chase or Mercy?"

"Steele's lips mashed thin, "None."

"I'm sure they're alright. Mr. Holt is a stout lad. And Mercy, well, *she's a pretty tough cookie*, as you Yanks would say."

"I don't think we've said that since 1947," countered Steele. "And I wish I could be as sure as you are." He motioned down the corridor, "Did you get anything out of her?"

"Not yet. We'll have to wait until the Nepatolin wears off. Then we'll have a go at her."

"I want to be there when you question her..."

■ ■ ■

"Who the hell is this? And what the hell are *those?*"

"Hush, Yadros," pointed the old man, "I told you there were *two* people. And those are their animals..."

"Animals," the other man held his hands out, gesturing something the size of a loaf of bread. "Not Animals," he threw his hand wide.

"You owe me Yadros..."

Their voices echoed off the walls of the service tunnels sounding tinny and distorted. Chase and Mercedes stood silently behind the old shopkeeper, holding the two bandaged German Shepherds in their arms, watching the exchange with curiosity.

"You owe me... blah, blah, blah, when do I get to pay off this lofty debt, Beliot?"

"You married my sister, Yadros," the old shopkeeper reminded his friend.

"Ach," waved the other, "the cost is too high, you should take her back..."

"Don't be ridiculous, a deal is a deal."

"I want to return her for manufacturer defects," insisted the man named Yadros.

"Well she was fine when you married her. She's been fine for ten years. If she's broken now, you're the one who broke her."

"She gained weight..."

"Then stop feeding her so much," retorted the old shopkeeper.

"She's grown surly and spiteful..."

"Then stop making her angry and be nice to her..."

"She's..."

Chase cleared his throat rather loudly, interrupting the exchange, "I hate to interrupt, but..."

Yadros pointed at an open transportation crate, "Get in."

Chase's eyes widened, "Excuse me?"

Mercedes stepped up next to him, Allie cradled in her arms, "Yeah. *What?*"

"The easiest way to move you around," began Beliot, the old shopkeeper, "and keep you out of sight, is to hide you in plain sight. These types of delivery crates are used by all the shops and restaurants to move products and inventory in and out of the station through these service tunnels. This is absolutely our best chance to get you to your ship unnoticed."

"Do they ever get searched?" asked Mercedes.

"Rarely."

219

"Almost never."

Chase raised a dubious eyebrow, "Uh-huh."

The packing crates were large enough for one person and one dog so Chase took Allie and Mercedes took Fritz. After packing assorted materials around them, Beloit shook their hands and wished them well before covering them completely with towels and linens. Much like a cocoon, there was little room to move but it was comfortable at least. The vented covers were latched down and two uninformed employees were tasked with delivering the crates to D-7 on hover-dollies. They would be alone, as each delivery traveled a separate route for safety.

■ ■ ■

Arms folded, Steele casually leaned against the corridor bulkhead, "How long has she been awake?"

"About an hour," Replied Derrik. "We have her set up for a Level Alpha Persuasion Protocol."

Jacked raised an eyebrow, "Come again?"

"She's been stripped down to civvies, the temp is set at sixty-three degrees, in total darkness with absolutely no sound. No food, no water, no blanket, no bed pad, no pillow..."

"Just the metal bed flat? She's got to be freezing."

The Lieutenant Commander nodded, "When we go in the lights will come up to a comfortable fifty percent, the heat will come up to seventy-six degrees and we'll bring her something to eat and water. When we leave it goes back to the way it was before we walked in."

"What's the end game?" asked Jack.

"To tell us everything we want to know, of course. Willingly, to get it to stop. We can do it all by conditions. Beta gets more severe, Charlie gets worse and Delta is simply hellish. It's all psychological, we never have to touch her. She'll begin to associate our presence as pleasant, and our absence as uncomfortable, she'll welcome us. Beg us to stay."

"What are some of the other conditions?"

Derrik Brighton shrugged, "Really hot, really cold. No light, total light. No sound, lots of sound. Water but no food, food but no water. Then we can alternate, play with her internal clock. Most people don't last until Charlie. I've actually had some fold during Alpha."

Steele ran his fingers through his hair, "How long will this all take?"

"Could be a few hours, could be a few days."

"Or we could just beat the truth out of her..."

Derrik frowned at Steele, "Think you'd really feel comfortable doing that to a woman?"

Jack sighed, making a face of distaste, "Nooo, you're right."

"Now, one rule; you don't talk. Nothing, not a peep. Understand? I will introduce you to her, you still don't talk. You don't talk even if she talks to you. One of the key factors is consistency and I need to be that voice of consistency..."

"OK, OK, I get it," waved Jack. His MOBIUS pinged, the holo-screen popping into view.

"Incoming from the boarding sentries, Mr. Mercury," reported the female voice.

"Connect, MOBI."

MOBI's face slipped to the side of the screen, the live video opening, the face of the Perseus sentry standing on the deck of the L-7 , appearing in frame. "Mr. Mercury, we have an unscheduled delivery, sir."

"What is it?"

"A sealed transport crate. The bill of lading says it's from *Beloit Curio.*"

"Does the bill say what's in it?"

"No, sir. It looks to be paid in full... There's something handwritten on it; *So Mote it Be...* I'm not sure what that..."

Steele launched into a run, "Stand by, I'm on my way!" he ordered, closing the screen. "Be right back!" he called over his shoulder as he pounded down the corridor.

■ ■ ■

The delivery person having vanished as soon as delivery was complete, left the two sentries standing alone on the L-7 docking spoke. "I've been hearing sounds from inside the crate, Mr. Mercury, but I can't tell what it is..."

Steele tromped to a stop, "Get it open, *get it open!*" He grabbed one of the fasteners and spun the locking mechanism to release the catch, moving to the next. Each man took a side, releasing the locks. Lifting the top off and dropping it to the deck, a cascade of linens and packing materials swelled up and poured out of the crate, a pair of arms tossing materials clear from inside. Allie's head popped clear as she attempted to clamber free and the

221

three men dug through the materials scattering it on the floor, revealing Chase Holt sitting at the bottom.

"Man am I glad to see you guys... it was getting a little claustrophobic in here..." He accepted a hand up, pulled to his feet, climbing out, a wash of packing materials falling away from him. "It was getting a little warm in there..."

"Good to have you back, Brother. Where's Mercedes? Fritz..?"

Chase looked around, distressed and Allie nuzzled his hand. "Crap. They're not back yet? I don't understand, they left before us..."

■ ■ ■

Steele was in no mood to sit in on the interrogation of the Red Moon's commanding officer, but it was a necessity. There were plenty of things he'd rather be doing... one in particular; getting everybody back to the ship safely.

"How many teams are out?"

Interrupted from his thoughts, Steele glanced over at Derrik as they walked down the corridor towards the interrogation room. "Ten teams of two. We're not leaving here till we get them back."

Derrik wanted to remind him there was a mission greater than any one or two crew members. Or that losses should be expected and are acceptable for the greater good of the mission success. But he knew Steele well enough to know that wouldn't go over well. Sometimes the right thing to say is nothing at all. He decided *nothing* was prudent at this time. He entered the code into the door panel and the door slid open, the lights flickering on, the heat kicking on to reduce the chill. He tossed a packaged sandwich on the stainless-steel table and set a bottle of water on it.

The two men sat on the stainless steel chairs mounted to the table across from Aleese Portwin, as she righted herself from the bare cot. "Come sit at the table," said Brighton, matter of factly. She rose stiffly rubbing her arms and sat on the cold metal chair across the table from them, eliciting a shudder. Brighton slid the sandwich and bottle closer to her. "Lieutenant Commander Aleese Portwin, Skipper of the Red Moon... I am Colonel Durock Brithauz, GIS, *Galactic Intelligence Service*."

"I know who GIS is..."

"Good..."

"Who's he?" she asked nodding in Steele's direction as she unwrapped the sandwich.

"His name is unimportant. He's a mercenary who works for the GIS."

"Well, tell him to stop staring at me like that," she mumbled, taking her first bite, "he's creeping me out." She swept her hand over her severely shortened hair, "And was this really necessary? You couldn't have come up with a better idea..?"

"You have bigger problems to worry about, Ms. Portwin. You are charged with transporting fugitives guilty of *Platricide* - planetary murder. That makes you an accessory..."

"I don't know what you're talking about," she countered, reaching for the bottle of water.

Derrik snatched it out of her reach and stood up, "We'll come back when you feel like telling the truth." He patted Steele on the shoulder who rose and both men quickly left the room, the lights going out, the heat shutting off as the door closed behind them.

"Hey wait!" she screamed. *"How about a blanket, it's freezing in here!"*

"Now what?" asked Steele folding his arms and leaning against the corridor bulkhead.

"The room is monitored; audio, infra-red and night vision video feed. We'll keep an eye on her behavior. She's going to be real thirsty later when we go back in..."

"The sandwich?"

Derrik nodded an affirmation, "Cured meat and a little hidden spice. She'll be parched when we go back in. I won't have any water, we'll serve her soup. She'll eat it but it'll be seasoned too." He tapped Jack on the shoulder, "Go ahead, check on your teams, I'll let you know if anything develops here."

■ ■ ■

A second unscheduled delivery on the dock had a rather upset young man detained by the sentries, waiting for Steele's arrival. The top had already been removed, a mess of packing materials and linens lay scattered around it, the top leaning against the wall of L-7.

The Sentry handed Steele the bill of lading, "Says the same thing as the first one did but the crate's empty, sir."

Steele locked eyes with the young delivery man and held up the digital sheet, "What can you tell me about this? And why are you nearly two hours later than the other delivery?"

223

"I don't know anything mister, all I know is I was ordered to deliver this here... I don't know what was in it, I wasn't there when it was packed." He waved his hands, "And I didn't open it, honest. It was like that when I got back..."

"Got back? What are you talking about? You left it unattended?"

"I had to," he shrugged. "The hover-dolly broke down. I had to get the crate off the dolly by myself and drag the damn dolly all the way back to Beloit's to get another one."

"And?"

"And when I got back, it was open, all sorts of stuff laying around it like somebody searched it..." He scratched his head, "Sort of the way it looks now..." he noted. "I had to repack it and..."

"Can it be opened from the inside?"

The young man scrunched his face like it was stupid question, "No."

"Dammit," hissed Steele. "Where did this happen? Where did you leave it when it was opened?"

"In a service tunnel on L-42."

■ ■ ■

Derrik Brighton slid the bowl of steaming soup across the table towards Aleese Portwin who was looking cold and frazzled. "Here, this will warm you up."

Her eyes accustomed to total darkness, she squinted, blinking away the tears, the light stabbing her eyes. She pulled the bowl towards her, warming her hands on its sides. "I guess I'm supposed to be grateful, right? A blanket would be nice."

He reached for the bowl, "I could trade you a blanket for the soup..."

She guarded it carefully, pushing his hand away. "Where's your friend?"

"He's a very busy man," replied Derrik, "he has other commitments right now."

"Since when did the UFW start using mercenaries?"

"Who said he worked for the UFW?"

She smirked, pointing her spoon at him, "C'mon, you're GIS... GIS is *UFW*. So, if he's working for *you*, he's working for the UFW."

Derrik pursed his lips, leaning back in his chair, "The GIS does many things the UFW isn't aware of. We have a very autonomous existence.

Sometimes our goals align, but they rarely concern themselves how we achieve those goals. More often than not, they'd rather *not* know."

"Am I one of those... *goals?*"

He leaned forward, his elbows on the table, his fingers steepled. "You are. Albeit a minor one. One the UFW would not concern themselves with. Which isn't good news for you." She sipped her soup, watching him stoically. "You have a unique opportunity however," he explained. "You can determine your own fate. I have offerings at my disposal that can be either extremely unpleasant or... *comfortable*."

She shivered as the heat in the room continued to chase the chill away. "Well if I have a vote..."

"Cooperate and we can do away with all this unpleasantness. It'll be much easier for all of us."

She eyed him carefully, trying to read him. "When you say *easier*, are we talking *painless?*"

"Painless, comfortable..."

Aleese Portwin wasn't a fool, she knew the punishment for the crimes of the operatives her crew had recovered was death. But she wasn't clear on what her participation would bring. "Are we talking in life, or in death?"

"That is your choice. And it depends on your level of cooperation."

"Life wouldn't mean much in prison..."

"No it wouldn't," agreed Derrik. "If I am satisfied with your cooperation, I have the option to free you."

"I can go back to my ship?"

"I'm afraid, that option isn't available Ms. Portwin. You will be relocated."

"What about my crew?"

Derrik shrugged nonchalantly, "Provide what I need and I don't care about your crew."

Still shivering, Aleese Portwin pushed the empty soup bowl away and hung her head, "Can I please have a blanket and some water?"

Derrik nodded and motioned his hand in the air, the door to the corridor swishing into the bulkhead, a crewman bringing in a blanket and water. Derrik activated his MOBIUS and rotated the screen so it faced her, setting it to record. "Describe your ship *in detail*. I want the names of all the operatives you picked up and their destinations; any other ships involved in the operation and names of anyone who is connected with the operation on a hierarchical level. If at any time I suspect you're holding something back, the deal ends and things will become very unpleasant for you. Understand?"

"I understand."

"Good, start with your name and rank and continue from there..."

■ ■ ■

Steele was heading back to interrogation to check on the progress when his MOBIUS chimed and announced the bridge was attempting to reach him. He put the screen in front of him as he continued down the corridor, "Mr. Reegan, give me some good news..."

Lieutenant Commander Reegan's expression was strained. "I'm afraid I don't have any, sir. All the teams have returned and checked back in..."

"Nothing at all?"

"No sir. I'm sorry."

Jack stopped walking, the pit in his stomach tightening, his eyes burning. This was a last resort. "Initiate contact with station security. See if..."

"It's funny you mention that Mr. Mercury, we were contacted by station security about the same time the teams came back, they are sending over two investigators."

Steele's eyes narrowed, "For what?"

"We were informed it was rather routine, that they interview crews whenever there is a mishap on the station..."

Steele's brow knitted, "Are they referring to U-11?"

"That would be my assessment."

"Dammit," he hissed. "They're not coming for tea and biscuits, they're on a fishing expedition..."

"Excuse me?"

"They're not coming to be nice-nice, they're up to something," explained Jack. He pinched his lower lip in thought, "Double the sentries and put another team inside at the airlock. No boarders without my presence."

"Aye, sir."

Steele started walking again, determined to get answers out of the Red Moon's skipper, on *his* terms if necessary. He was tired of waiting. "Keep me apprised," he swiped the screen closed and marched on with purpose, determined to take his frustration out on the task at hand.

Twenty feet from the door to the room where Aleese Portwin's interrogation was already well under way, Steele's MOBIUS chimed again bringing him to a stop. The screen appeared before him and he swiped the MOBI character out of the way, the image of Lieutenant Commander

226

Reegan appearing. "Yes, Mr. Reegan?" snapped Jack, unable to prevent aggravation from creeping into his voice.

If the Lieutenant Commander noticed, he gave no indication of it. "Sir, a cleaning service vehicle has pulled up to boarding. Did you or Mr. Brighton request some kind of work done..?"

"No of course not. Probably a station scam to add more service charges..."

"The woman says she's from the *Beloit Cleaning Service*... Oh, aaand it looks like the investigators have arrived as well..."

Beloit... Beloit... Beloit... why was that name so familiar? He broke into a dead run.

■ ■ ■

Steele stood at the open airlock to catch his breath and compose himself. "Don't worry sir," commented one of the Marine sentries. "The Sergeant out there has them pretty well occupied," he tapped his earpiece, "I'm listening in on the conversation."

"The service vehicle is what we can't figure out, sir," commented the other sentry. "She absolutely insists she has an appointment and refuses to leave."

"Thank you, boys," replied Steele. He tugged on his leather jacket, took a deep breath and strode down the boarding tube. The two investigators were speaking with three of the sentries next to the entrance to the boarding tube, the fourth, speaking with two women in the service truck; a small, unmarked, boxy, utilitarian hover vehicle. The sentry at the service vehicle discreetly motioned to him, urging his presence.

One of the investigators reached in-between the sentries at the boarding tube to get Steele's attention as he passed, "Sir, *sir!*" The sentry shifted his body and blocked the man. "Hey," he objected, "who is he? I want to talk to him."

The Sergeant smirked, "If you don't even know who he is, how would you know you want to talk to him?"

"We need to talk to everyone..."

"That's not going to happen, guys. Someone will speak officially for the ship and crew, but that's probably it."

"I am a security agent of this station, we are responsible for the safety and security of everyone and everything that comes ashore, including the ships at dock."

"Oh yeah, and I hear you've been doing a bang-up job," shot the Sergeant sarcastically. "But we have a schedule to keep and interviewing members of the crew is out of the question."

Steele appeared and entered the conversation with the investigators, taking over. "Jax Mercury, how can I help you gentlemen?" He waved his hand behind him, and turned to the Sergeant, "Would your men assist the ladies with their *cleaning* equipment? And I'm told it has some sensitive electronics so be careful not to knock it about?"

"Absolutely, Mr. Mercury."

A good head taller than the two investigators, Steele took them by the shoulders in a friendly manner, one under each arm, steering them away from the ship towards the open airlock to the station. "Walk with me gentlemen."

"And who are you?"

"I told you already. Jax Mercury."

"Yes, I got that, but who *are* you?"

Steele smiled warmly, "The man with the answers. I hear you have some questions."

The other investigator looked down at his e-Pad ready to take notes, "And what is your official title on the Perseus?"

Steele circled the air over the e-Pad with his finger, "I'll bet if you check your station records you'll see that I'm the owner of the Perseus. Or maybe you already know that and just enjoy wasting my time."

"And do you have your registration numbers and ship specs..."

"Again," said Steele, raising an eyebrow, pointing at the e-pad, "all in the station records *including* the insurance carrier. I'm beginning to think you two are..."

"How many crew members are on your ship?" interrupted one of the men.

Steele's brow furrowed, "How is that relevant to anything..?"

"Why do you need cleaning services for a brand new ship?" asked the other.

Jack was happy to see they had moved on from the procedural questions but it still had little to do with anything. As far as he could tell they were wildly fishing but the manner in which they were doing it was completely ineffectual. Perhaps they were looking for incongruities... it still didn't make sense to him. Maybe that was the idea; confusion. "Well thank you, we take pride in maintaining the Perseus. She's actually a couple years old and she was due for some carpet cleaning," he lied.

"Exactly how old is the ship?"

"Where are you going with this?" asked Steele, not attempting to hide his aggravation. "Get to the point. I thought you were investigating something. If not, you're wasting my time and I..."

"Do you know this man?" The investigator with the e-Pad turned it around, showing a screen capture of Derrik Brighton carrying a woman in a red dress, taken by a station security camera.

The worst thing to do when answering yes or no questions is to be too wordy, too positive, or too objectionable. Keep it short and concise. Steele shook his head. "No."

"How about this man?" The security agent flipped to a screen capture of Derrik Brighton with what looked to be three other men taken by another station security camera. The man in the middle appeared to be dead drunk.

"No."

"How about any of the other men in the picture?"

"No."

The investigator swiped to a new picture of Chase, Mercedes, Fritz and Allie. "How about this man and woman with these animals?"

"No."

"So you're not *really* the man with all the answers then are you?" commented the agent, sarcastically.

Steele remained emotionless. Blank. Unreadable. "No, *is* an answer. And it's a perfectly *acceptable* reply to the questions you've asked me."

"How about these two men?" The investigator swiped to a crime scene photo of two bloody men laying heaped together on the floor."

Steele pulled back, surprised at the content, "Wow. No..." Steele pointed at the screen, "He doesn't have any pants on."

The agent holding the device frowned, "We're aware of that. We're investigating the brutal murder of these two men and the possible kidnapping of the woman we showed you in the first photo. We also believe the murders are connected somehow with the incident on the U-11 spoke. I'm sure you've heard about that."

"Yes, it was on a station broadcast. Something about an accident while testing a jump system?"

"Yes, well, we don't believe it was an accident. And we suspect the man and woman in the photo with the two animals are responsible for the murders."

"What makes you say that?" interrupted Jack, fishing for details.

"Both men were covered in bite marks. And not a bite pattern associated with a hominid. We also suspect they may be connected to the incident in U-11; the crime scene was in close proxi..." The other investigator elbowed his partner, prompting him to stop talking.

"I see..." Steele shrugged. "Well, I'm sorry I couldn't be of more help."

"You can. By letting us interview the members of your crew that were ashore during these incidents. They may have seen something that is critical to..."

Jack shook his head, "I'm afraid not..."

"Hiding something, Mr. Mercury?"

"Hardly. No, I have a schedule to keep."

"But enough time to clean your carpets?"

The comment was dripping with sarcasm and Steele knew he was being drilled for a reaction. Either a capitulation to give them free access to his crew, or an angry, defensive response. Either of which they could interpret as due-cause to try to get what they wanted; access to the ship. But Steele had years of playing this game, though from the other side, never as a suspect or person of interest. Still, it was pretty easy to see the emerging patterns and these two were, for the most part, predictable. *Amateurs.*

Jack smiled a warm *go screw yourself* smile, "Gentlemen, I fully appreciate the scope of your task and the difficulties of your position. I really do. And if you can *prove* to me without a *shadow of a doubt*, that *each and every ship* currently docked at this station and the ones that left immediately after the event on U-11, are returning to cooperate in the same manner you are demanding of me and my crew, I will be more than happy to cooperate in kind. If not, I have no reason to believe the Perseus will be treated objectively and we are therefore being targeted as a scapegoat." They simply stared blankly at him. "Yeah, that's what I thought."

"Is that a yes or a no, on speaking with your crew?" asked the agent with the e-Pad.

Steele was finding he had less and less tolerance for stupid people but more restraint, which could be infuriating at times. He bit his tongue. "That would be a most definite, resounding, *no.* Thank you for your time, this discussion is over." He turned on his heel and walked away.

"Mr. Mercury, one more question..."

Steele simply waved without looking back and kept walking. *Kiss my ass.*

"Mr. Mercury, your ship is not cleared to depart until this matter is resolved! We'll get your cooperation one way or another..!" called one of the men.

Jack didn't even bother acknowledging, he just kept walking. *Yeah, you could try that, let's see how that works out for you.* Part of him wanted to go back and tell them how bad they were at whatever it was they thought they were doing. He would call it the shotgun approach; ask a bunch of unrelated, disjointed questions and see if they get any answers. No organization, neither one took a clear lead, no good guy - bad guy... it was sad actually. Of course they were just security. He wondered what that entailed, what training they might have gotten. Obviously not nearly enough.

The four Perseus sentries stood between the utility truck and the boarding tube, "Everything alright, Mr. Mercury?" asked the Sergeant.

"We're not out of the woods yet," he replied. There was nothing but a puzzled look, "We're not in the clear yet," he clarified. *Ah good, there was that look of understanding.* "Everybody aboard?"

"Yes sir. Fritz was taken to the infirmary to attend to cuts to his feet. Ms. Huang is in interrogation with Mr. Brighton and the suspect."

"The cleaning ladies?"

"Awaiting your release, sir. They have been compensated for their time and generous assistance."

"Good." Jack glanced over his shoulder at the empty L-7 dock. "Prepare to get underway, release the ladies now so they have time to get to the station."

"Aye, sir."

CHAPTER NINETEEN

NELSON'S POINT : *BREAKAWAY*

"Let's blow this pop stand, Mr. Reegan."

"Sir?"

"Get us the *hell out of here,* Mr. Reegan."

"Aye, sir. Getting us the hell out of here." The Lieutenant Commander jumped to his command chair, dropping into its padded contours and activated his screens. "Communications, get us the station's traffic coordinator." He tabbed to his engineering screen, checking the stats, "Main core temps look good..." he keyed his mic, "Engineering, this is the bridge, initiate main engine startup."

On a backdrop of the station in front of them, the same pleasant looking woman that welcomed their arrival appeared as an inset on the big screen, *"Welcome to Nelson's Point Trade Hub. I am traffic coordinator Maydena, may I be of assistance?"*

"This is Lieutenant Commander Reegan, of the Perseus. We are ready to get underway..."

"Wonderful. And might I say, what a beautiful ship." Maydena smiled politely.

"Wonderful," mocked Reegan quietly, tabbing through the holo-screens on his monitors. "All teams reported in, all locks secure, ship pressurized... The dock master has not released the boarding ramp or mooring arm..."

"Ahh crap..." Steele spotted them on the big screen through the observation windows of the L-7 spoke. "We have company, Mr. Reegan," he pointed, "looks like a boarding party."

Reegan pursed his lips, "Ms. Maydena, we are ready to depart but it appears the dock master hasn't removed the boarding tube or the docking arm..."

"Stand by Perseus..." Maydena's eyes never left the screen, her mechanical smile never faded. *"Perseus, main engine startup has been detected. Active main engines are not permitted this close to Nelson's Point Trade Hub. For your own safety and the safety of the station, please shut down your engines."*

Reegan's voice was measured. "Ms. Maydena, we are ready to depart. Please have the dock master release the docking arm and the boarding tube."

"I am sorry Perseus, we are not releasing any ships at this time..."

Reegan pointed at the upper right corner of the big screen, *"Bullshit!* You are releasing a yacht on L-16 as we speak..!"

Maydena ignored his interruption, continuing to speak, *"Station security has yet to complete its investigation into recent events. Please shut down your engines and allow the investigators to board your ship. Please do not risk damage to your ship."*

"Investigators my ass, that's a military boarding team," growled Steele.

Steele blocked his mouth with his hand in case the machine masquerading as a human had some ability to lipread, "Mute sound."

"Aye, sound off."

"If you don't mind, Mr. Reegan..."

"Your bridge, sir."

Steele stepped to the empty first mate's chair and tilted two of the holo-screens to face him, continuing to block his mouth from view. "Security teams to airlocks, prepare to repel boarders. All gunners to turrets, charge but do not deploy. Charge shields, charge GOD drive. Ready the ARC system..." He tabbed to the docking menu and pulled up the control screen for the upper mooring mount and activated the explosive bolts that held the unit in place. "Helm, plot us an escape vector." The bridge immediately became a flurry of activity.

"Escape vector set, sir."

"Sound up."

When the sound came back on, Maydena was still speaking. *"...do not risk damage to your ship and injury to your crew. Shut down your engines. The investigators are ready to board, please comply with their recommendations..."*

"Stop talking Maydena," commanded Steele. "And listen closely..."

"Patrol vessel approaching from the other side of the station," came a whisper. "Her shields are up and guns are armed."

Jack gave a subtle hand signal to acknowledge the information. "Maydena, your boarding team has thirty-seconds to reach the station airlock. If I see an attempt at breaching, we will tear the docking tube off your station."

"You will most certainly damage your ship."

"It's not going to do your station any good either," replied Steele.

"You do not have clearance for departure. I urge you to cooperate, the investigation will not take long..."

"The boarding team has entered the tube, sir."

Steele knew a breaching charge was unlikely to penetrate the armor plate covering the airlock door but he wasn't willing to risk it. "You were *warned* Meydena..." he growled, tapping the execute button on the control screen of the upper mooring mount. All the bolts fired simultaneously, a heavy thump reverberating through the Perseus' hull; the force of the charges blowing the mechanism free of the ship with such force it folded the station's docking arm at its wrist like a crushed soda can. *"Helm,* full reverse thrusters!"

The Perseus shuddered, the docking tube moving, extending some as it strained to maintain a hold on the collar around the airlock door on the ship's hull. A team of six men ran from the mouth of the boarding tube and up the L-7 spoke toward the station. "Helm, add some roll, let's twist ourselves free."

"Roll, aye."

Groaning and screeching metal transmitted its agonizing sound from the station's equipment through the hull of the ship as it tore free of L-7. Observation windows exploded outward from the torsion, casting glitter in space, the lights of the station refracting off the pieces. The mooring tube tore free of the ship with a shrieking squeal as it rolled, the bodies of the boarding team joining the glitter floating peacefully in a strangely macabre dance.

"Patrol vessel is looking for a firing solution, still blocked by the station."

"Activate ARC," commanded Steele. "Helm, get us out of here - *fast."*

■ ■ ■

The thump reverberated through the hull like a hammer on a metal drum and Derrik Brighton frowned, looking up, "What in bloody hell was that?" He was forced to grip the edge of the table and Mercedes Huang stepped back, slightly off balance, catching herself on the wall of the interrogation room as the ship shuddered.

Aleese Portwin looked up from her dissertation, wide eyed. "What's happening?"

"We must be pulling out of the station," replied Mercedes, looking out the door's window seeing crew members hustling past, down the corridor.

"Continue," Derrik urged Aleese Portwin. "You've got a lot of ground to cover yet."

Aleese began speaking again, only to be interrupted by the sound of squealing, protesting metal. "What is *that?*"

Mercedes frowned, listening carefully, "I don't know. Thrusters, I hear thrusters... we're rotating... main engines coming up..."

"OW! OW! OW!" screamed Aleese grabbing her head with her hands, tears running down her face. *"We have to stop! We have to stop! Please! Make them sto..."* A sharp pop snapped her head to one side as if she'd been slapped, her eyes separately looking left and right. Blood ran freely from her nose, the corners of her eyes and one ear as her head slowly lolled back to one side and she slipped down in her seat, her hands falling away, dangling limply.

"Oh my Lord!" Mercedes jumped forward not sure what to do.

"Dammit! Bloody fucking hell!" Derrik sat back and slammed his fists down on the stainless table, *"Damn, damn, damn!"*

"What the hell just happened Derrik? What do we do?"

"Nothing," he waved in disgust, slapping the table, "she's dead."

"What? *How?* What... I..." Mercedes was at a loss for words, and had no concept of what had just transpired.

"She was chipped," moaned Derrik. "Somebody pushed the flipping button before we got out of range."

"But..."

"A micro charge. Some organizations implant their officers that carry sensitive information." He rubbed his hands over his face, "To prevent the information from falling into the wrong hands." He sat with his elbows on the table and his chin in his palms, staring at the deceased Ms. Portwin, tears of frustration welling in his eyes. "Dammit, we were so close..." he moaned.

■ ■ ■

"Shields up," commanded Steele.

"Shields, aye."

Flying manually by flight stick, Ragnaar rotated the Perseus, pitching the bow downward, her hull parallel with the station as he accelerated away from Nelson's Point. "Patrol craft giving pursuit..."

"Second patrol craft being launched," announced Lieutenant Commander Reegan.

Steele dropped into the first officer's command seat, adjusting its screens. "Helm, full throttle. Tactical, prepare a decoy..."

"First patrol vessel is firing..."

Intense crimson slashes passed the hull high and to the left. "Looks like they're guesstimating," commented Jack.

"It's just a patrol vessel, their sensors aren't as advanced as a military ship," announced the tactical officer. "The ARC system is enough to give us a decent edge."

"Firing again..." Crimson slashes passed the Perseus low, directly underneath the hull. "Firing again..." There was a jolt, the lights flickering. "Direct hit astern, shields ninety percent..."

"They cannot match our speed," commented Ragnaar, "we will be out of range in thirty seconds."

Jack ran his fingers through his hair before calling up the readied decoy on one of his screens and setting an oblique flight path from their exit route to the gate for Citra 5.

"Grid clear, Mr. Mercury."

Since the Perseus has considerably superior sensor systems, both in accuracy and reach, it was certain the pursuing patrol vessel had lost track of the Perseus long before the Perseus did of it. They would stumble across the matching energy wake for the slower decoy and hopefully follow it.

Steele tapped the launch button on his glass keyboard, "Decoy away." He paused, tracking its flight path on the plotting screen, an inset window showing a live, reverse camera feed, the Perseus shrinking as the decoy and ship went their separate ways. "Flying true," he commented, satisfied. "Helm, break for Citra 5, reduce speed to minimize our energy wake." He turned to the Lieutenant Commander, "Mr. Reegan, the bridge is yours; I expect you can retire the gun crews now." He stood, leaving the first officer's command chair, "Well done everyone. Mr. Reegan, prepare a damage report and let me know if there is anything that needs attention."

■ ■ ■

Like a weight had been lifted from his shoulders, Jack took a deep breath as he walked the corridor, headed down to the medical bay to check on Fritz. He made a mental note to talk to Chase and Mercedes to see what the hell happened on U-11 to turn everything sideways so hard. It was almost inconceivable to him how much of a crapfest it turned into. Of course it nearly went from crapfest to shitstorm. They were *that* close. He didn't want to destroy the Red Moon, he wanted to disable the GOD Drive and track her in normal flight to see where she went. He resigned himself to the fact that everything happens for a reason, even if it wasn't immediately obvious. Yeah, well, he sure wanted to know how that reason played out, because he sure couldn't see an *upside* to it. Nothing he could do about it now though.

Derrik Brighton and Mercedes Huang were outside the interrogation room in the corridor quietly discussing something as Steele approached. "How's it going?" he asked casually, walking past, fully intending to let them continue their conversation. Without a word, Derrik held his hand out, stalling him, tapping on the security keypad with his other hand, the door sliding into the bulkhead. Derrik waved him in.

Jack's heart sank, the pit of his stomach doing a somersault at the visual of Aleese Portwin slumped back in her chair, covered in blood, mouth open, eyes staring in different directions. "Is... Aww, *what the hell...*" he groaned, turning back to Derrik and Mercedes still standing in the corridor. "She's a bloody mess! What the hell did you do to her?"

"Her head exploded," blurted Mercedes.

Jack heard the words but the comprehension was slow in coming, "Her head did *what?*"

Derrik rubbed his forehead with is fingertips, "She was chipped. Some of the agencies out here do it to prevent their officers from divulging their secrets. It has an explosive charge..."

"Oh my God, who agrees to something like that? How did it get triggered..?"

"Remote control or range limit. Get too far from the transceiver and it automatically detonates. Like if they're kidnapped..."

"When..."

"When we were pulling out of the station," interrupted Derrik. "No way to really tell for sure how it was triggered..."

"Doesn't really matter at this point, does it..." grumbled Steele, his jaw clenched. It wasn't really a question that begged an answer. "Please tell me you got something out of her first?" He took a deep breath, closing his eyes hoping for a positive answer.

"Some," replied Derrik. "Probably about twenty percent of what she was capable of giving us."

Jack rolled his head trying to release the sudden tension in his neck, "I guess it's *something,*" he lamented. He took a deep breath, letting it out slow, his jaw clenched. "Both of you; my office, half an hour." He walked away, his hands flexing.

■ ■ ■

Carrying the bandaged Shepherd carefully, Jack dropped to a knee, lowering the cradled dog to the sofa, gently setting him down. "Now, no picking on your bandages..." he admonished.

"Hello," mumbled Fritz, looking drunkenly around at the office full of people.

"The Doc gave him something for the pain," admitted Jack, 'he's a little loopy."

"Allie too," added Chase, "I left her in my quarters, she's out cold."

Steele dropped into the chair behind his desk with a weary grunt, "So... anybody want to explain to me how we blew up a ship with something little more than an EMP grenade?" Everyone started talking all at once and he was forced to whistle to bring the cacophony to an end, *"Enough..."*

"To be fair it didn't exactly *blow up...*" offered Chase after the cross-talk stopped.

Jack pointed at him, "It no longer exists, therefore the difference is merely semantics..."

"Actually," interrupted the Chief Engineer, "an in-place jump, which is what is most likely, transported that section of the ship, intact, somewhere..."

"Where?"

He shrugged, his hands wide, his expression uncertain, "Possibly wherever the last jump was logged - if it was still in the control system's cache memory. Or if something had been accidentally entered... in either case, if it was too far to reach it could drop out of jump almost anywhere... known *or* null space."

"That," pointed Jack, "does not answer the question; how something so minor could trigger something so major."

"Placement," replied the engineer. "Perhaps if we review the digital playback from Fritz's CABL system we will find answers there."

Jacks' eyes widened, "We can do that?"

"Certainly." He turned to the holo-chart table behind him and called up an administrative panel only an engineer would know how to access, his fingers dancing across the pop-up holographic controls. An empty video frame appeared, hovering above the table, numbers in the lower right hand corner running backwards. The engineer slowed the backward roll, finally stopping about fifteen minutes before the event, a still frame appearing; Fritz's eye-view somewhere in a corridor aboard the Red Moon.

Steele looked over at the Shepherd sleeping peacefully on the couch. "Can he tell..."

"No," replied the Engineer, taping the play button on the controls. "He is totally unaware."

The group watched the events unfold in crystal-clear holographic detail with high definition audio as Fritz and Allie made their way through the ship; hiding, sneaking and running.

■ ■ ■

The Engineer began narrating technical highlights as the two Shepherds entered engineering, the group oohing and aahing as events unfolded, leaning back and forth with the motion of the playback, as the dogs, working as a team, aided and protected one another. He rattled off some statistics about the engine size and energy to power ratio; good but not comparable to the Perseus. The unique configuration had two smaller GOD drives, each running in alignment with one of the two main engines – as opposed to one larger, independent unit like the Perseus. He estimated it was to conserve space on the ship. "Oh!" he exclaimed, pausing the video and putting his hand on top of his head.

"What?"

"Look where he dropped the device!" he pointed, pausing the video, Fritz's view looking down into an access opening from the catwalk. "That's the alignment crawlspace for the starboard GOD drive and main engine!"

"That's bad?"

"It couldn't get much worse..." replied the Engineer, un-pausing the playback. Fritz's eye-view looked up at an approaching crewman, glanced over his shoulder at Allie and back at the crewman. They could hear the shouts from the crew as Fritz lunged at him, his teeth clacking, the man retreating. With encouraging shouts from below the catwalk, the man advanced on Fritz a second time, swinging a heavy metal tool at him, a swish of air as the dog deftly ducked under the swing, lunging at the man's face, driving him stumbling back in fear. Fritz ordered Allie to jump and his gaze followed her down as she dropped to the consoles below, running across them. "Oh, I think it just got worse..." he paused the video. "She just jumped down on an engineering console and ran across several more. She may have inadvertently activated something..." He un-paused the video again, Fritz taking one last glance at the man staggering to his feet before ducking under the catwalk railing and dropping himself, to the surface below; making everyone watching, sympathetically feel the fall. The Engineer paused the video just before the moment of impact, Fritz's feet and the surface in focus. "The console is cracked, a GOD drive spool-up has been initiated..." he pointed at the program on the screen.

He un-paused the video yet again and the glass surface spidered under the Shepherd's feet, the eye-view changing, focusing on the exit as he ran across the consoles, musical notes matching his foot-falls before he dove to the floor and accelerated. "And there it is," he waved, closing the video frame. "A jump was initiated. The console was rendered inoperable, preventing them from regaining control. The close proximity of the EMP probably negated the system safeties and triggered an early event..."

"Couldn't they have used another console?" asked Jack.

"Possibly. It's on the other side of the bay... maybe with all the confusion it happened too fast. Or the broken console locked them out."

"Why would the EMP trigger without the remote?"

The Engineer looked at Chase, "You didn't?"

Chase Holt shook his head, "Nope. It started counting down all on its own."

The Engineer pursed his lips in dissatisfaction, "I didn't think that - what did you call it? Tennis ball? Would offer enough protection glued around the device. That fall into the inspection shaft from the catwalk is a good ten feet or more. It probably destabilized the mechanism."

"Best laid plans of mice and men..." remarked Jack sarcastically.

"No plan survives the first shot," added Chase.

"So what now?" asked Lieutenant Commander Reegan, leaning against the wall with his arms folded across his chest.

"You want to take that, Mr. Brighton?"

"Certainly Mr. Mercury." Derrik initialized the holo-chart table, "The Skipper of the Red Moon gave us some useful information; including all the names of the operatives they picked up off Earth. The hit the Red Moon took, destabilized their atmospheric control and cut their operation short by about half of their assignment. It required them to deviate to Nelson's Point for repairs. Realizing she couldn't fully fulfill her contract, two FreeRanger destroyers rendezvoused with her at the station to pick up the operatives and transport them home; they agreed to split the rescue bonuses. Each ship took a number of individuals and went their separate ways. She was not informed which operatives were on which ship - a security measure." He reached in and cycled through several star systems, "The only lead we have is, that one of the destroyers is headed here," he pointed, "Wyandek in the Ardollis System."

Lieutenant Commander Reegan took the nod from Jack Steele and left the room, walking out onto the bridge, the door to the ready room hissing closed behind him. "Mr. Ragnaar, plot a course to the Ardollis System, we're going to Wyandek."

"Ardollis, aye. You are aware Skipper, that is well inside FreeRanger..."

"Dark territory," Reegan interrupted. "I am aware, Mr. Ragnaar."

"We'd better not be entering dark territory empty-handed, Skipper."

"I agree. We'll have to pick up something along the way, then..."

CHAPTER TWENTY

EARTH - CHICAGO, ILLINOIS : *THE COLLAPSE*

It wasn't that the North American power grid was the only damaged electrical system on the planet. In fact, there were large swatches of the globe without power; but it was the only one that directly affected Bobby Fortuno's life. Chicago had power even through the riots, until the grid's cascade failure put it in the dark along with a good portion of the country's Midwest. Chicago was a huge drain on an already damaged and overtaxed system, but no one seemed to care about, or follow, the new power usage guidelines set forth by Department of Energy, or the pleadings of the Mayor to reduce the strain. So now they were paying the price. Blackout. No food or clean water, business or communications. Banks were shut down, credit cards didn't work, and people were desperate. In some areas, neighbors worked together, in others it was complete anarchy.

That's when Bobby called it quits. He almost called it quits that night on the south side, before the SWAT truck rolled through the neighborhood and rescued him, Nick Omanski and the good Samaritan, Denny Wilson. But he held on to the hope that things could turn around; that the police department would somehow be able to regain and maintain control of the city. But he had to face facts; the police department couldn't hope to do the job without proper communications, fuel, food or pay. Surprisingly enough, some guys were sticking with it. But the city had become a war zone and anyone in uniform was a target. Bobby had long since lost his adrenalin addiction, he wanted to get to his daughters and find a quiet, safe place to ride things out.

"Ready, Ski?" Bobby slammed the tailgate of the plain, unmarked, police SUV, packed tight. Sans cage, the detective's unit he liberated from the motor pool with the help of a friend who worked there, should be roomy enough and rugged enough to get him and his family to that safe place. Wherever it might be.

Without family or ties, Nick Omanski had no reason to stay any more than Bobby Fortuno. "Ready Sarge." Nick slid carefully into the back seat next to Bobby's ex-wife, Sharon, being careful not to disturb his two broken ribs. "Whoof," he grunted, settling in. "We stopping by to see Pop-Pop and Nanna before we head out?"

Bobby glanced over at Denny Wilson in the passenger seat as he stuck the key in the ignition, "Owners of Romano's Sub Shop," he explained. "Almost like family..."

Denny nodded, hanging his baseball cap on the muzzle of one of the M-4 carbines in the vertical weapon rack mounted to the dash, "Jus along fo da ride, boss. I be good wherever we go; so long's as it's outta' here." Despite his *gentle giant* demeanor, Bobby saw Denny's true character when things went sideways. When the big man expressed a desire to be included, Bobby Fortuno did not hesitate to adopt him into the extended family.

Casting a final glance in the mirror at the house behind him, Bobby eased the SUV out of the driveway. *Bye, house.* He sighed mentally, *And the mortgage was almost paid off...*

■ ■ ■

Surface streets were the best bet with the most options. The expressways, with their limited access on and off, creating a gauntlet of sorts with few exits, were littered with wrecks and intentional roadblocks of destroyed and burned out cars. Riding an overpass crossing the expressway below, Denny indicated an area on his side of the vehicle, "Damn, looks like Beiruit. Never thought I'd see dat kind of mess here... Makes me sad," he lamented. "I don't pretend to know anythin' about politics, but it pains me to no end knowin' our government sold us out to the aliens."

"I don't think it's all that simple Denny," replied Bobby. "There's a lot more here than meets the eye, and we don't know the whole story..."

"I don't think we know much at all," interrupted Nick. "I don't know that we ever will... Like your friend Steele, Bobby. What's that all about? Whose side is he really on? Maybe you shouldn't have let him go..."

Bobby twerked his mouth sideways in contemplation. "Jack? I rode with him for a couple years before he went to the Canine Unit; knew him for several years before that. Graduated the academy together, went on double dates; hell, we were at each other's weddings... Nah, Jack was always a straight shooter, always a stand-up guy. I can't ever remember him doing something that wasn't on the up-and-up."

"People change," offered Denny.

"Maybe some," agreed Bobby, shaking his head, "but not Jack. I refuse to believe it. I gotta believe this planet still stands because he did all he could."

■ ■ ■

There was a fire somewhere, the smell hanging in the air, hitting the back of the throat and making it itch. Bobby Fortuno rolled up the windows of the SUV and flipped on the A/C. The streets were uncommonly quiet, devoid of sirens or traffic; either vehicular or human. It was beyond unnaturally still, it was downright creepy. The North Side neighborhood was traditionally a quieter section of the city, but then again it didn't take much to trigger events of desperation or mayhem. "This is just eerie," Sharon mumbled, looking down a passing side street. "It looks like two in the morning instead of two in the afternoon... Where do you think everyone is?"

"Personally, I'd rather it stay like this," replied Nick.

The street was blocked ahead with abandoned cars extending several blocks, a traffic jam of silence. Bobby steered the SUV up over the curb, across the grass and idled down the sidewalk.

"You gots a crowd of people midway down the next block, boss," pointed Denny.

Bobby nodded, "I see 'em. We'll take the next right, cut around them through the neighborhood..."

"What if they need help?" asked Sharon.

"Not my job anymore," replied Bobby.

"So we're just going to ignore people who need help?" Sharon replied incredulously, annoyed at her ex-husband's callousness.

"We don't know they need help, Sharon..."

"You think everybody's gone bad, Bobby? Why don't you just see if..."

"Dey've spotted us, boss..." interrupted Denny.

"Maybe it's just me Sarge, but they don't look friendly," commented Nick from the back seat.

"No. No, they don't..." Bobby was already on the gas, giving it a goose to beat them to the corner, the V8 launching the SUV, the tires ripping up the grass, fences along the sidewalk whipping past, the vehicle barely fitting past the oak trees that lined the street on the curb side. "We got this..." He hit the brakes to make the corner, having to mash them hard, a blockade of cars scattered like a Tetris puzzle, blocking the street from sidewalk to sidewalk. *"Dammit,"* he hissed. He glanced in the rear view mirror contemplating a

244

retreat, only to see two motorcycles racing up the sidewalk a half block behind him. Small rocks and bottles started raining down around the SUV and he felt a familiar pang of distress, the group in front closing quickly. The crosswalk was open to the sidewalk on the other side of the blocked intersection and it only took a microsecond for him to make the decision. "Not this time," he growled through clenched teeth, dropping his foot off the brake pedal and stomping the accelerator. "Never play chicken with a two-ton truck," he muttered, steering straight through the center of the melee.

"Good God, Bobby, don't *kill* them!" shouted Sharon from the back seat.

"Sharon..." *thump.* "Honey..." *thump, thump.* "Please..." *thump.* "For once in your life..." *thump, thump, thump.* "Shut the hell up..." *thump.* And they were through, most of the group splitting like the Red Sea to get out of the way of the rampaging SUV. There were a few unlucky souls who paid the price for their attempt; bouncing off the vehicle like rag dolls, the wrap-around push bar protecting the front of the truck as it plowed through them like the armored tank that it was.

"Motorcycles are right behind us," announced Nick looking over the back seat out the back window.

"Got it. Everybody hold on..." Bobby let the SUV slow, drawing them in before slamming on the brakes, the ass-end of the SUV rising momentarily as he stomped on the gas again.

One brake check was enough. The motorcycles split; the left one glancing off an oak tree near the curb and careening into the traffic jam of abandoned cars, the bike imbedding itself in the side of a minivan, the rider catapulted over the top, disappearing from view. The motorcycle on the right ran through a picket fence, up the stairs of a house, off the porch and flattened itself into the side of a neighboring house, the rider bouncing off like a crash test dummy.

Bobby didn't slow. A couple blocks down, he crossed the grass and dropped the SUV off the curb, back onto the street beyond the stranded cars in a peacefully empty street.

■ ■ ■

The seven girls sharing the Myrtle Beach, beach house were no longer having fun. It wasn't a vacation any more. It wasn't a reprieve from their college studies, it was a nightmare. The world had gone mad during their stay and they were trapped there. There was still water and electricity, although there were restrictions. For them it was food that was the most limited. Many people had left the beach, attempting to get back to their homes, the lives they left behind. What little news was available, told Annie and Tina Fortuno that the lives they had left behind before vacation no longer existed. As far as they could tell, they were on their own. And though picturesque as it was here on the beach, the future didn't look very promising. It was going to be survival of the fittest.

The girls had taken to foraging the empty houses along the beach for food and supplies left behind by those who fled. They kept notes and a hand-drawn map on the living room wall of all the houses they'd visited, and the ones still occupied in an attempt to make the best use of their efforts.

Having found fishing poles and a cast net at one of the houses, they'd had meager luck fishing from the shore, meaning tonight's dinner included some unknown, unidentifiable fried fish with their Ramen noodles.

Annie Fortuno strolled through the open front door from the deck, "Well it smells good at least."

"I hope so, said the tall redhead with freckles. Better than those clams we dug up..."

Tina Fortuno wrinkled her nose, "I know we're trying to consume protein, but those things were disgusting."

"I've had worse," said the petite blond pulling her hair back and tucking it up. "I just wish we could run the air some..."

Annie shrugged, "Nice breeze, I'm OK with it."

The blond made a face of resignation, "In San Diego we run the air most of the year, you get used to it."

"Were not in San Diego," snapped Tina sharply. "And if we get caught using it, they'll cut off our power altogether." She checked her watch, "Half hour till power curfew, is dinner almost done?"

"Almost," replied the Brunette from Georgetown University. "About five minutes."

Tina nodded with a sigh, glancing at the blond, "Sorry."

The blond shrugged, "S'okay." The circumstances, uncertainty and pressures they felt were wearing on them all.

Though it was still light, well before sunset and a half an hour before power curfew, the lights flickered briefly before going out completely, the electric stove shutting down.

"Ahh, what the hell," grumbled the brunette cooking the fish. "It's not time yet..."

"Maybe they're having problems again," said the redhead.

Annie ducked back outside to the deck, looking up and down the beach, "Uuhhh... what the hell is *that?"* Everyone suddenly became aware of an uncomfortable low frequency hum which seemed to penetrate flesh, reaching into the body, making the skin crawl and tingle. The progress of dinner temporarily forgotten, the girls poured out onto the deck.

The long, dark, silent alien ship sidled sideways over the beach from the water, mere feet off the surface. The hum was more a feeling than a sound and it was disturbing to see something so sizable move so effortlessly and without sound. A blue glow reflected off the water and illuminated the sand beneath it.

Annie Fortuno reached out and grabbed her sister's hand, Tina giving a little reassuring squeeze though she was petrified, herself. "We're alright," she assured herself in a whisper. The girls moved closer to one another, many holding hands, terrified.

"I have to pee," whispered the brunette.

"I think I just did," admitted the petite blond.

"We should run and hide..."

"Don't be stupid," hissed Tina. "You can't possibly think that would work..." She swallowed hard, feeling more vulnerable and insignificant than she had ever felt in her life. "Whatever happens, we stick together. Understand?"

Silent nods were the only reply as they watched the frightening visage move closer to the house. There was a unified gasp as a panel the size of a garage door on the side of the ship popped open and slid up over the hull, an opening appearing behind it, a ramp extending to the sand. The ship continued to float there, now motionless.

"Whose is it?" squeaked the redhead.

"It's not ours," whispered Tina. "It's not from here..." Her eyes searched for something recognizable but there were no markings on the hull that were readable or made any sense.

"What do we do?"

"Whatever they tell us to do," hissed Tina.

A group of armored figures ran down the ramp, their footfalls sounding metallic. Out onto the sand, they still sounded robotic as they spread out in all directions, taking positions between the house and the ship. It was difficult to tell if they were live beings or mechanical. They looked artificial, but they certainly *moved* like they were human. Or at least some kind of human-type beings.

"It's the *Borg*," wept the brunette.

A flash of lightning with accompanying thunderclap erupted from a cloudless sky nearly made the girls jump out of their skin, a second ship appearing out of thin air, becoming visible above the first as it exploded out of a spontaneous cone-shaped cloud of compressed air. It streaked past, arcing around and returning, floating several hundred feet above the one on the beach. They could clearly see blue glowing panels on its belly. Much smaller, it was very sleek, with wicked, evil looking lines. Several girls began to cry as one of the things on the beach approached the stairs of the deck.

"What do you want?!" called Tina, as forcefully as she could, finding her voice. The thing waved at her, a *come here* wave. She shook her head, no. "Tell us what you want!" It shifted what appeared to be some kind of weapon in its hands and circled the group with the finger of its free hand, pointing to the sand at the bottom of the stairs. "You come up here," demanded Tina.

"Are you nuts?" hissed Annie. "For what?"

There appeared to be some dialogue between the units on the sand before the one addressing them turned its attention back to the girls above him on the deck. Its armored head shook a slow *no* and motioned to the stairs making a motion that Annie guessed meant he was too heavy. "He can't," she whispered. "He's too big."

He pointed directly at her and nodded.

"I'm not leaving without my stuff," lamented the blond, turning back to the door of the beach house. "This face," she defiantly vogued her fingers around her face, "doesn't go anywhere without makeup..."

A shrill, earsplitting squeal made the girls cringe and cover their ears, stopping the blond in her tracks. The armored thing at the bottom of the stairs pointed at her and shook his head, no. With one finger he made a stern *come here* motion, pointing to the sand with an aggressive *right now* motion. She began to cry, terrified, but did as she was ordered, followed by the rest of the group, sticking together, holding hands the best they could, descending the stairs.

The thing nodded, making a show of stepping aside and waving politely toward the ship with an *after you,* motion. It made a show of politeness but Tina's gut told her this was not going to end well. She felt a coldness, a finality... she wanted to run. But Annie's vice grip on her hand reminded her she could not in good conscience abandon her sister. Or any of the other girls for that matter. Whatever happened, they would all go together...

Tina Fortuno, always her father's daughter, critically scrutinized when she passed, what she could only sum up as a walking tank. They were bulky and metallic, with no discernible sound but moved fluidly like a man. Could it be a suit? She hardly thought so. *How would a human being move something that heavy?* She avoided eye contact, or rather, avoided looking at the gold visor where she expected the eyes to be. She shivered at the prospect of actually seeing the alien face behind the visor - if there was one.

When she turned her attention to the ship it became apparent, even in the fading light that the ship wasn't as completely black or smooth as it first appeared. The closer they got the more detail she could see, the more alien it became, the more insignificant she felt. Dread gave way to near panic, her heart hammering in her ears, the low hum of the ship making her skin crawl.

"You're crushing my hand," complained Annie.

"Sorry," mumbled Tina, "I'm afraid if I let go of you, I'll run..."

"I thought you were trying to keep *me* from running..."

"Yeah. That too."

Nearing the ramp leading to the opening in the side of the ship, the team of armored aliens withdrew from their positions on the beach, closing around the young women.

An armored hand pressed on the center of Tina's back, urging her and her sister up the ramp, producing terrified gasps from the girls behind them. "Hands off, tin man," barked Tina, pulling away, immediately regretting her outburst...

■ ■ ■

It took nearly forty minutes for the ten-minute drive over to Romano's Sub Shop and Bobby wondered how long it would take them to get clear of the city at that rate. Sitting on the sidewalk a few doors down from the restaurant, Bobby put the SUV in park. "Denny, stay here with the vehicle, keep your eyes peeled. Ski, you're with me."

"What about me?" asked Sharon.

"Stay in the car and do what Denny tells you to do," replied Bobby, opening his door and stepping out.

"How long will you be gone?"

249

Bobby shook his head and sighed, waving off her question dismissively.

Nick waved at Bobby from the front of Romano's "Sarge, I think their lights are on inside..."

"Can't be. There's no power, Ski."

"Maybe they have a generator..."

The front door stood propped open with a worn wooden wedge, lights on, a cool wash of air-conditioned air drifting out across the tile entry between the glass front windows, the restaurant empty. "Man, there's a whole lot wrong with this picture..." Bobby swept his windbreaker jacket aside, drawing his Glock from its holster, Nick Omanski doing the same. Cautiously entering, Bobby ventured a peek over the counter for anything or anyone hidden. Nothing. Fresh coffee brewed in the twenty-cup maker against the wall behind the counter. He touched the ice-cold glass of the refrigerated deli counter with his free hand as he passed, still full of meats, cheeses and drinks.

"This is creepy," whispered Nick.

Bobby nodded and did the silent *sshh* signal. He pointed to the open doorway leading to the back.

The stainless kitchen was spotless, everything in its place, upright glass coolers full of refrigerated food supplies. The sink, dishes, glasses and coffee cups in the drying rack were still wet, as if someone had just finished them.

Fearful of what he might find, Nick opened the stainless refrigerator from one side, his Glock trained on the opening. It was well stocked with milk, butter, fresh pies and a cake. He motioned to Bobby and shrugged, who shook his head in return, a puzzled expression on his face.

"Where the hell are Nanna and Pop-Pop,?" whispered Nick.

Bobby indicated a door at the back of the kitchen and made an upwards motion, "Maybe their apartment," he whispered.

Turning the handle gently. It opened with a squeak and he hesitated to listen. Nothing. Hallways and narrow stairwells are a cop's nightmare; a deadly funnel, a shooting gallery with no place to hide. "Let's go..."

Moving slowly, they backed up the stairway towards the first landing, looking up the next flight of stairs to the second floor and the apartment door. Though it was only a two-story building, the stairs continued up from there, probably to the roof.

Huffing in pain from his ribs, Nick was sweating profusely. "You OK, Ski?" hissed Bobby.

250

"Nick wiped his face on his jacket sleeve, "Yeah, Sarge. Keep going, I'm good."

Moving up the second flight of stairs nearly back-to-back, Nick Omanski covered the apartment door as Bobby backed up and covered the flight of stairs to the roof. With his foot on the top stair to the landing, the apartment door swung open startling Nick into a flashback of the ambush. He had to fight his reflex to fire, *"Jesus Christ, Nanna!"*

She froze in his sights, bags in hand, "Boys, you're late," she said with an uncharacteristic tone of irritation.

Bobby holstered his Glock and reached out, patting Nick on the shoulder, "Put it away, Nick." Omanski relaxed slowly, the sights falling away from his line of sight. "What do you mean we're late? Late for what, Nanna?" asked Bobby.

"We called you hours ago, Sergeant..."

"*Called* us..?"

"Ahh," interjected Pop-Pop, appearing in the doorway. "What she means is telepathically - with prayer..."

Bobby frowned in contemplation, "What? I don't understand. What are you saying?"

"Nanna sometimes has the ability to communicate with people through thought. She wanted..."

Nanna harumphed as she headed up the stairs toward the roof with her bags, "Tell them the truth Poppa, they need to know. There's no time for this foolishness, we need to be ready to go..."

"Fine," he sighed. The old man waved them into the apartment, "It will be easier to understand if I show you."

"You're leaving? Where are you going?" asked Bobby following Pop-Pop into the apartment.

"Wait," said Nick, "why is she taking bags to the roof?" But Bobby and the old man had already entered the apartment, leaving him on the landing alone. "Great," he mumbled, "just stand out here and talk to yourself, Nick..."

Ultra-modern and exceedingly high tech, it was not what Bobby would have expected of a couple in Nanna and Pop-Pop's age bracket. He envisioned dark, hand carved, old world furniture, a curio cabinet full of antique knick-knacks, musty oriental rugs and cuckoo clocks. Not glass, black lacquer and an entire wall of flat screens. "You must have a serious sports addiction, Pop-Pop..." Then the question came back to him, "How do you still have power?"

"We have a solar generator on the roof. But that's not important right now, Sergeant," explained the old man. "We are Watchers..."

"What the hell is a Watcher?" asked Nick staring at the wall of big screen televisions.

"And what are we supposed to be late for?" asked Bobby.

The old man held out his hands to stop the questions, "We are..."

"Oh for heaven's sake!" exclaimed Nanna, walking back in empty handed, continuing to admonish the old man in their native language, causing Bobby and Nick to frown; perplexed. She shooed Pop-Pop away from the conversation, "Take those bags up to the roof," she pointed. "Look boys," she began, motioning them together to stand side-by-side, gathering their hands and holding them in her own. "We don't have much time... so I have to make this brief and you have to understand me without questions, understand?" She did not wait for a confirmation or acknowledgment from either of them, continuing on. "Pop-Pop and I are something called *Watchers*. We are *observers*," she pointed up at the ceiling, "from out there. No matter our appearance to you, we are not humans from Earth. We did not come from the *old world...* At least not the one you're thinking of," she smiled. "I am sorry we had to lie to you about that, but it was necessary to..."

"You're *aliens?"* interrupted Bobby, still trying to reconcile that in his mind.

"No questions," she reminded him. "But yes, by your definition we are aliens. As I was saying; we were sent here to track your world's development and any difficulties created by outside interference. It hurts my hearts that intervention could not have come sooner on behalf of your people to prevent this fall..."

Nick's eyes widened, "Hearts?"

"That's what you heard?" complained Bobby. He turned his attention back to Nanna, "So you're just leaving us now? *Like this?"*

"That's why we called you here..." began the old woman, "we had chosen..."

"How did you do that, exactly?" interrupted Nick. "Call us, I mean."

Nanna opened he mouth to reply but all Bobby heard was a burst of automatic gunfire from the street below. "Denny!" he shouted, suddenly remembering he and Nick weren't alone. He broke away from Nanna's grip and headed for the stairs, Nick right behind him.

"Get to the roof!" screamed Nanna. "We don't have much time!"

■ ■ ■

Standing outside the SUV for a better view in all directions and improved situational awareness over sitting in the vehicle, Denny spotted the group of foraging young adults well up the street from his position. Unaware they were being observed, they raided cars, smashed storefront windows and busied themselves with searching for things they thought of value. It appeared to Denny much of their action was simple wanton destruction for the sake of destruction. And he knew what that looked like, he'd seen enough of it before. First hand. It never ceased to amaze him how quickly the human condition descended to animalistic, vindictive behavior. The fact that the behavior fed on itself, breeding increasingly more violent acts that quickly spiraled out of control, transcending even hate, put him on edge.

With no way to alert the Sergeant or Nick without calling attention to himself, giving away his location and risk the all-important vehicle asset he was tasked to protect, he was going to have to do something contrary to his training; defend in place. He eased the passenger door of the SUV open, sliding over in his seat.

"What's happening?" asked Sharon from the back seat.

"Ssshhh," he whispered, unlocking an M-4 from the weapon rack, "slide youself down and stay dere..."

"Why? What do you see?"

"Jus do it. And stay quiet..." he hissed, sliding down in his seat.

"Shouldn't you just talk to them?"

"No offense ma'am, but d' anyone ever tell you, you ask too many stupid questions?"

"You don't have to be rude," she replied, looking between the front seats.

Sitting on the edge of his seat his knee against the door, Denny positioned his foot on the bottom of it keeping it slightly ajar, the M-4 in his lap pointing at the floor between his legs. "I count ten of dem," he said, thinking out loud.

"There's two across the street to our left, too."

"I counted dem," he replied, "but thanks." Not only did he need to protect their only asset, the vehicle, but he could ill-afford to let them enter the open sub shop and possibly take Bobby and Nick by surprise. He kicked the door open as they approached, sliding himself partly off the seat, hidden behind

253

the windshield pillar. His foot held the armored door opened just far enough for the use of cover and a place to sight the carbine through the *V* made by the door and body of the SUV. Sighted in, he yanked back the charging handle in one clean stroke, chambering a round, a sound almost as distinctive and iconic as a pump-action 12ga shotgun. "Dat's far enough..." he thumbed the safety off, two clicks to full auto. "Turn yo ass around and head back d' way you came..."

The group of four in front of him stopped in their tracks. *"Or what, old man?"* snapped the kid in the front, waving his arms.

"Yo gonna have a bad day, sonny..."

"Look here," rapped the loudmouth, waving his arms again, "we got us a old nigga upin our hood... Go home nigga..."

"I don' much like dat word, sonny," interrupted Denny. "I sugges' you pick another; or maybe your momma dint' teach no better manners..." Denny was not fooled by his antics, watching the group as a whole, his peripheral vision tracking others as they moved to his left flank. "Dey do somethin' stupid, you go first, sonny..."

"Unless you go *first*, nigga!"

The kid behind the loudmouth had a sawed-off shotgun and Denny saw the barrels appear as the kid stepped out from behind his friend. A minor sight adjustment and Denny squeezed the trigger briefly, the M-4 barking out about five rounds, stitching him from his sternum to his collarbone, twisting him, his white t-shirt dotted with red splotches. The double-barreled sawed-off shotgun roared, as the kid's grip tightened, roaring again as its recoil wrenched it out of his hand, the loudmouth screaming in agony as the first blast caught him, nearly point-blank in the back of the calf, blowing it apart across the sidewalk. The second blast caught him in the back as he fell, gutting him from behind and he continued to scream as the others scattered like cockroaches. He continued to scream as a pool of blood bloomed out from under him, spreading across the sidewalk, while he tried to hold in his shredded intestines, his foot and ankle barely held on by sinews.

Denny quickly realized the additional screaming was coming from the seat behind him, "You hit lady?" The absence of a response instantly angered him, "Jeee*zus*, woman, *shut the hell up!*" He thumbed the M-4's selector switch to single fire, and casually put a round through the kid's head, ending his pain. "Shoulda gone home to yo' momma, kid," he muttered.

"Oh *my God!*" Sharon wailed from the back seat, "Why did you do that? He was just..."

"Trying to kill us," shouted Denny, finishing her sentence. "Sides, he was dead already; I jus' ended his pain..."

"You're a *monster!*" she shouted, *"An animal..!"*

Denny flinched as 9mm rounds smacked the windshield on an angle from his left flank, oblong bullseyes appearing in the glass, sharp flakes of dust filling the cabin. "You are free to seek better company..." he growled, leaning out, sighting in and returning fire.

■ ■ ■

Gun drawn and at low ready, Bobby slid to a stop at the restaurant's open door, dropping to a crouch to take advantage of the deli counter, the only cover in the all-glass storefront. *"Denny?!"* he called, shouting over the gunfire.

"Still here..! Don't come out, boss, they're all over the place!"

"Sharon?!"

"Annoying as hell, boss!"

Nick who was crouched beside him burst out laughing, clearing his throat upon receiving a scornful look, "Sorry Sarge."

"How many you got?!" called Bobby.

"Two down. At least eight left. Maybe more comin'."

"Can you make it in?"

"That ain't happenin', boss."

Spotting motion across the street, Nick stepped around Bobby, "Tango, twelve o'clock..." They fired simultaneously, empty casings pinging off the deli case to their right, the target dropping behind the parked car he emerged from. "Did we hit him?"

"Don't know..."

The plate glass store window behind the counter exploded, showering the deli cases with knife-sized shards of glass, the window collapsing with a crash, slugs whacking the back of the counter behind them. Bobby could see Denny standing on the rocker panel of the SUV's open door to get the elevation he needed to effectively return fire, the M-4 cracking off rounds in select-fire, the ex-Marine picking targets and spreading the love.

Screaming profanities, Sharon ran across the front of the store and Bobby reached out, grabbing her by the wrist, yanking her through the doorway; a sudden darkness falling across the street and buildings. *"He's a maniac! A lunatic..!"*

"Shut up and get back in the kitchen," he commanded, pushing her towards the back of the restaurant.

"He's going to run dry pretty quick," said Nick, watching Denny duck back into the SUV to reload. "How the hell are we going to get him in here?"

"I don't know," growled Bobby. "But if these clowns wise up, they're going to cut through the alleys and get behind him. We're blind here and we have no cover..."

"We'd have a better vantage point from the roof..."

"We have handguns Ski, not rifles. We're not going to be much help from the roof."

"We can keep their heads down long enough for him to make the run... we just can't leave him..."

"We're not going to *leave* him, Ski, we just need a viable plan..." Bobby's face blanched as Denny stepped out of the SUV, one M-4 carbine in each hand. *"Holy crap,"* he groaned.

Nick Omanski leaned forward to see what Bobby was seeing, his body snapping rigid, "Oh *Jesus!"*

Denny left the cover of the armored SUV heading for Romano's doorway and the street erupted in a mad riot of criss-crossing gunfire, flying glass, ricochets, shouts, screams, smoke and deepening shadows. Bobby Fortuno and Nick Omanski fired at anything that moved, all but oblivious of the bullets that buzzed by, smashing windows, deli cases, thudding into walls, tables and counters. Denny staggered then dropped to a knee, fighting to get back up before toppling over on his side, losing his grip on one of the M-4s, still firing the other while laying on his side.

"Denny's down! Denny's down!" announced Bobby, desperation creeping into his voice.

"My last mag, Sarge..." announced Nick, slapping a fresh magazine into his Glock's magwell.

"Keep shooting, kid... *Crawl Denny, crawl!"*

"Should we pull back?"

"Not until we run out of..." his slide locked back with an audible clack, the naked magazine follower staring up at him through the open ejection port. "Son of a bi..."

A brilliant blue streak momentarily illuminated the shadow that had fallen across the street and buildings, a parked car on the opposite side of the street disintegrating in an explosion that shook the ground, producing a fireball that rained smoking parts down in a hundred-foot radius. It was the first of many, appearing from above, riddling the street, obliterating cars, trees and building fronts, erasing nearly any place to hide, along with the gang of attackers. Bobby and Nick lay on the floor of Romano's, arms covering their heads, debris flying in all directions. As suddenly as it had started, it was over, a tart electric smell so palpable it could be tasted, mixed with the smell of burning metal and rubber.

"What the hell was that?" grumbled Nick, pushing himself up off the floor, looking around, a smoking tire laying behind them on the floor of the restaurant.

"Don't know, don't care," mumbled Bobby, getting up, a hubcap sliding off his back. "Not looking a gift horse in the mouth..." He ventured outside cautiously, scanning the street; swept clean of cars for a block, smoking craters in the street and sidewalk, trees blown into matchsticks.

Denny was covered with debris and Bobby gently rolled him over, "Denny?" He motioned to Nick, "He's hit, let's get him inside..."

"Ain't nothing but a thing, boss," mumbled Denny with a weak smile. He blinked, trying to focus on the sky, "What th' hell is dat, boss?"

When Bobby looked up he could actually feel the color drain from his face, a giant black shape hovering directly above them, mostly obscured by the building. "What... What in God's name am I looking at?"

Nick helped Bobby scoop Denny off the ground, getting him up on one leg, "Sarge, I think the technical term is UFO."

"Don't be ridiculous, Ski..." snapped Bobby.

"You heard Nanna..." he replied, "she *said* she was an alien."

"You actually believed that story?" Bobby shouldered Denny, Nick under the big man's other arm. "Shame on you Ski, you don't recognize batshit crazy when you hear it yet?"

"You gotta admit it's a pretty strange coincidence."

"It's one of our military transports..."

"You sure you want to stick with that Sarge?"

"For the sake of my sanity, yes..."

■ ■ ■

It took them a good five minutes to haul Denny up to the roof, Sharon complaining the whole time about the humming in her head and her itchy skin. Having been exposed to as much noise as they were, none of the men could hear *anything*. And each made note of feeling odd but wrote it off to gallons of adrenalin and its after effects.

Personally, Bobby felt drained but his anxiety about what was actually on the roof kept a trickle of adrenalin flowing. Stepping through the open stairwell door to the roof and into the sunshine made his knees weak, a dark ship the length of a football field hovering just a couple feet above the roof, the nose sticking out over the street. At least it *looked* like the nose. If that wasn't disturbing enough, two large armored robots stood at the far edge of the roof overlooking the street. His heart began to hammer in his chest and he felt light headed.

Nanna trotted toward them from what appeared to be a boarding ramp, more spry and agile than her advanced years should allow, calling them, "*Quickly*, this way boys," she waved.

"We're getting in that thing?" asked Bobby.

"Yes, of course..." she replied, turning and walking with them.

"Nah, I don't think so," he countered.

"You're not even *curious?*"

"I... *no.*"

"You are *lying* to me Sergeant Bobby Fortuno," she teased. The old woman put her arm around his, walking at his side, "You have no reason to be fearful. Besides, your friend is wounded, he needs medical attention. He will get excellent care with these people."

"Fine," agreed Bobby, gritting his teeth. "But then I'm getting off..."

"Why? There is nothing left for you here; at least not right now..."

"My daughters. I have to find the girls..."

"They are not lost," she replied, matter of factly.

"What do you mean? How would you know tha..."

With a knowing smile, Nanna gestured toward the top of the ramp without speaking, a massive armored figure standing there, an alien weapon cradled in his arms. Two girls appeared from the muted light of the interior, appearing in the sunlight, silhouetted by the dark opening.

Bobby's eyes widened in astonishment, *"Annie? Tina?"*

"Daddy..! Mom..!"

CHAPTER TWENTY ONE

NEW VANUS SYSTEM : DEEP BLACK'S - SCAVENGER ONE

Cheriska Skye's *Vulture* pushed through the corona of the gate into New Vanus with an explosion of color; only to be replaced by the striking, motionless waves and swirls of iridescent blue dust that stretched across the system. The tendrils of electricity washed across the ship's hull, releasing its grip, disappearing as the Vulture slid away. It took a moment for Cheriska to realize the colors she was seeing were not part of the gate transition, but the unique nature of New Vanus. It was breathtaking. A relatively new system in its terrible two's, *counted in eons of course,* the closest thing to habitable was a *Class 12a* planet which was relatively primitive and not terribly stable yet; a *Class 14* being optimal in maturity and stability with an atmosphere suitable for most humanoid life. That *Class 12a* would need a couple more eons to develop into a safely habitable *Class 14.*

Cheriska Skye hadn't exactly led a sheltered life, but she had begun to realize what a narrow scope it had been. It was painfully obvious she needed to get out more. Reflecting on her childhood growing up, she recalled the joy of gravity. *Real* gravity. And *real* air. The kind that rustled the leaves of trees with a quiet hush, the sound of night insects singing you to sleep... She was a young adult the last time she was planet side. Until now, so close to her destination, she hadn't realized how much she was looking forward to it. How much she missed it. She'd lived more than half her life in space. And not to be unkind, because Rikovik's Reef had provided a good living, but it didn't qualify as a planet. You could call it a planetoid all you wanted, it was still little more than a rock-ship hybrid monstrosity.

And nothing pointed out Rikovik's faults and shortcomings faster than visiting a *real* station, like Resurrection back in Irujen. Sure, it had been converted from a cruise liner, but the class, the style, the cleanliness... the difference was night and day.

Less than an hour from the gate into Irujen System, her Vulture had been greeted by a patrolling flight of armed UFW combat drones that assessed her ship before politely inviting her to visit the station. One drone escorted her ship, allowing her to communicate directly with the station while the rest of the drone flight continued on its patrol. The landing bay had been nothing short of spotless, the flight services exceptional, and the accommodations for visitors; professional, warm and friendly. Of course, as much as Cheriska would love to move Deep Black, lock stock and barrel, to a place like that; her particular breed of clientele would never venture within two systems of a place like Resurrection Station. Their business and survival often relied upon complete anonymity. So unfortunately, Rikovik's Reef, despite its societal miscreants, had a unique, shall we say, *charm*... that necessity dictated she call home. Of course, maybe it was time for a branch location. Certainly something to think about.

But Resurrection Station had shopping! *Lots* of shopping. And not the *bazaar, haggle with the natives in a cave* shopping; but the *would you like a glass of champagne while you shop,* kind of shopping. There had also been the *Ecosphere* - a park under a massive dome; a place that took her back to her childhood, laying in the grass, looking up at the stars. She walked barefoot across a meadow of soft grass, through swaying trees, feeling a breeze, discovering a small waterfall feeding a babbling brook that wound its way a quarter of a mile across the park. It was the closest thing to planet side she could imagine, and it only made her want it more. Spending a few days lounging, relaxing, and shopping was a necessary diversion from the confines of the Vulture, and put her mind in motion.

Resurrection Station was a bit of cultural shock to Cheriska after spending nearly two decades on Rikovik's Reef. No dust and grunge, no rust, no crime to speak of, air that smelled like, well, *air*. Fresh - not like poorly filtered, recycled, metal stink. She wondered if she could bottle that scent and take it with her wherever she went. Like back to the Reef. The thought of returning to that armpit wasn't an appealing one. Of course, *the sky is always bluer on the other side of the planet,* or so the saying goes.

■ ■ ■

Mesmerized by the swirls of iridescent color reaching across New Vanus and still basking in the afterglow of a shopper's high, Cheriska turned her seat sideways, stretching out and kicking her feet up on the arm of the empty copilot's seat, admiring her new boots. The autopilot navigated the Vulture across the system toward the gate to Velora Prime.

"Deep Black, Deep Black to Scavenger One, are you out there?"

Cheriska reached out and without really looking, tapped the comm, the vid-screen winking on, "I'm here. What's up, Too?"

"Just checking in, seeing where you're at. How are your travels going?"

Cheriska turned the screen a little, "Fine. I'm in New Vanus." She held up one foot, "Like my new boots?"

Too's face registered surprise, "Are they *red?*" she squinted. "I saw a few things come through the account..."

"It's called *oxblood,*" replied Cheriska, turning her foot and admiring the color, "whatever that is."

"They're nice..."

Cheriska detected something other than appreciation, "You don't like them?"

"They're okay."

"Hmm, maybe I should send yours back then..." teased Cheriska.

Cheriska Too stifled a hopeful smile, *"You bought me a pair?"*

"You didn't think I would forget my sister, did you?"

Too shrugged sheepishly, smiling, *"Thanks. I can't wait to try them on..."* Her expression suddenly turned serious, *"What the hellion is that?"* she pointed at Cheriska.

Not thinking, Cheriska glanced over her shoulder, realizing Too was referring to the sleeping creature laying across her shoulder, it's tail wrapped loosely around her neck. It had been so quiet and still, she had forgotten it was there. "Oh, yeah, it's a Love's Dragon. Isn't he cute..?"

"A what?!"

"A Breedlove's Dragon. They just say Love's Dragon for short. Remember that explorer, Dr. Breedlove? He's the one who discovered them... I forgot the name of the planet they come from..."

"Haven't some of those things killed their owners?" interrupted Too. *"Eaten their faces or something?"*

Cheriska waved her hand dismissively, "Thirty years ago, maybe. The original dragons were larger, more aggressive, unpredictable. He's since developed the species to be domesticated."

"How do you develop a species?" asked Too, dubious.

"I don't know; gene splicing, altering DNA, selective breeding I guess..."

"Pretending to be the creator," snarked Too. *"That's playing with fire."*

"They took that out too."

"Took out what?"

"Their ability to make fire..."

"They can make fire?!" exclaimed Too.

"No, not anymore," corrected Cheriska. "They no longer have the gland that produces the gas they could ignite with their clicker..."

"Oh this is a bad idea..." lamented Too. *"Clicker..?"*

"Calm down. The breeder I bought him from assured me he was harmless. The clicker is a metallic bone-plate on the roof of their mouth they would scrub with a sandy part of their tongue for a spark. But without the gland, nothing happens. What I thought was fascinating is that their saliva protected their mouths from burning..."

Too rolled her eyes, *"Wonderful, he can torch your face without burning his lips..."*

Cheriska shook her head, "You're impossible."

"Just remember that when he cooks your face before he eats it."

"Stop..." Cheriska stroked his long neck, and he stretched, still asleep, gurgling contentedly, "He wouldn't do that, look how beautiful he is..."

Too's eyes widened, as the sleeping creature flexed itself, *"By the Gods, he has wings? He can fly too?"*

Cheriska looked indignant, *"Of course.* I thought that was implied. If he didn't, he'd just be a Love's *Lizard.* What part of *dragon* didn't you understand?"

Cheriska Too rubbed her temples, *"Sooo many ways this could go wrong..."*

"How's the shop?" asked Cheriska, changing the subject.

"Everything's fine. We sold the good engine off the Syndicate yacht you reclaimed..."

"Really? To who?"

"Back to the Syndicate. To rebuild one of the yachts damaged back when that Jax Mercury guy torched their hangar. Did you know they lost five ships? Not including the one we salvaged."

"Do they know it was originally their engine?"

Too shook her head, *"No, the boys had it pulled from the wreck and stripped down to the powertrain already. It was cleaned up and in inventory when they called."*

"Good deal." nodded Cheriska. "It probably wouldn't go over well if they knew it came from one of their own ships."

■ ■ ■

Cheriska woke from a disturbing dream with a start, feeling for the wetness on her face, not fully awake. The Love's Dragon sitting in her lap stared up at her with piercing green eyes, wings folded against his body. Disoriented, the dream still vivid in her mind, she examined her hand for blood. Nothing. *Damn you, Too, for putting that image in my head...* She had to force the dream out of her mind.

"Where you licking my face?" she wondered aloud. The Love's Dragon stood on his hind legs, his tail resting on her thigh, front feet on the breast of her flight jacket, one wing wrapping her upper arm for support as he reached up to bump his forehead against her lips. The breeder had instructed her to watch for this behavior. "Smart little man," she smirked, "let's go get you something to eat." He scrambled up her arm, circled over her shoulder and perched himself up next to her ear, tittering excitedly, clicking his teeth. Cheriska had already learned the difference in sound between his teeth and the clicker. "Thank you for not eating my face," she joked, the dream fading from her thoughts. Rising from her command seat, she did a precursory check of the autopilot and progress on their route to the gate to Velora Prime. Satisfied, she headed to the ship's galley. "You know," she said reaching back to rub his chest, "we still haven't come up with a name for you... How *do* you name a dragon, anyway?"

Hand feeding him and watching him closely, it suddenly became apparent to Cheriska that his coloring had changed. He had turned from a brownish color resembling her leather flight jacket, to a gray similar to the stainless galley table he was standing on. She was sure she would have remembered the breeder mentioning that. Maybe he forgot? Or maybe it something he wasn't aware of? In any case, it was fascinating. She decided it was time to review the video file her MOBIUS had received about the Breedlove's Dragons.

Full and content, he gurgled, something that resembled a quiet chuckle. Arching his back he momentarily extended his wings before settling. Staring passively at her with sparkling green orbs he instinctively click-clicked, the little burp that escaped igniting in a puff of fire.

"Oh, *damn...*"

CHAPTER TWENTY TWO

CITRA 5 SYSTEM : *PERSEUS*

Jack Steele leaned back against the desk in his suite, his arms casually folded across his chest, the accommodations a little more spacious than the ready room off the bridge. "So we're doing *what* now?"

Commander Reegan, Derrik Brighton, Mercedes Huang, Chase Holt, Torn Dado and Ragnaar congregated around the chart table, Ragnaar reaching in and manipulating the holo-chart. "I recommend we make a detour; stop here," he pointed at a planet, "on G'Naroth Sarat in Bengaloo. Amanpoor to be exact."

Steele raised an eyebrow, Amanpoor is..?"

"A commerce port on G'Naroth Sarat."

"Of course," he said flatly. "And why in the middle of a pursuit would we do this?"

"We need to pick up some kind of cargo. Goods for..."

Steele's face went blank, "So we need to go shopping, Mr. Ragnaar? Is that what you're telling me?" he scoffed sarcastically. "I hardly think..."

"Bloody hell, hear him out," interrupted Derrik, "it makes sense."

"Sir," continued Ragnaar, respectfully, "as soon as we leave Citra 5 we're in confirmed FreeRanger territory. We're headed to Wyandek in the Ardollis System; that's five gates and nearly ten systems deep into dark territory. We need to make some preparations before we enter dark territory..."

"Alright, Mr. Ragnaar, you have my attention. Talk to me."

"First off, no one deadheads empty into dark territory. Ever. We need to have a respectable cargo load of marketable goods to trade or sell. We have to *act* like we *look*. Second, we need to transfer funds from our operating account to cash. Gold. About a million credits. Outfits out here don't take IOUs, they don't issue credit and they won't take transfers. Everything is cash only, off the books. Nobody wants a bribe they have to share with the FreeRanger Council."

"Steele nodded appreciatively, "Got it. What else?"

"As capable as this ship is, we may want to look up an escort company, see if we can find one with contacts or stations in the territory. Even if it's just for appearances, having friends, even if they're *paid* friends, never hurts. Start them off with a retainer, even though we don't need them right now."

Steele rubbed the stubble on his jawline, mulling over these new operational requirements. "Do all traders use hired guns?"

Ragnaar withdrew his hands from the holo-chart and straightened up, "Many, not all. Some have the benefit of a name the FreeRangers recognize. Companies that are friendly and cater to their needs are left alone for the most part. Some Captains travel in groups or convoys, some have full-time escorts. And then there are the ones that use the *hired guns*, as you put it. That money goes into the FreeRanger economy though, so some respect comes from the knowledge that you are already dealing with an accepted service. Quite often the fact that you are under escort contract is enough, the escort doesn't even need to be present."

Jack's expression was dubious, "Well isn't that convenient. Sounds more like a safe passage tariff than a protection service."

"Doesn't really matter how you look at it," offered Derrik, "as long as it works. Right?"

Jack ran his fingers through his hair, "I suppose." He turned his attention back to Ragnaar, "So what types of cargo should we be looking at?"

"Liquor is always a safe bet - some brands more than others; you saw that in Nelson's Point. We should be able to get whatever we want in Amanpoor. Then of course, there's parts, foods, delicacies; medical supplies; I've taken the liberty to create a list." The big man paused for a moment, weighing his next words carefully, "And there's something else that will give us credibility... buy us considerable favor almost anywhere we go..."

Steele saw the change in his demeanor, the Lieutenant was waiting for a prompt, "What would that be, Mr. Ragnaar?"

Ragnaar cleared his throat and shifted nervously, "Dust."

Dust. Glacier. Ice. Blizzard. It had an assortment of names; a blue-white powder that sparkled like freshly fallen snow. The premium illegal drug of choice throughout most of the known universe. *So now we're going to be drug smugglers. Swell.* Steele's first reaction was to say, *no.* In fact, *hell no.* But he was going to have to trust Ragnaar's experience and expertise. They were in the former pirate's backyard now. *In for a penny in for a pound...* He pursed his lips, the decision distasteful though he knew it was a necessary evil, "OK." He ignored the stunned faces looking back at him and pointed to Commander Reegan, "New course; G'Naroth Sarat in Bengaloo. Look to Mr. Ragnaar for directions for Amanpoor." He clapped his hands, "Let's get this done people, we don't have time to waste, we're in the middle of a pursuit here..."

■ ■ ■

Chase Holt hung back after everyone else left the suite, "Ok, I may be way outta my element here, Jack, but how do you expect to catch up to that destroyer if we're going on a shopping excursion?"

Jack was leaning into the holo-chart, the port of Amanpoor on G'Naroth Sarat enlarged so he could examine the detail, rotating the beach-ball sized planet with his hand. "We're pretty close to them right now. According to the integrity of the energy trail we're tracking, we're estimating they're just beyond our sensor reach. They don't know they're being pursued so they're cruising not running. We're faster than they are and we can GOD jump; they don't have that capability. We can still catch them - as long as we don't get stupid and waste a bunch of time..."

"Or Murphy's Law doesn't..."

"Bite your tongue," scolded Jack. Changing the subject, he went back to studying the holo-chart. "According to the charts, G'Naroth Sarat is governed by the UFW, but being on the border, Ragnaar says they play the neutral card, dealing with both UFW and FreeRanger clients. I have a feeling that most of the FreeRanger clients are supplied by third party deliveries though. I don't see them venturing here and setting a ship down on a planet where they might be caught vulnerable."

Chase peered closer at the images, circling the holographic planet with his finger, "No station, huh?"

"Not here."

■ ■ ■

The cockpit of the P-57 was snug but relatively comfortable and it was an unlikely but convenient place for a little undisturbed solitude. Perfect for a little studying, the only light coming from Steele's holographic MOBIUS screen, the bay dark around the fighter. "MOBI, what can you tell me about the history of the FreeRangers?"

"Stand by, Mr. Mercury, synching with the ship's historical database..." MOBI's dark-haired character looked back at him with a pleasant expression, a data stream scrolling across the screen underneath her. "Files found."

"Summarize, please."

"Detail is limited, Mr. Mercury, but according to the corroborating information in the database, the FreeRanger concept was born on or about interstellar date; 69037.281. That is one-thousand-four-hundred-eighty-five years, two-hundred-forty-seven days ago according to the interstellar calendar. The initial concept was in flux for several decades as support grew and became more mainstream. For the first century there was no structured leadership, merely a groundswell of support and interest. It became apparent some kind of structure and hierarchy was required to keep the various factions from infighting and cannibalizing the weaker groups. In fact, the organization didn't even have a formal name until, 69154.473. They initially called themselves the Dark Raiders..."

"Is that why pirate held sectors are called *Dark Territory?*"

"There is no mention of that anywhere in the historical files, but reasoning suggests that is quite possible."

"Continue, MOBI."

"By interstellar star date, 69317.186 they were battling a public relations image crisis bordering on nightmarish, brought on by decades of overzealous freelancers and very little control over the bulk of their membership..."

"Imagine that," snorted Jack, "they got a bad rap for robbing, stealing and killing."

"Bad rap?" MOBI's head tilted to one side in a familiar human fashion.

"Never mind. Continue."

"Later that year, with an organized council in place, the members were polled and a new name voted on, including set codes of conduct. The *FreeRangers* emerged as a cleaner, more civilized, business-driven model focused on profitability, led by a council of twenty-five members arranged in a hierarchical court. The Council President has the final vote as a tiebreaker if the council is split on a decision. The word *free* in the name reflects free men doing work unhindered by restrictive laws and taxes. It appears the *ranger* part of the name was found to be more positive than the negative connotation associated with the word *raider*. It was also perceived that they would police their own members to make sure their new code of ethics was followed. "

Even criminals have a code of conduct, though calling it a code of ethics might be a stretch. "When they were originally founded, what was the purpose of the organization? What were their goals?" asked Jack.

"According to the records, the initial goal was not only to insure their ability to conduct free, unfettered business and trade in whatever they wanted - wherever they wanted, but to completely avoid UFW taxes."

"Mmm, yeah, nobody likes paying taxes..." Steele rubbed the young beard on his jawline, compelled to shave, but put it out of his mind; knowing he needed to look the part. He was never really comfortable with a beard. "So they went from an advisory council to having a Navy. How did that happen?"

"The FreeRangers made a shift from a disorganized band of misfits to one with an educated and experienced leadership. Those freelancers who were originally raiders and opportunists were tasked with protecting FreeRanger interests like ships and stations from UFW interference."

"How do the protectors get paid?"

"The council implemented a flat rate tithing on all FreeRangers except the protectors. The Council reinvested those funds to expand FreeRanger territories and pay protector assignments. Protectors accept missions and assignments both with flat rate pay schedules and performance bonuses. They are also allowed to freelance. Funds received for freelance work are subject to the tithing rate but most contract work of that type is cash based and rarely reported."

"Tithing..." repeated Jack. "You can call it whatever you like, they're paying taxes. Hm, so the very thing they fought against, they accepted." He pinched his lower lip in contemplation, "You said they reinvested in expanding their territories, how or what did they do exactly?"

MOBI paused momentarily, the data stream scrolling under her animation. "Some money was invested in legitimate businesses, some was invested in equipment, ship development, stations..."

"So they have an entire economic base?"

"Oh yes, the BOFFIE manages..."

"BOFFIE?" interrupted Jack, frowning.

"*Bank of FreeRanger Financial Investments and Economy*. It is run by a sub-council on finance. They make recommendations to the FreeRanger Council based on economic trends, business development, technology advances and fleet needs."

"Yeah, let's get back to the fleet thing. So, they have freelancers... but we've encountered ships that looked more like organized Navy than amateur..."

"Searching..." MOBI's face cast a downward glance, looking like she was searching the data stream below her image. "Information found," she said, looking back up. "On or about interstellar star date, 69531.232, the very first FreeRanger shipyard went on-line. The facility had complete plans for five different ship designs and began building its first ship the day it went live. Ships produced were available to any FreeRanger or freelance entity and could be financed through the BOFFIE. Captured ships could be reconditioned at this facility, for a fee of course, and any new or unique design would be reverse engineered - the plans added to the production lineup."

"So the Navy?" Steele reminded her.

"The greatest portion of the production in the first several years, were armed ships. It is believed the largest military ship available at the time was an escort destroyer. There are no known statistics on production numbers or ship specifications in the database."

"How is their Navy structured?"

"The command structure is similar in configuration to what you would expect, except that the Navy is a combination of both, actual FreeRanger Navy and freelancers. In some cases, the freelance ships may be identical to those in the Navy with the same specifications, purchased or financed by their captains or owners through the BOFFIE. FreeRanger Navy *must* follow mission orders; freelancers have more freedom to accept or decline mission assignments and have more latitude on mission execution. Navy resupplies are provided; freelancers must pay for resupply - or acquire their own sources."

"Then that's their weakness..."

MOBI tilted her head again, "Mr. Mercury?"

"The fact that a large sector of their Navy is *profit* driven as opposed to *duty* driven. The lack of honor, integrity and dedication can make a big difference in the will to fight..."

The bay lights flickered, coming on, a soft muted glow illuminating the nearly empty bay. Steele squinted, Lieutenant Loech Braskus strolling up to the nose of the fighter and around the side to the ladder. "Can't sleep Mr. Mercury?"

Jack shook his head, "Just a quiet little place to do some studying, Lieutenant. How about you?"

The Lieutenant smiled crookedly, "A strange place to *study*, if you don't mind me saying..." He didn't wait for a reply, "I just thought I'd come down and check the birds before I hit the rack. We've got a little over four hours till we emerge in the Bengaloo System. Another three or four to G'Naroth Sarat. Being on the fringe of Dark Territory," he tapped absentmindedly on the fuselage with his knuckle, "it seemed like a prudent..."

"Oh, I totally agree," nodded Steele, closing his MOBIUS screen. Grabbing the frame of the canopy's windshield, he pulled himself to his feet in the cockpit. "I should probably get some bunk time too... I'll leave you to it."

CHAPTER TWENTY THREE

TERRAN SYSTEM - UFW REVENGE : *PICKING UP THE PIECES*

Off to her left, the Man-In-The-Moon smiled brightly at Lisa as she eased the Reaper underneath the Revenge and held it steady when prompted by her HUD. A pair of docking clamps reaching down from the belly of the frigate, locking onto the fighter with a *clank*, drawing it upwards. The throttles, now controlled by the docking computer, zeroed themselves and Lisa released the flight stick. Fitting into the impression in the hull of the Revenge, the Reaper became part of the bigger ship.

A sliver of light appeared from above, widening as the frigate's hull plating opened, a face peering down through the top of her canopy. *"Seal is good Ensign. You can release your canopy..."*

Shutting down her systems, she pulled the canopy release, the seal popping with a quick hiss, the pressure equalizing. While it motored back out of the way, hands reached down from above to help her and then Draza Mac step up and out of the cockpit. Standing on the deck, Lisa unlocked her helmet, wriggling it off, her reddish-auburn hair cascading out onto her shoulders.

The deckhand accepted her helmet, "Skipper wants you on the bridge, ASAP, Ms. Steele."

"What about me?" inquired Draza Mac.

"Nope, just the Ensign."

Lisa fist-bumped the Sergeant, turning for the elevators at the front of the bay, "I'll catch up with you later Mac."

■ ■ ■

Lisa exchanged nods with the Marine sentry outside the bridge door before passing through onto the bridge, the door disappearing into the bulkhead. She stopped, waiting to be acknowledged when the Ensign in the First Officer's command seat looked over her shoulder.

"Skipper?" asked Lisa, not seeing him anywhere.

"Ready room," she replied, thumbing over her shoulder before turning back to her duties.

Lisa couldn't really primp before entering; she was still in her flight gear. She mentally shrugged and walked in, the door sliding open, then closed behind her.

"Sup?" Brian flipped a small box in her direction, "This is for you..."

Lisa caught but bobbled the box before it settled in her hands. "What is it?" she asked, lifting the top open.

"Your new pips... Lieutenant JG."

Lisa's eyes widened, "Wow..."

"I talked to Pappy, since you're the only pilot for the Reaper, we thought it would be a good idea to have a couple more jockeys familiar with her. And we all know how well pilots take instruction from someone of an equal or lower rank; Pappy agreed the senior pilot needed a bump up."

"Wow..."

"Yeah, you said that," he joked. "So... you will be responsible for their familiarization and instruction on the Reaper. Flight scheduling shouldn't be too complicated, and then you can spend a little more time on the bridge as well."

"That's fantastic!"

"I'm glad you agree," he nodded approvingly. "The other pilots will be shuttling over later this evening; you can introduce yourself then." He motioned to her flight suit, "You might as well get changed, I have something else for you to do. And don't forget your new pips..."

■ ■ ■

The deck above the Revenge's small flight deck, *if you could even call it a flight deck,* was a catchall of sorts; cargo deck, staging area, deployment or recovery area... and fairly humble in size compared to any of the spaces on the Conquest. But today, its limited open space was filled with a cacophony of shouting, arguing and crying. Lisa raised her hands above her head for a futile attempt at attention. It garnered her nothing and she gave up on decorum. *"SHUUUUT UUUUP!"* she screamed, her fists balled. *Ok that worked a little too well...*

People froze in mid-argument, Marines froze in mid-stride or mid-conversation; all eyes shifting to her. She gathered herself up, smoothing her uniform tunic, "I am Lieutenant Lisa Steele... I understand you may be confused and frightened. There is nothing to fear here, you are safe." She turned to the Marines, still in their assault armor, saluting them, "Thank you gentlemen, you are dismissed. I will handle it from here." They returned her salute, glanced around the area, at each other, the group of frightened civilians and back to her with a nod before stepped away.

The group shifted, moving toward her, giving her a moment of pause. Maybe she had released the Marines a little too soon. "Ladies and gentlemen," she said calmly, her hands out-stretched. "I need you all to relax and stay calm, I will explain everything to you..."

The group parted as someone pushed through their midst, "Lisa? Lisa Steele - Jack Steele's sister?"

"That's right," she replied.

The man thumbed his chest as he approached, "Bobby Fortuno..."

"Oh my God, Bobby," smiled Lisa, "I almost didn't recognize you out of uniform." They reached out and shook hands, the crowd closing ranks but remaining respectable.

"My friend Denny, they took him away..."

"He was shuttled over to another ship," replied Lisa, "and last I checked, he was still in surgery..."

"What have you heard? Will he make it?"

"Honestly Bobby, he's in the best hands imaginable; the Conquest has one of the finest medical staffs in the fleet. I've seen them do amazing and remarkable things..."

"Fleet," muttered Bobby, deadpan.

"I know, I know, it's a lot to take in all at once." She turned to address everyone, "This will all be clearer soon..."

"Lisa, what, *who* are these *watchers?* And where did they go?" asked Bobby.

"They were sent for a debriefing, everything will be clearer soon..."

"Yeah, you keep saying that..."

She looked out over the crowd, "Can everyone hear me? Can everyone understand me?" Several couples raised their hands, puzzled looks on their faces. "Englais?" she asked them.

"Parlez-vous francaise..."

"Sprechen zie deutch..."

"Mowimy po popolsku..."

Lisa held up her hands stalling any more responses, "Bobby," she whispered, "I'm going to need your help keeping everyone calm and orderly, can you do that?"

"There's over a hundred people here, " he whispered back.

"I'm aware of that. It's either that or the Marines come back. Understand?"

He nodded, motioning Nick Omanski to his side. "This is my partner Nick. My ex-wife is the one over there in the red shirt," he indicated, "with my daughters."

Lisa admired the attractive family, "She looks like a keeper..."

"Yeah, you'd think that," he interrupted, "but no." He shot Nick a *shut up* look with a quick glance.

"Look," insisted Lisa, "If we can get everyone to just sit and relax I can bring crew members in to distribute translators, food, water, and get everyone comfortable.

"Translators?"

Lisa raised an eyebrow, "If you're going to question everything I say, this is going to take forever. You're going to have to trust me..."

"Because I should trust *kidnappers?*" hissed Bobby.

"No, you should trust *rescuers*," she corrected him. "In case you've forgotten, your ass was in the *frying pan*." She placed her hands on her hips, "So do I get your help or not?"

■ ■ ■

With a handful of temporary translator disks, Nick Omanski, Bobby Fortuno and his daughters helped Lisa get the people who didn't speak English, equipped to understand her so she could explain what was happening. It took a little patience but their diligence paid off, allowing her to communicate freely and keep everyone calm as members of the crew trickled into the bay.

Sitting on the floor with food and water, the group was wary but relatively calm, the initial case of cow-eyes having faded as the alien medical team moved from person to person to implant permanent translators. Bobby and his family opted to go first to demonstrate to the others that the procedure was safe and relatively painless; his ex-wife, of course, feeling the need to complain. Surprisingly, having heard just about enough, it was Nick Omanski who stepped up and silenced her with a few choice words whispered in her ear. Curiously, when Bobby inquired, his partner refused to repeat the magical, harpy-silencing words, responding with nothing more than a wink and a wry smile.

"Ladies and gentlemen," said Lisa sitting on a polycarbonate crate, scooting back, "I expect everyone can understand me now? Understand the crew around you?" Her questions were met with quiet nods. "Good. As you have seen, aliens are as real as you and me. Just like people on Earth, there are good and bad. And the way they look is just as varied out here as on Earth - in many cases even more-so as their genetics have adapted to the unique circumstances and environments from which they came. There are aliens living among us on Earth, and there are humans living out here in space. There are of course other planets like Earth, and..."

"Have you been to any of them?" asked a French woman.

"Just one so far. An absolutely beautiful planet called Veloria..."

"How many?" someone shouted. "Planets like Earth?"

"Hundreds... thousands," she replied. "Plus space stations the size of cities, habitable planetoids, ships that dwarf anything you can imagine... *Some* people out here have been born in space and lived their lives having never set foot on a planet."

"When you say *people*..."

"A general term for other beings you will meet," explained Lisa. "Just like different races on Earth, there are different races out here - as varied as the planets and solar systems they come from scattered across the universe. What you've seen today is just a grain of sand on a beach by comparison. For all the ways we differ, there are as many ways we are the same - quite remarkable when you think about it."

"These watchers, were they aliens?"

"Yes. They were here to monitor our technological progress to determine when we might be suitable for entry into the space-faring community. They also observed what was happening with the infiltrators..."

"So why are *we* here? Why us?"

Lisa thought about how to frame her answer, "Well, you all had the... *unique opportunity* to know a watcher in your area. Over the years, you and your families formed a mutual bond with them that reached a familial level. You were chosen, adopted as extended family - to such an extent that when things got desperate, they could no more leave you behind then they could their own flesh and blood." She held her arms out indicating size, "Remember the metal men? Those are our Marines in heavy armor. They were there to not only extract our watchers but to protect them *and* you. Our teams knew you were coming. They knew who you were. And as some of you saw," her eyes flicked over to Bobby and Nick, "they didn't hesitate to protect your families to get you safely out of harm's way..."

"So what the feckin' shite do we do now?" asked a barrel-chested Irishman with a red handlebar mustache.

"There are plenty of opportunities out here..." answered Lisa, her hands folded neatly in her lap.

"Don't be yanking me clackers, Molly, we don't know feck about space!"

"Lieutenant Steele," she corrected him, hopped off the crate, slowly strolling across the deck in front of them. "Look, I'm a prime example," she began, "I was in the same place you are now, about a year-and-a-half ago. Now I'm a pilot. I found something that fascinated me and they gave me every opportunity to make that happen. Anything you did at home you can do out here. And more."

"What if we just want to go home?" called a voice from somewhere in the back.

"Realistically, you're here because it was so bad where you were, that home currently doesn't exist for you. It's gone..."

"But wait..." said a woman waving her hand.

"If," continued Lisa, "or *when* circumstances change, and things calm down and we have some semblance of order, you will have the opportunity to go back. *If* that's what you really want. You may also be given the additional opportunity to do liaison work between the surface and the assets out here in an official capacity." She watched the woman lower her hand.

"If we decide to go back..." began Nick, looking introspective, staring at the floor in thought, "would we go back to where we came from?"

"You would most likely go back to the area you are most familiar with. But it will be open for discussion... especially if that area is still in flux."

"If we decide to stay *out here,* where would we end up?"

Lisa stopped, her hands clasped behind her, "The government of Veloria has graciously extended an open invitation to resettle there. Knowing of course that you left with little to nothing, there will be preparations made for you and your families, both in housing and career possibilities based on your experience..." Lisa could sense a *but* coming, "If you ever want to come back to Earth, you have to remember, space flight between planets is not so much different than airline travel between countries on Earth. It takes a little longer but the accommodations are much nicer."

"Like how long? How far is this... *Veloria?*" asked Annie Fortuno.

"About three months."

"Nah shite, that's a long feckin' time to be settin' on yer arse twiddling yer pipe without a nice Sally to feak," complained the red-haired Irishman. "And I won't be rattlin' some manky tramp with a face like a cats arse... No knobrot for this Mick, I like me plums jus' the way they are."

Despite her translator not being able to decipher all of the Irishman's colorful slang, Lisa got the general meaning in context, as disturbing as it was. She just wasn't sure how to respond.

"No indifference to your, uh, *plums*, I can... *appreciate* your concerns, Mr..."

"Shamus," he thumbed his chest.

"Mr. Shameless - *Shamus*," she corrected herself. *Shameless, oh boy.* She couldn't help herself, it just popped into her head.

"Ballsbridge, Dublin," he nodded proudly.

Balls-bridge... Oh God, this just keeps getting worse. "Ladies and gentlemen," she said, redirecting the conversation away from the redhead with the handlebar mustache. "We are at an extremely pivotal point in Earth's history. And like almost all significant times in history, it's messy. It's scary. It's dangerous. It's also remarkable and exciting. You have an opportunity to be a part of it or to be a bystander. You stand at the crossroads of one of the most remarkable points in man's time on Earth." She decided to use a conversation Jack had described with Voorlak. "You can choose to be like a man named, Herman Shimp, or take a leap into history with both feet like, George Washington."

"Who the shite was Herman Shimp for feck's sake?"

It took a conscious effort on Lisa's part not to roll her eyes. "No one knows. A nobody. He stood aside and watched history pass him by..."

"Aye brilliant, Lassie! Ya titsmacked me with that one... Though I s'pose I'd prefer St. Patrick o'r your Washington..."

Oh, God... shut up, shut up, shut up... Lisa took a deep breath and resisted even looking in his direction. "Man and Earth will recover. We will rebuild, better and stronger. We will be more prosperous. And we will join the interstellar community. Medical and technological advances will be staggering..."

"What would *we* be doing?" asked Nick Omanski, his arms folded across his chest.

"In some cases, you would be the new watchers in your area. Of course, we wouldn't send you back down until some stability has been reached. In your and Bobby's case, you would be our liaisons with the police and local government in Chicago. Not only to determine their needs and supply them the necessary tools required, but to help and guide them..."

Bobby was shaking his head, "No offense. Really... But I'm just a Sergeant and he's a Patrolman," he indicated Nick, "with two years on the job. You're dreaming if you think they're going to give two shits about what we think or say. No one under a Commander is going to... "

"You let *us* worry about that," she interrupted with a grin. "We can be *very* convincing."

CHAPTER TWENTY FOUR

BENGALOO SYSTEM - PERSEUS : *G'Naroth Sarat*

Jack Steele opened his eyes, a giant black nose filling his sleepy field of vision, "What the..."

"Bengaloo," rumbled Fritz, staring down at him. "Why you sleep on couch? Bed right over there..."

"I dunno," mumbled Jack, "I was studying..."

"This not studying," corrected Fritz.

"I know - I *was*, I must have fallen asleep."

"You get up now?" the dog asked, still standing over Jack.

"Have I been paged?"

"No."

"Are we on fire?"

"No."

"Then, no. I not get up now," insisted Jack.

"I'm hungry," grumbled Fritz.

"Then go to the galley and eat breakfast," muttered Jack.

Fritz hopped off the sofa to the floor, "OK, fine."

"Wake me when we get to G'Naroth Sarat," grunted Jack, rolling over on his side.

■ ■ ■

Squeak - squeak. Squeak - squeak. Squeak - squeak - squeak - squeak - squeak - squeak... "Oh my *God,* stop it," scolded Jack, his eyes still closed. "Where did you get a squeaky toy?" he mumbled, still mostly asleep.

"Allie gave to me," replied Fritz, his mouth full of soft, fuzzy plushiness.

"Or did you *take* it?"

"She gave," insisted the Shepherd.

"Are you sure?"

"Yes."

Steele could feel hot breath on his face and opened one eye, a giant black nose filling his field of vision. His other eye opened, revealing a continuation of the picture; a stuffed plush toy resembling a cheeseburger in his mouth. Jack snorted a chuckle.

"You still on couch."

"Yes."

"You get up now..."

Steele stretched, "We're at G'Naroth Sarat?"

"Orbit."

■ ■ ■

G'Naroth Sarat was a marvelous example of terraforming technology even though it was still a work in progress. About half the planet's landmasses were covered in a rich green tapestry of agriculture; the other half, sharp mountain ranges and dry, rolling, arid deserts. The weather control system produced clouds and rain once a day to cool the mean average temperature from the mid-eighty degree range to the mid-seventy degree range, and provide the needed precipitation for efficient crop development.

Not without its urban and industrial districts, the largest city on the planet, Amanpoor, ringed the space port like a bowl; the buildings reaching up like a wall around it. All approaches to the port were from the ocean side, crossing over the rippling blue water to the dull gray landing pads surrounded by emerald green ground cover.

A video inset flickered into existence on the main screen, *"Ground control to Perseus, good afternoon,"* began the traffic coordinator. *"We have you on final approach. Feeding you approach and telemetry control information... now."* An overlay of telemetry data appeared on the big screen with navigation lines, speeds and coordinates. *"You are cleared for set-down on pad, zeta-three-seven - indicated on your screen. Please be aware of possible cross traffic."*

"Zeta-three-seven, confirmed," replied Commander Reegan.

"Current temperature in the Amanpoor area is eighty-six degrees, wind from the west at ten. One hour of rain scheduled this evening at seven, sunset at eight-fifteen. Should make for an interesting sunset..."

"Thank you, ground control."

The video link with the traffic coordinator winked out. "He looked so real," remarked Chase standing next to Jack behind the Commander's seat.

"He was," replied Reegan, watching their descent. "They're not all AI like the one at Nelson's Point..."

"Bit of a Chatty Cathy, though," remarked Steele.

"A what?" asked Ragnaar.

Steele frowned, "Chatty Cathy - it's a doll from... *never mind,*" he waved.

The spaceport grew as they approached, the gray concrete oval landing pads of all sizes, surrounded by rich green landscaping that stretched for miles to the edge of the city. Low hangar-like buildings dotted the spaceport, dwarfed by the ships parked on the landing pads. All of it was toy-like, a perfect diorama, the colors so vivid, the wall of skyscrapers silhouetted against a turquoise sky. The flashing navigation lines directed them down to a pad several rows inland from the water.

A target icon flashed on the left of the screen moving right, "Cross traffic left, altitude thirty-four-hundred."

Ragnaar nodded, "I saw him. He'll pass over us by seven-hundred." He double-checked their glide slope and rate of decent.

"There have to be almost a hundred landing pads down there," whispered Chase, his eyes trying to take it all in at once.

"A hundred and seventy square miles of space port," remarked Commander Reegan. "And I'm counting five FreeRanger ships so far..."

Steel leaned over his shoulder, "Where?"

"Patrol gunships here and here," Reegan marked them on his command screen, the identifiers appearing on the big screen. "A cutter here," he pointed, "a destroyer here, and an armed transport over there..."

"Keep looking, see if you can find any more. And see if you can find any history on any of them.."

■ ■ ■

Z-37. The bright yellow numbers painted on the concrete stretched for fifty feet under the hull of the Perseus, nearly unreadable at an angle standing at the base of the ship's ramp. But in case you had a brainfart and forgot where you parked your ship, an illuminated can-sign marked the entrance to the underground metro, and another on the front of the low warehouse building that was nothing more than a sloping entrance to the underground shipping system. Cargo shuttles sat in the always-open doors waiting for tasking. Just beyond the concrete; manicured hedges and tailored ground cover.

Stepping off the ramp, Steele looked up at the graying sky. He knew what time it was, he didn't have to look, "Right on time," he observed.

"Sir?"

He shot Ragnaar a bemused smirk, "The weathermen at home can't even predict rain for the right day much less down to the minute..."

"Well to be fair, Mr. Mercury, they have the benefit of actual weather control here."

Steele watched the first few drops splatter on the concrete, "Our Air Force has a program that can make weather, it's called HAARP - *High Frequency Active Auroral Research Program.*"

"That doesn't sound much like a weather system," interrupted Ragnaar.

"No it doesn't, does it..." replied Jack. "That's the innocuous public name the government uses hoping not to scare the citizens. HAARP actually stands for, *High Altitude Active Rain Production.* The problem with it is, they can create the weather... but they can't stop it once they start it. And they can't steer it. They were hoping to create destructive weather as a guidable weapon and in the process of testing created a few rather devastating hurricanes, two of which hit our own country doing extensive damage. Not to mention the hordes of tornado spawns..."

"That is... regrettable. Is it still in use?"

"It was announced a couple years ago that the project was being discontinued. That the antenna arrays and equipment were being dismantled - but that was a lie to appease the conspiracy theorists, who've since developed new ways of detecting HAARP's ELF and VLF radio transmissions."

"What are we talking about?" asked Chase stepping off the ramp to the landing pad followed by Mercedes Huang.

"Weather control," offered Ragnaar.

Chase had to decide whether to feign interest or not. *Not.* "Ah," he nodded blankly. He held his hand out, rewarded by catching some hefty raindrops, "We'd better get going before it opens up on us..."

"Mmm," grunted Jack, turning for the underground metro entrance. "You guys got your shopping list?"

"Aye, sir," confirmed Ragnaar, exchanging glances with Chase.

"I'm still not real clear on what *we're* doing Mr. Mercury..." inquired Mercedes, trailing the three men.

"Fishing, Ms. Huang. We're going fishing."

▄ ▄ ▄

282

Steele wasn't sure what to expect but the tunnels leading to the underground metro were clean, mostly smooth, featureless concrete. Well-lit, lined with digital video screens the thickness of a sheet of paper, bombarding visitors with advertisements and commercials for every conceivable product, attraction, restaurant, club and business in Amanpoor.

Pedestrian traffic came to a sudden halt just before the entrance to the metro station and Steele eyed the other people around them coming from other landing pads headed into the city. "What's going on, Mr. Ragnaar?" he whispered.

"Security checkpoint." Ragnaar glanced at his shipmates, "Nobody is carrying anything, right? No weapons? Being on the border, they're very strict here."

"Wait," whispered Steele, "I thought you could get almost anything here? Small arms included."

"You can," replied Ragnaar, moving up in line. "But everything is transferred directly to the ship. No one can take personal delivery of a weapon."

Steele eyed the armed security team as they neared the checkpoint, "Doesn't seem to apply to them though does it..."

The team leader waved people through the checkpoint, "Keep walking, the train is waiting. That's it, move along..." He occasionally glanced over at the officer watching the scanner screen for any sign that someone might need to be stopped or questioned.

Approaching the open doors of the train, Steele took a deep breath, not realizing he'd been controlling his breathing. He felt naked being unarmed, and this place which had previously seemed shiny and welcoming, suddenly put him ill at ease. His little voice had been silent for a long time... months. But suddenly it felt the need to whisper in his ear. He wondered what it was trying to tell him.

Sitting in front of Jack and Mercedes, Chase and Ragnaar turned sideways so they could converse discreetly over their seat backs. Ragnaar glanced around and lowered his voice, "We'll be getting off before you at the *Trade Exchange* building, it's an underground stop. You'll be getting off in the city at *Central Street Square* after the train leaves the tunnels..."

Nearly silent, the magnetic drive of the underground metro propelled it through the tunnel on an antigravity bed across the width of Amanpoor's Space Port, stopping occasionally to pick up more passengers heading into the city from the landing pads.

"You've been here before," offered Jack, glancing at the people around them.

"I have," replied Ragnaar, leaning closer. "It's a fairly safe city but don't get complacent. *The Black Hole Bar & Grille* is an eight block walk from your stop. Walk it - no ground transportation and no shortcuts. It's in your MOBIUS," he added, tapping on the unit around Jack's wrist. "Don't forget to use it."

"No ground transportation?"

"It's not worth the hassle or the cost. The cabbies will drive you around the city for an hour for a ten-minute walk..." Steele nodded his understanding. "And for the love of the Gods, don't buy *anything* from *anyone* on the street..."

"Got it..."

Chase heard the announcement for the next stop, "That's us..."

"Hey," said Jack reaching out as Chase and Ragnaar rose from their seats. Chase shot his friend an inquisitive look. "Whatever you do, don't buy any Tribbles," teased Steele. They shared a knowing chuckle and a brotherly fist bump.

As the train rocked to a swift but gentle stop and the two men shuffled toward the open doors to the platform for the Trade Exchange, Ragnaar nudged Chase Holt's elbow, "What the hellion is a *Tribble?*"

■ ■ ■

In its day, the G'Naroth Sarat Security Service building was not only a work of art but a technogeek's dreamworld. Like any other government entity anywhere, it had seen better days... but the view was still good. Even though it was less than a third in size among the other buildings surrounding it, it held a prominent spot in the city skyline overlooking Amanpoor's Space Port, its all-black structure striking a somewhat sinister silhouette.

The Sergeant walking past the Inspector's office saw the rain pattering across the windows, the city lights and buildings distorted through the rain-slicked glass. "Damn, raining pretty good... Seems early today..."

The Inspector's attention did not stray from the report on his computer screen, "Uh-hum... Nah, seven-fifteen..."

The Sergeant neither criticized nor commented on the disjointed reply from the man in the windowed office. Perhaps one day, the Inspector would move over to the coveted side of the building that overlooked the Space Port and the ocean beyond it and *he* could eventually have the windowed office - even if it *did* overlook the city. "Say Inspector, did Data Bridge get a hold of you? They were looking for you earlier..."

"Yeah, sure..." The words sunk in and Inspector Brooker's attention snapped away from the report he was engrossed in, the dark stubble on his jawline marking a long day. "Wait, what? *Who* was looking for me?"

"Somebody over at Data Bridge. About an hour ago..."

Brooker ran his hand over the top of his shaved head in exasperation, "*Dammit.* Did they think of looking for me in my office?" He pushed away from the desk and rose to his feet, his chair rolling back and banging against the wall. "Do I always have to hold their hand?" He brushed past the Sergeant in the doorway, "Thanks Sarge..."

The Sergeant watched him disappear down the corridor, glancing out the twenty-third-story window at the soggy city one more time before heading off to resume his duties.

■ ■ ■

Brooker swung the door wide, strolling into the Data Bridge, lined with rows of security techs monitoring scores of monitors, large and small, recording data from all over the Amanpoor Region. "So who's the freaking genius that couldn't find me hiding so cleverly in my office?" he exclaimed. No response, the deafening roar of silence - broken only by the sounds of the digital video feeds. "Alright, fine. I get it. Nobody wants to admit to being so stinking bad at hide and seek... Does *anyone* have something for me, or did I just walk all the way over here for my frigging health?" He waved his arms , "So the Sarge just made it up..?"

A woman with short-cropped platinum hair rolled away from her work station waving him over, having called up the video playback. "Inspector..."

"Oh, good, I was beginning to think I was invisible," he snarked, sauntering over.

"Apologies, Inspector, we've had a shift change. This is what was caught in the incoming Zeta checkpoint." She directed his attention to the video.

"Help me out here, Sweetness, what am I looking at?"

"Here, this man," she pointed, "he has an implant." She switched color frequencies to something resembling night vision, catching a vibrant glow in the man's left eye.

"What's your point?" asked Brooker. "Lots of people have implants..."

285

She drew his attention to the readouts, "His heart rate changes but his breathing remains even. It just appeared odd to the operator." She indicated the other people with the man in the video, "These three people with him had no such reaction. Now, the data cores are still checking facials but this man, the big one with the face tattoo, is a known pirate. We haven't seen him here in five or six years..."

Brooker rubbed the stubble on his chin, "Well, being a pirate isn't a crime, at least not on G'Naroth Sarat. But it might warrant a look. Nothing on the other three then..."

"Not yet, Inspector."

"Send this to my office - and stay on this. It's probably nothing but this is your assignment until we know more. If I'm not in my office, use my MOBIUS."

"I understand, Inspector."

■ ■ ■

It wasn't until the train emerged from the tunnel and rain splattered the roof of the train that Jack and Mercedes realized the roof of the train was glass. It curved over the top and down the sides to about waist level, allowing an uninterrupted view of the city around them. The metro system rose several stories above the streets, the antigravity bed supported by the surrounding buildings. When a vehicle passed overhead he involuntarily sucked in, quickly realizing traffic passed around them at multiple levels, above *and* below.

"Hoh," huffed Mercedes, "It's - it's like Blade Runner or the Fifth Element... This - this is *unbelievable*."

Steele chuckled, "Says the woman who flew here across space. Through jump gates. Across multiple solar systems. On a star ship."

"Yeah, well... allow me my amazement, will you? I've just stepped into a movie I grew up with."

"What I find remarkable," whispered Jack, "is the amazing accuracy of foresight in some of our Hollywood directors like Ridley Scott and George Lucas..."

"Makes you wonder if they knew something we didn't," replied Mercedes, glued to the window.

Steele tugged on her elbow as he rose from his seat, "C'mon, this is our stop..."

■ ■ ■

At street level, clear awnings extended over the sidewalks, automatically activated by the rain. Under their protection, Jack Steele and Mercedes Huang wove their way along the crowded sidewalks past shops, businesses, massive corporations and the occasional sidewalk vendor selling all manner of goods.

"Smells good," commented Steele, his stomach reminding him it had missed an earlier meal.

"Remember what Ragnaar said," reminded Mercedes, wagging her finger at him.

"I know, I know. Just saying." Steele paused, looking in a shop window at nothing in particular.

"What are you looking at?" Mercedes wondered aloud, standing next to him, looking at the same nothing.

"I think we're being followed."

"The woman in the navy-blue jacket?"

Steele glanced at Mercedes out of the corner of his eye without turning his head, "No, where do you see her? I'm talking about the guy in the gray suit and hat across the street."

"I see him," said Mercedes shifting her body, looking at the reflection in the glass over her shoulder. "Are you sure about him?"

"He moves when we move, stops when we stop..."

"Hmm," snorted Mercedes, "Not too obvious then, huh?"

"Where's the woman?" asked Jack.

"Same side as we're on, about thirty-feet back. She ducked into a business when we stopped."

Jack took her by the hand and they walked leisurely, hand-in-hand trying to catch glimpses in the windows they passed. They paused and Jack gently spun Mercedes into a hug, looking over her shoulder. "Yep. Got her." The woman quickly hailed a cab, the vehicle descending from an air-lane above the street. "Dammit," he groaned, "she knows I made her."

"What do you suppose they want?" asked Mercedes as they unwrapped and walked on.

The cab eased past, ascending back into an air-lane above the street, the woman peering at them through tinted windows. Steele couldn't help but smile, catching it out of the corner of his eye. "I don't know..." It just reminded him how naked he felt without a weapon on him. Suddenly intrigued, he steered Mercedes through the front doors of a business with oversized spaceship models decorating the lobby and interior.

"Toys?" she asked, a sarcastic tone adding volumes to the single word inquiry.

"Dealership. I think."

■ ■ ■

Having been summoned on his MOBIUS, Inspector Brooker strolled back through the Data Bridge door, "What have you got for me, Sweetness?"

"You be the judge, Inspector..." Motioning to an empty chair, the female Data Bridge officer with the short platinum hair pulled up digital reports on her twin screens as he rolled up next to her. "The guy with the facial tattoo is a pirate named Ragnaar. He has, *or had,* a brother named Deeter, also a pirate. There are no records of either one having being seen in the last five to six years - either here or anywhere else... Until just recently." She tapped Ragnaar's image on the screen, "Our friend here, was spotted at Nelson's Point with this man," she tapped on Jack Steele's image.

"What about the other two?" asked Brooker.

"They were *also* seen together at Nelsons Point..."

"So they've switched partners?"

"It appears so. And these two," she pointed at Chase Holt and Mercedes Huang, "were wanted for questioning about an incident that happened at one of the station's repair docks..."

"What kind of incident?" he interrupted.

"Nelson's Point wasn't terribly forthcoming with the details, but the best I could gather, two bodies were recovered in the maintenance ring and it was in the same vicinity that a freelancer's ship was destroyed, right at the repair dock."

"What? How?"

"I heard *mysterious explosion*, I heard *GOD jump malfunction* where a section of the ship jumped leaving the rest behind in segments. Depends on who you talk to..."

Brooker shook his head, "I've never heard of a jump malfunction like that - I wonder if it's even possible." He motioned toward their pictures, "Do we have names for these two?"

"No. But here's where it starts to get involved..." She pointed at Steele's photo, "This guy, Jax Mercury, is the one who refused the station's requests for crew interviews. It's not clear if he's the captain or owner of the Perseus. When the Station refused to let his ship depart until the security teams could conduct the interviews, the Perseus forced itself free, tearing off a docking arm and destroying a docking spoke that was still attached. Then it outran a gunship that tried to pursue it..."

Brooker pointed to an image of the Perseus, *"That* thing?" He pursed his lips, "Sounds awfully guilty to me... Send out a service crew to visually inspect the exterior of their ship. See if we can confirm any damage without tipping our hand."

She nodded. "But there's more..."

Brooker's eyes narrowed, "More..." he repeated, deadpan.

"There's another hit on his name, about a year ago. It's lengthy. It occurred at Rikovik's Reef..."

"Ugh," he grunted, "garbage heap."

She pulled up a rough outline of the Revenge. "He docked in a frigate called the Raven, it was reported they were searching for salvage parts."

"Sounds reasonable enough..."

"Except there was some kind of firefight in the industrial sector near the establishment they had been directed to and several locals were killed. Video footage from a transport vehicle placed him in the vicinity. While security teams were searching for the suspects, his group temporarily disappeared. Mercury reappeared later, on the Island..."

"That's the *Syndicate* side of the Reef..." coughed Brooker.

"Aaand," she continued, "another firefight ensued. He broke out a harem of the Syndicate's girls, killed several of their men, stole a yacht, severely damaged the yacht basin, and destroyed two security patrol craft in the process of escaping to Aegeron Pass with the assistance of his ship, The Raven."

Brooker ran his hand over his shaved head, "Who, *what* is this guy? Pirates don't even mess with the Syndicate." He stared at Steele's picture on the screen, "Mr. Mercury is either lucky or crazy..."

"Or both," offered the Data Bridge officer.

"In any case he's dangerous." Brooker's stare persisted, "What are you, Mercury... Pirate? Freelancer? Contractor...?" He snapped out of his thoughts, "Where are they now?"

"Looks like the pirate and the other man got off at the Trade Exchange building, here," she pointed at the Metro map on the screen.

"Then they split up. Where's Mercury and the woman?"

"Got off the Metro at Central Street Square and proceeded up Central on foot. They don't seem to be in any hurry..."

He tapped on the edge of the monitor, "Cameras?"

She made a face of distaste, "That whole sector of Central has been a problem. Maintenance doesn't know if it's our controllers up here, or bad lines out in the field. They've been working on it for almost a week. Again."

The Inspector cursed under his breath, "Do we have anybody out there?"

"Two plainclothes observing."

Brooker straightened up and tapped on his MOBIUS, "Good, link us up. I'm heading out there."

■ ■ ■

Steele examined a model perched on a pedestal, admiring the ship's lines as he glanced past it through the showroom window across the street at the man in the gray suit and hat. The woman in the blue jacket had returned, sitting at an open-air cafe not far from her partner. The rain had stopped and the awnings were retracting against the buildings.

"Welcome to *Zin's*. Isn't she a beauty?" asked the salesman, as he strolled casually across the sales floor. "I'm Zin." He was impeccably dressed, and his pale, flawless, smooth skin, looked uncomfortably drum-tight. "I have one to test fly sitting on *alpha two-two...*"

"Tell me more about her," said Steele, running his finger along the lines of the ship while keeping an eye on the darkening street, lights flickering to life as the shadows deepened.

"You have a good eye, sir," complimented Zin, "the *Velocitor* is in a class by herself. She accepts a crew of four, with accommodations for two more, for a total of six..."

"Just in case you have... *passengers*," commented Steele with a hint of sarcasm.

"Exactly," continued Zin. "Designed for rather long range for a ship of her size, she has a small, *shielded*, cargo capacity, for that more... compact, *extra-valuable* cargo," he smirked smugly. "Very popular with certain sectors of the business delivery community."

Steele nodded his appreciation. *Like smugglers.* "Armor, shields, armament?"

"She comes well equipped, and she's *very* fast." The model lit up in sections as he spoke of the highlights; "Four gimbal-mounted forward guns, with a twenty-degree arc. One top turret with two guns - unobstructed firing arc. And one bottom turret at the stern with two guns that has a forty-five-degree arc. Her armor is a light composite - but very sturdy and she has very special, *fourth* generation, Garland-Pulmon particle shields. Very tough, very fast recharge."

"Power system?"

"Heavy duty, also by Garland-Pulmon. Well suited to keep all her systems fed with plenty of reserve. Even adequate for the optional GOD Drive..."

Steele was casually eyeing a third man who had joined the other two, a hover car lifting away, leaving him at the sidewalk cafe. "Can the ship you have in stock accommodate the drive unit?"

"Our demo *does* have a GOD drive. However, if you purchased a standard Velocitor it could be retrofitted with some modifications," nodded Zin. "With the drive, you sacrifice the extra two seats and a small portion of your cargo space..."

"A fair tradeoff," smiled Steele, turning away from the windows.

"You would of course have to bring her back *here* to the dealership for the upgrade..."

Steele nodded, "Of course..." He pinched his lower lip, "Uhh, considering you accommodate, er, *clients* from all walks of life..."

"Yes..?"

"I'm assuming you have a back exit..."

■ ■ ■

After a circuitous route to be assured they hadn't been followed, the customer service driver for Zin's dealership descended the limousine from an air-lane to the entrance of The Black Hole Bar & Grille. Opening with a hum, the vehicle's door swung up over the roof, allowing its riders an effortless exit.

Stepping out, Mercedes Huang smoothed her hair, "That was... *interesting.*"

Steele gave a nod to the driver as the door dropped, stepping up next to his partner in crime, "Yes. Yes, it was..."

"I'm not sure I understand how he knows when he's in his lane up there or not. Have you driven something like that?"

Jack shook his head, "No, in fact I was wondering the same thing. It feels a little unnatural in a car... Not like driving, not like flying..."

"Yeah," she agreed, "just... *weird.*"

Steele pulled on the heavy wooden door for The Black Hole Bar & Grille, "I'm glad no one was following us - can you imagine what a chase would feel like?"

Mercedes shivered, "Frightening thought..."

Sandwiched between two much larger buildings, it felt like the The Black Hole Bar & Grille was a historical survivor of some sort, from another era. It wasn't modern steel and glass, it was old school dark wood and roughhewn stone with a polished marble bar and dimly lit booths. Considerably more expansive inside than the outward appearance revealed, a three-man band played somewhere off in the darkness. The smells drifting through the restaurant only served to reawaken Steele's grumbling stomach. His artificial eye switched to night vision, revealing the extent of the crowded interior, groups of people congregated around the bar two and three deep, standing in between tables and booths.

"This is going to be a needle in a hay stack..." whispered Mercedes.

"Just drink, wander around and listen in. Shoot me something on MOBIUS if you hear anything interesting."

"You going to order something to eat?"

Steele took a deep breath, "If it tastes half as good as it smells, yes. You?"

Mercedes smiled wryly looking over her shoulder and winked seductively, "Somebody will feed me..." She disappeared in the moving crowd headed for the bar.

Finding an available high top table, Steele took some time to eat while he watched the crowd, scrutinizing, carefully searching for anyone in uniform, listening to the conversations of the people around him and passers-by. Mercedes drifted past, drink in hand, plucking a morsel of food off his plate as she passed, "Uniforms on the other side of the bar..." She kept walking, melting back into the crowd.

Finishing off the food on his plate, he rose and casually headed around the bar in search of FreeRanger Navy uniforms.

■ ■ ■

Sitting with her back to the bar, an empty seat to each side of her, watching the people on the dance floor, Steele instantly took notice of the redhead in uniform. "Excuse me, I don't mean to bother you, but my knee is killing me," he lied, "might I sit for a couple of minutes?" The Ensign looked up at him and silently nodded at the seat on her left while sipping her drink. Jack eased himself into the chair, playing the wounded soul, indicating the pips on her collar, "Ensign?"

She regarded him cautiously, "Yes."

"Thank you for the seat, Ensign." Steele held out his hand, "Jax Mercury..."

She shook his hand, wary of his politeness, "You're welcome. *Grinleeah,*" she offered. Steele was shocked by the intensity of her green eyes and he took a moment to consider where the reflections were coming from that created the glowing effect. "You're staring..."

Steele looked away reflexively, "Sorry, your eyes are so green..." He glanced back, "Probably sounds stupid but it almost looked like they were glowing - I was trying to figure out how..."

"I was flash-blinded as a child. My eyes are genetic implants from a large cat called a *Corsicat.*"

Steele raised one eyebrow in surprise, "I didn't know that was possible."

The woman nodded. "They are lab grown nowadays, they make excellent replacements for a multitude of reasons. The most distinct advantage, of course, is I see very well in the dark..."

"Who sees what now?" asked a man in uniform appearing on her other side.

"We were discussing my eyes," replied the woman. "I guess they're glowing in the lights from the dance floor."

The man with the Commander pips on his collar smiled, "Mesmerizing, aren't they?"

"Hypnotic," agreed Steele.

"Mr. Mercury," motioned the Ensign, "my husband, T. B. Yafusco. Tibby, this is Jax Mercury."

The two men shook hands, "I'm sorry Mr. Yafusco..."

"Tibby."

"Tibby. I'm sorry for intruding, I was just needing a few minutes to rest my knee..." he began to rise from the seat.

Tibby dismissed the idea with a casual wave, "Sit, sit. Grinah and I don't mind." He looked out toward the dance floor, "Besides, I think the

293

Lieutenant will be out there for a while." Following his gaze, Steele realized the FreeRanger Lieutenant out on the dance floor was being entertained by Mercedes Huang. Tibby motioned towards Steele's nearly empty snifter, "What are you drinking there?"

"Diterian brandy..."

"Ah, a lady's drink." He waved at the bartender for an additional glass. "Try something new," He poured a clear liquid from a bottle on the bar into a small glass with two cubes of ice in it and handed it to Jack. "Sip, don't gulp."

It felt cold on Steele's tongue but going down it was like flaming razorblades and his eyes watered almost immediately, a flush hitting his face and forehead. "Hoh..." It took his breath away.

Tibby grinned, "That's all right, Kleer grows on you," he waved. "So, I don't see any rank on you," he indicated Jack's collar, "what do you do?"

"Ship owner," wheezed Steele, still trying to catch his breath.

"Ah," nodded Tibby. "Who do you work for... fly for?"

"My company," replied Jack, regaining some of his composure. *Need to take smaller sips of this stuff.* "Mercury Transport," he fibbed.

Still half-seated in his own chair, Tibby leaned in across Grinah, "You're about the same age as we are, how did you manage that?"

Steele shrugged, "I was kind of sucked into it actually. My first ship was a wreck when I first got her. We sort of rescued her from the previous owner who had left her in such disrepair... It took us weeks with a full crew of volunteers to make her livable and flyable..."

"Volunteers?" frowned Grinah dubiously.

"Friends and family," offered Jack. "Lots and lots of friends. Engineers, mechanics... a lot of hard work, but she eventually flew. Then it was a matter of searching reclaim yards for parts to get her really ship-shape."

Grinah's green eyes sparkled in the play of the lights, "How long did it all take? To get her ship-shape?"

"About a year. Now the second ship..."

"Second ship?" Interrupted Tibby.

"Yes. The second ship we found about a year later..."

Grinah's head tilted, "You *found* a ship..."

"Brand new as far as we could tell," continued Jack, sipping the Kleer gingerly. Each time it seemed to be a little easier than the sip before it - though it always had a bite. "It was left in an abandoned hangar. Must have been there for some time, nearly all her cells were dead. We had to plug her in," he gestured, "just to get aboard her."

"Amazing," mumbled Grinah, not sure if she believed the tale or not.

"What type of ship was it?" asked Tibby.

"A nice little frigate."

"Whaat?" Tibby pulled back looking gobsmacked. "Who abandons a perfectly good frigate?" He moved back in, "Did you search her records for ownership?"

"That's the thing," offered Jack, "all her record files were wiped." He swiped his hand through the air, "Clean as could be. Universal charts, star maps, travel logs, crew roster... *all* gone."

T. B. Yafusco straightened up scratching his forehead. "You are one lucky... did you *look* for the owner?"

Steele shrugged again, "We stayed in the area for at least another month, flew her around; *nothing.*"

"By the Gods," muttered Tibby, sipping his Kleer. "So now you've got *two* ships..."

"Probably a good thing," added Jack. "Because the first one wasn't doing well. We didn't expect her to last forever, but she was falling apart fast. We couldn't keep up with all the repairs and maintenance she constantly needed. We had to retire her."

"Mmm, a pity." Yafusco straightened, "Sometimes even the professional shipyard reconditions don't hold together for very long. Something about the original hull integrity never being quite what it was..."

"And the stresses of space," added Grinah.

Steele accepted a refill of Kleer, missing the silent signals from the bartender. "Now the third ship..."

"Third?" objected Tibby, pausing the refill mid-pour. "You joke, no?"

Jack shook his head, "No, she's the one we came in on," he flipped his thumb in the direction of Amanpoor's port. He looked around and adjusted his thumb-point to what felt more right.

"And how did you get *this* one?" asked Grinah.

"I got this one from my Uncle Sam. His firm wanted us to test this new transport design - it's kind of a lend-lease deal. Whatever we profit during testing we share with his firm..."

"And if it breaks apart during use?" inquired Grinah.

"Yeah," smirked Jack, "That would be bad." He chewed on his tongue and bit the inside of his lips realizing they were going numb. *That can't be good.*

"So do you still have the little frigate too?" asked Tibby, leaning in again.

"Sure," admitted Jack. "She's under contract doing security escorts..." he fibbed. "More profitable than using her for our own escort. We just hire local if we need it."

Tibby nodded his appreciation, "Smart." He leaned against the bar, half standing half sitting on the tall barstool. "So why aren't you sitting behind a desk in a comfortable office somewhere?"

Steele smirked crookedly and waved at their surroundings as the lights flickered to the beat of the music, "What, and give all *this* up?" They all laughed. "So what about you two?" He circled the two of them with his index finger, "What's your story..?"

CHAPTER TWENTY FIVE

VELORA PRIME SYSTEM : *VELORIAN NAVY FLAGSHIP, WRONIN*

Closed to other visitors, the Wronin's Officers Club was empty except for one extended table. Alité Galaýa Steele, Queen of Veloria stood at the head of the table, surrounded by the ship's senior staff, the UFW Commander who had bought the Wronin to Veloria with his crew, and an assortment of senior UFW instructors. She glanced at the faces around her as she sat, "Gentlemen," she waved, "please, be seated." Lifting a warm bread roll out of the basket in front of her she set it on her plate and tore it open, steam rising from its sweet dough. "So tell me Commander," she began, looking to the UFW Officer at her right. "How is our ship, is she ready? Is our crew ready?"

"The ship is doing very well, your Majesty. And her crew," he indicated Walt across the table from him at the Queen's left, "as your Captain will confirm, has done exceedingly well. They have studied hard and worked even harder. My instructors are very pleased with the results. And though it was a bit crowded at first, it was a brilliant idea to parallel-train a secondary crew in preparation for the arrival of the *Hyperion...*"

The queen tore a morsel off her roll and set it on her tongue. "When is she due to arrive, Commander?"

"Twenty-three days, your Majesty, I checked this morning. She is currently running time trials and equipment testing near the Naval Yards on Tanzia."

"Wonderful! And the Wronin, when have you scheduled her shake-down cruise?"

Walt cleared his throat, "We have already done that, your Majesty. We have run her across Velora Prime thru to and around New Vanus and back, and through to Cariloon and Zender's Trek and back..."

"Aww," she pouted momentarily, "I should have liked to participate in that milestone of our Navy's rebirth..."

Walt's brow furrowed, "I apologize, your Majesty, I had no idea..."

"No matter," she rebounded, gesturing politely, "I will take great pleasure in the shakedown of the Hyperion, then." She glanced over at Commander

Walrick a few seats down the table from Walt, "Commander Walrick, how is the Wronin's squadron progressing?"

"We have two squadrons aboard the Wronin, your Majesty. And they are settling in quite nicely; I do not foresee any issues even if we were to deploy tomorrow."

"So they are ready then..."

"Yes, your Majesty."

"Splendid," she smiled, turning back to the UFW Officer at her right. "Commander, will you be staying on with us to familiarize our second crew to the Hyperion when she arrives?"

The Commander leaned back momentarily to allow a food server to deposit a plate of salad in front of him. "No ma'am. The Hyperion will have her own training crew to familiarize your people with her. Honestly, considering how well your secondary crew is doing, I don't expect that to take long... maybe two weeks."

Prime Minister Nitram Marconus paused, his salad-laden fork suspended above his plate, "Your Majesty, have you decided on a commander for the Hyperion yet? Perhaps the Admiral?"

Alité's eyes darkened at the mention of her husband, "The King is otherwise occupied with the UFW for the foreseeable future, Boney. You, Mr. Edgars and I, will have to discuss other possible options..."

"Have you heard from..." A sharp glance flashed in his direction from the Queen, cut Boney off mid-sentence and he wisely let the topic drop from the conversation.

"Your Majesty," offered the UFW Commander, "I am sure we could supply you with a list of viable candidates; officers with years of experience who have retired from UFW service but may not be entirely ready to give up the life..."

"I appreciate the offer Commander, please see that the Prime Minister Marconus gets that information..."

■ ■ ■

Commander Walrick was watching over the shoulder of the traffic control officers in the Wronin's flight tower, an armed shuttle with a purple stripe on it positioning to launch off the fantail. "Hold the Queen's shuttle there, wait for her escort flight."

"Aye, sir."

"Clear her escort flight as soon as they're in position."

"Aye, sir."

A set of four, heavily armed Warthog *D* series fighters with purple tails maneuvered past the waiting shuttle, snaking past in a line, heading for the fantail. A P6 Spectre with a six-man crew, set up for electronic and sensor dominance warfare, jagged purple slashes decorating its hull followed in close trail.

"Royal Guard you are clear for launch..."

"Royal Lead, copy."

The blue glow of their anti-gravity systems reflected off the deck as they eased out through the shimmering static of the stasis field and over the fantail into space. Handpicked flight crews, the Royal Guard were tasked with escort and protection of the Royal family and government officials like the Prime Minister whenever their craft left the ground, a personal security detachment riding with them on their shuttle.

"Royal Shuttle, you are clear for launch..."

"Copy that - launching. Thanks for the hospitality, Wronin."

Walrick let out a silent sigh of relief that things had gone well. Not that the Queen made him particularly nervous, no, they had grown up together. The layers of their friendship ran deep - only blood could bring them closer. No, it had more to do with making sure he lived up to the trust she had put into him. Quite often the burden felt suffocating, crushing. But she always took notice of his efforts and that always seemed to lighten the load.

"CAG, the bridge has a ship with no broadcast ping entering sensor range..."

Walrick moved over to the plotting table, "Show me."

"Here," pointed the traffic officer.

"How many flights are out?"

"Two."

Walrick pinched his lower lip for a moment as he scanned the holo-chart, eyeing the progress of the Queen's flight, heading to the surface. "Send Gray Flight to say hello," he ordered, touching their holographic icon. "And launch a third flight."

"Aye, sir."

"I just don't like the timing of their arrival..." he watched the movement of the Queen's flight.

"If it makes you feel any better, CAG," he indicated the unidentified craft, "they don't seem to be in any hurry..."

■ ■ ■

The shuttle's co-pilot looked back over his shoulder, Incoming message for you, your Majesty..."

"Send it to my TESS, please," replied Alité, sitting reclined in a semi-private cubby away from the other people on the flight. The holo-screen popped open and she grabbed a corner, angling it. TESS didn't even have time to announce the call, the video feed pushing her image to the side, filling the screen, the face of the Grand Matron of the Royal House looking a little disheveled.

"Lady Phyllis..."

"Your Highness..."

Alité glanced at the time on the corner of her screen, "It's past midnight your time, what is it that could not wait until morning?"

"It's that *boy* again, your Highness... I can't... I just... *Ooooo...*"

"The *Prince?*"

"Yes..." sighed the woman, trying to gather her composure. "I don't know what I'm going to do about that boy..."

"Alright, calm down Lady Phyllis. What did Colton do *this* time?"

"He's disappeared again. He's been gone for hours, and it's dark..."

■ ■ ■

Colton Steele was not your typical six-year old. Well, nearly six. There was nothing typical about him. Half Velorian and half human, his genes were quickly pushing him past his friends and classmates to the size of an average ten-year old, just barely under four feet tall already.

With a strong independent streak in him, he had few fears and an intellect far beyond his age. He learned quickly, was highly inquisitive, physically gifted, adventurous and he adapted easily. Despite all that and the fact that he was a Prince, it was harder than one might think to live up to all the expectations. None of his friends or classmates could understand, his teachers and instructors couldn't understand... But nature? Nature didn't judge. Nature didn't care one way or the other - it had no opinion. It was patiently waiting for him when he arrived, no matter how long it had been since his last visit. It didn't complain, it simply *was*. Perhaps that's why he loved it so much; it offered such a wide array of wonders without demanding much of him. It invited exploration, introspection and close examination without expectation. Of course, it required *respect*. You couldn't go running around willy-nilly without nature reminding you occasionally that she was not to be trifled with - like the day he trudged through that field of nettle flowers. In shorts. His legs were swollen and itchy for days. Who knew? That was the day nature taught him to be more observant. And, to wear long pants.

He learned something new each time he ventured out, far more than when adults were around... *Don't touch that, don't climb that, don't go in there, don't wander too far...* Adults could be such killjoys.

About twelve feet off the ground, Colton climbed into the no-spin hammock he'd hung from solid limbs of neighboring trees. It had taken a couple of tries to get it just right so he left it up permanently, his go-to resting place for days when he didn't make it back before dark. Another lesson nature had taught him; don't wander aimlessly in the dark. Find a place to rest. And as an addendum; don't rest on the ground, there are dangerous things in the forest that come out to hunt at night. He didn't fancy the thought of being something's midnight snack.

He hung his knapsack on a branch within easy reach above his head, along with his walking staff by its leather wrist strap. But his training Katana never left his possession, it lay alongside him in its sheath.

Laying back, the leaves above radiated light. A soft, barely discernible glow, a canopy of nightlights, their photo-reactive cells absorbing the light from the sun and storing it for the night. A breeze played through the trees with a hush, the leaves moving gently, their light dancing to the sound of chirping insects and twitters of night birds flitting through the branches high above.

But beyond that, it was the stars that twinkled through the gaps in the canopy above that fascinated him most. His mother was up there, in orbit, visiting Veloria's new ship, the *Wronin*, or something. And farther out there somewhere, his father. Whom he hadn't seen in about a year. He reflexively looked for his TESS, remembering he'd left it in his room so they couldn't track him like they did last time. He tried to remember the pictures of his father that he kept on his TESS - but try as he might, the face wasn't clear in his mind. Oddly enough, he could remember Fritz well enough. He missed his father. It seemed he was gone more than he was home. According to his mother, father had a *duty* that took him away. Something *very* important.

Though he wasn't so sure he understood all of that. Or cared all that much what the reasons were.

The sudden howl cut through the forest like a knife, Colton's hair instinctively standing up on the back of his neck. *"Volken,"* he whispered reverently. He'd only seen pictures of them, but he'd heard the story of how his father had barely escaped being killed by them. Terrifying. There was another howl coming from another direction, a little farther away. He looked up at the branches above him, then down at the ground below, *was he high enough?*

Fear is a necessary emotion to keep you safe, he remembered his father telling him. *You have to pay attention to it, but you cannot let it let it govern your actions. You must learn to control it. Panic is your worst enemy. If you panic, you cannot think.* "Your mind is your best weapon *and* your best defense," he whispered to himself, repeating his father's words.

The howls continued, echoing through the forest, some close, some farther away. He thought he could hear a chase, squealing, crying as some animal was caught and killed amid growls and howls. It gave him chills and he pulled his jacket up around him. The forest finally fell quiet again, the sounds of the birds returning and the hush of the breeze lulling him to sleep as weariness overtook him.

■ ■ ■

The Queen's shuttle had settled down on the grass at the top of the hill, inside the gates of the palace at the end of the long, tree-lined drive that snaked up from the city. Most of the charred lifeless trees that lined that drive and surrounded the grand residence had defied death, returning to bloom during spring rains of that year. With one major change... Their leaves were no longer green. They bloomed in shades of red and deep burgundy with veins of purple. At night, their photo-reactive canopy of leaves cast soft purple halos on the ground.

It was not known to occur anywhere else on Veloria and a fast spreading rumor was quickly becoming legend... *The trees, having absorbed the blood of the murdered royal family came back to life to rejoice in the birth of the new Queen, as a constant reminder to her and the Velorian people that Veloria would survive and flourish.*

It was never lost on Alité that the trees she had grown up with and played under had miraculously chosen to return to life in the national color of the

Velorian people. She glanced over her shoulder halfway between the shuttle and the stairs of the palace, her heart quickening, having heard the legend - that somehow seemed all too possible.

"Your Majesty..."

The voice of Lady Phyllis snapped her attention away from the trees and she glanced at her TESS as she reached the stairs, looking up to where the Lady stood at the landing. "It's nearly two o'clock, have you located him yet?"

"No your Majesty." Lady Phyllis held out her hand, Colton's TESS resting in it. "He left it *behind*. I think he did it on purpose..."

Alité plucked it from her hand as she passed, "I'm sure he did. What am I going to *do* with that boy?"

"I am terribly sorry..."

"Not your fault, Phyllis," interrupted Alité. "It's painfully obvious he is growing up *far* too quickly..." They passed through the doors into the grand foyer, "What we need to do, is figure out how he's getting out without being seen... maybe our security is compromised somewhere."

"I don't understand how a boy his age..."

"That's the problem, Phyllis," countered Alité as they crossed the open gallery headed for the north wing, "we're not a boy his age. We don't *think* like a boy his age..."

■ ■ ■

Angular slivers of rosy warm light played through the canopy of leaves, dancing across Colton's face as dawn chased away the darkness. His face and jacket damp from the morning dew, he opened his jacket and dried his face with his shirt. Looking over the side to the forest floor he listened intently, scanning the shifting shadows - the forest was still asleep. If he was lucky, he could get back to the palace and his room before anyone noticed he was gone. He sat up in the hammock, his legs hanging off either side and slung his Katana over his head, laying it across his back before collecting his other things from the branch above him. With the knapsack buckled in place, his sword underneath sticking out above his shoulder, he let the walking staff fall to the ground below, barely hearing it hit the forest floor.

Dropping off the tree and collecting the walking staff that equaled his height, he strode off in the direction of home with the barest of light reaching through the trees. His father had a special electronic eye that allowed him to see in the dark... he could see a definite use for that.

Even at a hustle it was still probably a thirty or forty-minute hike back to the palace. And that didn't include getting back in. Unfortunately, in this light, a hustle probably wasn't wise, he'd have to make up time as light improved.

As the forest awoke it came alive with sounds; birds, insects, animals, flitting, scurrying running... *running?* Colton jumped off the trail and peered around a tree. Nothing. Shifting quietly, he peered around the other side. Nothing. *Was he hearing things?* No, he heard it again along with the thudding of his heart in his ears. With a crush of foliage and galloping feet, a pair of *Ridgeback* feral hogs burst from the underbrush and dashed across the trail behind him crossing back into the forest on the other side, grunting and squealing, trampling noisily through the ground cover.

He let out a sigh of relief and continued walking. While the Ridgebacks could be nasty little creatures, he was fairly confident they posed no real threat to him. He could hear them circle through the forest to his left, scrambling about, making a ruckus. It sounded like another pair off to his right, rutting and fighting, their footfalls sounding like a small stampede. He decided it might be a good time to *hustle* and put some distance between him and the hogs. He trotted for a while, slowing when their sounds fell behind him. Maintaining a hurried pace, he focused on the trail ahead.

Each time he heard something out of the ordinary he paused to listen as the forest played tricks with his hearing, deadening sounds, creating echoes. Like it was playing with him. It made him jittery and that irritated him. He felt like he wasn't alone but pushed it out of his mind as nonsense. *Nothing is out there but those damn hogs... and they're not stalking you. That's ridiculous.* He walked on, determined to ignore his imagination which kept prodding him for attention.

The soft galloping footfalls and grunts that materialized on the trail behind him startled him, prompting him to look over his shoulder, "Stupid hogs..." He barely caught the dark blur in his peripheral vision as his legs went out from underneath him, dropping him to the ground on his back with a jarring thud. Being up-ended, he lost the walking staff and when he opened his eyes it was just in time to see it before it cracked him across the face with a solid *whack.* Grabbing his face in an attempt to rub away the stars in his tearing eyes, he was tempted to cry, but a guttural growl sent a spike of adrenalin racing up his back that instantly replaced pain with fear. *Hogs don't growl like that...* Looking through his fingers a Volken stood at his feet, hair hackled, teeth bared, staring *through* him with piercing green eyes.

Uncovering his face slowly, Colton cocked his head, staring at the animal who was no more than about thirty inches tall. "I thought you'd be bigger..." He eased himself into a sitting position, the animal backing up as the boy rose slowly to his feet with the aid of his walking staff. "Easy does it, my friend... I'll go my way, you go..."

He could feel the moist heat of the growl behind him on his neck and panic nearly struck him rigid. He turned ever so slowly, looking over his shoulder, the nose of a much larger Volken just inches from his face. There were two, side-by-side, but he could only focus on the closest one. He swiveled and took a step back, forgetting about the smaller animal behind him. He wanted to cry now more than ever but he was too afraid to even do that. He took one step back, then another. He was still holding his staff but his hands were numb, he couldn't remember how to use it. His body was on fire with electricity and all he could do was jitter and shake.

"To survive you must think." The voice went through him like it came from inside him, and all around him at the same time. *"To fight or defend you must be able to think. Bury the fear... Breathe, Colton. Breathe..."*

As he took a deep breath, his mind cleared enough to realize the smaller of the three Volkens was leaning against his left leg, *beside him* facing it's two larger siblings. Colton let the staff drop to the ground at his feet and slowly reached back for the hilt of his Katana, drawing it out slowly. He was fighting tunnel vision and only just realized a fourth Volken had appeared from the shadows behind the two in front of him. It *dwarfed* them. With a short guttural bark she commanded the two litter mates to move aside as she stepped between them, pushing them aside with her muzzle, moving forward, her saber teeth nearly as big around as the walking staff he had dropped.

Her size stunned him, left him breathless, a monster of nightmares. His mouth was paste-dry, his heart hammering so hard his body shook, the adrenalin flooding him to the point of nausea. The only thing separating them was the blade of the Katana which he could barely hold up, his hands trembling. He could see it in front of him but he couldn't feel it in his hands. *I don't want to die. I don't want to die. I don't want to die...*

"Just stay very still, Colton... breathe..."

She towered over him, the boy amounting to nothing more than a snack. She looked down at him, her head reaching down, sniffing the blade of the

305

Katana, the polished metal fogging with the humidity of her breath. She moved her muzzle past the blade and sniffed his face and hair, inspecting him. He felt lightheaded, seeing nothing but darkness until she pulled back. She moved close again and bumped his chin with her nose.

There was a wet snort in his ear that made him jump, a guttural snarl so evil, so low, tears ran down his face. He dared not turn his head to look. The two adult Volkens snarled and snapped at each other, barking, their teeth clacking, their saber fangs flashing back and forth inches from his face. He was frozen in place, his feet anchored to the ground. *They were fighting over who would get to eat him...* The female swung a mighty paw at the newcomer, nails extended, and Colton could feel the swish of air as she connected with her target. With a bark and a grumble, the newcomer begrudgingly strolled away, leaving the boy to be eaten by the others.

She bent down, sniffed the Volken at his side, and bumped its nose with her own before turning away and strolling back the way she came, barking a call to the two adolescents. One stubbornly remained and the Volken at Colton's side advanced, snarling at his larger litter mate. With another call from the adult, it too turned and left, disappearing silently into the shadows leaving the young boy and the runt of the litter alone together.

No longer able to control his muscles, Colton collapsed in a heap on the trail, his body drained, his mind numb, physically and mentally exhausted. The Volken laid on top of him and curled up.

■ ■ ■

The first thing Colton had done upon waking from his slumber was to roll over on his hands and knees and vomit, his arms shaking to hold him up as he emptied his stomach. Not that there had been much of anything left in it anyway... Since he was alone in the underbrush, he had to assume the Volken dragged him there, though he wasn't sure why. Barely able to control his wooden hands, Colton ate his last two power bars and finished off his water hoping his stomach wouldn't reject it all. Uncomfortably wet, he realized he'd peed himself sometime during his ordeal, *Great. Just great.*

His arms felt like lead, he could only imagine trying to stand and walk... alone. It was then that he spotted the Volken hiding in the underbrush mere feet away watching his every move. "Did you bring me here to protect me, or eat me?" he had asked. The Volken simply rose and moved to the trail, a slight limp in his gait. He watched the boy over his shoulder and waited.

306

The remainder of the hike had been grueling, carrying a nearly empty knapsack that felt like it was full of rocks, dragging a walking stick that was as heavy as a tree trunk, all on heavy rubber legs that barely motored along. But no matter how slow he trudged along, the Volken youngster never left his side. Several times it stopped, listening intently, scanning the forest with its intense green eyes before trotting a few steps to catch back up. It was as if it was bound to Colton by the strong cord of a moral obligation.

■ ■ ■

The subterranean emergency shelter buried in the rocky hillside behind the palace was no longer in use and had been walled off from the building during the renovation but the air handling system still functioned and remained connected to the royal residence. Colton had found it by accident, crawling through the duct work from his bedroom. Sure, it took a couple weeks of exploration but when he climbed out in one of the rooms of the shelter it was a whole new exciting world of exploration. The fact that it had a hidden exit into the forest made it an even sweeter discovery. Although in retrospect his secret exploration days might be coming to an end. For a couple of reasons - today's events included, his rapid growth would soon prevent him from navigating the air ducts. Whereas he could previously crawl on his hands and knees, he was now having to do a slow, laborious, belly crawl. Although he had to admit, the *slow* part had a lot to do with his painful exhaustion. It was a lot easier when you didn't feel like you were going to drop dead.

Sliding his knapsack and staff along in front of him, his small headlamp lighting the way, Colton checked over his shoulder, the eerie green eyes of the Volken youngster shimmering in the darkness behind him. "Good boy. You're doing really well... we're almost there. Stay quiet, OK?"

Reaching the grate for his room, Colton waited, listening. It was silent, the light in the room muted. *Had it gotten dark already?* The Volken youngster was tired of waiting confined in the small space and tried to crawl over him, whining. *"Sssssshhhh!"* corrected Colton, holding him back. Gently unclipping the grate he eased it down to the floor...

■ ■ ■

Nearly running down the wide marble corridor, Lady Phyllis led the Queen, hand-in-hand, "He's *back*, you Majesty. I don't know how or when, but he's back!"

"No one saw him return?"

"No ma'am. A palace security detail noticed his door was closed - we left it open, remember?"

Alité adjusted her tunic as they neared the room, "Did they check?"

"No, they thought you might like to address him first, they are posted outside the room."

Rounding the corner to the next corridor, two plainclothes palace officers stood outside the double doors of Colton's room, previously Alité's childhood room. The Queen exchanged nods with them and one of the officers leaned to open the right-hand door and nudge it open without leaving his position, "Your Majesty."

She eased the door open, entering quietly, Lady Phyllis at her side. Colton slept on the floor on the other side of his bed, fully clothed, his back to her, only his head and shoulders visible, his knapsack tucked under his head as his pillow. A mixture of emotions rolled around inside of her; anger, relief, admiration, love, frustration. She was torn as to which was going to surface first, fighting off anger as least productive. *"Colton,"* she called from the doorway.

Ears appeared over the bed like the rising sun, slowly, steadily - except the sun didn't have shimmering green eyes. Or saber teeth. The two women recoiled and Lady Phyllis screeched, the Volken springing to the top of the bed, taking a defensive stance above the sleeping boy. Before the security officers had a chance to enter the room, Alité's Katana was clear of its sheath with a *zwing* and in position for a fight, the polished blade shining even in the muted light. *"COLTON!"*

Colton rolled over, reaching up, grabbing the Volken by the tail, *"Jax, NO!"* The animal spun quickly around and Alité leapt in for a strike, Colton snagging his front paws and dragging him off the bed on top of him, *"NOO!"* He screamed at her, one hand outstretched, trying to roll away with the animal on top of him. She stalled the blade mid-swing, afraid of hitting her son whose arms and legs were wrapped around the Volken. Colton nodded toward the security detail in the doorway with their weapons drawn, *"Get them out and close the door!"*

"Let him go!" commanded Alité, repositioning her blade.

308

"No, mother - he is *my friend!* Get them out! *NOW!"* His arms and legs were starting to scream in pain, he was not sure how much longer he could hold Jax. Although he didn't seem to be fighting to get loose. "Put your blade away!"

"Colton he is a *wild animal.* He's *dangerous!"*

"He is a *puppy.* And he's my *friend.* He *protected* me and *saved my life!"* Tears rolled down his cheeks; both from the pain in his body and the emotional bond he was forming... *"Pleeease,"* he pleaded.

The animal, no matter how initially frightening, seemed to be comfortable and content laying across her son's body, his initial aggressive posture and attitude gone. She waved behind her at the security detail, "Close the door." Reaching back, she sheathed the Katana. A quick glance told her Lady Phyllis wasn't as convinced, standing behind an overstuffed chair in the corner. "Do you want to leave?"

"No I'm fine right here..." she replied meekly.

Colton's arms and legs could take no more, dropping off the Volken who remained draped across his boy, tongue lolling out the side of his mouth past a set of juvenile saber teeth. "I think she gave him to me," panted Colton, flexing numb fingers.

"Who?" asked Alité. "Who gave him to you?"

"His mother. At least I think it was his mother..."

"Colton you're not making any sense..."

"I think he's the runt of the litter. His bigger brothers were picking on him... Well," he corrected himself, "maybe they were his sisters - they *were* pretty mean... But his mother nudged me with her nose," he said tapping his chin, "right here."

Alité blinked, trying to understand exactly how he could know this, and/or how much was created by the imagination of a five-year-old boy. She glanced at Lady Phyllis who simply shrugged. "Darling, how do you know all of this?"

"The mother," continued Colton, "she kind of scolded his siblings... Gods, she was big," he breathed. "Then the father showed up..."

Alité' eyes narrowed, it was becoming almost comical, "The father," she repeated deadpan. She dropped to her knees and sat on her heels.

"Yeah, and he was *really* angry. The father and mother argued..."

"Argued..."

"Yeah, right in front of my face - by the Gods I was *sooo* scared..." He looked down at his now dry pants, "I think that's when I peed myself."

309

Alité's eyes widened.

"Anyway, she punched him in the face," Colton motioned with his fist. "And then he left. I really think he wanted to eat me but she wouldn't let him. Then she said goodby to Jax and they all left. Except Jax. He stayed with me."

Alité blinked, doing her best to separate fact from fiction, "Jax..." she repeated.

"Yeah, that's his name."

"Who told you his name? Did his mother tell..."

"Don't be silly," waved Colton, "They can't *talk. I* named him Jax."

"I see. Why Jax?"

"Well, father's whole name is Jackson but everyone calls him Jack for short. And I didn't think it would be a good idea to have *two* Jacks - but that gave me the idea to call him *Jax.*"

"From the mouth of babes," mumbled Lady Phyllis.

Alité held out her arms, "We will discuss this more at dinner - come give your mother a hug. You had me very worried..."

"I'm sorry, mother." Nudging Jax off of him, Colton got to his feet and on wobbly legs walked over to his mother for the embrace he needed. The Volken puppy circled around them, sticking his nose in her ear with a huff, rubbing against her body - his own version of a hug.

After kissing his head, Alité held her son out at arm's length with one hand, covering her nose with her other hand, "Dear *Lords*, you stink! To the *shower* with you, mister... Phyllis, burn those clothes..."

"What about... *Jax?"* motioned Lady Phyllis.

"Phyllis, if you can get them *both* in the shower, you will have my undying gratitude and admiration..."

CHAPTER TWENTY SIX

AMANPOOR : *BLACKOUT*

Bright white flashes of light strobing through his head woke Steele, a pain lancing through his eyes like a hot poker. "Oh my *God*," he moaned, rolling over and letting his bare feet drop off the bed to the carpeted floor. The palms of his hands automatically went to his eyes, applying pressure like he was trying to keep his eyeballs from exploding out of his head. His head swam and his stomach made snarling noises like it was angry for the abuse it endured. "What the hell happened last night?" he muttered to himself, trying to hold his head together lest his brains leak out.

"You ignored my advice and drank Kleer like your friend at the bar..." said a very feminine voice from somewhere behind him in the dark.

Startled, Steele's reflexes launched him off the bed and into a wall which wasn't supposed to be there, painfully bouncing his nude form backwards, back onto the bed. "What the hell!" he complained trying to scramble back to his feet. "Computer, lights! *Lights!*" He thudded heavily into the wall but caught it with out-stretched hands, turning his back to it, leaning against it, trying to steady himself in the heavily tilted room while his artificial eye searched the darkness in night vision mode. *Maybe the room wasn't slanted, maybe it was his head...* "Lights," he repeated weakly.

"We don't have computer controlled lights here," came the feminine voice from the darkness. There was a click that produced light from a light fixture over the night stand on the other side of the bed which initiated a sharp spike of new pain through Steele's eyes. His hands shot up to shield them and keep them from bursting into flames. "Unh," he grunted, squinting. "Who are you, where am I..? Holy crap!" he complained, looking down. "Where the hell are my clothes?" He reached forward with some effort and snagged a pillow off the bed to cover himself.

"Geez, you try to do a guy a favor..." she mused, propping her pillows against the headboard and sitting up, her naked breasts clearing the bed linens, a cascade of hair rolling off her shoulders like waves of molten bronze.

Steele looked away, "Oh, ahh, um... you're naked."

"Yes I'm naked," she said flatly, "that's how I sleep. What's wrong, you don't like my breasts?"

"Oh they're fine," he waved not sure where to look.

"*Fine?*"

"Yes, well, they're very nice," he offered, trying not to offend.

"Nice? *Nice?* They're *spectacular,*" she corrected, admiring them while moving them appreciatively with her hands. "And what's more, they're *real.*"

A cold chill raced up his back and Steele pointed at the bed drawing circles in the air, "We didn't... um... do... you know..."

She raised an eyebrow and crossed her arms defiantly, "Have sex?"

"Yeah," he said slowly.

"You could do worse," she frowned. *"A lot worse."*

"No, I..."

"What kind of girl do you think I am?" she scolded. "Some kind of tramp? You think just because you're good looking and you have your own ship I'm going to sleep with you?"

"No, I..."

"Ok we *slept* together," she waved, "but nothing happened," she pointed at him. "Understand?"

He nodded, his brain sloshing around in his head. "I just thought..."

"Because we're both naked? *Puh-lease.* You could barely walk or talk." She drew circles in the air in the direction of the area he was hiding with the pillow, "You really think your equipment would have been up to the task?"

"Wait, what's wrong with my equipment..?" he slurred.

"Nothing that I could see, other than you'd need a crane to get it up after drinking that amount of Kleer."

"Oh," he said sheepishly. "Then how did I get..."

"You don't think I was about to let you sleep in my bed with your boots on, your clothes smelling like a bar, do you? Of course not," she snapped, "so I stripped you down. Your clothes are in the steam closet, they'll be clean and fresh by morning."

"Oh..."

She pulled the corner of the blanket and linens back, "Now come back to bed and warm up, you're shivering. That's the Kleer doing that, you need to sleep it off." He climbed back into the bed and she wrapped him in the blanket, rubbing his back with her warm hands, his skin cold to the touch. "I recommend you avoid ever drinking that stuff again, you don't seem to have

312

the system for it... Not everyone can handle it, it's harsh stuff." She pressed her body up against his, causing her to momentarily shiver. "Don't get any funny ideas, I'm just trying to bring your body temperature up..."

"Thanks," he replied softly. "I'm married. I would never want to..."

"I know," she replied, "I saw your ring. And if you wouldn't, she's a lucky woman..."

"Actually, I'm the lucky one..." Some of the murky details of the night, mired in muddy shadows filtered into his mind's eye, broken into disconnected segments. "You were the bartender..."

"That's right."

"Why did you bring me here?" he asked.

"Because I could tell you were not a Kleer drinker when your friend suggested it. I didn't trust him, I knew you weren't going to handle it well. I brought you home at the end of my shift so I could keep an eye on you, some people have violent reactions to it."

"Thank you..."

"Pattiwillow."

"Thank you, Pattiwillow... I like that name," he muttered as he drifted back off.

■ ■ ■

"Get off me! *Get off me..!*" Like a flash of lightning in his brain, Steele sat bolt upright in bed, kicking at the covers and sheets entangling his legs, pushing himself back against the headboard. *"DD217!"* he shouted aloud. But he was alone, and in a place he didn't recognize. *Where the hell was he? And why couldn't he remember anything? Except DD217. DD217 - what the hell did that even mean?*

A well-appointed studio apartment; the bedroom, living room and kitchen occupied one big space, facing a wall of windows that reached nearly floor to ceiling. Getting out of bed and standing on wobbly legs, he had to temporarily lean on the wall on his side of the bed to steady himself. *I remember the wall...*

Oblivious to his nudity, he wandered over to the window wall, examining the city street several floors below. Pedestrian and vehicle traffic was light but when a delivery vehicle passed by the window at eye level in an air-lane, he stumbled backwards in surprise, "Shit!" He caught himself on the arm of the couch, a chill racing up his back, his muscles trembling. Nothing looked familiar, least of all flying vehicles - a pang of fear knotting in his stomach. *Was he dreaming? Why was he twitching – it was uncontrollable and very annoying.*

Exploring his surroundings, a small device on the breakfast bar produced a popup hologram, the image of a woman addressing him, "Hello Jax, I'm..."

"Pattiwillow," he said with the recording, running his hand cautiously through the image. "Interesting..."

"I need you to listen carefully; take a shower, it will help you feel better. Your clothes are behind you on the ottoman. If you are hungry, find something to eat in the kitchen, but do not leave the apartment. That is very important, *stay in the apartment until I get back from work* - they called me for a daytime shift at the bar... I should be back soon."

■ ■ ■

Showered, shaved and dressed, Steele stood at the windows watching the world below, not really feeling any different than before. Having looked through the steam in the mirror he *had* recognized who he saw, but the name Jax didn't seem right, although he couldn't justify the reason why. And other than the familiarity of Pattiwillow, everything else was foreign to him. Images in little fragments passed through his mind without making sense or reason.

He stared down at the heavy gold ring on his finger, the winged horse and the strange symbols on its sides holding no meaning for him. Likewise, the gold medallion and chain that hung around his neck, the image of Saint Michael slaying what looked to be a demon. He only knew the name because it was on the medallion and could only assume it was religious in connotation. But the opposite side had a skull and crossbones, laying atop, but bracketed by an open, spread architect's compasses from above, its points overlaying an architect's square from below; a strange departure from the image on the flip side. The screen of the strange device on his wrist was dark, giving him no indication of its purpose or use. He examined it closely but had no idea how to remove it or activate it. He could only hope Pattiwillow could provide some answers as to his past prior to him waking up, because no matter how hard he dug, there was nothing there but empty darkness.

Although not quite as intense as before the warm soothing shower, he had to make a conscious effort to maintain control of his muscles. He was mildly successful at best. The old man in the corner, wrapped in his hooded cloak, looked on with quiet concern, sipping his Diterian Brandy.

■ ■ ■

Inspector Brooker slid the MOBIUS across the desk in front of Mercedes Huang, "You're free to go."

She snatched the device up angrily and rose from her seat, "It's about time..." she grumbled, fastening it around her wrist. "Got bored asking me the same questions over and over, did'ja?"

"Well, we really don't have enough to hold you..."

"*Enough?*" she snorted defiantly. "You don't have *anything*."

"You be sure to say hello to your boyfriend if you find him," prodded Brooker. "We'd still love a chance to chat with him..."

Just a couple inches shy of six feet tall in her boots, Mercedes leaned in, squaring off with the detective, eye-to-eye, "You can kiss my ass *Inspector*. Instead of helping me you held me. If something has happened to him it's on you."

"I can live with that," he replied without emotion.

She wore a wicked little smile, "You might *think* that, but Karma's a bitch...*"

Brooker looked puzzled, "Who is Karma..?"

Mercedes didn't answer, turning on her heel, *I am. And it's pronounced, fuck you.*

■ ■ ■

Rather than contact the Perseus on her MOBIUS she stripped it off. And while her initial impulse was to smash it against a building somewhere, knowing full well it had been tampered with while it was out of her possession, she left it on a vendor's cart in full view for someone to steal. *Let them follow that.* Making sure she hadn't been followed, she ducked into a boutique and bought a change of clothes before heading to the ship, hoping to disguise herself from the surveillance cameras.

Derrik Brighton paced the ready room full of officers, "Where have you been? You've been gone nearly forty-eight hours!"

"I can tell time, *you ass,*" countered Mercedes, tossing the hat from her quick-change outfit on the floor.

"Where the hell is Steele?"

Mercedes Huang stood her ground, "You think I'd have come back without him if I knew where he was? Get off my back, and let's go find him!"

"We don't have time for that. Steele's going to have to survive on his own for a bit..."

"What the hell are you talking about?" interrupted Chase.

"You heard her," countered Derrik, indicating Mercedes, "that FreeRanger destroyer that pulled out last night was the DD217, one of the two destroyers we were looking for..."

"Our plan was to intercept the DD62 in the Ardollis System," argued Commander Reegan, "I don't like chasing a new target... The DD217 may have dropped her assets here already and is empty for all we know..."

"And we're nearly two days behind schedule," countered Derrik. "By the time we catch the DD62 in Ardollis, she may already have touched down on Wyandek and dropped her assets *there*. The DD217 is still trackable if we leave *now.*"

"And what if the DD217 assets are here?" asked Mercedes. "We'd just be letting them go..."

"If they're here they're already in the wind," countered Derrik.

Reegan folded his arms defiantly, "Sorry, this ship isn't going anywhere without Mr. Mercury."

"Thank you, Commander," offered Mercedes touching his shoulder. "Chase, let's go find..."

"I think you're forgetting I'm second in command for this mission," Derrik reminded them. "The Admiralty and the GIS are in agreement on this mission and I don't intend to let things..."

"You need *my* ship and you need *my* crew," interrupted Reegan. "And you're not going to get either one. Understand? I'm in command of this vessel..."

"And I'm in command of this mission now. Follow my orders or I'll relieve you of command, Mr. Reegan."

"No, sir."

Derrik looked to Ragnaar who had remained silent, "Mr. Ragnaar..."

"No, sir." The big man folded his arms defiantly.

Derrik resorted to resigned calm. "Gentlemen, we all know how this is going to go if I have to notify Admiral Higdenberger. Your careers are over. Mr. Ragnaar here may end up in Federation prison..."

316

"Where I come from," urged Chase, "you don't leave a man behind. And you definitely never leave a *Brother* behind. Period."

"Don't play the *Brother* card on me, Holt. You do whatever is necessary to accomplish the mission," argued Derrik. "No *one man* is more important than the mission."

"That one man is the most important man on this mission, a friend and a Brother... He is family..." His jaw set, it looked to Mercedes that Chase was getting ready to escalate to violence and she pushed him toward the bridge door. Out, out, let's go, *let's go..."* she urged.

"If you leave the ship," Derrik called after them, "you're on your own..."

The door slid closed leaving them on the bridge with an audience. She grabbed Chase by the hand and lead him off the bridge, past the Marine sentry and into the corridor. *"C'mon,* we have work to do. Maybe if we get lucky, Reegan can stall long enough for us to find Jack and get back." They hustled down the corridor, "You know what to bring. I'll meet you at the ramp in five... now *go."*

■ ■ ■

Lieutenant Torn Dado stood at the ramp, a day-pack slung over one shoulder when Chase Holt and Mercedes Huang arrived, Fritz trotting alongside Chase. "Where do you think you three are going?"

Chase and Mercedes exchanged blank glances.

"Not without *me*, you're not."

"This may not be the best career choice, Tornado," offered Chase.

"Yeah." The Lieutenant turned and lead the way down the ramp past the Marine sentries, "You coming or what?"

The trio trotted down the ramp after him, "Wait," called Mercedes. "We appreciate the offer and all, but why are *you* going?"

Torn Dado stopped mid-stride and turned on his heel, pointing at her, "Can you fly? How about you?" He pointed to Chase, "Can *you* fly? Because if you can't, you're going to need me. Unless of course, you intend on calling this rock home. Because I don't trust that jackass," he nodded in the direction of the ship, "as far as I can throw him."

"Pilot's a good idea," nodded Chase stepping forward.

"Torn Dado held out his hand, "Hold on... I know he might be useful," he motioned toward Fritz, "but he may be an even bigger liability. He should

317

probably stay here. From what I gather, this place doesn't look too favorably on loose animals."

"He's more than just an animal - you get that, right?"

"I do."

"He could be *very* helpful..."

"Not if animals are restricted and they seize him."

Mercedes gave Chase a sideways glance, "Now that he mentions it, I didn't see one dog, cat or bird while I was here... Or bugs... I haven't seen any bugs either."

Chase frowned, "So no one on this entire freaking planet even has a pet? *What the hell?"*

Mercedes bit her lip, "If they do, they're not allowed outside anywhere that I saw."

Chase rubbed his forehead, "Aarghhh." He looked down at Fritz, "I'm sorry buddy, I know you want to help, but I don't want to create more problems than we already have... Besides, your feet still need to heal."

Fritz dropped to a sit with a *harumph.* "Find him," he grumbled, staring down at the bandage on his paw.

"You *promise* to stay here?" asked Mercedes, wagging her finger at him.

The Shepherd looked up and nodded.

"Say it," she urged.

"I *promeese,*" he annunciated slowly, his nose wrinkling.

■ ■ ■

Sitting on the couch and trying to make sense of the slivers and images floating randomly through his mind, Steele tried to assemble them like puzzle pieces. He had not yet been successful at matching anything that made any sense; and staring out at the city below was the best diversion he had at hand. Hearing the apartment door swing open behind him, launched him off the couch - full of questions and hoping for answers.

Pattiwillow was all smiles, "Ooh, Jax, you're up, that's wonderful!" She saw the instant darkening of his expression when her neighbor followed her into the apartment, "It's alright, Jax, this is my neighbor Freedrich, he's a doctor. He's agreed to come over to check on you..." She crossed the apartment and took him by the hand, "How are you feeling?"

"I can't remember anything..."

"Your hands are trembling..."

318

"Yeah, I can't get them to stop."

Freedrich was a slightly portly man with a heavily receding hairline, dressed in a pale blue uniform. His manner was professional but cautious, approaching Jack with restraint. "Sit my friend," he waved at the couch. "We just want to be sure you're going to be alright. Patti, says you consumed quite a bit of Kleer..."

"I guess."

"It can be dangerous stuff." Putting a wireless earpiece in his own ear and holding a two-inch disk with his fingertips he slid his hand inside Jack's shirt, "Just listening to your heart..." He moved it around, "Lungs sound good but your heart seems to be working hard... Just the one heart then, eh?" Freedrich straightened up, his fingers hooking on the chain around Jack's neck, the medallion pulling free to the outside of his shirt. "What's this then?" he admired, lifting it to take a look. He rolled it between his fingers, flipping from the Saint Michael image to the other side, "Oh my," he breathed.

"What?" asked Steele, looking up at him.

The Doctor pulled a thin panel with a hand impression on it from a small bag he carried, wiping the surface with a sterile wipe. Taking Jack's hand, he placed it into the indentation and held it there. "Just keep it there, you're going to feel a few pinpricks, nothing too uncomfortable."

"Ow..."

"Jax, do you know what that image means?"

"I don't remember."

"Do you have anything else like it?"

Steele held up his wobbly left hand with the ring on it, "Like this?"

With his free hand Freedrich examined the ring, holding Jack's hand still, the symbols clear to him. "How long have you had this ring?"

"I don't know..."

Prompted by the unit, the doctor released Steele's hand, flipping the device over, examining the data on the screen, "He's *very* toxic yet. He needs to be treated before there's permanent damage. You should have called me earlier Patti."

What does it mean?" asked Pattiwillow.

Kleer creates severe dehydration and can affect the Myelin Sheath of the nerves causing them to shrink and deteriorate. He can't remember anything and the tremors are because his nerves are having a difficult time transmitting - he needs immediate medical attention..." He shined a small light in Jack's eyes looking for pupillary light reflex. "He has a CABL eye..." he noted, staring in. "I wonder how extensive his CABL system is... it may be what's keeping him alive...

"The symbols, Freedrich," reminded Pattiwillow, "what do they mean?"

"That I can't take him to the hospital for treatment, too many questions. I need to call a friend for help - he'll know where to take him. He needs fluids and detox if he's going to survive."

"I wanted to call *his* people for help, but I can't activate his MOBIUS..."

"That's because he's so toxic his body chemistry doesn't match the profile on his MOBIUS, it simply doesn't recognize him..."

"Save him..." whispered a voice in his ear.

"I will do everything I can..." replied Freedrich turning to the sensation of a hand on his shoulder.

"Save him..." whispered the voice in his other ear.

He spun his head around, Pattiwillow staring oddly at him. "What..?" she asked slowly.

"Take him to the Architect's Temple," said the whisper.

"Get us a ride!" Freedrich pointed at her. "Quickly! I know where to take him!"

She ran to the glass wall and tapped a yellow button on a frame between the windows, lighting a call signal around the window outside. Within moments a car service pulled up to the fourth-floor apartment, hovering outside, the vehicle's door opening over his roof as he edged up to the building. The apartment's glass door opened inward allowing Pattiwillow, and Jack Steele, with the assistance of Dr. Freedrich, to step from her living room into the waiting vehicle together.

"Medical emergency," announced Freedrich, flashing his hospital ID to the driver as the car door sealed shut.

"Amanpoor Med Center?" asked the driver reaching for his emergency lights switch.

"The Architect's Temple," he corrected, catching Steele as he collapsed in the seat next to him.

"Permission to go *code three*, Doc?"

"Yes, permission granted. *Please - make it fast."*

"You got it Doc," replied the driver, accelerating hard. "You picked the right driver, they called me *Flash* back when I was Canyon racing in Drifters..." The graphene photovoltaic paint on the vehicle alternately flashed red and white, the radio's emergency transponder broadcasting a siren signal on all vehicle frequencies in the immediate vicinity, directing traffic to other lanes away from the temporary ambulance screaming past them, weaving between the buildings, the red and white halo of color reflecting off their surfaces. "Used to race all the time with my friend Dar until he went into the military..."

An enclosed glass walking bridge between buildings zipped past over the top of the car, "Yeah, *Redline*, he was a real phenom. But like everybody else on the circuit, he got burned out. Me too, it's exhausting..." He weaved between lanes. "But days like today bring it back a bit..." he grinned. "Can't say that I don't miss it sometimes. *Hold on...*" He leaned instinctively as they rocketed around a corner, sweeping past towering buildings of glass. "Any excuse to go fast - part of the job I love."

Freedrich had his earpiece in, moving the disk around Jack's chest, his skin pale and clammy, "I think we're going to lose him..." He patted Jack's shoulder, "Stay with us, Jax."

The city suddenly dropped away behind them, the buildings shorter and more spread out, dwindling to almost nothing, giving way to farms and rolling fields with surrounding forests. A large pinnacled structure on the horizon reached out of the canopy of trees. "Not while I'm driving, you won't," countered Flash, shoving the throttle to the far stop, the car jetting across the traffic-less sky. "We're touching down in sixty seconds..."

■ ■ ■

Not having been exposed to the outside world firsthand with his initial visit to Amanpoor's Trade Exchange, Chase Holt instinctively ducked when the red and white flashing car zoomed past them overhead, sounding like a giant bumblebee. *"Flying cars,"* he said disdainfully, "that is *not* something I'm going to get used to..."

"Well how do *your* cars drive?" asked Torn Dado, reaching for the door to The Black Hole Bar & Grille.

Chase shrugged like it should be obvious, "On the ground like they're supposed to."

Torn Dado shook his head, *such antiquity.* "What's the plan, Ms. Mercedes?"

"Money talks and bullshit walks. And I got a shit-ton of credits for anyone willing to talk..."

■ ■ ■

When Pattiwillow and Dr. Freedrich returned to the waiting car, Flash was leaning against the fender paging through his MOBIUS, "Back so soon? I thought..."

"They wouldn't let us in to stay with him," interrupted Pattiwillow.

"You think he'll be alright?" asked Flash, closing his MOBIUS screen.

Freedrich, rubbed his forehead with his fingertips, "I honestly don't know, he was barely breathing... If I had him in the ER... maybe. Here..." he shook his head, "I just don't know what they can do for him here. But this is where the voice told me to bring him..."

"Voice?" hissed Pattiwillow. "What voice? You didn't say anything about a voice."

"There was no time. And it was as clear as you speaking to me right now..." He ran it in his mind again. "Yes. And something tells me I did the right thing - they were waiting at the door with a hover-gurney like they were expecting us."

Flash looked surprised. "What did they say?"

"Nothing. They checked his medallion and ring, took him in and closed the door on us."

"Medallion?"

"The mark of the Grand Architects of the Universe. And his ring had Knights markings on it..."

"Mmm," nodded Flash, waving them into the vehicle. "That makes sense then, that's who these people are..."

"They were dressed in hooded robes," interrupted Pattiwillow, "like monks."

Flash climbed in through the driver's door, "Yep, I've seen them. It is said they created the Heavens, the planets, the stars, the gates... Everything that has lived, draws a breath... everything there is, or ever was."

"Have you ever been inside?"

"No. I don't think anyone gets in without being part of the order. I've dropped people off here, but I've never picked anyone up," he lied. "No one from my company has *ever* picked anyone up from here," he lied again. "I have a feeling once you go in, you don't come back out..."

"So I won't ever see him again?" asked Pattiwillow.

"I seriously doubt it, young lady," replied Flash, easing the car up into an air-lane.

Freedrich cleared his throat, taking Pattiwillow's hand, "As fast as he crashed, I believe his organs were shutting down. I don't expect he will ever regain consciousness. But if it makes you feel any better, I'm sure they will make him comfortable in his final moments..."

"No, that *doesn't* make me feel any better," she snipped.

Freedrick slumped back in his seat, taking a deep breath, "I wish they would have talked to us..."

Flash smirked, "Sounds like they already talked to you," he wiggled his fingers near his ear, "whispered in your ear. They can do that you know."

Freedrich didn't move, his eyes closed, "Felt a hand on my shoulder too... strange sensation; warmth, trust..."

"That happened to me once, back when I was still racing." Flash tossed it off with a casual wave of his hand, "Turned out to be my mechanic playing a joke on me." He shrugged, "Nearly pissed myself just the same..."

CHAPTER TWENTY SEVEN

G'NAROTH SARAT, AMANPOOR : *ABANDONMENT ISSUES*

Always open; the music, food, alcohol and party never stopped at The Black Hole Bar & Grille. Mercedes Huang turned away from the bartender, scanning the patrons and staff in the muted light. "Dammit, she's not here."

"What did he say her name was?" asked Torn Dado, unable to hear over the music.

"Pattiwillow. Patti for short."

"When's her next shift?" asked Chase, leading the trio through the crowd toward the front door.

"She was in earlier for a few hours and went home to *tend to a friend* - his words. She's due back at about nine tonight."

Chase glanced at his MOBIUS, "Almost three hours... Y'think this *friend* she was *tending to,"* he added air quotes, "could be Jack?"

Mercedes shrugged her shoulders, "You know him better than I do, would he shack up with a barmaid?"

"That's not what I meant. *And no,* I don't think so..."

"Well, you're the one who added *air quotes,"* she countered, adding her own air quotes.

"I don't know what *that* means," interrupted Torn Dado, imitating the air quotes, "but it's really annoying, please stop. And, no - the officer I know, would not do that."

"By your own admission," said Chase pushing the door of the club open, "he was mixing with FreeRanger officers..." The trio paused outside on the sidewalk. "Could they have known who he was somehow? Maybe drugged him?"

"I didn't get any sense of that..."

"Could he have drunk too much? Gotten ill?" offered Torn Dado.

Mercedes looked down at the sidewalk, playing the images of the night in her mind, "He *seemed* fine. It all looked very friendly. I didn't see any body language or attitude that would indicate anything abnormal..."

"And you were..."

"Dancing mostly," replied Mercedes looking back up at Chase. "That way I could keep an eye on him. There were only a few instances where we were out of sight of each other; like bathroom breaks."

"What was the plan if you got separated?" asked Torn Dado.

"Meet back here at the club the following day. Just stay here until we both showed up."

"And?"

"We got separated somehow... I don't even remember at what point. But I searched the club, he wasn't here. They guy I was dancing with was on the same crew so I went back to his hotel hoping I'd run into Jack at the hotel if he did the same thing."

Chase frowned, "So you shacked up with this guy..?"

"No," she waved, "I ditched him and slept in the lobby. They must have called the police; I was arrested and detained until late that afternoon. They were looking to arrest Jack too. I didn't want to lead them to him so I went back to the ship, hoping he'd reported in... I even ditched my MOBIUS because they confiscated it and returned it before releasing me."

"Probably bugged," nodded Chase. "Why did they want to arrest him?"

"The Inspector kept asking about a place called Rikovik's Reef..."

"That's a planetoid in what *used* to be the frontier..." volunteered Torn Dado.

"I don't know if it's the same person, but apparently, a Jax Mercury was involved in some kind of bru-ha-ha there..."

"If *bru-ha-ha* means big trouble - yes there was," admitted the pilot. "And yes, he is."

"Just great," sighed Mercedes. "Then of course he was asking about Nelson's Point..."

Chase looked concerned, "What did you tell him?"

Mercedes rolled her eyes, *"Nothing.* God, I'm not a freaking amateur. He let me go hoping to track me to Jack."

"Message coming in..." Torn Dado pulled up the screen of his MOBIUS, his expression darkening, "Terrific..."

"What's going on?"

"We're on our own... The Perseus took off."

"Whaaat? *Dammit,"* Chase punched the air. *"That blows.* They didn't even bother calling us to give us a chance to get back! That's not cool."

"So what do we do now?"

Mercedes stepped between them, grabbing each one by an elbow, guiding them up the street, "Change of plans."

■ ■ ■

"Welcome to the Grand Tower Hotel, how can I help you?"

Mercedes slid her ITC card, *Interstellar Trade Credit,* across the front desk counter at the hotel clerk. "We need a room."

"How long will you be staying with us?" asked the clerk, picking up the card with pale spindly fingers.

Mercedes tried not to notice the clerk had a rather arachnid appearance, "Not entirely sure, let's start off with several nights." She tried to figure out if it was a man or woman without staring.

"We'll set you up for five days for now. Will that work for you?"

"Yes... thank you."

The clerk slid three disks about the size of a quarter across the counter with her ITC card, "Here are your keys. If you keep your key in your pocket, your MOBIUS device will direct you to your room, as well as alert you to the dining schedule, menus and room service. Will there be anything else?"

Mercedes pulled up the screen on her MOBIUS and turned it toward the clerk, "We're looking for a friend we're supposed to be meeting, have you seen him? His name is Jax Mercury..."

"I have not," replied the clerk, checking the photo with one eye, checking the database on her own screen with another. "No mention of him in any of our guest stays." She looked up, "I will add a notation to your account to notify you if he checks in."

"Thank you..."

Chase grabbed her by the elbow as she turned away from the desk, steering her attention toward a man walking out the hotel entrance toward the street. "Am I seeing things," he whispered, "or does that look exactly like the that traitorous horse-faced ass, Secretary of State?"

"It does... Where's your little pog-thing that had the list on it?"

"The e-RIP?" *electronic - Report In Progress.* "I transferred the info to my TESS," he whispered.

"Look on your MOBIUS" she directed, following the man out the door. "Any files you had on your TESS may have been transferred over..."

■ ■ ■

"Maybe you'd prefer to drive, lady?" complained the driver.

"If you don't mind, yes," replied Mercedes.

"Pssch," snorted the driver, "then get your own car."

"Let the man drive," urged Chase pulling her back into her seat as the cab whistled through traffic.

"He's going to lose him..."

"No he's not," countered Torn Dado, pointing ahead, "look, he's actually catching up."

"He's heading out of the city," announced the driver. "Once we clear the traffic he'll be an easy target."

"You'll have to fall back then so we're not so obvious..."

"Yeah, you may not believe this lady, but this isn't my first time..." countered the driver gruffly.

Not unlike someone turning on a bathroom shower, the seven o'clock rain washed across the car prompting Chase to check the time on his MOBIUS, "We need to be back in less than two hours if we want to catch the barmaid before she gets to work."

"We're going to need a vehicle," whispered Torn Dado. "It would be best if we had our own..."

Mercedes scooted forward in her seat again, "Where can we rent a car later?"

"Back at your hotel," replied the driver, passing between trucks.

Within a few minutes the city dropped away behind them giving way to sprawling suburbs, which in turn gave way to ranches and rolling hills. Dropping out of the air-lane the driver followed the other vehicle off the highway exit, falling back. "He's headed to the Cork & Cleaver," he pointed, "top of the hill. It's a vineyard and restaurant - pretty pricey. Want me to follow him up?"

■ ■ ■

"The driver was right," whispered Torn Dado, "we're really not dressed for this place." The simple name, Cork & Cleaver, lied about its elegance. And the *aromas*, well, Torn Dado couldn't remember anything smelling this good since before he was deployed on the Conquest - his parents taking him to one of the finest restaurants back home, for a sendoff. "I want to live here..."

327

"On this planet?" asked Mercedes.

He flashed her a grin, "In this *restaurant.*"

The maitre d' glanced at them with a disapproving eye, but escorted them through the restaurant and seated them nonetheless. Toward the back, near the kitchen. Mercedes snagged the maitre d' by his sleeve, eyeing the table where the Secretary of State was sitting alone. "Listen," she said in her best seductive kitten voice, "I realize we're not entirely *dressed* for the occasion, but we only have one night here and we were told that this was absolutely the *finest* restaurant with the *finest* service..." she rubbed his arm. "I would be *sooo grateful* if you could sit us over there," she nodded at a more desirable table. "I *promise* we will take *very* good care of you..." She smiled coyly.

■ ■ ■

Torn Dado slid into the booth across from Chase and Mercedes with his back to the Secretary of State. "I *cannot* believe that worked."

Mercedes swept her hair back, "What are you saying? Are you saying I'm not attractive enough?"

Torn Dado shrugged, "Sure, you're just not *my* type. I..."

"Oh, *please...*" She scooped up his hand, resting her other hand on top, drawing little circles on the back of his hand with her thumb while caressing his palm with her fingertips. She locked eyes with him, "I know I've never mentioned it before, but you have the most *amazing* eyes" she purred, "they glitter like *gold*. And your hair..." she made a deliberate reach across the table and stroked the hair at his temple, "it's like silk... You can't tell me you haven't even *thought* about what my skin would feel like against yours... naked, pressed together, sweaty..." she whispered seductively.

His eyes had gone glassy, dilating, "I... I..."

She released his hand and sat back, "And *that's* how it works."

"Oh, damn," chortled Chase. "That's cold."

Torn Dado looked put-off, angry and embarrassed all at the same time. He opened his mouth to reply but Chase cut him off, eyeing the other table, "Ooh, we have another player..." His eyes narrowed, "She looks familiar but I can't..."

"That's Germany's President, Chancellor Angela Merkel," whispered Mercedes. "Can you get a shot of her from here?"

Chase activated the e-RIP program from his MOBIUS taking a 3D photo, the software making a comparison. "It's a match," he whispered back. "Incoming," he nodded toward the table, another man arriving. *"No idea who he is."*

"Wow," breathed Mercedes, "President Tayyip Erdogan. Turkey... We've got a real unholy alliance going on here."

Chase had taken another 3D photo, "Confirmed," he said, closing the screen. "This can't be a coincidence."

"No it can't," replied Mercedes. "I have a feeling Amanpoor is a dispersal point for this group. That FreeRanger ship dropped them off and now they wait here for a ride home to be arranged..."

"So the Perseus is chasing an empty ship," offered Torn Dado.

"That'd be my guess," remarked Chase with distaste.

Mercedes fished through an open zipper in her day pack under the table pulling out what looked like a makeup compact, "Torn, head outside, see if you can reach the Perseus - give them an update."

"Got it." He slid from the booth and headed for the door, nearly running into an extremely well dressed patron being escorted through the restaurant by the maitre d'.

"Makeup? *Now?"* whispered Chase, watching a third man arrive at the table. He took another 3D image that produced no match. He saved it just the same.

"Sssshhhh," she hushed him, sliding the open compact past her water glass aimed at the table across the restaurant. She covered the small earpiece in her ear and adjusted the direction of the compact. *"Hello, hello, greeting, greetings..."* she mumbled out loud, watching them shake hands as the man sat down, the waiter immediately bringing him a drink. She narrated for Chase's benefit, *"I trust your trip went well... We are sorry under the circumstances that we did not have the lead-time to evacuate everyone..."* The man slid what looked to be ITC cards across the table to each of them, *"Lord Toberus sends his regards and thanks you for your service. He apologizes for being unable to personally visit with you today, but he cannot, obviously, be everywhere at once. He is a busy man after all. You will find two-hundred-fifty-million credits in your new accounts..."*

"Uh oh, somebody's not happy," she interjected. *"Alfano Toberus promised..."*

"Oooh, that pissed him off," she added. *"We do not use first names when referring to Lord Toberus. Never ever use that name again."*

"We were promised seven-hundred-fifty-million..." Mercedes nodded, "And greed rears its ugly head... good job horse-face."

The newcomer leaned in, his general attitude darkening considerably. *"I will remind you that your assignments were and are incomplete. Failed. And I will point out that while others have surely been captured or perished, here you are... at the courtesy and will of Lord Toberus. Free to move on with your lives, despite the fact that his investment of extensive time and money is now lost."* The man rose from the table, *"I have more meetings to make so I will take my leave. Consider your employment terminated and your compensation complete. Our ties are permanently severed. Goodbye..."* He turned and departed, passing Torn Dado on his way back into the restaurant.

"What did I miss?" asked the pilot, sliding back into the booth. Chase put his finger to his mouth, quieting him, indicating Mercedes' little device.

"This is unacceptable... Alfano Toberus is going to hear from my counsel," recited Mercedes. *"I didn't spend my entire life on that cesspool for a paltry two-hundred-fifty-million credits; I left more than that behind!"* She glanced up at Chase, "Horse-face is *pissed...*"

"I can see that. So, who is this Lord Toberus? Or Alfano Toberus?"

Mercedes pulled the earpiece from her ear, "Now they're just bickering like children." She left the compact where it was, allowing it to continue to record but stowed the earpiece back in her pack, her eyes flicking up to Torn Dado. "Did you get the Perseus?"

"They're out of range."

Chase wiped beads of moisture off his water glass. "Great, what the hell do we do now?"

Mercedes gave him an evil sideways glance, "What's the punishment for Platricide or planetary subversion?"

Chase cleared his throat, "Death..."

"Exactly."

"But they're supposed to be captured and tried..."

"There is no trial, Chase. When these people are caught they go straight to detention for execution. Look at your list, it doesn't say; *Wanted Suspects.* It says *Guilty of Platricide and Planetary Subversion.*" She searched her pack by feel, withdrawing a micro hypodermic, checking the label and sliding it under her napkin. "You don't think the Perseus will ask that FreeRanger ship for directions, do you? No, they're going to destroy it, hoping to get these people," she nodded at the other table. "They need to be eliminated and we're *here*. It's our job, like it or not."

330

Torn Dado seemed to take in stride, "You going to poison them?"

"Yes..."

Chase kicked his pack under the table, "So I packed clothes and some electronics and you packed *poison?*"

"I packed the tools of my trade. And yes. Poison is one of those tools..."

"I thought you told Jack you weren't an assassin."

"I lied. Well, sort of..."

"So you're *sort of* an assassin?"

"Our agents are all trained for this sort of thing, but women have a greater advantage; we can often get closer to the target than men. So, I've had a few opportunities..."

Chase looked at her like he suddenly didn't recognize her. Never having met one before, he was starting to understand Steele's dislike for spies. "Hmm. What do you have... Ricin? Polonium 210? Or something old school like Arsenic?"

"Polonium is Russia's choice and I wouldn't touch it with a ten-foot pole. That shit's radioactive - and it takes forever. People handling Ricin often kill themselves by accidental contamination. It also has a high possibility of collateral damage to unintended victims - like investigators and healthcare workers. So, the Agency developed a proprietary hybrid called Zephyr X. Like Arsenic, it's colorless, odorless and tasteless. I carry Zephyr X60 and X10..."

"What's the difference?"

"About an hour. Reactions differ depending on the dose and sensitivity. X60 takes thirty minutes to an hour, X10 takes ten minutes or less. They are both fairly safe to handle... more or less."

Chase raised an eyebrow, *"More or less?"*

"It's usually administered by injection or ingestion. But if you get it on mucous tissue - like in the nose or eyes, it will be absorbed pretty readily."

Torn Dado frowned in contemplation, "So how are we going to do this..?"

■ ■ ■

Sitting on the aisle side of the booth, Mercedes cupped the micro hypodermic, no bigger than a lancet, in the palm of her hand. "Here he comes," whispered Torn Dado from the other side of the booth, looking past her. "Three... two... one... *now.*"

Mercedes stepped from the booth in front of the waiter with his tray laden with food. "Whoa!" she exclaimed, helping him steady his tray, assisting him to contain the plates that threatened to slide off the tray. "Oh, I am *soo sorry,* my apologies," she smiled, locking eyes with him. "You've got everything, right?" He nodded in amazement that he hadn't lost anything. "Sorry again," she touched his hand and walked past, heading to the restroom.

"Oh, she's *good,*" Torn Dado whispered.

"Did she do it?" inquired Chase, watching the waiter deliver the food to the table they were stalking.

"It was so fast, I couldn't tell." The pilot checked over his shoulder at the table of criminals watching the waiter take his leave. "I guess we'll find out soon."

As Mercedes returned from the restroom, the waiter was right behind her with another loaded tray, pausing at a distance to wait for her to be seated. She looked over her shoulder, "I promise I'll look before I jump up again..." He merely smiled politely before depositing salads in front of each of them.

Chase waited for the waiter to be out of earshot, "Well?"

She held up empty hands, the used lancet flushed down the toilet in the ladies' restroom. "I got a really good dose on one, another with a decent dose but I completely missed the steak. Who has the steak?"

"The one you call Horse Face," replied Torn Dado. "And... I gotta ask... what the hellion is a horse face?"

Mercedes nearly spit a mouthful of salad out of her mouth, Chase taking the opportunity to reply. "A horse is an animal with a long, narrow face. It's an insult."

"Ah, OK. So, they're ugly animals?"

"Well no, horses are generally thought of to be attractive, powerful, graceful animals..."

"Then I don't get it."

"It's not an insult to the horse, mind you," added Mercedes. "But it speaks to the odd proportions of the person with said, horse face."

"I see..."

■ ■ ■

Chase motioned with his fork, "Someone's not looking too well..."

Chancellor Merkel was looking rather pallid and sweaty. Mercedes checked the time on her MOBIUS, "Right on time - forty minutes. She must have gotten the heavier dose..." The Chancellor grabbed her chest in pain, crying out in anguish.

Horse Face half stood, looking around, "Help! Help! Is anyone a doctor?"

"I have an idea... Watch my back." Mercedes grabbed her pack from under the table, rising hastily, nearly taking the waiter with her for a second time. "I'm a doctor!" she shouted.

"Ohh, what the hell is she doing?" hissed Chase leaning over the table. "*This* wasn't part of the plan..."

Mercedes dropped her pack on the floor, easing the Chancellor off the chair to the floor, "She's having a heart attack! *You!*" she pointed at Tayyip Erdogan, "Get over here, I need your help!" With all the movement and action, she slid the Chancellor's ITC card from her jacket pocket and palmed it. "I need to do chest compressions, you're going to breathe for her..."

On one knee opposite the Chancellors body, Erdogan shied backwards, "I don't..."

Reaching across the body, grabbing Erdogan by the lapels and pulling him closer, nearly on top of the *patient*, Mercedes growled in his face, loud enough for everyone around to hear, "You help me or she'll *die,* you coward. If she dies, it will be on *your* head." She rose to one knee, pulling at his jacket, "Take your jacket off and put it under her head," she snapped, wrestling it off of him. As she folded it she felt for and found the ITC card, sliding it discreetly from the pocket as she stuffed it under the Chancellor's head. Both cards went into the pack as she reached for an individually packed moist wipe. She checked the barcode label before handing it to him, *Zephyr X10*. "Sterile!" she yelled at him. "Wipe *your* mouth, wipe *her* mouth... *I* compress, *you* breathe, got it?!"

He nodded mechanically, tearing open the foil pouch, "Yes."

She began the useless compressions on the deceased Chancellor's chest. Other than a little perspiration Erdogan wasn't showing any real signs of contamination yet and she wasn't leaving until she knew she'd gotten him. She looked at the Secretary of State, nearly calling him Horse Face, "You!" she pointed at him, "Hold her legs..."

He half-stood, glancing around, a look of fear crossing his face, hedging on panic. Maybe he'd figured it out. She never gave him credit for being that bright. Maybe it was just suspicion, maybe a good guess. But Mercedes Huang knew the look of a man about to run for his life. She glanced at her

333

own table, Chase and Torn Dado's attention riveted on her. She nodded in the direction of the Secretary of State as he made his move jumping up, his chair clattering to the floor as he broke for the door. Chase and Torn Dado following him out, everyone's attention on the center of the restaurant.

She was compressing and Erdogan was breathing, his palor changing, the color leaving his face, streams of sweat running down his brow. He was starting to pant, probably disregarding it to exertion.

"You alright?" asked Mercedes. "You don't look so well..."

"I am fine," he wheezed.

Erdogan was starting to wobble, his arms shaking from exhaustion, the lack of blood and oxygen taking its toll. Veins visibly throbbed on his forehead, his hair slick with sweat.

"Feeling tight? Weak? Chest hurt?"

He stopped, glancing up at her, looking ghostly, laboring to breathe, pain radiating up into his left shoulder and jaw, his lips turning blue. "Gaaa..." he grunted.

He had a minute left, maybe two if he was lucky. "The people of Earth send their regards," she winked, an evil grin curling the corners of her mouth. "Enjoy your stay in hell, you filthy pig..."

■ ■ ■

Ditching the chaos, Mercedes ran out into the darkened parking lot, an ambulance racing up the drive, lights and siren wailing. Nonchalantly slinging her pack over her shoulder, she turned and walked in the opposite direction across the lot, another ambulance and two police cars swinging off the main road at the bottom of the hill. *Where the hell are you guys?* At the end of the fourth row, headlights flashed briefly, the vehicle backed into a spot in a dark corner of the lot. She cut between the cars, dropping low to avoid being seen by the emergency vehicles as she zig-zagged her way across the lot toward the waiting car.

Torn Dado glanced in the rear-view mirror, "Buckle up..."

"You sure you know how to drive one of these things?" asked Mercedes.

"Doesn't everybody?" he quipped.

As soon as the police and ambulance techs cleared the drive, disappearing into the restaurant, he was into the throttle, lights off, rocketing across the parking lot to the drive. Adding lift, he illegally cut across the landscaping, already at an air-lane height by the time he reached the road. He slowed to swing the on-ramp to the mostly empty highway and headed for the distant rolling hills and the desert beyond.

Mercedes examined Horse Face, the sizable black eye visible even in the darkened interior. "He's out cold, how hard did you hit him?"

Chase shrugged, "I've wanted to pop this lying, treasonous coward in the face every time I saw him run his stupid mouth on TV. I guess maybe I hit him a little harder than I thought." He waved it off, "He'll live."

"Until we're done with him," added Mercedes, "then we dump his worthless carcass out here somewhere. Did you get his ITC card?"

Chase pulled it from his pocket and handed it to her, feeling a little like a common mugger. "Yep."

■ ■ ■

The cruise back from the desert was filled with more silence than talk. Until they passed the off-ramp for the Cork & Cleaver. "Looks like all the emergency vehicles are gone...." remarked Torn Dado, reducing throttle.

"Mmmm, looks closed now," added Chase, looking past him from the passenger seat.

Her legs stretched out across the back seat, arms folded across her chest, Mercedes sighed.

"*What...*" grunted Chase, his voice dripping with aggravation.

"Nothing..."

"What?" asked Torn Dado, quietly.

"Little hint," offered Chase, "When a woman says nothing, it's not nothing. It's always something - it's *never* nothing."

"Huh?"

Mercedes swung her feet off the seat, facing forward suddenly becoming more animated. "*You're* the one who gave me the thing!" she waved.

Chase glanced over at Torn Dado, "See what I mean? It's *always* something." He turned to look over his shoulder, "Yeah, I put it *on his leg...*"

"But it wasn't *doing* anything..." she insisted.

"Until you put it *in his pants!*" snapped Chase. "Who told you to put it down his pants?"

"I wanted it to *scare* him!" gestured Mercedes.

"Well it *worked!* It *scared* him - then it *killed* him!" He rubbed his forehead, "I've heard guys get wounded in combat scream less than that... it was *horrifying...*"

335

"Guys?" prompted Torn Dado.

"How was I supposed to know it was going to *kill him?*" shouted Mercedes.

"Guys?"

"Oh I don't know," mused Chase, "the fact that it looked like a *big hairy tarantula with a scorpion's tail* wasn't clue enough?" He tried to blink away the images, "God, I've never *seen* seizures like that..."

"Or that shade of purple..." added Mercedes. "At least we know how many of them were let off here..."

"Guys!"

"But not their *names*," complained Chase. "Because he screamed himself to death before he could tell us..."

"GUYS!"

"WHAT?!" shouted Chase and Mercedes in unison.

Torn Dado reduced throttle, pointing at the highway ahead, "Road block, *ROAD BLOCK!"*

Four police vehicles blocked the highway ahead, two on the ground and two hovering in the air-lane.

"Go around them..."

Torn Dado shot Chase a look of incredulity, "You didn't just say that."

"I don't care what you do flyboy, get us the *hell* out of here," insisted Mercedes. "Go dark and get off the highway..."

Torn dado rolled his eyes, backing the throttle down. "In what *universe* would that work?"

"Well you're a fighter pilot," exclaimed Chase, "do some fighter pilot stuff!"

"In case you hadn't noticed, this is *not* a fighter, and I am *not* a magician!"

"Well you'd better think of *something*," urged Mercedes, "or you're going to be in the prison cell next to ours..."

Torn Dado brought the vehicle to a stop in air-lane of the empty highway about a mile and a half from the roadblock, several cars in line on the ground at the checkpoint, "Maybe they're not looking for us."

"That's wishful thinking. And if you're wrong, we don't get a do-over." Mercedes pointed off to the right of the highway, "Now go dark and get us off the road."

The pilot flipped off the switches for the lights and eased the car off the roadway, "Turning off the lights doesn't make us invisible, you know. I'm still on their sensors." As the vehicle left the roadway it descended, dropping to about twelve inches off the ground, the tall grass whipping over the nose as it plowed through.

"Dude, get us off the ground," urged Chase, "they're going to be able to see exactly where we went..."

"Most vehicles do not have an anti-gravity system designed to fly, just to float over the surface of the road..."

"Then how..."

"We can achieve an air-lane over the highway because certain roads have an embedded power grid that act as magnifiers, allowing the vehicle to do so. This is no doubt a rental vehicle so it's systems are not capable of much more."

"What about emergency vehicles?" inquired Mercedes.

"They can fly *and* outrun us."

"Swell..." Mercedes was sitting on her knees, facing backwards, looking out through the rear window, "I don't see anyone behind us..."

"We need to dump the car quickly," explained Torn Dado. "Their sensors will have recorded the make, model and license of this unit. They don't need to chase us if they don't want to, other units will find us..."

337

CHAPTER TWENTY EIGHT

XIAN PI SYSTEM, PERSEUS : *OFF THE GRID*

"Red alert! All hands to battle stations! All hands to battle stations!" The alarm klaxon whooped throughout the ship, every corridor and room bathed in red flashing light.

Shocked awake, Fritz vaulted himself off his human's bed in the muted light, the pall of acrid smoke heavy in the air. He slid on the carpet, the bandage on his foot tearing away as he scrambled for the door to the corridor, the door automatically sliding open allowing him passage. His heart hammering, he skidded to a stop in the center of an *empty, quiet* corridor. *What?* Looking left and right he could hear voices towards the bridge and he trotted in that direction. Two marine sentries chatted casually outside the bridge entrance. He stopped short of engaging them and turned back, heading for the executive quarters normally occupied by his human. The door opened, disappearing into the bulkhead and he re-entered the room, the air clear, his errant bandage laying on the floor where it had torn off. Sitting down in the middle of the room, he surveyed his surroundings, unclear as to what had transpired. He sniffed the air pensively - nothing. No smoke, no Jack. He eyed the bed and considered returning to it but his grumbling stomach changed his mind.

Dogs aren't nearly as forgetful or short on memory as most people accuse them of. No, they just have a different attitude and perspective of the world; if it doesn't physically hurt, they usually disregard it and move on. Sometimes they sniff it or piss on it before moving on, but Fritz simply discarded the dream.

Strolling down the corridor toward the galley, the German Shepherd passed members of the crew going about their daily duties. Some said hello, some ignored him - he greeted them all just the same, with a toothy smile and a wag of his tail. He needed more; he needed a hand resting on his head, an ear scratch, a belly rub, a hug... someone to talk to him like Jack did... He *needed* Jack. All he could do was be patient. Unfortunately, patience was not one of his best virtues. The instinctual canine part of him told him it was his fault that Jack wasn't home, he'd done something wrong, he had been bad, that his human was angry with him and he was being punished. Fortunately, Fritz had the logic of the CABL part of his brain to correct that instinct and expose it for what it was, misinformation. But he still admonished himself for not accompanying Chase and Mercedes; he *knew* he could have found his human. This thought was instinctual *and* logical, since he had the tracking skills and abilities. This saddened him greatly, knowing Jack's absence was not his fault, yet it was, because he could have made the difference in locating him and bringing him home. This was the irritating conundrum that plagued him, the very thing that made him unique... at least for a dog. Personally, at this moment he was not appreciative of it. What he was truly aware of, was that missing his human was physically painful.

It helped having Allie around. A little. But she was stuck in the instinctual canine remorse and she didn't have the logical advantage he had. Well, sometimes it was an advantage - sometimes it was a plague. Still, he looked forward to seeing her. Ragnaar had been taking care of her and proved to be the best friend the two Shepherds had on the ship; making sure they had the food, water, exercise and human interaction they needed. Outside of his size and gruff exterior, the ex-pirate turned out to be a largely misunderstood teddy bear.

Ragnaar lifted an eyebrow, wrinkling the tattoo across his face, "Tore you bandage off again, huh?"

"Fell off," grumbled Fritz.

"Sure it did," remarked the big man with skepticism, taking a knee in the grass of the ship's small garden. Allie wandered around on her own. "Paw," he demanded, holding out his hand. Fritz sat and boldly handed over his paw. "Not this one," Ragnaar let it drop, pointing at the other one, "*that* one." Fritz tentatively held it out as ordered, allowing the man to examine it, looking between his toes and checking his pads. He was gentle in the process, humming to himself, something Fritz found rather soothing. "It's healing well. I think you can go without a new bandage..." He pointed towards Allie, "Go play, let me check in with the bridge..."

■ ■ ■

After merely five minutes alone Ragnaar returned to the two dogs who sat in front of him as he dropped to a crouch, "Listen you two, there's something going on - I have to head to the bridge." He patted the two of them simultaneously, "Fritz, can you look after Lady Allie for me? Take her to see Cookie in the galley, he'll make sure you both get something to eat..."

Fritz nodded. Not only could he communicate with Allie in canine body language, actions, gestures and dog-speak, he also knew her human commands, which she obeyed well. "O-kay," he annunciated.

"You two be good," he said, giving them one last affectionate tussle before rising.

They watched him go before returning to their interrupted socializing and exploration of the garden. They leaned on each other, pushing and nudging as they roamed, never straying more than a few feet from one another.

As predicted, the man in the galley nicknamed Cookie, a pale, wiry man, with an orange-red crewcut and a ready smile, had a sizable portion of eggs and sausage for each of them. He generously took time away from the counter and other crew members to be sure the German Shepherds had whatever they needed before returning to his duties. Side-by-side, the two dogs politely ate their fill, occasionally looking up from their food to check their surroundings. When the lights flickered momentarily, they took no notice.

■ ■ ■

Ragnaar flagged the Marine sentry at the bridge entrance, returning a casual salute, passing through the automatic doors as they split down the middle and disappeared into the bulkheads.

Lieutenant Commander Reegan looked relieved as the Lieutenant entered the dimly illuminated bridge, crew members faces awash in the light of their stations, "Ah, Mr. Ragnaar, please take the helm."

The satiny, translucent silver lining of the jump tunnel on the big screen, reflected hues of wavering gold and deep copper, errant streaks of light passing across the ship's bow. Ragnaar eyed it with curiosity. "Helm, aye." The Ensign at the helm relinquished her seat with a nod, looking exhausted, requiring the Lieutenant to take immediate manual control of the ship as it wandered off course, working to maintain attitude and direction. The ship shuddered, the nose wavering and he flipped a questioning glance over his shoulder, "Skipper? Are we experiencing solar wind? In a *transition tunnel?*"

"Yes, Mr. Ragnaar."

"This is not good. Is not good at all..."

"I am *aware* of that, Lieutenant."

"Distance to Gate?" he inquired, leaning to his right to look at the navigator's screens, maintaining his hands on the manual flight controls.

"Only three hours," replied Reegan. "We are hoping the tunnel will mitigate the event."

"It will not," countered Ragnaar,

"It appears a star perpendicular to our route has experienced an SPE," *Solar Proton Event,* offered the Ensign at astrometrics. "It occurred four hours after entering the gate From Edenlight to Madrassas..."

"No travel advisories?"

"Within moments of the occurrence being recorded..." replied the Ensign.

"But nothing *pre-event?"* Ragnaar was busy adjusting attitude thrusters to stabilize the ship and reduce the need for constant correction but the solar winds were not constant and fought his best efforts.

Reegan sipped a cold coffee, making a face of distaste before responding, "There is no way to tell if it was a monitored star or not, Lieutenant. And being in a gate transition, we have no way of telling from our position, which star it might be. It may even be from a star in null space - if there are any in null space that is."

Ragnaar eyed the rosy copper coloring on the right side of the satiny, translucent lining of the jump tunnel, "I do not believe we will make it to the gate, Commander. I advise that we break Dark Protocol and inform Admiral Higdenberger of our situation..."

"I'm afraid that's impossible, Lieutenant," replied Reegan, "the interference is too heavy, we're dark whether we want to be or not. We've even lost sensor contact with the DD217 ahead of us."

"How close were we when we lost contact?"

"We had nearly caught up with her in Edenlight; she entered the gate just three hours before us. She should be fairly near the exit to Madrassas..."

"Commander, I suggest we increase speed in an effort to reduce our time in the tunnel..."

"We are already at maximum safe protocol for transition, Lieutenant."

"Yes sir, we are. But I will remind you that the protocols are a broad fit, mean average, for all ship types and sizes. Our overall size, mass and energy wake, do not compare to something, for instance, the size of a capital ship. Smaller ships like the Perseus are penalized unnecessarily; our safe margin is *easily* twenty-five to thirty-five percent higher than the prescribed protocols."

Commander Reegan rubbed the stubble on his jaw in contemplation, "Hmm, I trust your judgment, Lieutenant. And it makes sense." He nodded toward the screen, "Let's push it..."

■ ■ ■

Something was wrong, Fritz could sense it. He could *feel* it. He paused in the middle of the corridor, Allie stopping next to him, looking at him with curiosity. She moved around him, trying to get him to look at her. He closed his eyes and concentrated, relaxing... he could feel movement beneath his feet, a gentle swaying that was so subtle, he nearly missed it, oblivious to the sensation when he was on the move. He continued on, quickening his stride, Allie keeping pace. "Hurry Allie..." Instinctually, he headed for the state room he shared with his human - whether it was the safest place or not, it was the most familiar, and therefore comforting.

■ ■ ■

As if it was birthing a ship through fire, the mass of undulating, swirling, crimson, orange and yellow plasma exploded, the jump event spilling the DD217 out into space, short-lived tendrils of energy dragging across her hull. The bridge lights flickered, half of the ship's systems going dark.

Commander T. B. Yafusco was on his feet next to his command chair, one hand on the armrest, glancing down at his darkened command screens, "Did we make it? *Did we make it?* Where are we..?"

"Madrassas, Commander. We made it."

Tibby put his hands on top of his head, inhaling deeply, letting it out through his teeth, "Thank the Gods..." He let his hands drop loosely to his sides and looked out at the Madrassas System stretched out before them. "I've never been so relieved to see normal space."

Sitting in the first mate's seat, Grinah cleared her parched throat, "I've never seen a gate corona like that, it looked like we were on fire..."

"Frightening," muttered Tibby, replaying it in his head, "a total absence of more than half of the color spectrum, I've never seen anything like it."

"Damage reports coming in," noted Grinah, tapping on her ear piece. "Main propulsion down, thrusters only. Shields off line. Point defense systems off line, main gun batteries down..."

Tibby laid his hand on the shoulder of the helmsman in front of him, "Do you have manual control?"

"Aye, sir."

"Good, point us at Lindmore, it's the fourth planet. Just keep us moving."

"Aye, sir."

"Do we have communications?" he asked of no one in particular.

"No. Internal comms only, and no sensors, Commander."

Tibby sat casually on the arm of his chair, "Alright people, let's get things back up and running here. As soon as we have communications, send out a travel advisory for the Madrassas - Edenlight jump corridor. Show it as temporarily impassable..."

"What about that ship that was behind us?" whispered Grinah. "You think they'll make it?"

"I don't know," he replied, looking pensive. "After we get up and running again, maybe we'll loop back towards the gate and see if they've cleared it. Nothing else we can do. When they disappeared it could have been the level of sensor interference we had, or they may have fallen out of jump." He glanced around the darkened bridge, "And at this point, even if they do appear in the next two or three hours, we're in no condition to help them until we get ourselves squared away."

Grinah leaned in, "I guess those people we dropped at Amanpoor will be stuck waiting for transports if they're heading to Bengaloo through Edenlight for pickup..."

Tibby shrugged, "We don't know if all of Edenlight is affected, but if they're coming through Madrassas to use this gate," he thumbed over his shoulder, "they'll be waiting a while. Not that it's our problem," he waved, "we made the drop and we got paid. Which puts us solidly in the black, by the way," he added, rubbing his fingers together like he was rubbing a coin. Glancing around at the bridge again, he indicated with a nod, "As long as *this* doesn't cost us a bunch of credits to fix..."

■ ■ ■

Ragnaar's adjustments were nearly constant, no amount of thruster trim could compensate for the solar winds that seemed to ebb and flow. Having experienced much the same type of occurrence in open space with much different effect, he was convinced the difficulty had something to do with being in the confines of the jump tunnel. A stabilized worm-hole made of

343

energy, anchored at each end by generators in the form of gates, he was sure there was a mathematical equation to calculate the resulting disturbance of a Solar Proton Event beating on a Genesis Gate's jump tunnel, but it was well beyond his mathematical abilities. There *were* people who could handle that math, he just wasn't one of them.

The Ensign at astrometrics spun in her seat, "Commander, I'm reading a marked increase in both helium and HZE ions..."

Reegan glanced at his screens, the estimated time to the gate was still about an hour and a half away. "Cause?" He was pretty certain he already knew the answer.

"The leading edge of a Coronal Mass Ejection."

Though it was not the answer he wanted to hear. "Going to yellow alert," he warned, tapping his control panel. Yellow lights flashed throughout the ship, the warning tone sounding briefly, security and compartment doors closing automatically, protecting the various sections of the ship.

The bridge crew eyed the flaring walls of the jump tunnel as it appeared to waver, changing from a rosy copper to a deep red, waves of bright red and orange swirling and pulsing in ever-changing patterns.

Having run nearly the length of the ship, Commander Derrik Brighton appeared on the bridge, out of breath, "What's going on? Have we caught the bastards?"

Reegan motioned toward the screen, "No..." He lowered his voice, "But this little chase of yours just might be the end of us."

"What are you talking about, *Reegan?*" his name spoken with animosity.

Without words, Reegan rose from his command chair, the two men roughly equal in height and size, he moved the GIS agent to the back of the bridge by a vice-like grip on his elbow. "I've had about as much as I'm going to take from you..."

Brighton tore his arm free, posturing aggressively, "In case you've *forgotten* who I..."

"No I haven't forgotten *anything,* Mr. *Brithauz.*" interrupted Reegan, unflinchingly. "You're Higdenberger's darling little spy. Personally, I don't know why, you haven't made a decent call since you stepped aboard the Perseus. *My ship...*"

"My mission," asserted Derrik.

"What... you mean chasing down planetary terrorists on a ship that we were unable to confirm was carrying them? Because *you* chose to abandon members of the team, *our team*, that was attempting to gather that information. Is *that* the mission you're referring to?"

Brighton took an indignant posture, "You are fully aware that Higdenberger *approved* that action."

Reegan leaned in close, "Because you *lied* to him. And you *omitted* details that were crucial to him assessing the real situation to get the answer *you wanted*." Reegan saw the flicker of surprise that flashed across the GIS agent's face. "Yeah, thought no one knew about that private little call you made..?"

"How..."

"I told you," interrupted Reegan, "this is *my* ship. *My* crew. I find everything out eventually. You are just a *guest* here - and at this point, an *unwanted* guest. Push me. Go ahead. I promise you won't like the results." His peripheral vision registered the arrival of two Marine sentries, "If, *if*, we make it out of this mess," he indicated the big screen, "we are heading back to Bengaloo by the fastest route to collect the people you decided to abandon."

"They weren't mission critical..."

"Neither are you," Reegan reminded him. "And right now, survival has replaced mission. Because this is the position *your* decisions have put us in. Believe me when I say, you have no friends here." He repositioned himself, stepping back, "Let me ask you something, have you ever been to null space. Know anyone who has?"

Derrik folded his arms defiantly, "Null space is simply the space beyond the marked systems, the un-navigated space between known space. It's not some bloody mysterious place with *no space*," he waved his hands mockingly, "it's not *limbo space* for cripe's sake."

Reegan's mouth curled on one side, "You'd better hope not, or I'm going to make sure you're the first one to experience it *first-hand*..." He glanced at the Marine to his right, "Confined to quarters. No visitors."

"Is that a *threat*, Reegan?" snapped Derrik, as the Marines took control of him. "You heard him, he threatened to space me..."

The Marines were stone-faced, "I didn't hear anything," said one, turning to the other, "did you?" The only reply was a silent head shake. "Nope," said the first, "we didn't hear anything."

Reegan turned away to head back to his command chair and paused mid-step, "Make it the brig, gentlemen..."

■ ■ ■

Commander T. B. Yafusco and Ensign Grinah returned to the bridge from the Captain's ready room, Lieutenant Dash Zarnev currently occupying the command chair. "What's our status, Lieutenant?"

Dash glanced over his shoulder, "We're making progress, Skipper. Shields are up..."

Tibby was saw the warm glow of the shields on the starboard side of the ship, "I see that."

"As you've noticed," he indicated the view screen, "we're still experiencing effects of the solar storm, which have gotten more intense. Sensors are picking up increased ion activity."

"We have sensors back? Wonderful..."

"We have comms back on line as well, but transmission and reception is highly distorted. We haven't successfully reached out at all yet. Main drives are going through restart protocol," he rose from the seat to relinquish it to Yafusco, moving over to the first mate's chair, "so we should be under way in about half an hour."

Grinah stood behind Tibby's chair, her hands resting on his shoulders, "What about our weapons systems?"

Dash Zarnev held no animosity to being questioned by Grinah, even though she was a subordinate officer - everyone on the ship knew the relationship between Grinah and Yafusco. No one questioned her authority; when she spoke, it might just as well have come from the Skipper himself. Besides, she never took advantage of her position, it was more like they were a command team - and they worked well together. "Weapons systems come right after engine startup, ma'am. We prioritized flight over fight, and we have eaten through most of our stock of spare bio-relays, but we still have some left. We hope to get the greater portion of the weapons systems back on line."

"Shopping list?"

"Yes ma'am, the Skipper has one I started on his right screen, probably about the third or fourth tab down," he pointed.

"Let's hope Lindmore will have what we need," commented Tibby, paging to the list.

■ ■ ■

346

It was only forty-five minutes to Madrassas gate when Commander Reegan looked up from his command screens, prompted by the collective gasp of the bridge crew, fixated on the big screen. A massive gap appeared on the right side of the jump tunnel, darkness and flecks of light visible as the normally silver satin wall, turned fire red, orange and yellow, dissolving like melting nylon, disappearing...

"Mass Ion Wave..!" shouted the officer at astrometrics. "By the Gods, readings are..."

"Shields up!" ordered Reegan as the ship gave the impression it was sliding sideways.

Ragnaar fought with the controls as the Perseus washed sideways, stern first, then rolled like a football, wobbling, until he managed to fight it to a neutral position, finally getting the flecks of light outside to stop their sickening gyrations.

"Thank you Mr. Ragnaar. All stop." He closed his eyes for a moment to clear the image of swirls from his mind.

"All stop, aye."

Reegan rose from his command chair, "All stations, damage report. Astrometrics," he pointed, "figure out where the hellion we are." He stood in the center of the bridge, staring at a spread of stars near and far, having no idea if they were stars he knew or not. Whether they were in real space or what was referred to as null space. Was null space like Derrik Brighton had claimed, simply un-navigated space in-between systems? He'd heard about the ships that came before the gates, the generational ships that flew for hundreds of years to reach a single destination. But surely a modern ship like the Perseus wouldn't fall to that fate... could it? The null space of stories, legends, was a nightmarish place where the physics of space travel didn't exist. Where nothing existed, where physical properties didn't exist. Since the Perseus remained, perhaps not all the stories were true. His mind toyed with the possibility of flying a hundred years with a modern ship and never reaching anything. "Astrometrics?"

"She's still working, Commander. This may take a while."

"Damage report?"

"Nothing yet, sir."

■ ■ ■

347

Reegan remained unmoved on the couch in his office when the comm chimed, "I'm here, go ahead."

"Xian Pi, Skipper. We're in the uncharted space outside of the Xian Pi System..."

"Xian Pi..." mumbled, Reegan swinging his feet off to sit up, "where the hellion is that? I've never heard of it..."

CHAPTER TWENTY NINE

AMANPOOR : *THE TORTOISE AND THE HARE*

Inspector Brooker tapped the glass screen of his MOBIUS, the holo-screen popping open, "Talk to me Sweetness..."

The female Data Bridge officer with the short platinum hair stared back at him, "We picked up the bartender from The Black Hole Bar & Grille. So far she hasn't been forthcoming with any information."

"The other bartender said she was the one serving them, correct?"

"Correct. She reportedly left with a man from that party. By the description, it may be the Jax Mercury person you're looking for. The description of the woman he arrived with, is very close to the one you had in custody for questioning. There was no sign of him at her apartment but call records show she requested a car service at her apartment yesterday..."

"Have we tracked down that service yet?"

"Not yet inspector. It was a small independent so we're still looking."

"I wish we had better control over those small operations," the Inspector lamented. "How about our waiter friend from the Cork & Cleaver?"

"Still working with the image generation program," she replied.

He shook his head, "Something tells me this is all part of a something *much* bigger. This Huang woman was able to elude us much easier than she should have; I don't like it when people disappear like that. It smells too professional... like the Cork & Cleaver. Which makes me really concerned over what our friend Mr. Mercury might be doing in the dark this long. Anything on the guy we found with Huang's MOBIUS?"

"Just a vagrant..."

Brooker sighed heavily, "Keep digging."

He felt a tap on his shoulder, "Sir?"

Brooker turned to the officer behind him, "What have you got?"

The officer pointed down the highway, past the roadblock, "He stopped. He's just hovering there..."

The Inspector turned back to his MOBIUS, "Gotta go, Sweetness. Keep me up to date." Brooker closed the holo-screen, turning to the officer behind him, "Do we have an owner I.D.?"

The officer shook his head, "No, it's a rental. We'll have to contact the agency..."

"And he just went dark," noted the Inspector. "What the hellion does he think he's doing?"

"He's pulling off the highway..." the officer replied, squinting into the darkness.

Booker laughed out loud, "Where does he think he's going in that thing?" He wiped midnight dew from the top of his bald head, "Idiot. He's not going to get far over natural terrain, it doesn't have the power. Our detail is staying here - plot his course and send another unit before he falls off our sensors..."

■ ■ ■

Torn Dado yanked on the wheel turning on a ninety-degree tangent from their direction, "What are you doing?" complained Mercedes.

"We're low and slow. By my estimation, we have fallen off their sensors. They know our course... Somewhere on that course they will be waiting for us. I don't plan to drive right into it."

"Alright... so what's your plan?"

"Not getting stopped comes to mind. Maybe it's just a DUI checkpoint..."

"Where would drunk people be coming from way out here?" pondered Chase.

"I don't know. There is another city beyond where we stopped in the desert..."

"How far?"

"About an hour beyond it at highway speeds."

"Are you thinking of doubling-back to the highway?" she asked, leaning forward between the seats.

"It had occurred to me. But if they tagged us already, the first one to scan the transmitter on this car will realize it's on a wanted list..."

"Any way to disable it?"

Torn Dado shook his head, "Same result, they'd be all over us for that."

Chase leaned back and slid down in his seat, "What a fucking mess... I didn't sign up for this shit." Combat was easier than this; you see a bad guy, you engaged and killed a bad guy. Well, as long as the Rules of Engagement allowed that. Because the damn politicians kept screwing around with them - like they knew anything about war or combat to make any intelligent decisions. Allowing politicians to change ROE criteria was like letting the blind lead the deaf, dumb and stupid. Driving cars. In traffic. It had gotten to the point where you had to wait to get shot at first before you took action. Then they would ask if anyone on your detail was actually hit before you took action. That's when he refused to re-up and go back. Still, it had to be easier than this shit.

"Think of it as a search and destroy mission," smirked Mercedes.

"No offense, but your and my ideas of a search and destroy mission are vastly different. And for my version, I am sorely under-equipped."

■ ■ ■

"This is Brooker, go ahead."

The face of a uniformed officer sitting in a patrol cruiser appeared on the MOBIUS holo-screen, "Inspector, we have two units here at the intercept point. We've been here for over fifteen minutes. Your stray vehicle is a no-show."

"Any chance they got past you before you arrived?"

"No sir, we were in the area."

Brooker responded to the chime on his MOBIUS indicating a second call, "Hold on, officer, I have another call." He tapped MOBI's face on the sidebar, "MOBI, split screen." He grabbed the tab of the spit holo-screen and pulled, separating it into two screens, "Sweetness, what have you got?"

"We're making progress..."

"Good, hold on." He turned to the officer on the other screen, "Do a sweep on their approach vector, see if you can pick them up." He looked at the empty highway, "We're done here, I'll send two from this end to assist you." The officer nodded and the screen winked out, leaving him with one again. He snapped his fingers as he turned, getting the attention of one of the officers attending the checkpoint, "We're done here," he pointed up at the two cruisers hovering in the air-lane, "Send them up to where our friend disappeared off the road and see if they can pick up the trail. They'll meet two units coming from the other end."

"Yes, sir."

"Alright," he said, turning his attention back to the screen, "tell me where we are..."

"Our bartender, Pattiwillow, still isn't talking and the magistrate is threatening to release her in the morning if she's not charged with something..."

"That's alright, we know where to find her. What else?"

"Detectives canvassed her building and a neighbor, a doctor over at Amanpoor Medical Center, claims he attended a gentleman in Pattiwillow's apartment. A man that meets the description of our friend Jax Mercury. He also admitted she *called* him Jax."

"So where is our friend Jax Mercury now?" inquired Brooker.

"He doesn't know. He claims he instructed her to get him prompt medical attention and then he left. Apparently, Mr. Mercury consumed too much Kleer..."

"Kleer," muttered Brooker disdainfully, "why does anyone drink that poison... So, the doctor didn't offer any medical attention, just a recommendation? Just advice? That sounds rather odd, doesn't it?"

"I thought so," replied the Data Bridge officer. "Detectives are checking the admission records of Amanpoor Med Center."

"Good. Any word on the car service?"

"Not until morning when we can request credit records from her bank. Then we'll know who may have transported them and where they went." She looked down for a moment, looking through her notes. "Almost forgot, we have an image of our Good Samaritan at the Cork & Cleaver..."

"It's our friend, Mercedes Huang, isn't it..."

"Yes, Inspector."

"Dammit, I knew it," he snapped. "What the hell is going on here? It's not a coincidence I can tell you that..."

■ ■ ■

"I've got lights on the horizon behind us," called Mercedes kneeling on the back seat, facing backwards, looking out the rear window.

"Are they chasing us?" asked Torn Dado, weaving around obstacles and terrain deformities in the dark.

Mercedes bounced around, managing to hold onto the unbuckled straps of the shoulder harness, "I'm not sure. I just know they weren't there a minute ago..."

"Step on it," urged Chase, "I don't feel like going to prison tonight..."

"I'm going as fast as I can," countered Torn Dado, "hitting a tree isn't going to do us any good either." Tall grass whipped over the nose, the vehicle shuddering as it plowed through bushes and shrubs, bouncing over irregularities in the ground.

Mercedes bounced off the roof, "What the hell was that?"

"We bottomed out. It's going to happen; I can't see well enough to slow down or avoid them... Now if I could turn the lights on..."

"Don't you dare!" she scolded.

The car shuddered and bounced, vaulting over something unseen, everyone feeling momentarily weightless as it crashed down again, a spray of water dousing the car, Torn Dado hammering the throttle wide open to keep the weak anti-gravity from sinking in the marshy ground. Covered in mucky water and slime, visibility zero, something heavy slammed against the windshield, spidering the glass, creating an inward bubble, Chase's arms coming up to protect himself.

Wrestling with the beaten vehicle, the Torn Dado managed to maintain control as it careened across the ground. Trees flew past on either side, branches screeching across the roof like fingernails on a blackboard as the car bounced and slid. Glancing a passing tree with a fender, sent them pinballing from tree to tree, the metal body painfully squealing with each agonizing hit, spinning the car around, catapulting it off higher ground backwards, crashing to a road a couple feet below, grinding across the pavement of the highway in a shower of sparks, coming to rest on the median.

Half on the floor, upside down, Mercedes righted herself in the back seat with a groan, "What the hell happened?"

Chase glanced at the darkened dash, "I think we killed it."

Torn Dado tested the controls, rotating the car around, "All her electronics are out but she's still running..."

Chase looked up and down the empty highway, "Which way?"

Torn Dado elbowed the broken window out of his door, the glass falling away, the glittering nuggets scattering across the median. He peered into the darkness and back, "I wasn't trying to, but if we're back on the main highway, it should be this way," he pointed left, "to the city beyond the desert."

Mercedes stretched out on the back seat, rolling her neck, "I don't see as we have much choice..."

Torn Dado flipped on the lights, only half of them still working, steering to the left and aiming the vehicle up the empty highway.

"I hope Horse Face paid for the extra rental insurance," remarked Chase.

■ ■ ■

Ribbons of color shimmered across the horizon as the sun neared its edge, though it would be some time before any of that light reached down to the streets between the tall buildings of Amanpoor. Inspector Brooker closed the door of the unmarked patrol vehicle and drug himself to the entrance of the G'Naroth Sarat Security Service building, wondering if his bed missed him as much as he missed it. Maybe a nap on the couch in his office - he couldn't even form full thoughts anymore...

They had searched the remainder of the night, whomever was in that rental car had slipped away in the darkness. Brooker had already admonished himself for not allowing the units to immediately give chase, but at the time it had been pretty clear that the vehicle would not have been that hard to collect. Someone in that car knew what they were doing. Like they knew what they were doing at the Cork & Cleaver. Maybe. Could it be possible *both* people died of natural causes? Maybe. It was more likely something more sinister... but the lab would have to figure that one out, visual and physical evidence present didn't provide anything out of the ordinary. The open end was who was the third person at that table and where did he go? Was *he* the one in the rental car? Could that be why he abandoned his friends? Maybe Mercedes Huang being there was a coincidence. Perhaps the missing third person at that table was *Jax Mercury.*

"By the Gods I need some sleep..." He closed the door to his office, laid his duty weapon on his desk and stretched out on the couch...

■ ■ ■

Chase Holt rubbed his dry eyes, "I can't believe the sun is coming up already..."

"Bengaloo," noted Torn Dado.

Chase looked at him sideways, "*What?*"

"The star. Its name is Bengaloo. And it's not really rising, the planet is..."

"Oh for fuck's sake," grumbled Chase, "I know how it works."

"Oh. I just meant ..."

"Whatever," waved Chase, agitated rubbing his eyes with the heels of his hands. "It's bright and it's killing my eyes." His nerves were abuzz - feeling the old familiar sensation of sleep deprivation that was so well known to him in a combat zone; irritability, tingling fingers and hands that felt more comfortable carrying an M249 Bravo than empty, exhaustion mixed with sleeplessness, vigilance bordering on paranoia...

Torn Dado's yellow eyes flashed with curiosity. He opened his mouth to say something, thought better of it and closed it again. He checked behind him, Mercedes asleep in the back seat. Easing the battered rental over onto the shoulder, he slowed down, looking at the highway junction ahead. "It doesn't go any further. Left, or right?"

Chase shook his head, "I don't know, I haven't seen anything familiar. This can't be the same highway we took out into the desert last night."

"I agree. Since we headed left on this road, another left may risk heading back toward Amanpoor."

"So we're completely lost and just guessing at this point..." it was more a statement than a question.

"Yes," replied Torn Dado, unblinking.

"Just clarifying," confirmed Chase, lips pursed. "Fine, go right."

Torn Dado eased back onto the road, staying on the ground, the damaged car unable to hold height in an air-lane. "We need to get rid of this thing before somebody spots it..."

"I know," grunted Chase, staring blankly at the road ahead.

■ ■ ■

A quick knock on the door preceded it swinging briskly open but Inspector Brooker remained unmoved on the couch with a hat over his eyes. "What," he grumbled flatly.

"I have some updates, Inspector."

"Morning to you too, Sweetness."

The platinum haired Data Bridge officer sighed, "Good morning, Inspector Brooker."

He smiled under the hat, "Coffee?"

"No thank you, I already had some."

"Funny, Sweetness, funny. Ok, what's going on?"

"We got a call back from the rental company for that car - the gentleman who rented it was the same one at the table with our two casualties last night."

"Any sign of him or the vehicle?"

"No. But the rental company did say their logistics show the car went dark last night near route forty-one."

Dammit, it was him. "Alright, put out an *All Watch* out on him and the vehicle. Have the rental company notify us immediately if it somehow reappears."

"Right. It turns out," she continued, "the three of them all arrived on that FreeRanger destroyer, the DD217."

"Interesting..."

"Along with twenty three other people."

Brooker pulled the hat off his face and swung his feet off the couch, sitting up. "That's a pretty big dump, what's up with that - they running livestock?" He played with the brim of his hat, "Do we have a list?"

"There's no reason listed for travel on the travel logs but we do have an arrival list. And it looks like all but a couple are waiting for connecting flights to arrive. Many of them are staying at the Grand Tower Hotel."

"How *convenient*. Round them up. Let's see if we can figure out what's going on here... *Somebody's* got to have a big mouth."

"All of them?"

"Yes, as many as we can find. And let them know in no uncertain terms this is not a *request...*"

"Yes, sir. Oh, and Ms. Pattiwillow's bank responded; the credits she paid out for the car service went to an account for an anonymous funds transfer service..."

"Damn gypsy drivers," frowned Brooker.

■ ■ ■

Among farms and rolling fields with surrounding forests, a large, pinnacled structure of red stone reached out of the canopy of trees on the opposite side of the four-lane divided road. "Stop!" shouted Chase. *"Stop! STOP!"*

"OK, *OK!"* countered Torn Dado, throttling back, sliding the car off onto the shoulder as a truck flew past in the air-lane above them. "What's the problem?"

Chase was out of the car on the side of the road almost before it came to rest, the door swung up over the roof. "I've never seen anything like it..."

Mercedes climbed out, leaning on the mangled rear fender, half awake, "What's with all the shouting?" She followed Chase Holt's gaze at the building across the road and rubbed her face, "Where are we?"

"It's massive..." whispered Chase, reverently.

"What is it?" whispered Mercedes in return, somewhat mockingly.

Chase pointed at the familiar symbols in the stone on the building, "I think it's a Masonic Temple..."

"You are mistaken, my friend," corrected Torn Dado though his missing window, "that's the sign of the Ancient Architects." Chase walked around the front of the vehicle, and broke into a trot across the highway. "Chase! You *don't* want to go there! They are not friendly to outsiders!"

Mercedes rolled history backwards in her mind's eye, less than a year; *was it really that recent? It seemed like an entire lifetime... someone else's life.* She recalled her brief education on Masonry by Agent Mooreland back in The Barn. From what she could remember, Chase was right, they sure looked like Masonic symbols and images. "Wait up!" she called, pausing for a vehicle to pass before sprinting across the road after him. She caught up to Chase as he walked up the long tree-lined drive to the front of the temple, catching his sleeve," What are you thinking, Holt?" her tone inquisitive.

"That if Jack needed help, he may have come here."

"We don't even know where we're at... How would he have even known about it, much less find it?"

"Same as we did," responded Chase. "By accident."

"Look, I'm willing to accept a shot in the dark, but we're really reaching here..."

Chase paused, taking the time to meet her gaze, "When it comes to things happening and falling into place when you're involved in Masonry, I've learned to trust the energy that flows through it. I don't know if I'd call them miracles, but things happen. Things that are far more than just coincidence. Strange, bizarre things..."

"Ok, I get it," she said, patting him on the chest, "you believe in magic..."

"Don't patronize what you don't understand," he warned. "It's a bad idea to arrogantly assume you know better."

Torn Dado jogged up, carrying all three of their pack bags, "Who knows what now?"

Mercedes flashed him a surprised glance, "Where did you put the car?"

"Way back in the trees on the other side of the road," he nodded towards the highway. "It's invisible to traffic. Probably the air too. We're on foot from here on in, though," he added, handing Mercedes and Chase their packs, "that thing's done."

▪ ▪ ▪

Sitting at his desk, Inspector Brooker was holding his hat tightly over his face, *"Aaaaarrrrgggghh!"*

"Inspector?" The Data Bridge Officer stood in the corridor outside his door, leaning in.

He slid the crushed hat up off his face letting it sit crookedly on the top of his head. "Sweetness," he said flatly, a mixture of despair and aggravation on his face.

"Problem?"

"I *hate* these people..." He waved his hand dismissively, "Scratch that, I *despise* these people..."

"I..."

"Do you know..." he began, sweeping his hat from his head, crushing it on his desk, "how many people we got, again..?"

"Fourteen."

"That out of fourteen people, not one of those fourteen claim to know any of the other thirteen? And *two* of them are *married!"*

"How do you know they're..."

"They have the *same last names* and old fashioned wedding bands..."

"I didn't realize anyone wore those anymore..."

"And *by the Gods*, she's an arrogant witch," he continued, ignoring her interruption. "No one knows *anyone*. They're all *complete strangers*. And no one recognizes the photos of our two casualties or the missing person." He let go of the hat and it unrolled somewhat on its own. "They claim they've never even *seen* each other before." He threw his hands up, "We even showed them the digital replays of them coming through the checkpoints together and they were *totally unaware* they all came off the same ship. I couldn't see one tell and voice analysis didn't come up with anything either. These are either trained liars or complete psychopaths."

"What are you going to do?"

"The magistrate isn't going to let us keep them, I've got nothing to hold them on. So, I'm going to let them go... all except the married couple. I'm going to pit them against each other, see if we can stir something up. I could probably sell *that* to the magistrate..."

■ ■ ■

The building looked ancient; stone, wood, stained glass, not the shining metal and glass of the ultra-modern, alien, Amanpoor. But it was beautiful, perfectly crafted and meticulously maintained. Two giant, metal lion statues, one on either side of the long drive, one standing, one reclined, guarded the entrance to the courtyard before the entrance. Two enormous gold pillars bracketed the double-door entryway to the building itself, ornate stone carvings adorning the structure.

The interior was just as impressive; painted, arched ceilings thirty feet high, stained glass far above letting in a spray of color from the morning sun, reflecting off the black and white tile floors, the main corridor reaching away from the entry, lined with massive, ornately carved, wooden pillars.

"Stay here," ordered Chase, pointing at a wooden bench against the wall that resembled a church pew. Forewarned, Mercedes and Torn Dado silently sat themselves on the wooden bench, the thin pad doing little to make it comfortable. It almost forced the body to sit upright and straight, looking forward at the opposite wall. The man in the dark, floor-length, hooded robe, stood at attention beside the bench, the gold-adorned staff in his right hand, clacking the floor as their butts hit the bench. Another man, dressed and equipped identically, his face nearly invisible in the shadows, stood directly across from him, standing next to an empty bench.

"They look like monks," whispered Mercedes.

"Something like that," whispered Torn Dado in return. "Only much more."

She leaned forward to look around the pilot and the monk-sentry, watching Chase disappear down the endless corridor with the monk who had greeted him with closely spoken words, guarded posture and some kind of hidden greeting. "Where do you think they're going?" she whispered.

"I'm sure I have no idea," he whispered back.

"Is it a church? Because it looks like a church... just a lot bigger," she whispered, leaning forward again. "This corridor has got to be a thousand feet long."

"I suppose you could look at it that way," he replied quietly, not really feeling comfortable holding a conversation - no matter how quietly.

"Man, this bench is uncomfortable," she commented, rising to stretch her legs.

The clack of the sentries' staffs on the floor echoed in the entry foyer as they stepped towards each other, turning in unison to face her, blocking her from the corridor, the wood of their staffs clacking together in an X.

359

"Sit. Down," hissed Torn Dado through clenched teeth.

She held her hands up in surrender, backing up and sitting down silently. The sentries stepped back in unison, their staffs whacking the floor as her butt met the pad on the bench.

"Don't do that again," hissed the pilot.

"Don't worry, I won't..."

"This is not a place to test your curiosity."

"I can *see* that. I wasn't trying to do anything more than stretch my legs..."

"Yeah," replied Torn Dado suspiciously, not truly believing her.

■ ■ ■

Chase Holt allowed himself to be gently lead down the corridor, guided by the monk's arm around his, "We've been expecting you, Mr. Holt..." Although not as tall as Chase, the man was sizable; six feet tall, 300 pounds, with silver wavy hair that reached his shoulders and a long beard.

A chill raced up his back, "You know my name..."

"We know many things..." said the man in the robe, his hood cast back over his shoulders.

"You have me at a disadvantage, sir, *I* didn't know I was coming..."

"Pike," offered the man holding his arm. "And yet, here you are."

"I uh, try to recognize when an opportunity is put in my path."

"Good," responded Pike, patting his hand, "your mind is open and receptive." He squeezed Chase's hand for emphasis, "Then recognize what I am about to tell you next, my Brother; energy exists in a delicate balance between dark and light..."

"Uh, huh," replied Chase, unclear.

"Between dark and light - between good and evil, between God and the ungodly... the balance *must* be maintained. If you upset that balance, my Brother, chaos ensues. For one cannot truly exist without the other."

His brow furrowed in contemplation, Chase mulled that thought. "So good can never triumph?"

"Triumph yes, be completely victorious, no. Neither good nor evil can be permanently banished; for neither light nor darkness is definitively finite. Good and evil for the same reason cannot be measured except within the narrow scope of man's laws. And being that those laws are created by man, they are flawed - as the creators of the laws are flawed. Because it has definitions does not mean the definition is fitting, reasonable or complete in

360

its execution." Pike touched his forehead with his index finger, "Here's an example, albeit a simple one; a man writes a law making it illegal to spit on the sidewalk. Sounds pretty simple, does it not? But what is his reasoning for it? Health? Morality? Aesthetics?By creating this law, does he mean it is acceptable to spit in the street? Or inside a house - or a business? What about a walking path? Has he considered the reason someone is spitting? What if it is necessary?" He waved his hand, "But I digress, we've gotten off the topic... which is; be wary you do not become that which you seek to destroy."

"The agents guilty of planetary subversion?"

Pike patted the young man's hand. "You must *stop.*"

"When you say *you...*" Chase said slowly.

"Your little group. And I will be painfully blunt Brother Holt, your actions are destined to end badly if you continue. *Very badly.* You are walking a fine line between light and dark; your perception is that you walk the path of righteousness. But that fact, which is so obvious to you, will be lost when observed from a different angle. Understand this; luck was with you, but the well of luck is not inexhaustible. If the next time you reach for a quench, the well may not provide enough supply for the thirst."

Chase Holt's mind leapt ahead, envisioning a life devoid of luck. "Does the well ever refill?"

"It does. Slowly. By time, circumstance and deed. But if you continue to dip into it so liberally, it will almost certainly be too low to provide you what you require when you need it most."

"I understand," admitted Chase, admiring the works of art and history they passed, in all its forms.

"You are at a crossroads, my Brother. Take great caution in which path you choose... one way continues your journey, the other ends it. Rather abruptly, I might add."

"You understand why we undertook this task?"

"I do indeed. But your task was twofold, was it not?"

"Jack..." nodded Chase.

"Yes."

"Have you seen him? Has he been here?"

"He has," admitted Pike.

"We need to find him, is he still here? "

"He is not. He was here for a time, but he has left. He has been tried, was not denied and is willing to be tried again."

361

Chase was listening carefully to every word, weighing their meanings, "Sooo... he's OK then."

"He is," confirmed the monk. "His path is long and arduous, he has much to do."

"We need to catch up with him, then."

"I'm afraid that is not possible, Brother Holt; the Grand Architect of the Universe has you on a separate path. Your journey, if chosen wisely, while no less difficult, is long and filled with its own trials. It would serve you well to remember your obligations."

Suddenly feeling abandoned and overwhelmed in a life he was unprepared for, Chase was reaching for something, anything, that resembled stability and familiarity. "Will we ever see Jack again?" he asked slowly, an uncomfortable feeling of despair washing over him.

"Possibly, but not for some time. No matter our paths, we all are traveling upon the *Level of Time* toward that undiscovered country..."

Chase nodded, clarity approaching. *No matter where you started in life, or how widely you traveled, all roads eventually merged,* "To that house not made with hands, eternal in the heavens..." he muttered.

■ ■ ■

Continually rolling a gold metal token given to him by Pike, between his fingers in silent contemplation, the trio walked the drive back the way they came in. It wasn't until they passed between the giant lion statues that a realization hit Chase like a slap in the face. He stopped, mid-stride, frozen in place, the token paused between rolls. "Pike..."

"What's that Lassie?" commented Mercedes, "Timmy's fallen down a well?"

Chase shot her an evil glance, "*Albert* Pike..."

"What's that Lassie? Bark a little slower, I can't understand you..." She shrugged, "You say that like it's supposed to mean something to me."

"Ever head of the book *Morals and Dogma?*"

"I might have heard of it in college..."

"It's; *Morals and Dogma of the Ancient and Accepted Scottish Rite of Freemasonry.*"

"Yeah. Kind of explains why I never read it," she commented.

362

Holding his temper, Chase took a deep breath, "Albert Pike was the author. A thirty-third degree Mason from the 1800's, he's the only Confederate General with an outside statue in Washington, D.C."

"Hmm, I think I've *seen* that statue..." she brushed her hair out of her face, "So, what's your point?"

"I just met him."

"That's not possible..." she waved dismissively.

"Why not?" asked Torn Dado, jumping in.

"He died over a century ago," replied Chase.

"No-no-no," countered Mercedes, shaking her head, "it's not possible..."

"Unless it is," mulled Chase. He walked on, rolling the gold token between his fingers again. "I told you, strange things happen when you believe in the energy."

"So what now?" asked Torn Dado.

"We're on our own," replied Chase. "Jack *was* here, but he's not now."

Mercedes tried unsuccessfully to snag his arm, "Wait, what?" she asked, catching up. "If he's not here, where is he?"

"They didn't say."

Mercedes jumped in front of him with her hands out in front of her, stalling him, "And you didn't bother to ask? What the hell... Exactly how does that conversation go? They tell you he's come and gone and you just nod and say, *OK?*"

With one arm he swept her aside, "It wasn't my place to ask - if they wanted me to know they would have told me."

"That doesn't make any sense, why wouldn't they tell you?"

"We have divergent paths. He has to walk *his* alone, we have to..."

"Oh, *come on!*" she objected. "You can't possibly believe the crap that's coming out of your mouth..."

"Actually," injected Torn Dado, "even with my limited knowledge of the Ancient Architects, I would tend to believe everything they told me..."

"Then you're just as gullible as he is," she snapped, thumbing towards Chase.

Chase paused, turning towards her, "Do you believe in coincidence?"

"What?" She searched her mind, "It depends..."

"At what point do you stop believing something was a coincidence?" He stayed her rebuttal with a wave of his hand, "Because maybe I should run this backwards for you; the series of very intricate events that lead us here..." He began ticking them off on his fingers, "We weren't looking for this place,

363

nor did we know it even existed. The one place on the planet we *needed* to find, but had no idea we were *required* to find. We were, and still are, *completely and totally lost*. We guessed which way to turn when the road we were on connected to this one. We guessed which way to turn, in the dark, on a road which we *thought* was the highway to the desert - but wasn't. After running a vehicle off-road, that, was by all description, completely inadequate for the task. While avoiding a roadblock. After eliminating three enemy targets on a *wing and a prayer*. And there's got to be a half dozen just in the restaurant..." he added, losing track of which finger he was on. He dropped his hands, "We followed a *single* man to a restaurant to be awarded with *multiple* people involved in the overthrow of our planet, a multitude of star systems away. A man which we *accidentally* recognized in an alien city where we knew *no one*, save a barmaid we were searching for, but never found." He thumbed at Torn Dado, "And isn't it convenient that we have a chauffeur since you or I cannot operate these vehicles..." He waited until he saw some form of reaction before cutting her off, "*Aaaand...* lost, abandoned and seemingly destitute with no way to survive, in a place we are unfamiliar with, we find ourselves blessed with seven-hundred-fifty-million credits." He folded his arms, "Coincidence? Because that's *a lot* of damn coincidences..."

Mercedes glanced back at the building without speaking, her arms folded.

"If we were at home, I'd say let's go play the lottery..." Chase threw up his hands, "Oh wait, *we already did,* and *we won...*" he pointed at her.

"Seven-hundred and fifty-million," she mumbled.

"And it goes a lot further back than that," he added quietly. "Think back to the first time you met Jack. *I've* known him for years. Everything between then and now; every event, every nuance - and here we are - this is where the energy lead us." He nodded towards the Architects Temple, "So if they have something to say, I'm going to listen. If there's something they choose *not* to tell me, I have to believe there's a reason for that as well."

Mercedes let her arms drop with a sigh, "OK I get it. What do we do now?"

"First, no more hunting targets, we're off the case..."

"But..."

"We're done," he insisted, pointing a finger at her. "More importantly; *we disappear.*"

"How do we..."

364

Chase indicated a car that had pulled up into the Temple's drive, the door opening up over its roof. "We ride there."

"Where's *there?*"

"The city past the desert," he replied, steering Mercedes toward the car.

Hovering on anti-gravity, the car dipped as the trio climbed in. "Where to, folks?" asked the smiling driver, looking back over his shoulder, the door dropping back into place.

"Sandorra," answered Chase, holding the gold token up close enough for the driver to see the markings of the Ancient Architects on it.

"I understand," he nodded, rotating the car around, sliding out into light traffic, accelerating smoothly, rising up into an air-lane. "So how is everyone this morning? Good I hope. It's a bit of a ride to Sandorra, so make yourselves comfortable, there's drinks in the console," he tapped it with his elbow. "If you need anything or have any questions - my friends call me *Flash...*"

CHAPTER THIRTY

DEEP BLACK, SCAVENGER ONE : *VELORIA*

Despite the fact that it was, at first, a little touch and go with the heavily-armed Warthog fighters that had rampaged out from the Wronin to intercept her, Chariska was proud of how well she managed it, remaining relatively unflustered. Being that the Scavenger One wasn't armed with anything more than a couple salvage cutting lasers, went a long way to convince them her arrival was nothing more than pure coincidence. After verifying her ship's registration, they seemed satisfied she was of no threat and on legitimate business.

Her sensors had picked up the small flight of ships that had departed the big Velorian cruiser parked in orbit above the planet, bound for the surface, but she had no idea of their significance. Her sensors hadn't displayed any information other than the fact that they were there. In retrospect, that should probably have triggered some suspicion that there was something out of the ordinary about them. Her best guess was the response of fighters had some significance tied to that flight - but they weren't saying. Despite their *all business* demeanor, they remained professional and amicable, thanking her for her cooperation. Not that she had much choice, mind you, but with what she knew of Veloria's recent history, she could certainly understand their caution.

She was both surprised and appreciative of the escort to the surface, a pair of fighters showing her the way to something they called the ASP, the *Air and Space Port,* which was the main travel and trade hub for the planet. Until a new approach and departure navigation assistance setup for the planet was completed, new visitors could expect to be led by the hand to control approach traffic.

Twice they passed departing flights heading back out of the atmosphere, almost exactly on their approach vector, coming within a mile of each other.

She took note of the gorgeous colors as they approached, the deep greens of the terrain and vibrant blues of the oceans. Dropping out of descent about a mile above the ocean they passed over a giant metal spindle sticking out of the turquoise water that upon approach and closer observation grew much larger than it initially appeared. Partially hidden in the depths of the water, definition broken by rolling waves, a wide shadow looked almost as big as a full space station.

"Gray Three to Deep Black, you got me?"

Cheriska broke her gaze away from the silver spindle and the rolling turquoise below her ship, glancing to her left, the pair of Warthog D's maintaining formation out her port window. "Go ahead, Gray Three."

"OK, Deep Black, your speed and altitude are fine. Stay on this heading and follow the canyon inland. In three minutes you'll get directions from ASP Control to guide you in."

She eyed the approaching coastline, "Thank you Gray Three..." The Breedlove's Dragon she had yet to name circled round her neck, standing on her shoulder, looking out the left side of the cockpit, tittering in her ear.

"Blue skies, Deep Black. Welcome to Veloria." In near perfect unison, they winged over, breaking into a left arc, taking them back over open water. Half way through their turn they leveled off before pulling up, their twin engines flashing blue white as they streaked nearly vertical, the atmosphere compressing around them as they disappeared, a tandem sonic boom rolling across the sky, two small clouds forming, a pair of vapor trails pointing to the heavens.

■ ■ ■

On her approach to the ASP, sun had given way to broken clouds. By the time Cheriska had the Vulture tucked into the rental hangar and buttoned up, a light rain had started across the facility.

Her duffel felt a little heavier here. Flexing her legs, she set the security on her Vulture from her MOBIUS and closed the screen. Heading across the hangar floor she waved a thank you to the ground crew. It was not her imagination, real gravity felt a little heavier; not uncomfortable, but noticeable.

Duffel bag in hand, she strolled out of the open hangar door and stopped halfway to the waiting hover car, closing her eyes and turning her face upwards, oblivious to the curious stare of the puzzled driver. The Breedlove's Dragon tucked his head under his wing, clutching her leather jacket. She hadn't felt rain since she was twelve, over twenty years ago. And by the Gods, the sweet smell of fresh, rain-washed air... *it was so amazing.* Childhood memories came rushing in at her; she remembered having a

Corsicat as a childhood pet... *Magui*... she had completely forgotten about her. A mixture of feelings and emotions washed over her, tears mixing with the raindrops running across her face. It was *exhilarating*...

"Hey, *lady*..." called the driver from his open window, a touch of impatience in his voice.

She bought her gaze back to the real world and blinked away the raindrops. "Yeah - yeah, don't get your shorts in a wad..." she replied, a smile crossing her face, stepping towards the car.

■ ■ ■

Having been excused from the dinner table, Colton Steele was rolling on the floor with the Volken puppy, family and friends still eating and conversing. Lady Phyllis, the Grand Matron of the house enjoyed an occasional meal with the family, regarded as such. Coffee cup in hand, she leaned over to Alité whispering closely, "Is it possible that thing has grown already?"

Alité watched her son and Jax play, her attention unbroken. "I hardly think so," she shook her head, "it's only been a week. At least I don't see it..."

Lady Phyllis leaned back again, "I *swear* he looks like he's grown."

Prime Minister Nitram Marconus and his wife Willamena, both considered family, sat across the table from Alité, chatting with the others around them. The Prime Minister's TESS chimed, her face appearing on the glass screen. He excused himself from the table to take the call, returning a few minutes later, a bewildered look on his face.

"Something wrong, Boney?" asked Alité.

"I... it was a very strange call. It seems there's a woman going through security at the ASP who says she's here on Veloria to see you..."

"Me?" Alité's eyes went wide. "Who is she?"

"Cheriska Skye. Daughter of Alfano Toberus."

■ ■ ■

A small six-person armored shuttle sat on the circular palace drive just beyond the steps to the entrance, the side door open, the Prime Minister's four-man Peacekeeper security detail in and around it, waiting patiently in the persistent drizzle. Standing under the covered pergola at the entrance to

368

the palace, Alité laid her hand on the sleeve of Nitram Marconus' jacket, "Boney are we even sure this is possible? I always thought Walrick and LaNareef were his only children..."

Your uncle was a terrible womanizer."

"I'd heard that, but..."

"He had mistresses everywhere," continued the Prime Minister, "and there was one particularly terrible scandal, where the woman died."

"I don't remember that."

"You were still a child, my dear. All the evidence pointed to Alfano as the murderer, but at the request of your grandfather, the King, the evidence was buried to save the royal family from a nightmare that could have destroyed Veloria. Your grandfather penned an irrevocable decree that Alfano could never hold a position of power here on Veloria or within the empire - he knew your uncle was grossly unfit."

"I don't understand, why is he using Toberus, when the family name is Galaýa?"

"Alfano decided using your great, great, great grandfather, Magistrate Toberus' name, was a defiant affront to the entire royal family. His sick little joke. When your grandfather handed down the crown to your father before he passed, it was clear Alfano was going to continue to be a problem for the family. He gave your father the ultimate power to deal with Alfano permanently if it became necessary, but your father could not bring himself to do what was his Kingly duties demanded of him. He was a just and honest man, but some thought, and I'd have to agree, a little soft on some of the hard decisions."

Alité eyed him suspiciously, "I'm not sure I understand what you're saying..."

"If you father had put Alfano down like the animal he became, your mother and father would likely have died of old age..."

"And Dakkah and Mozzy would still be alive..."

"Your brother and sister," he said gently, remorse in his voice. "Not necessarily, he had already poisoned LaNareef's mind against the family. Poor boy, he was never as strong as Walrick."

Alité positioned herself in front of the Prime Minister, hands on hips, a mixture of emotions fighting for position. "Why didn't you tell me these things before?"

Boney laid his hand on her shoulder, his years of wisdom, medical experience and familial knowledge poured out in his voice. "It is in the past, my dear. Nothing you do in the present will change the past. And burdening you with ancient history that you cannot change would have only served to distract you from the tasks you had at hand."

"But I'd like know where my father failed," she wagged her finger at him, "so I can avoid the mistakes he made..."

Boney squeezed her shoulder, "I don't see much chance of that, my dear Queen; where your father lacked in warrior fortitude, you seemed to have gotten an extra helping. You have no trouble making the hard decisions, in fact you excel at them."

Alité leaned in, "Are you saying I'm a *hard* woman?"

Boney recognized a verbal joust when he heard one, "I prefer the word *strong*. Strong of mind, strong of will, strong of commitment and dedication..."

Alité could find nothing to argue there and stepped back with a wry smile, he'd bested her. She waved him off, "Go. Go find out who she really is and what she wants."

■ ■ ■

Cheriska sat in the armored shuttle between two Peacekeepers, across from Prime Minister Marconus and two more Peacekeepers. She had no defined expectations on how things would transpire but the two-hour-long interview was not as stressful as she could have imagined it, had she tried. Other than inspecting her birth documents and a painless DNA test, the interview was more a discussion and the Prime Minister had been gracious and accommodating. She wasn't sure why that surprised her, but it did. She had the distinct feeling it could have gone *much* differently though, if she hadn't been exactly who she said she was. The Breedlove's Dragon on her shoulder, who was relaxed and calm now, showed signs of distress during the interview, pacing and posturing across her shoulders, though he never became aggressive. She was going to have to pay closer attention to him in the future, he definitely seemed a good barometer of the situation.

"Does he have a name?" asked Boney, nodding in the direction of Cheriska's dragon.

"Not yet," she replied, "I'm hoping something strikes me as appropriate."

■ ■ ■

When she entered the palace, it was a little smaller than she'd pictured it would be, but its columned entrance, polished marble entry and arched ceilings suddenly left Cheriska feeling severely self-conscious - she was horribly under dressed. When she saw the Queen approaching from the salon dressed in a smart, perfectly tailored white suit and sheer cape, she went from self-conscious to mortified. Professional but feminine, the Queen walked with poise and confidence, something that Cheriska was quickly losing faster than a tree sheds leaves on a windy, Fall day.

Alité smiled widely, extending her hand even as she approached, "Welcome to the house of Steele, cousin. I am Alité."

Cheriska took the hand offered her and dropped to a knee, her head bowed, the Breedlove's Dragon venturing off her shoulder and down her arm to sniff the Queen's hand. She caught him with her free hand, preventing him from going too far. "My apologies..." she offered. "Cheriska Skye."

Alité pulled up on the woman's hand, grabbing her by the elbow and helping her to her feet, "You are family; family doesn't kneel here." She pulled the surprised woman close for a hug, the miniature dragon unsure of where to retreat. When they parted, he ended up standing on Alité's shoulder.

"I am so sorry," said Cheriska reaching out for him. He ducked under Alité's long hair and emerged on her other shoulder, seeming to enjoy the sensation. Cheriska ran her hand through her short-cut hair, "I think he likes your long hair..."

Alité giggled, "He's adorable. What's his name?"

"I haven't given him one yet..."

Alité put her arm out, resting her hand on Cheriska's shoulder, "Go home to mama, little man," she encouraged. With a quick rub on her cheek he obeyed, running across the bridge to Cheriska. "He's precious. You *must* to come up with a name for him..."

"If you have any suggestions, I would welcome them..." Alité turned to lead them to the salon, "I apologize for not being properly dressed, your Majesty..."

"Alité," she corrected her cousin. "Just Alité. And I see nothing wrong with the way you are dressed. You are clothed for travel and function; I often dress the same way."

■ ■ ■

Since the other dinner visitors had departed during the Prime Minister's absence, all that remained for an evening nightcap were; Alité, Cheriska, the Prime Minister and his wife, Willamena. Having bathed and tucked young Colton Steele into bed with his Volken companion, Lady Phyllis joined them, setting a platter of cookies on the low table in the center of the group.

"You must try these," urged Alité, "Lady Phyllis makes the most amazing Pattahoolia cookies..."

The conversation lasted several hours, drifting from Cheriska to the Prime Minister to Alité and back around again. Every little bit seemed to fill more of the voids for everyone; the missing history, the tragedies, the survival, the recovery, the return home... Cheriska learned the relationship between Alité and the Prime Minister stemmed from her childhood and his position as the royal family physician, where he garnered the nickname, Boney, that she still used today. And that he seemed to be an endless wealth of historical information, about both, Veloria and the royal family. He had actually known her father, Alfano Toberus and it pained her deeply to know how much damage he had done and what kind of chaos he had created. At least in her own life, when he was gone, he was forgotten; she remembered him by only the tiniest of margins. She could only recall bits and pieces of her early life - her childhood didn't really exist in her memory until her aunt, Rafaella, rescued her from the orphanage on Darius.

But for Cheriska, the real tragedy was the magnitude of misery and destruction, her father, had affected the royal family and the people of Veloria. *That fact constantly stuck painfully in her throat.* "By the Gods, I am *so, so, sorry* for what he did. I cannot imagine what it must have been..."

Boney reached across and patted her hand, "No, no, no, Cheri my dear," he interrupted, "you cannot take the burden of evil perpetrated by another, upon yourself. As an innocent child you had no control of your life, much less anyone else's. If it has come to be, as it has, we must trust, that to some extent it is part of a larger plan contrived by someone with an understanding of things well beyond our own comprehension."

"And," added Alité, "since Alfano abandoned a staggering amount of finances; fifty-million-credits by your account, we can only assume that he is no longer among the living; a man of his nature would never have done that willingly. We can only hope his demise was deservedly horrifying and painful." She scrutinized a cookie between her fingers, "May the demons of hellion thoroughly torture his soul for eternity..."

■ ■ ■

Despite the late hour and Alité's offer for them to stay, Boney and Willamena had excused themselves to return home for the night, leaving Cheriska and the Queen alone after Lady Phyllis retired for the evening. After a night of discussing history, conversation turned to lighter subjects including the present and the future. Sitting together on a sofa, propped on pillows and snuggling with lap warmers, they chatted like sisters, the Breedlove's Dragon curled in a slumbering ball between them.

"I can't imagine the pressure you must be under, after all you've been through, to literally have the weight of an entire planet resting on your shoulders..."

Alité stared down at the sleeping dragon for a moment before looking back up, "I couldn't do it without Boney, and some other very dedicated people..." She paused for a moment, "And as my husband Jack says; *One step at a time. Keep putting one foot in front of the other and soon you find yourself standing at your destination.*"

Cheriska looked surprised, "Oh. I didn't know you were married."

Alité looked momentarily pensive, "Several years now. My, it has gone by *so* fast..." She smiled weakly, "We don't get to see him much."

"Well why not?"

Alité shrugged, "His duties take him away from home..."

"That's just sad," commented Cheriska, stroking the sleeping dragon. "What does he do?"

Alité chewed her lip, "I'm not sure I should be telling you..."

"Who am I going to tell?" shrugged Cheriska with a cherubic smile.

Alité rolled it over in her mind for a moment, it wasn't exactly a secret, after all. "Other than being the King of Veloria, he is a high-ranking officer in the UFW Navy."

Cheriska's eyes widened, "Really? That sounds very time consuming. I'm surprised you ever get to see him at all!" She took a moment to process that information. "How... I mean you're the Queen, you're royal family... how did he become King? I'm not sure I understand..."

"I coronated him before he left. There were concerns that if something happened to me, that Veloria would be left without a leader. Jack is my husband and a natural born leader. I thought it was a wise choice."

Cheriska nodded thoughtfully, "I understand." The Breedlove's Dragon had rolled on his back, his wings open and relaxed as she rubbed his belly. "But he was never a part of any royal family then?"

Alité waved it off, "That never mattered to me. He is a *good man.* His bravery, integrity and honor are what make him the man he is." She leaned toward the coffee table, activating a small holo-pedestal sitting on it, a picture winking into existence of Jack standing under the nose of a Cyclone fighter in his leather flight jacket, taken on the flight deck of the Freedom. "And he's not too bad to look at..." she smiled proudly.

The recognition was instant. Cheriska's mouth dropped open.

"Mommy! Mommy!"

Alité turned away, never seeing her reaction, "We're here in the salon, Colton..."

"Mommy! Mommy!" he cried, running through the rotunda where the hallways met, prompting her to rise to her feet, the Katana that never left her side clutched in her hand by the Saya. He raced through the doorway, the Volken puppy on his heels.

"Colton, what's the matter?" She caught him with her free hand as he crashed into her and grabbed her around the waist, the puppy sliding to a stop and catching sight of the Breedlove's Dragon at the same time. The Dragon was faster than the puppy, launching himself off the sofa and taking flight before the animal's curiosity spurned him into action. He hovered high enough that he was out of reach as Jax eyed him intently.

"Mommy! Daddy's home! Daddy's home! He's in my room...!"

It took a second for Alité to process that claim, "Colton, daddy's not coming home yet, were you dreaming? Were you asleep?"

He let go of her waist and pulled on her hand, "No, mommy, no; *daddy is here.* He's in my room! He scared me at first," he admitted. "Come see," he dragged on her, "I'll show you..."

The Dragon had settled high atop a fireplace mantle, well out of reach of the Volken puppy, clicking in aggravation. After a final glare, Jax decided to break away and follow his boy, galloping after him as they headed to his room.

A security team waited patiently outside Colton's room, the lights on, the doors open, "The room is clear, your Majesty," announced the man closest to her.

Alité stood in the doorway, "Colton, I don't see anything, do you?" she asked softly.

"Oh no!" He exclaimed, "The lights hurt his eyes!" He pointed to a corner of the room next to a chair, "He's there, don't you see him?" he said, reaching for the lighting controls.

"Sweetie, I don't see anyth..." As the lights dimmed, a tall figure appeared exactly where Colton had indicated, and she swept her son clear before the Katana come out of its sheath with a *zwing*. The long dark hooded cloak obscured the figure's face but she felt a familiarity, waving the security team, who had instantly appeared on either side of her, back. "Voorlak?" she whispered. The face turned up toward her and for a brief instant she caught a flash of green in the left eye from the lights in the corridor behind her.

■ ■ ■

Helmet dangling loosely from one hand, Lisa Steele plodded down the corridor of the Revenge to her quarters, exhausted from a day in the cockpit of the Reaper with too few breaks. *Mmmm, a hot shower and a meal...* The meal secondary to the hot shower to release the aches from hours of being in the same position in a confined space. Screw it, maybe a power bar and a drink from the mini fridge would suffice, she could always eat breakfast in the morning... Unless maybe it *was* morning. Well then she'd have dinner. *Whatever*.

The door to her quarters slid open and her German Short-Haired Pointer, Gus dropped off the sofa to greet her, his stubby little tail successfully wagging the entire back half of his body along with it. "Hey Gusstifer," she smiled, reaching out to rub his wiggling frame with her free hand, tossing her helmet on the bed, "man, mommy's pooped."

She straightened up, and began the task of removing her flight gear. Chest rig, sidearm, e-Pad holding her flight and mission notes from her thigh strap... Stripped to her waist, save her 2ndSkyn under garment, she sat on the ottoman at the foot of her bed to get to her boots when her earbud chirped, *"Lieutenant Steele, are you still plugged in..?"*

She stopped mid-task dropping her head to her chest, *ugh.* She touched the earbud activating the mic, "Steele here."

"Lieutenant, the Admiral is requesting your presence for a briefing on the Conquest."

She recognized Brian Carter's voice, "Now?"

"Now, Lieutenant."

"Permission to speak freely, Skipper?"

"Granted."

"Whiskey, Tango Foxtrot - I've been in the cockpit for nearly eleven hours..."

"I'm aware of that Lisa," he admitted.

"I *just* got my bag off... I could *really* use a shower and a bite."

There was an uncomfortable pause before she got a response, *"I think we can buy you a few minutes, Lieutenant. But step it up. Service dress in twenty minutes on the deck. We'll taxi you over."*

"Thank you, sir. Any idea what's going on?"

"Apparently above my pay grade, LT."

"Hm, I'll fill you in when I get back." Her earpiece blipped as she canceled the mic and tore at her boots.

■ ■ ■

Lisa wiped a clearing in the fogged mirror, combing her wet hair back, gathering it into a ponytail. "Not my best look, but it'll have to do," she lamented. She could live without the kind of makeup other women used but her hair was a different matter. *Oh, well.* Mostly dry with her towel draped over her shoulders she padded naked, out into her open quarters, her standard officers uniform laying neatly across the bed.

She caught the visitor comfortably sitting on the sofa next to Gus and she snap-turned for a better look, her modesty spinning her away to sling the towel around her for cover, "Jack! You're back!" she grinned widely. "You ass, how about some warning!" Snugging the towel, her heart hammering with surprise, a rush of warmth and affection washed over her body like a hug. She wheeled back to greet him, arms wide, and Gus wagged at her from the couch, his butt wiggling a happy dance. Alone. There was no place else to go in the suite, no place to hide, but that did not stop her from stepping to the center of the room and doing a 360° pirouette to scan around her. Her eyes narrowed and she clenched her jaw, " Jack, if this is some sort of a joke," she growled, stepping to the sofa and sweeping her hand through the empty air, "it's *not* funny..." She stood, hands on hips and did another 360° circle, "What the hell, am I losing my mind?" She patted the dog on the head, "Mommy's overtired, Gusstifer."

■ ■ ■

Though Lisa had been in the cockpit for nearly eleven hours, she had been operational for nearly sixteen hours. Escorting shuttles and equipment ships from orbit to the surface and around the planet - escorting ships of dignitaries, evacuees or medical personnel, acting as an initial liaison when applicable... and this had been going on for weeks. Off-duty hours were short, breaks were few and far between, and the natives weren't always friendly.

When Bobby Fortuno and his partner Nick Osmanski were dropped back off in Chicago, Lisa had a feeling they were going to be thankful for the special body armor and pulse rifles they were provided by the UFW Marines. In a spectacular moment of monumental government stupidity and total loss of common sense exhibited by city officials and upper brass at the police department, the massive delivery of highly-advanced, self-sufficient communications equipment, alien body armor and *death ray rifles*, as one reporter called them, was rejected upon delivery to O'Hare Airport.

The well-attended meeting, held in an expansive hangar, stacked with shipping-container sized crates of equipment, was to be returned to the UFW because of ignorance, or pride, or because somebody's brother-in-law didn't make some side money on the deal. Or something. Yeah, because Chicago.

In her temporary role as a liaison for the delivery, her complete loss of patience in the meeting prompted a rather drastic, but effective tactic; she shot the Mayor.

Taking Omanski's pulse rifle from him, she turned and shot the Mayor, a Police Lieutenant wearing a ballistic vest and then Osmanski himself. The only one left standing and conscious was Osmanski, of course. She considered shooting the reporter with the big mouth, but by then, there were so many people on their feet and in the way, it wasn't possible.

Not her finest moment. But it *was* convincing. Especially when the Mayor and Lieutenant could walk away a little while afterward with no ill-effects. Yeah, that was Lisa Steele; *making friends, winning hearts, changing minds, and influencing people.*

It had been weeks of that and she was dog-tired. She wondered if all the other pilots were as worn out as she was. Lisa checked her fingernails as the shuttle settled to the deck of the Conquest.

"You're good to go, Lieutenant," came a call from the cockpit.

■ ■ ■

377

Fleet Admiral Warn Higdenberger waved Lisa to a seat on the opposite side of his desk, the CAG, Captain Paul Smiley, standing off to one side. "Am I in trouble or something?" she asked suspiciously, her eyes flicking between the two men, looking for some sign or indication of what the meeting meant.

"You're not in trouble," replied Pappy, dryly, his hands clasped behind him, standing at an uneasy, at-ease.

Taking her seat, Lisa's ears felt hot, her cheeks warm, her stomach somersaulting, "What's going on?" Warn Higdenberger shifted uncomfortably in his seat, leaning back before leaning forward again, resting his hands on the edge of his desk. His face was dour, solemn, and his prolonged silence wasn't helping Lisa's nervous need to bounce her knee, which she was fighting to prevent.

"Admiral Jack's Steele's shi..." he shifted to a softer posture, "your *brother's ship*, the Perseus, is missing. The Perseus ported at Amanpoor, on G'Naroth Sarat, in the Bengaloo System as part of their mission." Higdenberger slid an e-Pad across the desk containing mission notes, "It relaunched from Amanpor in pursuit of a target it was tracking. We believe, but it was never confirmed, it may have left Admiral Stee... ahem, *your brother,* behind on G'Naroth Sarat, along with three other crew members. The Perseus was last pinged in Edenlight, entering the gate to Madrassas before she disappeared. There has been no contact with the Perseus, your brother, or any other members of the crew since..."

Lisa was listening and examining the mission notes on the report at the same time, "This was *five weeks ago!*" she interrupted angrily. "Why are you just telling me now?"

"We had to wait to see if they were possibly following *Dark Protocol...*"

"Five weeks," she growled, sliding the e-Pad back with an angry flick of her wrist. "There's no excuse for that." Rather than bounce her knee, she stood, turning away to pace, "And what are we doing now? Let's go look for them!"

"Please, sit dow..."

"I can't sit down," she snapped, "my brother and his crew are out there somewhere and you haven't done a damn thing in *five weeks!"*

"Lieutenant Steele," insisted the Admiral, "please understand that Dark Protocol has a considerable amount of leeway - and there may be functional reasons they haven't made contact; not because they're *unable,* but because it may jeopardize the operational security of their mission."

She folded her arms defensively, "Then if everything is all hunky dory and copacetic, why tell me now?" She spread her hands wide, "And how long do you intend to wait before you actually *do* something?"

"At ease, Lieutenant," warned Pappy.

She grabbed her forehead, "How can I be at ease? It sounds to me like you've left him out there without a *backup plan..."*

"Your brother knew the risks going into this assignment..."

"Assignment? Wait, why do I get the feeling that there's a whole lot more to this thing than I was told?"

"This plan was a year in the making, Ms. Steele," began the Admiral, "and much of it was your brother's doing." He saw the surprise on her face and held his hand up, "Let me finish. Initially, he was going undercover to infiltrate Dark Territory and rub elbows with the Pirates. The goal was to gain some insights to their operations, structure, strength and assets. To do that he needed a special ship; one that looked and operated like a transport but was able to defend itself in a pinch. He needed to be able to operate in their world, so it had to look the part without any signs of its true nature. The ship was built in secrecy, by a new shipbuilder never before used by the UFW, and was chosen for the job based on their willingness to not make another of its kind, unless it was by my personal request."

"So," she folded her arms, "you're telling me this whole demotion thing, losing the task force - is all an act..."

"Jack's rank has never been remanded," offered the Admiral. "We felt it was a necessary part of the operation. That was for the thousands of eyes watching."

"And the whole pursuing the escaping agents thing?" she pointed at the hologram of Earth hovering over the chart table.

"A lucky bonus," offered Pappy. "One of the reasons everything appeared rushed, it was unplanned. We hoped the Perseus could track the agents, possibly capture or eliminate a few, gather some intel... Ultimately we wanted to see who they were connected to. There are some theories that this goes beyond Pirate and FreeRanger influence... that there may be UFW entanglements. Since no one would consider a transport ship traveling in the same direction as a threat, or suspicious, it seemed like the perfect opportunity."

"In any operation like this, the less people that know, the better," explained Higdenberger. "In retrospect, we probably should have included you more closely in what was going on..."

"Ya think?" she gestured widely.

"We were hoping you might assist us with a special assignment to help us find him," said Pappy. "Your inexperience notwithstanding, your actions in the recovery of your brother's crippled yacht and how you handled yourself as Lisa Stone on Rikovik's Reef, was innovative and resourceful. Those kinds of instincts and critical thinking may be key to locating the Perseus and her crew - your brother included. Because you know him better than anyone else, you know how he thinks - we are counting on your insights."

Lisa's jaw set, "I don't care how we do it, we need to find him..." she hissed through clenched teeth, "cuz if he's not dead, I'm gonna kill him..."

CHAPTER THIRTY ONE

G'NAROTH SARAT, SANDORRA : *WHEN THE CHIPS ARE DOWN...*

Sandorra, one of the oldest communities on G'Naroth Sarat, started out as a frontier mining town and had grown into a strange, eclectic, oasis in the desert. Old mixed with new, rustic mixed with modern, modest mixed with extravagant. While occupying a similar sized footprint as the much more modern Amanpoor, the tallest building in Sandorra, stood at only ten floors at the center of the city, surrounded by an assortment of more modest structures.

The city spread out in all directions, ringed with green swatches of farmland, trees, small lakes and ponds. Sandorra was a multicolored blotch in the middle of a rugged, inhospitable desert made up of coarse sand, stony ridges and rust-colored low mountain ranges with a definite Western American feel. Chase imagined that it was similar to what Vegas had probably looked like in the 50's and 60's.

The mines were still in operation, scattered about, miles out in the desert. A small air and space port sat outside the city in another direction. Sandorra was mostly a blue-collar city, full of people that worked hard - with scraped knuckles and dirt under their fingernails. People that played hard and craved adult diversions... some of those diversions morally cleaner than others.

That's where the *Sandy Hill Bar & Casino,* came in. A house of drinking, gambling and ill-repute, replete with loose women of low moral fiber. A place that had been a staple of activity for well over a hundred years. Until recently - about a year to be exact, owner and proprietor, Waycom Hill, aged 107 years old, a picture of health, died suddenly - in what were deemed questionable circumstances, with no known family to inherit the business.

In a type of probate court, the city had finally decided to see if it could be sold as-is, after having been shuttered since Waycom Hill's demise. No one knew what really happened to the old man but no clues were found to indicate anything other than natural causes. But there were rumors. Rumors of something dark, or *someone* dark, that the old man owed money or favors to.

"Are you paying attention?"

Chase Holt turned away from the open door of the small private room completely padded in what appeared to be blue velvet. "Uh, yeah…"

"Try to keep up, will you?"

Mercedes turned away to catch up to Torn Dado and the inspector from the city, but Chase Hold snagged her arm, "Lemme' ask you a question," he said in a low voice, "you *do* realize this place was a whore-house too, don't you?"

"Yeah, I think I got that," she replied, raising an eyebrow, "I'm not a nun for God's sake."

"What the hell do we know about running a casino and whore-house?" he whispered.

"Well," she whispered back, "I don't know about you, but *I know,* when someone says they want to play the slots, they're not always talking about the machines…"

"Ha, ha, very funny."

"*And,*" she added with a smirk, "that some slots take coins and some slots don't."

"Ugh," he grunted, rolling his eyes, rubbing his forehead. "C'mon, I mean it. It's a logistical nightmare…"

"We'll *figure* it out," she insisted. "Now let's catch up."

■ ■ ■

The Sandy Hill Bar & Casino dated back to a time where building materials were sparse - everything and anything would be repurposed for life, work and business… including the ships people arrived in. The back half of the casino and bar sat in the refurbished cargo hold of an old freighter that Waycom Hill's father flew. When expansion took place, rather than scrap the original casino and start from scratch, it was simply added upon, melding the new with the old.

"So everything is working?" asked Mercedes, indicating the machines and bar with a sweep of her hand.

"Oh, yes ma'am," confirmed the inspector. "As you can see, you have full power and running water. None of the equipment has been touched so it's in the same condition as the day it was closed up."

"Anyone really know how he died?" asked Torn Dado.

"Mr. Hill? I'm sure there are people who know more than I do," admitted the inspector, "like the investigators. All I know is, he was found by the day-manager coming in for her shift. He was in his office slumped over his terminal. I remember something about an unfinished letter on his terminal that nobody could understand. Could just be a rumor though, I suppose."

"Maybe written in code?"

The investigator shrugged, "Could be, I don't know. With the scores of people that worked here, not many people really knew him. At least not well. He was supposed to be a pretty private guy." His brow furrowed, "Hard to believe though, considering the business."

"Did you ever meet him?" asked Chase.

"What? Me? Meet him? Uh, no. Never. I've never been here before. When it was open, I mean. I'm married, I would never come to a place like this."

Mercedes and Chase exchanged glances and she wondered if it was as obvious to him as it was to her, that the inspector was lying. "Well OK then," she clapped her hands once, "we'll take it."

"What?" blurted Torn Dado.

"Yeah, *what?!*" exclaimed Chase.

"We'll take it," she repeated, smiling at the stunned city inspector.

Chase grabbed Mercedes by the elbow and angled her away, "What the hell are you doing?" he hissed quietly. "We haven't even discussed this… not to mention that it's is a shit-ton of money for this place."

"Let's just say I'm a sucker for a mystery. Besides, we have at least ten shit-tons of money. We need a place…"

"There's lots of *places*," insisted Chase. "Lots of places that aren't a shit-ton of money…"

"Look," she countered, "you never know who will walk through that door looking to pass the time; your average Joe, ship's captain, cop, politician, *spy…*" she smirked. "What better place to skim information from people with loose lips, eh? The drunk, the one having a good night at the tables, the one getting his *pipe cleaned?*" She stared into his eyes, "Please tell me you understand where I'm going with this…"

"It could be an information jackpot…" he said flatly.

"Exactly." She good-naturedly wiggled her finger in his face, "Yeah, I see what you did there… casino - *jackpot.*"

■ ■ ■

In the captain's old ready room off the bridge of the freighter, is where Waycom Hill ran his casino on a daily basis. It smelled like two-hundred-year old ship, leather, electronics, stale cologne and perfume. "Remind me to send Flash a thank-you card for steering us in the right direction on this..."

Chase Holt wasn't sure where to sit, eyeing the blue velvet sofa with disdain, "Are you sure about that?"

"C'mon, it wasn't even on the market yet. He introduced us to the city..."

"Man this guy really liked blue velvet," mumbled Chase examining the sofa closer. He spun around, "That's not what I'm talking about, this place is a dump."

"A dump that makes mountains of cash," corrected Mercedes, nodding at the terminal screen. "According to his books, we'll make that money back in less than a year..." She waved her hand dismissively, "Besides it just needs a good cleaning."

Chase blurted out something between a snort and a laugh, "There's not enough bleach on this planet..."

"Oh, *stop.*"

He waved it off, "I can save us a whole lot of time and money; I'll just pour bleach in my eyes and we'll be good."

"You want some cheese with that whine?"

"I dunno'," shrugged Chase, "when I think of *outer space* and stuff like that, I think; advanced, clean, modern... not something that looks like it came out of a dystopian, post-apocalyptic video game."

"You've been watching too many movies," commented Mercedes, absorbed in what was on the terminal screen. "And apparently, playing too many video games..."

"Bite me," grouched Chase.

She straightened in her seat for a moment, rigid, her eyes wide, "Do you hear that?"

Chase waited for the punchline, "No. What..." he said, deadpan.

"Where's Tornado?"

"Went to get us lunch."

"Could he be back already?"

Chase checked his MOBIUS, "No, why..." he replied slowly, his curiosity deepening, hoping it wasn't an elaborate ruse on her part.

Her eyes narrowed, "I hear *humming...*"

Chase raised an eyebrow, "*Motor* humming, or *la-de-da*, humming?"

Mercedes raised slowly, quietly out of her chair, "*Somebody* humming."

384

■ ■ ■

Chase and Mercedes stood at the open door to the bridge peeking around the bulkhead doorframe, watching the tall blue figure leaning over the controls of the tactical station that had been adapted to casino security. The multitude of screens winked on as each security camera powered up.

"Why is there a big blue man on the bridge?" whispered Mercedes.

"I don't think it's a man," whispered Chase.

"You think it's a woman?"

Chase gave her a sideways glance, *"What?* No. No, I don't think it's *human."*

The tall blue figure stopped his humming and paused mid-task, motionless. Straightening up, he spun around, pointing at them, emitting an ear-piercing sound; a bizarre cross between a scream and a siren. Hands over their ears, Chase and Mercedes screamed to equalize the pressure in their ears and mitigate the painful sound. It all stopped abruptly as the two sides stood looking at each other, the two humans still covering their ears.

"*Intruders!* Security is being notified, do not attempt to flee!"

Chase let his hands drop, working his jaw to pop his ears and get them to stop ringing, "Don't do that again," he pointed at the blue figure. "Who are you?"

"I am Red, Chief Mechanic of the Hollister and Head of Security for the Sandy Hill Bar and Casino…"

"But you're blue," corrected Mercedes.

"I am Red. You are being detained until my security team arrives. Mr. Hill will want to speak with you - he will decide what is to be done with you."

Mercedes started to speak and Chase stalled her with a touch, "Listen Red, Mr. Hill isn't here anymore… we're the new owners," he indicated himself and Mercedes. "I'm Chase, this is Mercy." He stepped out of the doorway onto the bridge slowly. "We're not intruders, we belong here." He stopped, standing still with his hands in plain view as the blue figure moved a step closer, the four camera lenses in the relatively featureless face, studied him. "So is *Red* your name?" Two larger lenses, placed where the eyes would be, focused, the two smaller ones at the brow-line above where a nose should be, remained unmoved.

"Yes. I am Red." His head tilted a little to one side, a little like a curious dog, "When will Mr. Hill return?"

385

"Red, do you understand death? A cease to function?" Chase could feel Mercedes move up close behind him.

"I understand the concept." His posture seemed to change, softening.

"Well, Mr. Hill has ceased to function. It was about a year ago. Do you remember that?"

"I do not have enough memory to store a year's cycle," responded the machine. "I periodically back up and store to the Hollister's main frame." His voice seemed more somber. "Mr. Hill has ceased to function..." he said quietly, like he was making a mental note.

"Hollister," repeated Mercedes, "is that the name of this ship?"

"Yes. The ship is Hollister. I am the Chief Engineer. The Hollister and I have been in service for 232 years, nine months, fifteen days, forty-one minutes. We are old."

"Yes you are," nodded Chase. "But the ship isn't operational any more..."

"Incorrect, Mr. Chase. The Hollister is *fully* functional."

"But the doors didn't even work," Chase pointed at the door to the captain's ready room.

"They are not automatic, they are manually controlled."

"Oh. So, the Hollister can *fly?*"

"Yes, but not immediately, Mr. Chase. The Hollister is anchored to the ground, but all her systems are well maintained." He motioned to the bridge, "For instance the Hollister supplies all the power and water needed, for itself *and* the casino."

"When was the last time the engines were run?"

"To give you a date would require checking the ship's database. But I will estimate - one-hundred-years."

"How can you be sure..."

"I am *certain* they will start," Red asserted.

"Why are you called Red when you are blue?" indicated Mercedes.

Red held out his arm, flakes of blue paint missing, red showing underneath. "I am Red. Mr. Hill liked blue."

Chase and Mercedes shared a sideways glance, "I think we noticed that," replied Chase.

"So why didn't he call you Blue, then?" asked Mercedes.

"He liked the color, blue. He did not *dislike* the name, Red."

"Hm, of course."

"Would you rather be red?" asked Chase.

"I am Red," replied the blue machine, tapping his chest.

386

Chase shook his head, "Would you *prefer* to be red in *color* again, is what I meant."

Red looked down at himself, examining his arms and hands, the red areas showing through the worn, sloppy, blue paintjob. "I suppose it would be a refreshing change, yes."

"I think we can make that happen, Red," nodded Chase. "Can you show us around the Hollister and the casino? We need to know where everything is and how it all works…"

■ ■ ■

It took three weeks of cleaning, painting, remodeling and redecorating before the Sandy Hill Bar & Casino didn't look like you could pick up a disease simply by walking through the entrance. In fact, it was downright cozy. All the blue velvet was gone, replaced by tasteful shades of rich burgundy and gray, trimmed with gold. Several of the private rooms would now accommodate actual massage therapy. Whether the girls decided to offer a *happy ending* or not was up to them. Sandorra was morally and ethically neutral when it came to alcohol, gambling and women who chose to exchange sex for money. There were no social ambiguities or preconceived notions about adult entertainment like casinos and brothels; although adding *brothel* to the Sandy Hill Bar & Casino name, seemed a bit much.

With nearly triple the cameras - all with audio, there wasn't a room, table, game or corner where a conversation or action could go unrecorded. And the common areas of the Hollister were secretly covered in the same fashion, to protect against unscrupulous employees.

Even after being closed a year, some of the old employees found their way back, whether it be to apply for a position, or out of simple curiosity. Some made the cut, others didn't pass Mercedes Huang's expert scrutiny. As for the girls, they needed *the look*, but she was looking for special talents; girls who could pull their own weight in a conversation, whether it be by feminine guile or gifted dialogue. You can't farm intelligence if you can't get someone talking. She rehired several, who came back after moving to other clubs when the Sandy Hill closed. She was certain that was going to cause some bad blood with the other clubs but that was the least of her concerns. Through the whole process, Waycom Hill's death never left her mind. She examined it from every angle and she was certain it was murder.

387

Unfortunately, Waycom was dust in the wind and the autopsy was woefully inadequate to be able to affirm or deny any theory. With no body to exhume, there was no evidence.

Chase stuck his head in through the open office doorway, "You coming down? It's almost time."

Mercedes rose from her chair, checking her MOBIUS, "Ooo, grand opening time... Do we have a crowd?" she asked following him out onto the bridge. She closed the door, locking it with her keycard.

"We actually do," he confirmed.

"That's awesome," she said brightly, hazarding a wave at the three security techs sitting at the old tactical station surrounded by rows of flat panel monitors, "You boys ready?"

"Yes ma'am..."

■ ■ ■

"The guy at the bar is waiting for you," motioned Chase, as they walked through the empty casino. "He wouldn't say who he was - but he sounds official."

Mercedes couldn't tell who he was from the side in the shifting lights coming from the stage. "And you let him in anyway? Good job." Chase just shrugged in response. "Meh," she shook her head, "probably some inspector who wants a bribe for something."

Chase shook his head as he broke away, heading for the entrance, "I don't know; he asked for you, specifically." He tapped his ear comm, "Ok guys, let them in, we're open for business!" He adjusted the slug-thrower in the shoulder holster under his jacket; the damn thing was heavier than it looked. But it felt good to be strapped again. Over two-hundred years old, from the Hollister's meager crew armory, they were lightly used and in near perfect condition. Enough to supply all the Casino's principals, security teams and even Red, who had a cavity in his outer thigh where it snapped securely into place.

■ ■ ■

"Ah, Ms. Huang, how good to see you again..."

Mercedes unabashedly made a face of distaste, "Inspector Brooker. Sorry, I can't say the same." She motioned to the bartender for a drink for herself, "Can I get you a drink?"

"Thank you, no."

"Would you like to game? I can comp you some chips…"

"No, no," he waved.

"Massage? Handjob? Blowjob? Full-ticket ride?" she offered with an evil Cheshire cat grin. "We have a very talented staff."

He took off his hat and set it on the bar, "We still have some unfinished business, you and I."

"If you don't like girls I'm afraid I can't help you. There's another club up the strip that has boys…"

Inspector Brooker pursed his lips in consternation, toying with the hat he'd set on the bar. "You done?"

"For now." Mercedes sipped her drink, "How did you find me, Brooker? A little out of your jurisdiction, aren't you?"

His head tilted to one side, "I have my sources. You spend nearly a hundred million that's not yours and it's bound to make waves."

"Who said it's not mine?"

"You and I both know *where* you got it Ms. Huang. And *what* you did to get it." He reached into his jacket and pulled out a set of electronic handcuffs, setting them on the bar next to his hat. He slid them towards her, "Put them on."

She laughed in his face, "I don't know what you're talking about."

"Well, we can talk about that, in Amanpoor." He nudged the cuffs, "Put them on,"

Two of the casinos security officers appeared at Mercedes' side, looking imposing. "Is there a problem, Ms. Huang?"

Inspector Brooker swept his suit jacket open revealing his gold shield and sidearm, "Go away, boys."

In unison, they both opened they tuxedo jackets, revealing their slug-throwers and Deputy shields. "I don't think so." They remained steadfast at her side.

Mercedes reached back and patted the hand of the closest one, "It's alright, guys, we're fine. My friend here, is just showing me his kinky toys." She waited until the security team was out of earshot, "The off-duty guys like the pay and extra benefits, better than overtime pay."

Brooker nodded. "And loyalty, I'm impressed. That's hard to find."

389

Mercedes cracked a crooked smile, tossing her silken black hair over her shoulder. "You know what else I hear is hard to find? Proof."

Brooker leaned in, "I could just put these on you and take you…"

She crossed her legs casually at the knee, "Yeah, you could *try*. But not without my *permission*," she hissed. "And in the *extremely* remote chance you actually managed it, you'd never make the door." He started to speak and she cut him off, "You're in *my* house now. *My* house, *my* rules." She pointed to a man surrounded by girls getting ready to enter a private room, exchanging pleasant waves with him. "See that guy? Deputy Chief of Sheriffs for Sandorra…" She tapped her chest with her fingertips, "*My* house." She slid the electronic cuffs back to him, "So take your little party favors and get the fuck out of my club. You're a long way from home."

Brooker picked up the cuffs slowly, deliberately, "I *will* catch you and your friends."

"No. You won't." She stood up and smoothed her suit, the bulge of her slug-thrower showing on her waist under her tunic. "Word of advice, find a new hobby. Forget about us, move on. It won't ever work out like you hope it will."

■ ■ ■

A white-skinned, silver-haired girl with long legs, danced to a seductive, bumping beat on the stage beyond the bar, the music not too loud - but loud enough that Chase couldn't hear the words being spoken, as Mercedes escorted the man with the suit and hat, past him to the front entrance. She gave Chase a curt, *everything's fine* nod as she passed.

Chase surveyed the club; many of the tables were full, the stage had an attentive audience, waitresses were busy distributing drinks, the private rooms were occupied and the casino off to his left through the polished steel archway of the Hollister's cargo entrance, was off to a good start. *This might actually work.* It was fairly easy to separate patron from employee by their difference in attire and Chase visually checked the security people scattered throughout the club. Even Red was on duty for the grand opening; a black tuxedo jacket covering his, restored-to-red, frame. He had positioned himself in a shadowy corner near the entrance, in order to scan the faces of patrons as they entered, searching for security threats.

Chase exchanged pleasant smiles and a nod with a waitress as she passed him. The exploding tray of drinks she had delicately balanced; it's shower of sparkling glass and spray of colorful alcohols didn't immediately register as real, even as it pelted him. He glanced around trying to get his bearings, until he felt the familiar sensation of some invisible, high-speed, whisper of death that snapped angrily as it passed just inches from his face. Combat flashbacks triggered a flood of adrenalin and instincts; he dropped to a combat crouch, one hand shooting out and dragging the waitress to her knees, his other hand clearing the slug-thrower from its holster.

Mercedes was his first thought as he turned towards the open rectangle of light, the right-hand door of the entrance open, the man with the hat and Mercedes silhouetted for a brief second before he was quickly pitched backwards, his hat airborne. Her silhouette disappeared almost simultaneously, spun off her feet among a slew of incoming rounds splintering the wood of the doorframe and thudding heavily against the copper-covered wood doors. Angry snaps over Chase's head accompanied evil hissing as rounds passed through the open doorway and into the club. He scrambled low toward the doorway, beaten there by Red who was in full heroic stride, leaning into a sprint Chase didn't realize he was capable of. Having popped the slug-thrower free from its holding place, Red became a silhouette as he dashed into the sunlight, gun in hand, distinct metal *whangs* like hammer blows on a car as he took hits to his body without slowing.

Straddling the fallen, Chase arrived at the door, peeking low, firearm first, Red having reached the center of the street, in a proper combat crouch, fired at a fleeing vehicle that raced up the street. The slug thrower clanked as it fired, the recoil never moving Red's hands or arms, locked in a vice-like grip. After more than a dozen shots he paused, straightened and relaxed, snapping the weapon back into his leg, a dull thud echoing from up the street as the car crashed into vehicles parked along the curb. "Targets neutralized. They are dead," he announced matter-of-factly, stepping quickly back toward the entrance.

"Get your ass out of my face," groaned Mercedes, rolling onto her side to sit up. Chase rose and stepped over her, "Where are you hit?" A security team passed them in the open doorway and sprinted down the street, guns drawn.

Up on one elbow, she gingerly lifted her holed tunic, the slug-thrower on her hip crushed in its holster, a softball-sized bruise already forming under it on her hip. "It hurts worse than it looks..." She felt a sudden spike of panic, "The Inspector!" She swiveled her head and rolled to her knees with a wince, pain stabbing into her abdomen from her hip. "Brooker..." she urged, hovering over him. "Call an ambulance!" she shouted. *"Good God, let there be ambulances here,"* she pleaded.

Inspector Brooker's eyes fluttered open, staring vacantly up at Mercedes, the slug crease along his skull above his ear creating a small puddle of blood on the pavement under his head. He blinked slowly, "Let me up," he mumbled, his eyes rolling.

Mercedes leaned on the bar towel over the hole in his shoulder, a security agent compressing a towel over a hole in his stomach. "You've been shot Brooker, you have to stay still."

"You did this..." he breathed.

"Yeah Brooker," sneered Mercedes, "because I couldn't come up with a better plan than putting myself in the line of fire along with you. Don't be stupid."

"It would make you look innocent," he wheezed.

"Holy shit, you're a stubborn ass," she countered. "Stop talking or I might decide to *let* you bleed to death."

"So you'd *like* to see me dead..."

Mercedes couldn't help but grin at the irony, "Not on my watch, Brooker. Go get yourself dead in somebody else's backyard. You're not doing it here."

■ ■ ■

Amid the crush of Sheriffs cars and evidence technicians, Mercedes leaned against the fender of one of the squads parked across the sidewalk, dried blood up to her wrists, answering questions. The Deputy Chief of Sheriffs came over and put his hand on her shoulder, "How are you holding up?"

"A little sore, Deputy Chief, but I've been worse. How was your massage?"

He grinned widely, "Simply wonderful, thank you." He patted her shoulder, "Don't be afraid to get yourself checked out, Ms. Mercy." His eyes shifted to the interviewing Sheriff, "You take care of our girl, here..."

"Yes, sir." He leaned closer, "They're still going over the vehicle, it doesn't look random..."

The Deputy Chief frowned, looking concerned, "A hit? On who?" He flipped a thumb in the direction of the departed ambulance, "The Inspector? Or, the *club?"* he nodded toward the bullet-ridden entrance.

"That's not clear yet, Chief. But these guys were prepared..."

392

The Deputy Chief chewed on the inside of his lip, "I suppose it could be one of the other clubs wanting to eliminate the new competition. Let's keep a car on the street - two guys in a plain wrapper. And let's have someone with the Inspector - around the clock until we know who the target was."

"Yes, sir."

He turned back to Mercedes, "And you, young lady, no out-and-about," he waved his hand in the air, "without at least one armed escort until we clear this up."

"Thank you, Deputy Chief."

He winked at her, "You can tell the girls I'll see you all next week."

CHAPTER THIRTY TWO

PERSEUS, XIAN PI SYSTEM : *LOST*

It had taken the ship's database a good thirty minutes to find Xian Pi on the holochart in his office, Reegan pacing as the computer searched for the images. When it finally came up with the system hologram, there was no surrounding chart. He had asked the computer to clarify but it had no other data. Yet. Obviously, Xian Pi wasn't an island, the computer was making an assessment based on the data it had from the system to compare its star, number of planets, matching planet types, sizes, moons, positioning, orbits and the like, all gathered from old probe data that passed through the system several centuries ago. The data about the system still existed but the trajectory, probe origination and trip's log details were long gone. As a result, the computer was struggling to place Xian Pi on the map, so-to-speak. It knew, with relative certainty, *where* it was, just not what was around it or in which direction. It remained occupied with scanning its surroundings to compare stars, constellations and known charts to plot their position relative to the rest of the universe.

The fact that the ion storm was still rampaging all over the region didn't make it any easier on the sensors or computer to accurately detect, read and calculate what it should with any reliability. It was having to execute multiple scans, multiple readings, and scores of recalculations. In the meantime, the Perseus wasn't going anywhere. What was the point? You might as well try to find your way out of a vast open field, blindfolded.

Commander Reegan keyed his mic, "Do we have communications yet?"

"No, Commander."

"Damage report?"

"Nothing to report yet..."

"What the hellion," he muttered. Frustrated, Reegan stormed out of his ready room, across the back of the bridge and out the bridge door, tossing a simple nod at the Marine sentry as he passed, headed down the corridor.

■ ■ ■

The heavy iris blast door opened like the lens shutter on a camera, *"Chief!"* bellowed Reegan, as he entered engineering. "Where's the Chief?"

After a hasty salute, a Petty Officer thumbed over his shoulder, "Checking the GOD systems, sir..."

"Chief..." called Reegan, winding his way through engineering.

"Just finishing up my inspection, Skipper," announced the Chief from above him. He traversed the catwalk to a ladder and slid smoothly down. "Amazing really, how well she held up. The new tech of this shielding has worked remarkably well..." He started walking back the way Reegan had come in, the Commander following him.

"Chief..."

"I don't suppose that Miro Class Destroyer ahead of us fared nearly as well..."

"Chief..."

"She may have made it through the gate, but I'm sure she toasted some of her bio-relays - they're fast but not as robust..."

"Chief!"

"I'm sure if we had made the gate she would have been an easy target..." He paused, turning, "I'm sorry, Commander, you had a question?"

Reegan had to stop short, *"Yes* Chief, I need a *damage* report..."

"I have run every diagnostic I can think of," he commented, turning away, walking on, pointing at systems and naming them along the way, "I am just astounded..."

"CHIEF! Do we have any damage or not?"

The Chief paused, tuning to face Reegan, "No, Commander. All systems check out as unaffected. She has a clean bill of health."

Reegan took a deep breath, "Chief, for the love of the Gods, in the future, please just say that."

"She is a new ship Commander; we did not know how she would be effected and a thorough assessment was critical..."

"Chief..."

The engineer nodded, "Of course. I will endeavor to keep my assessments and review shorter in the future."

"That's all I'm asking," called Reegan, heading for the iris which was already opening for him. He keyed his mic, "Helm, we're done sitting still. Get us moving, head to the center of the system."

"Aye, Skipper. Getting under way."

■ ■ ■

The only thing remarkable about Xian Pi, was how unremarkable it was. There was nothing special about it, nothing noteworthy, and by the looks of it, nothing new since the probe passed through it centuries ago.

Reegan dropped into his command chair, "Report," he ordered, pulling up his control screens.

"Looks like Xian Pi has one habitable planet, Commander..."

"How habitable?" he asked.

"According to the probe's information, the fourth planet is midway between a Class 12a and a Class 014. Vegetation, water, atmosphere, climate, all appropriate for life. Considering the time lapse since the probe's visit, it wouldn't have changed much, though it may have some early signs of habitation by now."

Reegan pursed his lips in thought, "Size?"

"28,558 mile circumference."

"Any update on celestial charts as to where Xian Pi is?"

"Not yet sir, though it appears it's running across some dualities in its comparisons – I'm expecting some results fairly soon."

Reegan nodded a thoughtful acceptance, there was no rushing the computer's scans, measurements or calculations. He steepled his fingers, "Well, we're here. Let's go take a look at that fourth planet."

■ ■ ■

The emerald green fourth planet hung there in orbit around Xian Pi's sun, two small moons circling it, one gray, one reddish brown. A little over one-half of the unnamed planet was covered in water and it had its share of mountain ranges and small deserts, but no visible ice of any kind. Layers of clouds wound around it like tufts of cotton candy.

"Send a sensor probe for low orbit - let's get some high definition scans. Standard setup."

"Aye, Skipper, preparing probe." The astrometrics officer programmed a flight path for the sensor probe, the keys pipping under his fingers. "Setup complete. Launching probe." A small flare trailed the garbage can sized unit away from the Perseus, arcing down towards the planet. "Flying true..." A marker on the big screen tracked its path and location as it quickly diminished to a single point of light, lost in the backdrop of the planet.

"Helm, all stop."

"All stop, aye."

Well beyond the orbits of the moons, the Perseus hung in space facing the slowly rotating emerald marble, sunlight reflecting off a calm ocean above its equator.

"Sir, I'm getting rather odd readings from the moon it just passed..."

"Explain, Ensign," ordered Reegan.

"Sir, the density is way off what I would expect for a body that size..."

"Which one?"

"The red one, Sir. It was..." The marker and flight path disappeared from the big screen, the astrometrics officer snapping rigid in his seat, "Hellion... we lost it!"

"Tactical," Reegan pointed, "scan for that probe. Did we lose communications or did we lose the probe?"

"The probe is gone, Sir."

Reegan pointed at the astrometrics officer, "Was it showing any signs of malfunction?"

The Ensign was scrolling through the data stream, "Nooo," he said slowly reading the data. "She was running clean and free, Skipper."

"Did it *hit* something?"

"Nothing visible in any spectrum, Commander," replied the officer at tactical.

"Yellow alert," announced Reegan, tapping his control panel. The warning tone sounded briefly, yellow lights flashing throughout the ship. "Astrometrics, prepare another probe. Have it take a really good look at those two moons as it passes. Tactical, full shields. Helm, pull us back, give us some space."

"Helm, aye."

"Aye, shields up."

For the second time, a small flare trailed the garbage can sized unit away from the Perseus, arcing down towards the planet. "Flying true..." The bridge crew studied the big screen as it tracked the path of the probe, a scroll of data streaming in on the right side of the screen as it neared the moons.

"All gun crews reporting in, weapons live, targeting passive mode," reported tactical.

"Nearing the red moon..." announced astrometrics, "5,351 mile circumference... 1.57 g/cm³ - density, 9.701 m/s² - gravity..."

397

Rubbing his hand across the stubble on his chin, Reegan's brow furrowed, "How is that possible, it sounds like it's hollow..."

"Detecting natural geological rock... various metals... and *an echo..?*" He jolted upright and spun in his seat, "Skipper we have a shielded fusion energy signature..!"

"Red alert!" The alarm klaxon sounded, plunging the ship into eerie red flashing light. "Bring Commander Brighton to the bridge!" added Reegan.

"Contacts, Skipper! They're coming from the dark side of the red moon!*"*

"Probe destroyed!" The astrometrics officer turned back toward Reegan again, "Last look, the contacts are coming from *inside* the red moon, Commander."

"How many?" asked Reegan, forcing composure.

"Three... seven... *fifteen!* A mix of heavy and light fighters and two gunships...

"We should deploy weapons Skipper..."

Nervous, Reegan shook his head, "Negative. Hold position. We look unarmed, our best advantage is surprise. We'd lose a running gunfight; we need them close."

"How close, Skipper?"

"Point blank... Where they have nowhere to go."

■ ■ ■

Fritz looked back over his shoulder, "Allie, you stay," he annunciated, "I'll be right back." She remained curled up on the bed in Jack's quarters, looking apprehensive. Fritz knew she didn't want to be alone, and truthfully, neither did he, but he needed to see what the alarm was about. The electronic tag riveted to his collar gave him the same security clearance Jack had, allowing him passage through secured areas. As he approached the door to the corridor, the lock winked from red to green, opening, allowing him out of the room - closing behind him, relocking. Having waited until the alarm klaxon had stopped to avoid interference with any crew members rushing to emergency stations, the passageway was void of personnel.

Fritz could smell no smoke, there was no confusion, the ship was rather quiet; the crew tending to their emergency duty stations. Making his way toward the bridge, he passed several hatchways to turret stations and could tell by their status panels they were manned and armed. But the guns were silent and the ship's engines were obviously at idle, their normal rumble almost non-existent. As his electronic security tag allowed him to pass through a set of secured blast doors sectioning off the corridor, a pair of armed, armored, Marine sentries trotted past him in the opposite direction, prompting him to quickly sidestep them to avoid being run over. It startled him but they took no notice, hurrying to their assignment without so much as an acknowledgment, their heavy boots clomping down the passage behind him.

Another pair of Marine sentries, similarly equipped, stood post outside the bridge entry. He looked up as he neared and got a simple nod, neither one of them offering any objection to him entering the bridge.

The bridge was crowded and busy, every station manned, every seat filled. Derrik Brighton stood between the Captain and First Mate, chatting with them both, looking over their shoulders and gesturing at a swarm of ships on the big screen headed toward the Perseus, a rust colored moon behind them, a green planet in the background. There seemed to be great concern over the approaching ships and the Shepherd wondered why the Perseus was simply sitting still. With one smooth jump he effortlessly landed atop the holochart table at the rear of the bridge for a better vantage point and sat quietly observing the crew, unnoticed, his butt blocking a substantial portion of the system's hologram.

■ ■ ■

"I'm telling you," whispered Derrik, "those are Gogol gunships; the task force ran into a couple of them in Whisperfire, when we were headed to Terra."

"What about the rest of those ships?" asked Reegan.

Derrik shook his head, "Not Gogol, I can tell you that - their fighters are very distinct. These don't even look like FreeRanger equipment, they look more like *Vantage Raiders*."

"Never heard of a Vantage Raider..." commented Reegan.

"It's not a *what*, it's a *who*. Vantage Raiders are the throwbacks to what the FreeRangers were *before* they were the FreeRangers. They are the dirty, outlaw, pirate scum, that can't even bloody qualify as FreeRangers. They have no laws, no code of honor..." He wiped the perspiration off his forehead, "What the Gogols are doing with them is the big question..."

"Lieutenant Braskus to bridge; P-57s armed and ready for launch."

399

"You *can't* let them go out there," urged Derrik, leaning over Reegan's shoulder, "it's almost seven to one."

"Only as a last resort," Reegan assured him. He keyed his mic, "Stand by Lieutenant."

"We're being targeted, Commander," called tactical.

Light fighters slashed past on either side of the Perseus, close enough to see the figures in their cockpits. "Showing off," commented Derrik. "Trying to unnerve you."

Reegan nodded, stoic. "But if they destroy the ship they don't get the goods."

"Incoming comm..."

"On screen," ordered Reegan.

Arriving first, a line of four fighters abreast sat off the bow of the Perseus, the others circling around like buzzing mosquitoes, the Gogol gunships still cruising up from behind.

A video insert appeared on the big screen; a helmeted pilot, his face obscured by his reflective visor, stared at them. "I am O'Berk. You are trespassing in this system; you will surrender or be destroyed."

Reegan did his best to remain stone faced. "As you can see, Mr. O'Berk..."

"Incoming comm..." someone whispered, another video insert appearing on the big screen alongside the first.

Another pilot, his reflective visor obscuring his face, addressed the bridge of the Perseus, "I am Mozoreth. You will surrender or we will destroy your ship."

Reegan pursed his lips, "As I was explaining to Mr. O'Berk..."

"O'Berk?" The pilot's head turned away from the camera, "O'Berk, this is *my* capture!"

"Like hellion it is." O'Berk turned away from his own camera, searching the darkness outside his cockpit, "I was here long before you, Mozoreth; you are late, as always, you worthless piece of shit."

"I should kill you for that, you fat, spineless..."

O'Berk laughed, "You've tried before you ignorant babaloon, and as with everything, you failed. I will destroy this ship rather than let *you* take it..."

"Commander," came a whisper, "his missile targeting just went live..."

With the ship's shields set at thirty percent of their full military-combat capacity to match their appearance of a civilian ship, the Perseus would not withstand more than one missile hit. Reegan's fingers hovered above the shield controls, "Mr. Ragnaar," he hissed, "full military throttle on my mark..." The former pirate nodded a curt acknowledgment without speaking.

A slash of blue neon and a searing bloom of light quickly dissipated in a corona of debris and sparkling particles as O'Berk's fighter disappeared, his video square winking out simultaneously, leaving a gap in the line of fighters off the nose of the Perseus.

"Incoming comm..." came another whisper.

"On screen," snapped Reegan, gripping his armrests. "What the hellion just happened?"

A video square winked in. "Captain, Nņeågõlshierseotollém," announced the Gogol, blinking translucent eyelids across his large glassy eyes, "*Toberus Interstellar Investments.* You'd better have something on that ship worth saving," he pointed, "Or I will have to pay for that fighter... and *that* will not make me very happy." Glancing to his side, it appeared he was looking at the video inset of Mozoreth when he drew a line with his finger across his throat. When the pilot's video inset disappeared, the Captain appeared satisfied and turned back to the screen.

Reegan cleared his throat, "Captain, may I call you Nagol?"

"That is acceptable," replied the Gogol Captain, "I know you *pales* cannot manage our names." The saurian had a greenish hue to his thin, smooth skin, veins visible beneath the surface. "So, tell me what you are doing out here in our little dead-end system..." He folded his arms across his chest and leaned back. "And you might want to explain how you avoided our security."

"Commander Reegan," said Reegan touching his chest, indicating himself. "Completely accidental, I can assure you, Captain. We were in a transition between Edenlight and Madrassas when an SPE occurred. We were an hour short of the Madrassas Gate..."

The Gogol Captain looked off screen for a moment, prompting Reegan to pause, waiting for his full attention. "Please continue," waved Nagol.

"As I was saying, we were an hour short of the gate when the tunnel began to dissolve and we dropped out of transition. This is where we ended up. We only knew we were in Xian Pi, from archive information gathered by an old probe that went through here several centuries ago..."

The Gogol Captain studied Reegan carefully, dubiously. "Interesting how you ended up here and not in *null space...*"

"I agree," gestured Reegan, "and we were very relieved..."

"Especially," interrupted the Gogol, suspicion in his voice, "since the gates you mentioned are some thirty jumps away." The look he saw on the faces of the freighter's bridge crew registered true surprise and astonishment, which gave him some satisfaction. "The solar storm *has* been rather troublesome," he confided, undecided whether he completely believed the tale or not. "So," he leaned closer, "tell me what you're carrying. Make it interesting. Give me a reason *not* to take your ship and hold your crew for ransom."

Reegan verbally reviewed a litany of items in the cargo, a range of medical supplies, food, parts, small arms, weapons, liquor... Captain Nagol nodded along, seemingly unimpressed by any single item on the list, but generally appreciative of the diversity of the cargo. "All useful things I'm sure we'd be interested in adding to our inventory," agreed the Gogol, "however, nothing truly *outstanding*. I fail to see enough to compensate for our efforts... I suspect we may have to consider more drastic measures..."

"Dust," said Ragnaar.

Captain Nagol, paused mid-sentence, his mouth open. He pointed at the helmsman of the Perseus, "Him... *You.* What did you just say?"

"Dust," repeated Ragnaar. "Good quality."

"Blizzard? *You have Blizzard?!* See!" clapped the Gogol. *"That's* what I meant by interesting!" He leaned in again, "How much? *How much?"*

"Ten kilos," replied Ragnaar, calmly. "And we can, of course, get more. But that would require our ship and crew remain intact and operational."

"Mmm... *ten kilos."* The Gogol Captain wrung his hands in contemplation. "I think we should discuss this further. You will accompany us..." he waved to his bridge crew and within moments the fighters were dismissed, breaking formation, heading slowly back to the red moon, the two Gogol Gunships remaining. "We will escort you in..."

"We go in there, there's a bloody good chance we won't come out again," whispered Derrik.

"We have no place to go," breathed Reegan. "We don't know which way is out of this damned system..."

The Gogol ships moved into the flanks of the Perseus, Captain Nagol remaining on screen, "Just follow the fighters..." he pointed. "You may even meet Lord Toberus," he smiled crookedly, "on rare occasions, he enjoys meeting out guests..."

"I think we can take them," whispered Derrik.

"We need cartography updated or we're running blind," hissed Reegan.

■ ■ ■

There was something distasteful, something suspiciously sinister about the way the Gogol Captain said *guests*. Fritz wondered if anyone else picked up on it. It didn't sit well with him. And it didn't jibe with other Gogols they'd met, who seemed to have a strange code of ethics that bordered on altruistic and chivalrous. There seemed to be an odd infatuation and admiration for higher learning when it concerned the Ancient Architects, though he didn't fully understand it all. He jumped off the holochart table, reaching the railing overlooking the command pit, in one bound. He stood on his hind legs, hooking his front paws over the railing and barked, everyone jumping in their seats with a start.

"Not the time, *dog*," waved Derrik.

Fritz gave him a narrow-eyed look and wrinkled his nose, showing his teeth, clacking them once for effect.

"Ho! What have we *here?!*" exclaimed the Gogol Captain.

Fritz turned to the screen and bobbed his head once, acknowledging the Gogol, annunciating slowly, laboriously, "Ģreirggådariopshé senvou mé, I uso té strument Ö té cōnstruktures, as markez Ö té antiqos arkuitekos..."

The Gogol Captain sat momentarily motionless, open-mouthed, the video square suddenly winking out.

"What the hellion just happened?" asked Reegan, spinning in his seat to stare at the German Shephard. "What did you say?!"

Derrik was wide-eyed, "He spoke *Gogol* to him," he mumbled slowly, stunned. "He said, *Greg sent me, I wear the tools of the builders, marks of the ancient architects.*"

"*You* speak Gogol?"

"No. No, Steele, er, *Mercury* did it when we ran into those Gogol ships I was telling you about..."

"Incoming comm..."

Reegan turned back and pinched the bridge of his nose between his eyes, "On screen."

The Gogol Captain reappeared in a video inset, obviously transmitting from somewhere off the bridge, somewhere private. "I have heard of this animal. The one who speaks... *and* the man that owns him." He looked around suspiciously, "The Imperial Gogol Senate has issued an edict..." he waved his hand, "never mind," he hissed. "Dump your cargo. *All of it. Quickly.* I am sending you a feed of the star cartography for the entire region. Get to TriGate as fast as you can and jump. Do not attempt to return

403

unless you have at least one-hundred kilos of Blizzard." He looked around nervously, "Ǥreirggådariopshé has learned much with the *pale*, Professor Walt Edgars - the Senate is thankful for the time he tutored." He leaned in, "Now *GO. Quickly.*" The square winked out.

■ ■ ■

"Emergency dump complete, Skipper. We're closing up now."

Reegan glanced at the hull status on his right screen, while eyeing the star chart on his left screen. "Copy that," he replied into his comm. His eyes shot up to the big screen, watching the two Gogol gunships rotate around to recover the drifting cargo. "Navigation?"

"Course laid in to the TriGate. It's an obtuse angle from the moon base."

"Thank the Gods for that," commented Reegan, "I don't want to go near that thing..." The hull schematic on his right command screen flashed green, indicating the hull was sealed, the graphs showing the shields automatically restoring themselves to full coverage across the ship's belly. "Helm, get us out of here, *now!* I want a slow increase to full standard power, let's not attract any attention from those fighters.

"Skipper, we still have our pilots and gun crews at stations..."

"Well aware of that, tactical. I want some distance behind us. Ten or fifteen minutes will tell us if we're clear..."

■ ■ ■

"I've never seen anything like it, have you?" asked Reegan, sitting on the edge of his desk in the Captain's ready room. Ragnaar and Derrik Brighton huddled around the holo-chart table with the Chief Engineer and the ship's two fighter pilots, examining the gate that was centered in the vacant, navigable space between three separate star systems.

"No. And it's easily a two or three-day standard run from any one of these systems just to get to this gate," pointed Ragnaar.

"Why would it get placed way out here?" asked Derrik.

"It is relatively centered between the three," observed Ragnaar.

"The only thing I can think of," offered Lieutenant Loech Braskus, his P-57 wingman at his elbow, "is all three of these systems have habitable planets and the Architects expected them all to need it." He indicated Xian Pi, "The planet here is still pretty primitive but it probably has resources... we don't know about the other two yet, do we?"

"We do," confirmed Ragnaar. "One is space faring, one has not quite entered that phase just yet."

The other pilot nudged into the conversation, "Are we going to go take a look at them?"

"No," replied Reegan, quickly. "That's way off task. And our presence out this far is precarious at best, I don't want to push our luck."

"It may take us a month or more for us to get back to a sector we're familiar with," added Ragnaar.

"And we don't dare send any long distance comms from out here," said Derrik, stuffing his hands in his pockets. "We're going to have to maintain dark protocol for security."

Reegan eyed Derrik with mistrust, his brow furrowed, "So, we're not going to have any more problems, you and I?" he motioned between them.

Derrik withdrew his hands, raising them in casual surrender, "Sorry, mate. We had a mission. I did what I thought was necessary to accomplish that mission." He dropped his hands and leaned on the holo-chart table, hunched-over, staring at the star chart. "But we have a *new* mission, and it's all you. Get us back in one bloody piece."

"Hm," grunted Reegan. "I guess I just don't remember that being such a big concern of yours when you got us into this mess."

Derrik stiffened, "Well, maybe I should have..."

Ragnaar stepped forward defiantly, straightening to his full six-foot-six-inch height, folding his arms across his chest, his physical size imposing, "Am I going to have to separate you two?" he growled. "Because if I *do*," he turned his gaze towards Derrik, "you know who's going out the door head-first."

No matter how hard he bit the inside of his cheek, Reegan couldn't stop the smirk. "Thank you Lieutenant." He checked his MOBIUS, "We GOD jumped two hours out from the moonbase, well out of their sensor range. We will drop out of GOD two hours from the TriGate…"

"Why not just jump *to the gate,* Skipper?"

"As a precaution Mr. Braskus. We want to be out of sensor range if there's anyone patrolling the gate. No need to give away a secret we've managed to keep so far. We'll send a probe towards the gate, if it's clear, a short jump and we dive through the gate."

"If it's not?"

"We will assess the situation as it arises. We have about seven hours, if anyone needs some down time, take it now."

■ ■ ■

"Sir, the probe isn't picking up anything at, or near the gate."

Quickly reviewing the probe's sensor readout, Reegan looked up from his screens, "Excellent. Helm, prepare to jump to the gate. Tactical, send the probe all the way to the gate, we'll scoop it up before we jump through to Zostinar."

"Aye, GOD drive spooling up, bubble forming…"

"Jump time to the Zostinar gate?"

"Less than ten minutes, Skipper."

"Good… good." Reegan rubbed the stubble on his chin absentmindedly.

"What's on your mind, Reegan?" asked Derrik suspiciously.

The Commander waved casually, "Just thinking…"

"That it's been too easy?"

Reegan found himself nodding, "Maybe, I don't know, I can't define it… But something feels off. Something isn't right."

"You're starting to sound like Steele."

Reegan pursed his lips, "I don't see that as a bad thing." He tapped the alarm on his command console, the yellow alert tone sounding, warning

406

lights flashing throughout the ship. "Yellow alert, all gun crews to stations, pilots to their fighters…"

"Jumping…" announced the helmsman.

■ ■ ■

Five minutes from the gate to Zostinar, the Perseus dropped out of GOD, exactly as planned, shedding its multi-colored bubble of energy, the neon tendrils slipping from the hull as she lined up to recover the garbage-can sized probe back into the hold.

Reegan was still on edge but relieved to be so close to the gate and so close to leaving the dead-end Xian Pi System behind them. He hated to admit it, but maybe he was being paranoid for nothing. "Shields to full standard," he ordered. "Mr. Ragnaar, how do you suppose our friend, the Gogol Captain, will explain letting us go?"

"I do believe Captain Nagol will capitalize on our ability to supply more Blizzard Dust, Commander. In many regions, it is far more useful than gold; harder to get and of higher value, due to demand outstripping supply. It was a calculated risk on his part but he is probably highly respected by his employer - Lord Toberus. I expect he will have a persuasive argument for his decision."

"Gate event!" shouted tactical. "We have a ship coming through the gate from Zostinar."

Reegan tapped the red alert button, the klaxon sounding twice, emergency lights switching from yellow to red. "Gunners stand by to deploy and engage," he announced on comms.

Swirls of color across the gate burst outward, the corona splitting open as the bow of a ship punched through, electric plasma dragging back across the hull. "She's *big*, Commander…"

"Ident ping?"

"No, sir. And nothing in the database on her design… She's definitely not UFW."

"Yeah, I wouldn't expect UFW to be this deep in Dark Territory," remarked Reegan. *"Man*, she looks rough…"

407

"A light cruiser," offered Ragnaar, examining her lines on the big screen. "I don't see any affiliation marks on her," he pointed. "But you're right, she's definitely seen action."

"She emerged with weapons online; shields are powering up, Skipper."

"Comm coming in."

"Full military shields and jam all frequencies *on my mark,*" ordered Reegan. "Comm on screen," he motioned.

A video square winked in on the big screen, a rough looking man with wild, curly, blue-black hair and a full beard streaked with gray, filling the frame. "Nice little ship," he gruffed, his voice like rough gravel. "What are you doing here?" His right eye squinted.

Reegan chose not to acknowledge the insult disguised as a compliment. "We are in route to pick up more supplies for Xian Pi, since they are so needed here."

With a look of extreme irritation, the man glared at Reegan, "Don't play stupid with me, I am *not* in the mood. What are you doing here, *at the gate?*"

A chill raced up Reegan's back, the hair standing up on the back of his neck. A whisper from his tactical officer called his attention to a notation on his center command screen; *Two minutes - pass port-to-port. Broadside?* He offered a curt nod in response to the inquiry as he answered the captain of the cruiser, "I thought I was pretty clear, Sir, we are preparing to exit Xian Pi and…"

"Listen to me," interrupted the man, wild-eyed, "I can tell *what* you're doing, I want to know *how* you got here from Toberus so quickly…"

"Toberus?"

The man looked nearly insane, forcing calm, *"Toberus Interstellar Investments,"* he said slowly and deliberately. "Now, how did you get to the gate from TII in *eleven-hours?* That's a *fifty-seven-hour* run, *at best!*" He did a double take as someone off the screen made comments, diverting his attention. *"What?!"* He turned back to the screen, an intense look on his face, his eyes narrowing, "Do you have one of those *drives? A gate drive?"* His mouth cracked into an evil grin showing off uneven gold-capped teeth, "You *do!* That's the *only way* you could have done it…" He shook his head,

"That Gogol *puke* has done it this time… Toberus will *gut* him," he sneered. "If I bring you back in one piece, he may let *me* do it."

Reegan eyed the countdown on his command screen; twenty seconds until the ships were side by side, another sixty seconds to get the Perseus into the gate.

The captain of the cruiser circled his finger in the air, "So turn your little ship around and we'll escort you back to Toberus." He grinned wickedly, "I mean, I *could* shoot it full of holes but then it wouldn't be worth as much. Or," he waved dismissively, "I could send a boarding team over and just kill you all…" He squinted with one eye again, "But it would be best for all concerned if you were cooperative…"

Reegan watched the countdown on his command screen out of the corner of his eye; *Three… two… one… "MARK!"* The tactical officer maxed the shields at full-military, the systems responding instantly as he simultaneously engaged the ship's photo-reactive skin, rendering the Perseus nearly invisible to the naked eye. The communications officer employed an electronics jamming suite and the video comm square turned to static snow.

Reegan tapped *DEPLOY* on his controls, the gun turrets swinging out all along the sides of the hull, a main turret rising out of the top and another extending out of the bottom. They began firing immediately at the point blank range of about ten miles, creating a cacophony of sound; the *Zawunk-Zawunk* of the main guns thumping the deck, the rapid hammering of the smaller turrets vibrating through the hull. "Torpedo solution!" he ordered.

The Perseus shuddered as return fire blasted her shields.

"Port shields, fifty percent!"

"Combat roll!" ordered the Commander, "Present starboard gun batteries."

"Torpedo solution entered!"

On Reegan's command, the torpedo rack swung from the hull, swiveling to bear, firing two spreads of two, MK*25V, high-speed torpedoes each, two sets of fireballs streaking away in an arc toward the cruiser. "Torpedoes away…"

"Tracking… tracking… One destroyed… Two destroyed…" Searing flashes of light midway between the ships marked the early demise of the

409

two torpedoes, quickly followed by two more against the cruiser's hull. "Two solid hits! Her hull is breached!"

The Perseus shook violently, the cruiser continuing to return fire, the Perseus mere seconds from the gate, wiggling tendrils of neon color reaching out for its hull, rejected by the ship's shields. "Sir, we have to drop shields or we won't jump…"

Selecting all the remaining torpedoes left in the starboard rack, Reegan launched them all, six MK*25Vs streaking out in pairs toward the cruiser. "Let them deal with those…" He keyed comms, "All guns keep firing." Glancing up at the main screen, the nose of the Perseus neared the corona of the gate, her hull surrounded by a bubble of plasma, held away by the shields. He couldn't wait any longer, *"Drop shields."*

The multicolored plasma silently splashed down around the hull like a falling tidal wave, swallowing the ship whole, a hard impact jolting its frame, warning alarms ringing, lights flickering, several systems dropping offline. The satiny walls of the transition tunnel to Zostinar was a welcome sight and Reegan slumped back in his seat, "Damage report."

"Working on it, Skipper."

"Sitrep; any chance that cruiser will turn around and follow us to Zostinar?"

Rotating his seat, the tactical officer nodded towards Reegan, "I sent the full damage assessment to you; I highly doubt it. She may not even make it back to Toberus Interstellar. She was holed amidships on her port side, several turrets damaged or destroyed, shields down… and our last look before we jumped was before that final flight of torpedoes finished their run. That was quite a spread - set from bow to stern, if they didn't kill at least half of them, she may not even exist anymore. Our initial engagement took them by surprise and she wasn't in the best of shape to begin with."

Reegan keyed his comm mic, "Stand down all gun crews and pilots. Well done, people," he added, clearing the red alert.

"Damage report coming in; we lost a turret on the starboard side, another two damaged. Starboard engine is damaged but operating at fifty percent. There was a minor fire but it was contained with minimal damage. The GOD drive is currently offline - more details to follow. The photo-reactive skin shows extensive damage all along the starboard side. Overall though, I'd have to say we were pretty lucky."

"Hm," grunted Reegan. "Pretty lucky would have been passing them in here" he indicated the big screen, "where they couldn't fire on us…" He scratched his head, "We should be able to send a couple magnetic crawlers out on the hull for a survey, right?"

"Yes, Sir."

"Good, let's do that - see if we can get a handle on our needs before we reach Zostinar; no telling what we're going to encounter next. And have any of the free hands help the repair crews…"

CHAPTER THIRTY THREE

THE HOUSE OF TILLDAWN : *AWAKENING*

Completely relaxed, he at first, felt nothing. The world was without sound. It was without pain. It was without cold, or heat. It was without fear. There was only peace. A deep, penetrating contentment. He slowly became aware of a light breeze and a feeling of dampness on the exposed skin of his face and hands. To him though, it was a new sensation, it meant nothing - his world was without form or meaning. He drew sweet air into his lungs and could feel his heart beat for what seemed to be the first time. He was without memory. He was without identity. *But I think, therefore I am.* He was pleased in the knowledge that *he was, he is.*

It required some effort to open his eyes, like it was the first time for this as well. They resisted at first, like his eyelids were magnetized. His successful effort was rewarded with only darkness. This, for some reason, disappointed him. He did not know what to expect, except he expected more than nothing. But it came slowly, gradually as his eyes took in the splendor that surrounded him, an unbroken spread of sparkling points of light. An uninterrupted canopy of stars. It pleased him that he knew what they were. As his vision cleared he was able to discern stars of color, albeit subtle. He could not hold his eyes open for long, his eyelids heavy, feeling as if he could rest there, undisturbed, for an eternity; the peace he felt, so complete. As his eyes closed again he realized he knew the names of the stars... each and every one of them; his mind's eye tagging each one with an invisible label. *Curious.*

He drew in a deep breath, a wave of sensations flowing over him, aware of his body without movement, feeling every molecule of his being, awaken from its slumber. The thought of time crossed his mind without meaning, having no definition for the concept. It concerned him that there were things he could not define or identify, while seeming to know the names and locations of everything he saw above him. *Patience.* Something told him patience was the key; all manner of knowledge, reason and explanation would eventually be revealed to him. There would be no more questions, only answers. *Answers*, the last thought to pass through him as he drifted away, back to the nothingness from which he had come.

■ ■ ■

It had a name; warmth. It radiated across his body with gentle caresses and the sensation that penetrated his body reached his muscles, energizing them, waking them. A red glow filtering through his eyelids filled his mind, blotting out all thought except curiosity. He fought with his eyelids, succeeding in forcing them open, his will stronger than the magnets holding them closed. The canopy of stars had been replaced with a cloudless sky of intense blue, a fiery ball of light creeping up from behind a line of trees about a thousand feet away. One-thousand-twenty-two-feet to be exact. How or why he knew that, wasn't clear. There was a tall brick wall just beyond the tree line that cut the following forest away from what was inside it.

Laying, in a semi-upright position, he managed to roll his head to the left and right, the wall continuing around on both sides, unbroken, the area filled with all manner of plants and trees arranged in manicured and explosively colorful gardens. His mind felt assaulted by the organized chaos of colors and shapes, suddenly filled with the names of each and every species his eyes crossed. He looked back up at the sky again to clear the debris from his head, wondering if he could learn to control that. Birds flitted overhead and he knew instantly what they were and their specific genus.

His eyelids were no longer heavy, he closed them because he wanted to, not because he had to and envisioned the field of stars he'd seen previously. Unsure why, several stood out as familiar. He chose one and his mind focused on it, producing images and sensations. He chose another. And another, discovering he could produce images of anything he chose, even simultaneously. But that quickly became an uncontrollable mess of overwhelming imagery and sensation. He focused on only one, the others falling away, and he mentally stepped into the picture... *he was there.*

■ ■ ■

Whether mentally exhausted or frustrated with the lack of results he could produce, he opened his eyes again, the sun having cleared the treetops. The gardens begged to be walked, the brick pathway winding away from cobblestone patio. Sitting in a contoured recliner, the long, dark robe he found himself in was loose enough for most movement, but not enough so to allow him to straddle the recliner as he would have felt inclined to do. He flexed his hands and arms before pushing himself into an upright sitting position, swinging his bare feet off one side. The cobblestone was smooth and worn, still cool from the evening temperatures. It required less effort than he expected to rise to his feet, feeling neither weightless nor heavy. It was an odd sensation he couldn't define as he had no reference for comparison. Strolling off the patio to the brick garden path, he looked back, realizing he hadn't been alone, several other people on recliners not far from where he'd been, lay motionless. He wasn't sure what to make of this strange place, or the massive building the patio was attached to. *The House of Tilldawn.* He wasn't sure how he knew that.

The stone building looked like it had been there a thousand years, a cross between a castle and a cathedral, it's size stretching well over a thousand feet to the left and another thousand feet to the right. Exact numbers appeared in his head and he pushed them out, not concerned with that particular detail. *Hmm, he could control it.* He stopped at the edge of a reflection pool, a fountain above and behind it, a small waterfall pouring into it. He dropped to a knee to put his hand into the pool to test the water and the hooded face in the reflection was familiar yet unfamiliar. Pulling the hood back to reveal more didn't improve the recognition and he ran his fingers through the unruly hair that topped his head.

"Jack..."

He almost fell face-first in the water, turning to meet the deep, mellow voice. The man was shorter, much older, bearded and wore the same long, hooded robe. "Is that me?" he asked, touching his own chest. Other than the sound of the breeze through the trees and distant twitter of birds, they were the first real sounds he'd experienced - and they seemed exceedingly loud. Like he needed to adjust the volume.

"Jack Steele," replied the man. "Yes, that's you." Reading the blank stare, he realized the man's transition was, as yet, incomplete. He laid his hand on the man's shoulder, and squeezed gently, "Here, let me help you..."

With the flood of information, Jack Steele's eyes popped wide and he took a step back, his hands up in a defensive posture, "Wh... whe... where... what..." his head snapped left and right, eyes searching the area around him scanning for threats, his mind racing forward, an avalanche of information crashing inward like a tidal wave, his heart racing, breathing heavily, suddenly stressed into a fight or flight position.

The cloaked and hooded man opposite him, stood at ease, his hands out in a supplicant gesture, "Easy Jack." He pulled his hood back, revealing a lined, aged face and gray beard. "You're safe here."

Jack snapped from fight mode to upright and focused, recognition locking in. *"Voorlak?* What the hell are *you* doing here?" He looked around, "And *where* is here?" He looked down at his arms, the robe hanging loosely off him, draped nearly to the ground, "And why the hell am I dressed like *Obi-Wan Kenobi?"*

"Who..?"

Jack waved it off, "Forget it. I mean it's comfortable and all, but I don't really go for the whole Friar Tuck look..." He scanned his surroundings with a scrutinizing eye. "What the hell is this place?" he muttered under his breath.

"Friar tuck..?"

Steele took a deep cleansing breath and shook his head, "Never mind. Just point me to my gear and let me get back to the Perseus. I'm MIA and I need to get back, we have a job to..."

Voorlak's voice was measured, calm, "You ship is gone Jack. It has been for some time."

Jack's head bobbed back like he'd been slapped, *"Gone?!* When? How long?" He pulled up his left sleeve looking for his MOBIUS. "I have to call them... Where's my... my thing?" he tapped his arm, the name momentarily escaping him.

"You no longer need devices, Jack. You mind is..."

"Wait, stop," commanded Steele, his hand out in a stalling gesture. "No more talk. I thank you for your hospitality, but I need my gear. I'm out of here," he backed away, "I have a job to do..."

"Wait, Jack... you can't go..." waved Voorlak.

"Really? *Watch me..."*

"Jack," urged the old man, his voice uncharacteristically intense, "we have *much* to discuss."

"That's funny," countered Jack continuing to back away, "considering I haven't gotten a straight answer out of you yet. Like how long my ship has been gone - or how long I've been here..." He backed into something solid and spun away as a reflex, two hooded figures standing behind him.

"Is there a problem, my Brother?"

"He was not long enough in Chrysalis," responded Voorlak. "He awoke early."

Steele spun himself toward Voorlak for an explanation, seeing two more hooded figures standing alongside the old man. He glanced back over his shoulder, the first two to have arrived, still behind him. "Bad idea," he growled through clenched teeth. "Gear. *Now.*"

Voorlak recognized a caged animal when he saw one, nodding once, "Brother, his belongings - if you please."

"Brother, your belongings," offered the hooded figure behind him, holding out a bundle of clothes, boots and assorted other things.

Steele turned to accept them, eyeing the man suspiciously, knowing he didn't have them a moment before. "I'm not going to ask how you did that... frankly I don't give a damn." He backed away with his things, the five men converging to face him, Voorlak in the center, standing shoulder to shoulder, watching him with curiosity. "Not a lick of privacy, huh?" Jack stripped the robe from his body, dropping it to the turf, exposing his muscular body, "Whatever." Pulling his clothes on, item by item, they watched and waited patiently. He slid the MOBIUS on his arm before donning his leather jacket. "Which way out?" he asked politely, adjusting his collar. The five of them stood there looking blankly at him, motionless. "Uh, yeah," he waved non-nonchalantly, "that's alright, I'll see myself out..." He turned and strode toward the garden wall that he estimated was the wall at the front of the building, a thousand feet distant. He had no concrete basis for that decision, just a gut feeling. An urgency prompted him to trot. Then run. Pushing himself, he ran harder, leaning into a life-and-death sprint that should exhaust him, but produced no ill-effects. He was not tired *or* winded as he pushed harder yet, the wall approaching at a speed he should not humanly be capable of. The wall was taller than it looked, maybe seven feet; *seven feet ten inches,* his mind informed him. He slowed, planning to leap and catch the lip and pull himself over the top.

He leapt and nearly went over the wall without using his hands, landing on his feet, at the top, balancing. Standing atop the wall he looked back, the five men near the patio, facing him, watching. On the other side of the wall was an entry drive, bracketed by two massive lion statues facing the road that bordered what appeared to be the edge of the property; traffic moving swiftly along on the ground and in the air. With a brief wave, he dropped effortlessly down over the wall to the turf below. He marveled at the lack of effort the eight foot drop required; it was nothing more than jumping off a single stair.

416

He strode off, looking up the drive toward the road... That wasn't there. Nothing he expected to be there, was there. Full stop. Inside the back wall, the garden lay spread out in front of him, the five men in robes waiting for him where he'd left them. He looked back over his shoulder at the wall behind him. He turned back and leapt, no hands, landing atop the back wall... sprawling fields, rolling hills and trees lay beyond the wall and the back of the cathedral. He jumped off without looking to the garden this time, dropping back into the garden on the other side of the front wall. Once more he turned back and leapt to the top of the wall; the drive, the lions and the road lay beyond him. He pulled up the sleeve of his leather jacket and attempted to activate the MOBIUS on his arm - to no effect. The dark, lifeless screen stared back at him. Experiencing a toxic mix of confusion, fear, panic and desperation, he fought the urge to jump off the wall toward the road again. He resigned himself to the knowledge that he couldn't leave. That it wasn't just Voorlak's *wish* for him not to leave, he wasn't physically *capable* of leaving. *What the hell was this damn place?*

■ ■ ■

Sitting alone together in the shade on two loungers facing one another, Voorlak laid the folded robe on Jack's lap. "However you're most comfortable, my boy. It may take some time for you to adjust... it's normal. Especially since you awoke from Chrysalis early..."

A hooded figure appeared causing Jack to start and Voorlak stalled the man with his hand. "I'm sorry for interrupting, your Worshipful, there is an Inspector Brooker from the G'Naroth Sarat Security Service here to see a Jax Mercury..."

"Thank you Brother," waved Voorlak, dismissing him, "I'll handle it."

The way the monk had addressed Voorlak hadn't been lost on Jack. *Worshipful.* Jack rose and dropped the robe onto the lounger, "It's alright, I'll handle it... *Worshipful.*"

Voorlak looked up at him, "We are *Brothers*, Jack. He is not. At least not yet." He nodded toward the interior door, "You have a visitor to attend to... do try not to frighten the locals..." Jack nodded and turned for the door, "Four weeks, Jack. You've been here and your ship's been gone for four weeks..."

■ ■ ■

417

Three men sat on the wooden benches in the foyer of the Temple; a bald man in a suit on one side and two uniformed officers on the other side. A Temple sentry in a dark, floor-length, hooded robe, stood at attention beside each bench, gold-adorned staffs in their right hands. They remained unmoved as Steele passed them, entering the foyer.

"You must be Inspector Brooker," Steele extended his hand, "Jax Mercury, what can I do for you?"

The man rose and shook Jack's hand, not letting go, "I can't believe it's actually you, Mr. Mercury. I have quite a few questions for you." He locked an electronic handcuff around his wrist. "Now if you'd turn around please..." The sentries jumped into action, their staffs clacking together to block the uniformed officers from interfering.

"*Brothers*, stand down," ordered Jack. He turned around, offering his other wrist to the Inspector as the sentries returned to their posts, watching intently, the uniformed officers moving to take him by the elbows. "See, Brooker, this is going to pose a problem..."

"How so, Mr. Mercury?"

"Well, I cannot *leave* here. You will have to ask your questions here..."

"That's not how this is going to work, Mr. Mercury. I am not bound by the superstitions of this... well, whatever this place is," he waved dismissively. "I have a triple homicide to solve and somehow you're in the middle of it." He nodded in the direction of the sentries, "And if they interfere again, I can take them with us for obstructing an investigation."

Steele shrugged lightly, "Brooker, what you don't seem to understand is, the laws you're so fond of out there, don't apply *here*. Least of all, the rules of physicality."

"Yeah, you're boring me, Mercury." He nodded towards the door, "Let's go boys." He swung the door open, leading the way.

Two steps behind him, Jack followed him out, an officer on each elbow. They stepped toward the sunshine and entered the foyer at the opposite end of the building, a set of Temple sentries in dark, floor-length, hooded robes, moving from their stations to block the corridor; gold-adorned staffs clacking together in a X between them. Jack rather enjoyed the stunned look of the officer on either side of him. "Oh," he mused, "we have to go back, we forgot the Inspector." They rotated around and walked through the doorway, entering the foyer in the front of the building, a bewildered Inspector wondering where his officers and prisoner had disappeared to.

418

"What manner of trickery is this?" Brooker demanded, forcefully grabbing Steele away from the officers. Steele shrugged and scratched his forehead with a free hand, "I did tell you..." Brooker's eyes widened in disbelief as Jack handed him his high-tech handcuffs. "Oh, you might want these back - they look expensive." He grabbed the Inspector and spun him towards the door, "Let me show you how this works..."

■ ■ ■

Returning to the front foyer, Steele sat down on the bench and crossed his legs. "Since I *cannot* leave, maybe you would like me to answer your questions here?" he indicated the bench next to him.

It took a moment for the open-mouthed Inspector to gather himself and respond, "How..."

Steele shrugged, "I'm new here. Don't really know myself. *You* can leave, I cannot. That's all I know." The stunned Brooker waved the uniformed officers outside before dropping himself onto the bench. "Now you were saying something about our superstitious laws?" prompted Jack.

Brooker shook his head blankly and waved it off, "I never believed..." He blinked hard, looking at the sentries before leaning forward peering down the ornately arched corridor toward the other end of the temple. "My detainers," he mimed opening cuffs, "how did you..."

Steele shook his head, "Honestly, I don't know. I just didn't want them on and they fell off."

The inspector nodded his head loosely, "I've never seen anyone defeat them before - I... I didn't know it was possible."

"So you mentioned having some questions about a triple homicide?"

■ ■ ■

Steele sat back down on the lounger across from Voorlak, "How many of my people got stranded here?"

"Three," replied the old man. "They've settled in Sandorra. It's across the desert, about four-hundred miles from Amanpoor. Mr. Brooker has no idea where they are and Sandorra is outside of his jurisdiction. It's a frontier type of town and it's a little rough, but my sources tell me your people are very capable and have access to substantial funds to maintain themselves, until either your ship returns, or another can be contacted to pick them up.

Sandorra has their own landing port so there will be no need for them ever to return to Amanpoor." Voorlak could see the discomfort of the man he had come to know and produced the one thing they had a history of sharing. Something familiar. "Ditarian Brandy?" He handed Jack a brandy snifter, setting one on the cobblestone at his feet, pouring for the pilot before his own. "What's on your mind?"

Steele took a swallow, the familiar warmth sliding down his throat, the flavor waking his taste buds. He realized the snifter was nervously shaking in his hand. "Why can't I leave here..?" His stomach rolled, "Am I... *dead?*"

A weak smile crept into Voorlak's face, "No, Jack, you're not dead. But you're not alive anymore either. At least, not in the respect that you think of as *alive*." He watched Steele's eyes well with tears. "You are in some ways, *less*, but in many ways, you are more. *Much more.* You are neither living, nor dead, you are something... *new*."

Jack sipped his Brandy, steadying the glass with both hands, "Like what... like an angel or something?"

The old man made an accepting face, "Or something..."

Steele took a breath to steady himself and try to digest what was not making any sense as of yet. "I remember dreaming. Of friends and family, of my sister, of Alité and Colton..."

"You weren't dreaming Jack, you were visiting. It often happens during Chrysalis."

Jack frowned, "Are we talking teleportation?"

"Psychokinetic projection," corrected Voorlak. "We can do more than just visit, as *astral projection* would suggest. We can become solid and interact with our surroundings, physically and with our minds. Which is the *psychokinetic* portion of the equation."

I don't remember being able to *do* anything," commented Jack.

"Because you never finished Chrysalis..."

"You keep saying that word, what the hell does it mean?"

"Transformation," replied Voorlak. "You only finished about half of Chrysalis."

"But didn't you say I've been here a *month?*"

"Well yes. But it takes time to absorb all the knowledge there is. And was..."

"I will know *everything?*" interrupted Jack. *"Everything* everything?" He waved his arms wide.

"An oversimplification of course," agreed the old man, "but suitable for this conversation." He took a sip of his brandy. "Just as you are different from your fellow humans, and humans are different from other humanoid aliens across the universe, in some ways you are the same. What ultimately makes you unique is your life, your experiences. Your perceptions, your responses. And your history before you, were *you,*" he motioned at him. "That's all in there." He made a circle in the air around Jack with his free hand, "That's all part of the mix that makes Jack Steele, *Jack Steele.*"

Jack looked surprised, "Reincarnation? Because I really don't know if I believe in reincarnation or not."

Voorlak smirked, "Funny how the universe doesn't really care much about what you believe or not, eh? It just does what it does." He shrugged his shoulders theatrically, waving one hand, "Because aliens, right? Who believes in *aliens?*" He pointed at Jack, "But *you* believed. Didn't you? Yes, you did... You somehow *knew* this was all out here... It was more than just a gut feeling. You never talked to anyone about it, but you *knew*... That wasn't by coincidence, or by accident, or premonition... that was *memory*. There was some small part of you," he touched Jack's knee, "some small sliver of past life memory. You were so sure, yet your reasoning wouldn't let you believe it. But you'd been out here before - you'd *lived* out here. In fact, we had even *met* before."

Jack sat up rigid. "Really? You remember me from a previous life?"

"No way for me to tell *who* you might have been, just that we have..." The old man upturned his snifter to drain the last of his brandy.

"Do I still have a soul, then?"

"Of course..."

Steele was beginning to see some understanding, "So when we are reincarnated it is with the same soul, then - yes? It is recycled with us?"

"Yes," replied Voorlak. "When you are *recycled*, as you so interestingly put it, you retain your soul with the intention that as you age, travel through time, you learn from your mistakes and improve, becoming a better and better being, from one iteration to the next."

"That's what you meant when you told me once, I was an *old soul*..." Steel pinched his lower lip, "I always thought you meant it figuratively..." Clarity was so close. He took another swallow of brandy.

"That was a slip of information I hadn't intended. I'm surprised you remembered it... but yes, that was what I meant."

"So then if I have reached... what... the end of my," he made a cycling motion with his free hand, "recycles; I move up the ladder to something new?"

"Something like that..."

"And I get to keep my soul..."

"Yes..."

Jacks eyes widened, "Where do the souls come from? Are they endless? I mean, will they run out eventually? What happens then?"

Voorlak stalled the sudden avalanche of questions with a hand, "As much as I'd love to explain it all to you, my Brother, in your present condition, you do not have the capacity to understand the complexities of the birth of all there is. And *that* is where we have to start."

Like a flash of lightning, a massive segment of knowledge exploded in his mind, jolting Jack to his feet, "Mars... *Mars!*" The old man just watched him, wide-eyed. "Mars was where humanity was born... *Our* humanity," he corrected himself, "not everyone else's."

"Yes. What else do you see?"

"Mars was colonized... no... or was Mars the Garden of Eden? I can't tell," he rubbed his forehead, " it's not clear."

"Your humanity has started over more than once, Jack," clarified Voorlak. "You started on Mars, outgrew it, moved to the stars and didn't look back. By the time Humanity finally returned to your solar system, Mars was a dead planet, used up. But Earth had come into maturity and Humanity started over there."

"But we've found no signs of civilization on Mars. And that doesn't make sense, what about what I was taught about the Bible and God..? It would mean the scientists were right, God doesn't exist..."

"Easy Jack, easy..." motioned Voorlak, rising from his seat. "They are both right, they actually mesh together in a way they haven't discovered yet. You will understand all of this better when you finish Chrysalis. There is much to learn, much to absorb..."

"I don't think I'm supposed to know all this yet... No..." Jack was pacing around the lounger with nervous energy, his mind racing; "What if I didn't? What if I don't finish this Chrys-whatever it is. What if I don't want to? You said I'm not dead, what if I go back? I don't think I'm ready for this. It doesn't feel right. No. No, it doesn't feel right at all. It feels wrong. There is so much I haven't finished. This can't be the way it's supposed to be. I, I *can't*." He remembered the look on his wife's face, the anguish she attempted to hide from their son. There was so much left undone; Earth, Veloria, the fleet, his family... There was abrupt clarity and calm. He stopped pacing, locking eyes with Voorlak, taking a calming breath, letting it out slowly, "I can't do this, I'm not ready and it's not time for me. I have to go back. You have to send me back. You know I'm right..."

"You don't know what you're asking, Jack," said Voorlak, his eyes pleading.

One after another, hooded figures appeared around him, each one materializing like a ghost emerging from a fog, until there were twelve, Steele himself, being the thirteenth. The shadow of the hoods hiding their faces made it impossible to see who was speaking except for Voorlak, whose hood was still back over his shoulders.

"The initiate has a point, Brothers, he *did* come to us earlier than expected."

"But he has already completed half of the Chrysalis," Voorlak reminded them.

"Exactly. Half. Exceedingly rare for someone whose time is at hand. It proves he came to us too early."

"But should he not stay once he has begun, Brothers? He certainly cannot return to his previous self with what he has gained here..."

"Agreed. He could not be allowed to exist in the same plane as the *Normals* as an *Elevated*. Even if his experience is incomplete."

"Brothers, what is the procedure for a *Reversion*?"

"He would lose what he has gained," offered Voorlak. "He would return healthy and whole, but without knowledge or memory of his experience. By chance, he may retain some recollection of having visited the Temple, but nothing more."

"The Brethren find this procedure as acceptable?" There was a unified *aye* in response. "Does the initiate have anything to say on his own behalf?"

"You may speak Jack," coached Voorlak.

Steele cleared his throat, "I can't pretend to know the full ramifications of what is happening here. What I *can* say is, that I am honored to be here and I hope, in the future, when the time is right, I will get the opportunity to return. I truly appreciate what you have done for me and your compassion in this matter. Thank you..."

"It is more a matter of pragmatism than compassion, my Brother. It is rare, but early arrivals have occurred before. Even more rare, is for an initiate to awaken early. Even rarer yet, is the knowledge or feeling of ill-timing and will or desire to go back. Arriving here should not be taken lightly. However, harmony being the key to all societies, especially ours, we could not in good conscience force you to stay. The solemn and binding oath you take upon yourself, must be taken of your own free will and accord. There are no guarantees of course, but perhaps we will see you again at a more appropriate time."

Steele looked to Voorlak, "What happens now?"

"We will take a ballot."

Jack ran his fingers through his hair, "I'm confused, I thought you all agreed..."

"On the procedure, not the outcome..."

His heartbeat quickened; something had changed and he couldn't put his finger on it, "I don't understand, what other outcome is there?"

"You do not feel you are ready to be here," said a barrel-chested figure, a heavy white beard hanging out of the hooded shadow. "We must decide to send you back in good form, or let you pass."

"Pass?" That word sent a spike of adrenalin up his back, "Pass to where..?"

"Pass to that house not made with hands, eternal in the heavens... *Die*."

"Oh - wait, wait, wait..." Steele waved.

"The initiate will retire from the chamber while the Brethren ballot. Senior and Junior Stewards, escort Mr. Steele."

Chambers? But we're outside... Jack might've run if he felt it might do any good; he knew better. "How will I know..." in mid-sentence, he found himself in the Temple's front foyer, facing the outer doors, "what you have decided..." It took a moment for recognition and comprehension. He spun around, the two sentries were blocking his way, their staffs crossed in an X barring him from the Temple. "Oh, man, oh man, oh man..." he mumbled, pacing, rubbing his arms, his body suddenly covered with creepy-crawly, pins and needles. "Crap, crap, crap... This isn't good, oh man, this isn't good... Oh my God, what am I gonna' do... *Alité, if you can hear me, I love you...*"

EPILOGUE

VALHALLA OR PURGATORY : *THORNE AT MY SIDE*

He waited for his eyes to register shapes or light in the darkness but nothing happened, the blackness was absolute. *Were his eyes even open?* He made a physical effort to open his eyes and blink - he could feel them... He took a deep breath. He knew he was breathing but there was nothing of note... except... *leather*. He could smell leather. He moved his body and could hear the familiar creak. It took him a moment to realize he was clothed in his flight jacket and when he searched his other senses, taking a physical inventory, he could feel his pants and flight boots. *Where the hell am I?*

Extending his arms to either side, his knuckles struck hard, smooth, cool surfaces about twelve inches away, causing a spike of panic. He reached out in front of him, touching another surface almost at arm's length, the stress deepening. His mind foggy, he couldn't remember anything, least of all where he could possibly be. *Am I dead? Dear God I'm in a coffin...Wait... what if I'm alive? I'm breathing, right? Holy fuck, I've been buried alive!*

"HEY!" he shouted, slapping the surface above him. "Let me the fuck out of here!" He pounded with his hands, alternately kicking, his boots thumping loudly on the metal surface. Terror gripped his guts like a vice, a hundred *B* horror movies running through his head...

"Jack Steele, I am detecting extremely high levels of dopamine and adrenaline. Your heart and respiratory rates are far above normal. Are you in distress?"

"Hell yeah, I'm in distress, I've been *buried alive!"*

"You are not. You are in a pure oxygen sleep chamber."

"What..." he said flatly.

"Please calm yourself."

"Where the hell are we... *am I?"* he corrected himself. "And who are *you?"*

"I am assuming you mean other than being in a pure oxygen sleep chamber... Cartographically speaking, our location is unknown." A holographic screen appeared above his wrist, "I am your MOBIUS, of course."

The glow of her hologram washed across him and he squinted from its brightness even though it was dimmed for total darkness. He let his head drop back to the pillow and let his arms drop to his chest, breathing deep, trying to calm his nerves and his heart.

"That is much improved."

"Why can't you tell where we are?"

"I have no outside signal to connect to, there is no available network."

"Crap. How do I get out of this damn thing?"

"It is most likely voice activated with a manual control somewhere..."

"Think I found something," muttered Jack. His fingers fumbled in a slot along his right side in the pad he was lying on, locating a small lever he could lift with his fingertips. The seal on the chamber released with a *pssshhh* like a soda can and the surface he was on moved out into the open, the side folding down, allowing him to swing his feet off the pad and sit upright. "Lights, ten percent..?" The small eight-foot by ten-foot room appeared around him in a dull, muted glow, a small desk and chair, the sleep chamber and a tall skinny locker the only things in the room besides him. "Oh man," he sighed... "am I in prison?"

"I cannot answer that question."

He stood up carefully, testing his legs, a little unsteady. "Feel like I haven't walked in a while..."

"I have no records of activity before..."

Steele swiped the screen closed, "If you can't add anything useful, *shut up,"* he quipped, annoyed. A small refrigerator built into the wall next to the desk, under the locker, had bottles of water and some sort of snack bars. Selecting a few items, he ambled towards the door which split in half on a diagonal, disappearing into the bulkhead without hesitation. Stepping over the hatch threshold sailors often referred to as knee-knockers, he found the passageway dimly lit, no brighter than the room he'd left. It stretched in both directions. Listening intently, he heard nothing other than the noise of absolute silence in his ears. It felt unnatural.

■ ■ ■

Steele walked the passageway, helping himself along with his hands on whichever side was closest, his legs seemingly weak. Wherever he was, it was certainly utilitarian. Clean but plain, and by all appearances, relatively new. The narrow corridor came to a *T* and he decided to go straight, hoping

426

the hatchway in front of him would lead to something revealing. Like the one in his cubicle, it split in half on a diagonal, disappearing into the bulkhead and he stepped carefully over the knee-knocker...

A spread of stars reached across his field of view and around on either side, tears welling in his eyes as he surveyed the work stations on the ship's bridge. Not understanding his emotions, he moved from station to station, examining them closely, searching for anything familiar. The layout and darkened stations were totally foreign to him, though he felt comfortable within the space. *Is this my ship?* He ran his fingers through his hair, and stood at the front of the bridge staring at the vista displayed on the screen, several live video insets showing remote cameras at various angles. Camera Angle Three, showed landing gear and the belly of the ship; as well as anchor spikes holding the ship to the surface of a sizable asteroid drifting on the edge of a field. Scanning the inserts he spotted another, displaying a ship from an outside profile view. *Was that this ship, or an additional ship?*

Steele backed himself to the command chair, watching the screens, dropping into the seat. "Who's ship is this..?" he whispered aloud, surveying the unfamiliar bridge, digging through his memory and finding nothing.

"It's my ship..."

Steele spun the command seat to meet the voice at the back of the bridge, a figure about his own height standing inside the hatchway. "Lights, twenty-five percent..." He squinted as the lights came up, "And who are you?"

"Jack, it's *me*... Don't you recognize me?"

Steele's eyes narrowed, his brow furrowed, recognition slow, suddenly firing a flash of familiarity. *"Michel Thorne?!"*

"Sup, Brother."

■ ■ ■

Michel Thorne; a wide-shouldered, sandy-haired Belgian with blue-gray eyes, a broad, ready smile, a wicked sense of humor, and an IQ that Jack always felt had no bounds. Plain and simple, the guy was one of the smartest people he'd ever known; genius category stuff. And a friend he'd known for over two decades. No slouch himself, easily considered gifted, Jack often felt like a dull rock trying to cut butter compared to Michel's intellect. But that never seemed to affect or interfere with the long, topic-driven discussions, or bar-b-que fueled joke fests around the pool on weekends.

Michel was a computer and math wiz that did a stint as an ethical hacker working security penetrations, exploiting vulnerabilities and weaknesses in hardware and software for anyone needing to test their systems, including government agencies. That was long before the position was widely recognized, or even required *white hat* certifications. He had several offers to work strictly government gigs, but the restrictions were so heavy, so security sensitive, he became concerned about his family and chose the public sector, never looking back. And the money in the public sector was much better - that never hurt either.

Michel slid the mug across the table in the ship's small, empty cafeteria, "You still do the tea thing, right?"

Steele nodded, pulling the mug towards him, sliding the creamer over towards his friend for his coffee. "What the hell are you doing out here, Mike?"

Michel never begrudged Jack the incorrect use of his name in any form or manner he chose to use it, but he was the only one allowed that luxury. "I could ask you the very same question, buddy. How is it you found yourself floating out here all alone in an emergency life pod?"

"I was? I don't remember anything."

Michel nodded, "Yep. There you were, floating along, pretty as you please, right across in front of us. Almost ran your ass over."

Steele snorted, a curl at the corners of his mouth, "Well, thanks for not doing *that*. And thanks for picking me up..."

Michel blew steam off his coffee, "Any idea how you ended up out there?"

Jack shook his head, "No freaking idea. I can't remember anything except my damn name..." He sipped his tea.

"Well you remembered *me*..." Michel smiled crookedly, "eventually. You always were a little *slow*..."

Steele almost snorted tea through his nose, "Screw you," he smirked. "I love you too... Wait," his eyes widened, *"Pattiwillow!"*

Michel's eyebrows lifted, "What's that now?"

"A name. I think... A woman."

"Well, *that's* helpful," commented Michel dryly.

"No it's not," countered Jack.

"Yeah, you're right," snarked, Michel. "It's not worth shit. Think of something better."

"Something *better...*" muttered Jack shaking his head, "Y'know, I forgot what a pain in the ass you can be." He watched Michel's expression jump to joke mode, cutting him off, waggling his finger, "No. *No.* Quit it. No ass jokes, no... " He watched his friend pout in an exaggerated fashion and suddenly the years slid away and they were sitting around the pool again, the bar-b-que sizzling with burgers or steaks; he could almost smell them grilling. "Mikie, where's Rosa... Rosa and the girls?"

Michel snapped back to serious, "Safe. With my mom and dad. I moved them back to Kepplar about six months ago..."

"What do you mean, *back* to Kepplar?"

"Back. As in *return...*" smirked Michel.

"I know what *back* means, asshat," chuckled Jack.

"Back, as in *home,*" replied Michel, more seriously. "I was born on Kepplar 22B. Mom and dad moved to earth when I was little. You remember, my dad was an engineer; he came for work. I guess they visited once, a few years before I was born, and decided to come back to live."

'Well that explains a lot..."

Michel's head tilted to one side, "Like what?"

Steele tapped his skull behind his ear where the translator disk sat beneath his skin, "Why you could pick up languages just by listening to them. I remember sitting in a restaurant with you, listening to two guys speaking Greek in the next booth and all of a sudden you're in a conversation with them... speaking *Greek.*"

Michel dismissed it with a wave, "Dude, that was all me. I didn't get a disk until about four or five years ago when I started coming out here. You forget, I grew up in Belgium. You travel around Europe a bit and you pick up everything; German, French, Italian..." he ticked them off on his fingers.

"Yeah," interrupted Jack, "I *lived* in Chicago - I never *picked up* any Spanish, Polish or Korean..."

Michel shrugged, "We're wired different. No sweat, man." It was silent for awhile; there was much to talk about but he could tell Jack was struggling. "Look, dude, I think you're still under the influence of whatever is in your system. You were pretty heavily sedated in that lifepod. Why don't you sleep it off for a little while longer?"

Steele bobbed his head, his eyelids heavy, "If it's all the same to you, I'd rather not go back in that box, I'll stretch out on the bridge..."

Michel smiled, "I get it. The command chairs are pretty comfy. I'll come get you when our sleep cycle wakes..."

■ ■ ■

Michel Thorne stood in the center of the bridge of the Marauder Class gunship his father had helped design. The *Black Widow* was the first prototype ever built by the new startup, *Antwerp Shipworks*, and it had been a three-month odyssey to track her down and liberate her from the disgruntled partner who had stolen her and disappeared. Fortunately, retrieving her was bloodless, Thorne being able to hack into the secured ship and rewrite her code and registry to reflect the proper ownership. The ship was restored, renamed, crewed and gone before the thief ever knew it was missing from his stable. Before leaving, the crew recorded all the ships in his collection, disabling a fair selection before departing. Those records were anonymously sent to the UFW Ship Registry Service, to deal with as they wished.

Back in rightful ownership, the prototype, Black Widow, would be used to build interest and sales for Antwerp Shipworks' first release - and what better way to prove her viability, than to actually put her into service making money.

Standing between the command seats, the monitors and keyboard of the Captain's station tilted in his direction, Michel Thorne turned to his First Officer. "Anything show on recordings during our sleep cycle, Tom?"

"Two passes about three hours apart, Skipper," answered his First Mate. "Nothing to indicate they detected either of us."

"Good," he turned to his keyboard and called up several new camera views. "All gunners scan your sectors..."

"Aye, all gunners standing by."

Thorne leaned in and checked his First Mate's screens, "Is the *Palladium* ready?"

"Awaiting your command, Skipper."

Thorne sent a view of her to an inset on the big screen, "Tell her to cut loose."

"Aye."

The cargo hauler lifted off a neighboring asteroid, rising well above it, her gear retracting, before turning and moving off, away from the Black Widow, the blue glow of her main engines brightening. "Full scans, all spectrums," ordered Thorne. "Helm, pull our anchors."

The anchor spikes, forcefully fired into the asteroid's surface, were hydraulically ripped out, a metal against concrete squeal reverberating up into the deck as they were withdrawn into the landing gear before the gear retracted into the hull. The Black Widow floated free and Jack Steele, semi-reclined in the Captain's seat, opened his eyes, realizing he was no longer alone on the bridge. "Uh-oh..." he brought the seat upright, angling to slide out and relinquish his position.

Thorne patted his shoulder, "You're fine, Bro, stay put." He watched the diminishing Palladium on the big screen, "Anything on those scans?"

"Nothing yet, Skipper."

Michel Thorne straightened up and folded his arm across his chest, calm and collected. Watching. Waiting. "C'mon out and play, boys," he breathed.

It suddenly occurred to Jack... the Palladium was *bait*.

"The Palladium is turning away from the field toward the gate..."

Thorne checked the command screen facing him, "Right on time. If they're out here it'll be any minute now."

Jack's curiosity was piqued, "Who are..."

Thorne stalled his friend's inquiry with a raised index finger, his attention split between his command screens and the big screen, scan data scrolling on one side.

"Contact..." announced the Radar Officer. "One ship. A light Cutter, hanging on the edge of the field. No specs with the passive scans..."

"Wait it out," cautioned Thorne. "She's not alone." He nudged Jack with his elbow, "You're going to want to pay attention to this, because you're going to want one of these baby's after you see this..."

"Two more contacts, smaller, possibly heavy fighters, hanging on the edge of the field, Skipper."

"What are they waiting for?" mused Michel, skewing his mouth in thought. "Helm, move in, slowly, keep us on the dark side of these rocks."

"Aye." The nose of the Black Widow swung towards the contacts and she skirted around the asteroid, weaving methodically through the edge of the field, asteroids passing on alternate sides of the ship like a skier on a slalom course.

"Skipper, we've got a total of three fighters now, leaving the field to pursue the Palladium. The Cutter is staying put."

"Close on the Cutter," commanded Thorne, "stay concealed." He reached over and turned the monitors and keyboard to face Jack, "Keep an eye on these," he clapped his shoulder, "you're going to like what you see..." With an ear-to-ear grin he stepped up behind the helmsman and slapped the back of his command chair, "I got this." Michel slid in as the helmsman slid out, the controls never without a hand on them, a practiced swap that required precise timing to avoid a collision with any one of the thousands of city-block or larger, rocks around them. "Watch your right-hand screen, Jack."

Steele's right-hand screen displayed live; overhead, profile and stern schematics, the systems in use, and deployed equipment, their stats and condition.

"EWO, you with me?"

"Aye Skipper."

Michel Thorne was a talented pilot, sliding the Black Widow back and forth, up and down, asteroids flashing past on all sides in a blur. "Prepare to jam all frequencies. As soon as I hit her, link up and rip her data." His hands danced across the controls in front of him between the stick and throttle, the systems coming to life on Jack's screen. "Main weapons systems live. Shields up and gunners weapons-free on engagement..."

Thorne swung the Black Widow clear of the edge of the asteroid field, surprised the Cutter had yet to recognize the threat as his gun pipper came to rest on her stern. With his thumb he flipped the cover up on his launch button, a deployed pod of Stryker rockets waiting.

"Her shields are coming up, Skipper, main engines engaged..."

Having selected *all guns*, Thorne squeezed his weapons trigger, "Too little, too late." The amount of noise surprised Jack; twin seventy-five-millimeter auto-cannons roaring away, reverberating through the hull, accompanied by a set of pulse lasers screaming. And that didn't even account for the turrets that added to the cacophony, wacking away at the Cutter as they screamed past. The big screen switched to a rear view as the darkened hull of the Cutter shrunk behind them, her shredded stern glowing, one engine floating free, the other just debris and microdust strung out behind her as she coasted along, powerless. "Damn," Michel retracted the rocket pods, I didn't even get a chance to use them..." He rolled the ship, pulling her in a tight arc to pursue the fighters that were set to intercept the Palladium. "Did we get our data?"

"Aye, Skipper, a full rip."

"Good. She still jammed?"

"Permanently."

"Nice job." Let the Palladium know we're coming... on an open channel. These doorknobs can decide if they want to stay or go."

■ ■ ■

Thorne dropped himself into the seat across the table from Jack, setting his food down, "Food's not too bad," he smirked, *"but we could probably do with a better chef,"* he said a little too loudly.

"Hey, I heard that," came a voice from behind them.

"I knew they would run," continued Thorne. We essentially popped their base..."

"Base? That was a pretty small ship to be a base. That thing could never take in those fighters."

"Doesn't have to," countered Thorne, sipping his drink. "They do the same thing we did; set down on an asteroid. They can EVA back and forth between the fighters and mama. Pretty easy - they probably have permanent anchors sunk into the rock, a supply stash, maybe even a small pod building or two. They set up for two or three weeks and pick off a load or two and they head home to unload." He took a bite of his sandwich, "They dogged us last time we went through here, so I decided to see if we could set them up."

"Kind of a gamble..."

Michel shrugged, "Life is a gamble. You gotta play to win. I like my odds though." He tapped on the table, "She's pretty sweet, isn't she? I can set you up with one, we could run together. I'm sure I could get dad to arrange a lease option to buy or something if you're strapped."

"Before I do anything, I need to get home, Mike..."

"Your head clearer?"

"Steele nodded, "Yep. Remember most everything. Most. Still some gaps though."

Michel put both elbows on the table, leaning closer, "I'm sure we could arrange something, but I'm not headed back to Earth anytime soon..."

"Not Earth," countered Jack, "Veloria, it's in Velora Prime."

"Velora Prime..." Michel slid back in his chair, "Hey isn't that where the UFW had a huge fight last year with the FreeRangers?"

"That's the one..."

"I remember seeing that on the GalNet News. Weren't there like 30 ships or something destroyed in that fight?"

"If you included fighters," offered Jack. "Not capitol ships."

Michel leaned in again, speaking in hushed tones, "I heard that whole thing was over a ship the FreeRangers had offered a bounty on... I can't remember the name of the ship though..."

"Yeah, well," Jacked waved it off, unsure how much to reveal. "How much do you know about when I disappeared?"

"I remember it scared the crap out of Rosa when two guys in black suits came to the house to ask me about you. She freaked because I was away on business. *Out here."*

"Mmm, sorry about that. How long have you been coming out here?"

"About two years before you disappeared," replied Michel.

Steele shook his head, "So all those times, you were gone for business for like a month or two..."

"Yeah. Out here."

Steele folded his arms and leaned back, "You prick, you lied to me. On-site work for a client... *ass."*

Thorne laughed, "What the hell was I *going* to tell you? Like you would have believed me?" It was silent for a moment, "So how did *you* get out here?"

"If I told you I'd have to kill you," joked Steele. Michel rolled his eyes and Jack leaned in, "Are you now, or have you ever, worked for the FreeRangers?"

Thorne recoiled like he'd been slapped, "What? *Hell no!* You know me better than that. I may not always play by the rules but I have *ethics* for God's sake. Whatever we say doesn't leave this table..."

"Fair enough," nodded Jack approvingly. "I disappeared because I was accidentally abducted. Long story," he waved. "The ship the FreeRangers had the bounty on, was the *Freedom...*"

"That's it!" snapped Michel, "The Freedom - yeah I..."

"That was *my* ship," continued Jack, thumbing his chest. "We lost her in that fight. Along with some very good people..." his expression darkened, "That still bothers me..."

"Ass, you're full of shit," argued Thorne with a dismissive gesture. When Steele remained stone-faced, he knew it was the truth. *"Your* ship? Like, as in, Captain? Wasn't that a *cruiser?"*

"Converted into a Jump Carrier," countered Jack. "I had some remarkable people working on her - we were very blessed to have found them. Since we were freelancing for the UFW at the time, I was offered a choice; a replacement ship or a full commission..."

Michel tilted his head, waving a *come on* gesture, "Aaand?"

"Rear Admiral, Task Force Lancer; an Oijin, Squadron-Class Carrier, a Chimera-Class Battleship, two Freedom-Class Carriers, a Halceón Class Jump Frigate, a Missile Destroyer and some assorted support vessels."

"Whaat?!" Michel stared questioningly, but Jack's expression never wavered, "Dear God, you're not kidding..."

Steele absentmindedly tapped his index finger on his lips in thought, "Still not sure if it was the right choice or not. I don't think life was any easier *before*..." He sighed, "But it sure was less complicated."

Michel Thorne was not often at a loss for words, but his wheels were spinning, a million questions, and where to start? "So how... when..." He wiped his hand through the air like he was erasing an invisible chalkboard, "OK, you've got an entire task force, but you were out here, alone, in an emergency pod..." His hands went wide in a grand gesture, "What's up with that? How did that even happen?"

"That's where the blank is... I was on a special assignment. We were on G'Naroth Sarat in Bengaloo..."

"The whole task force?"

"No-no, single ship. We stopped in Amanpoor to pick up some... supplies."

"I *know* Amanpoor," confirmed Michel, "and I know you can pick up a lot more than... *supplies*. What did you get yourself into?"

Steele waved it off, "It wasn't *supplies*, it was just supplies. Forget the supplies, it had nothing to do with the supplies, it was just our excuse for going there."

"OK," said Michel, not totally convinced.

"Several of us went to a place called the *Black Star*... or something..."

"Black Hole Bar & Grill," corrected Michel, "yeah I know it."

Sighing heavily, Steele continued, "Anyway, the name I remembered earlier; *Pattiwillow*, she was the bartender. But that's where the blank starts."

"Think she drugged you?"

Jack pondered that for a moment, "I hadn't considered that. But I am now."

"Wait, so your last memory is from Amanpoor, on G'Naroth Sarat? Is that what you're telling me?"

Steele rubbed his forehead in consternation, "Yeah."

"Jack, we're in Madrassas; two systems and a temperamental star from Bengaloo. The corridor just opened back up two weeks ago... How long is your memory gap?"

Steele pulled up his sleeve, indicating his MOBIUS, "I don't know, she had no connection earlier."

"We go completely dark when we're in sleep cycle." He pointed at Jack's wrist, "Try her now, she should be fine."

Steele pulled up a holoscreen, MOBI connecting him instantly to the Black Widow's network, reaching GalNet, the news logo appearing in the upper corner next to the date. He stared at the date, willing it to be something else... *sixty-three days?* "Sixty-three days," he said slowly, his voice deadpan.

Michel's eyes widened, "Two months? Man, this is bad..."

"I have almost two-hundred missed contacts and personal messages..." His eyes burned and a lump grew in his throat, "Oh, my God... They must all think I'm dead." He rubbed his face with both hands, "Mike, I need to call my wife..."

Mike pointed to the crew's showers, "Go get cleaned up and pull yourself together, we'll set up a call from my office.

■ ■ ■

Space was at a premium in a ship like the Black Widow, so the Captain's office was small in comparison to what Jack had become used to. Off the main passageway instead of the bridge, Steele stepped over the knee-knocker into the office, the door closing quietly behind him. "You look better," commented Thorne, sitting with his feet up on his desk.

"I feel better." Jack sat across from him, "Any idea how long I was in the rescue pod?"

Thorne slid an e-Pad across the desk at his friend, "The guys ran through the computer before we dumped the pod, there was nothing but climate and life support settings. No manufacturer, origin, dates, recorded files... no anything. Like a generic unit. Never seen anything like that."

Butterflies in his stomach, Jack sighed, not bothering to look at the report. "Hmm. OK, let's make this call..."

"I'm proud of you, Brother," smirked Michel, "getting all married like an adult and stuff."

"Oh, shut up..."

"Whaat," gestured Michel, cracking a sarcastic smirk, "you've been single forever, it was time. I'm thinking if you waited this long, she's got to be something special, right?" He pulled his feet down and leaned forward, his elbows on the edge of the desk. "She's hot, isn't she... I know you, Jack, she's probably a looker... Is she sane though?"

"Mikie," grunted Steele in an admonishment, rolling his eyes. His MOBIUS forwarded to the big screen on the wall, an animated holding image of a waving purple flag emblazoned with the Velorian Royal Crest in white, the same winged horse that was on Jack's ring, greeted them.

Michel Thorne caught the parallel instantly, "Is that a Royal Crest?" He pointed at the screen.

"Mmm, hmm."

"Isn't that the same thing that's on your ring?" he indicated Jack's hand with a flip of his thumb.

"Mmm, hmm."

"What did you do," laughed, Thorne, "marry a Princess or something?"

"Something like that." Out of the corner of Jack's eye, he caught Thorne's expression mix surprise and disbelief.

An unfamiliar woman's face appeared on the screen; she was middle-aged, not unattractive, but matronly, and again, out of the corner of his eye, Thorne's expression changed to disappointment. "I am sorry," apologized the woman, "the Royal Family is not accepting any communications in this time of mourning. We appreciate your..."

"Excuse me," interrupted Steele, "who are you? And why are you answering Alité's personal device?"

Her demeanor switched from pleasant and condescending to indignant in a flash. "And who are *you...*" she snapped. "I will thank you to keep a respectful tongue in your head, and address Her Majes..."

"Admiral Jack Steele," he cut in, leaning closer to the screen, his voice measured. "And I'd *really* like to speak with my *wife*, Alité Galaýa Steele." The woman's expression went momentarily slack, color draining from her face, frozen in place, her mouth open mid-sentence. "*Now* would be good," he added.

There was a moment where Steele could swear she vibrated like a child doing the pee-pee dance. "I, I, I... *my apologies,*" she stammered, looking panicked, "please wait... *please.*" There was a high-pitched wail, cut off as the video feed dropped back to the holding screen, the flag waving at them again.

"What the hell was *that?*" blurted Thorne.

The seconds ticked away feeling like minutes, the screen winking back to a live picture, Alité Galaýa Steele, Queen of Veloria, staring back at her husband. Her eyes quickly changed from near black to brown to a vivid purple, her expression of irritation melting away, her eyes moist, her hands covering her mouth in surprise. "You're alive!" she gasped, tears running down her cheeks. "My King," she breathed, her hands lowering.

"My Queen," smiled Jack, fighting back his emotions lest they overtake him.

He heard a whisper to his left, *"Please tell me those are pet names..."* Steele reached across the desk and rapped his friend in the hand as discreetly as possible.

Alité's eyes shifted, "And who is this?" She wiped the tears away, awkwardly managing composure.

"Alité Galaýa Steele," Jack nodded toward Michel, "my friend of more than twenty years; Mr. Michel Thorne, of Antwerp Shipworks, Captain of the Black Widow. Michel, my wife; Alité Galaýa Steele, Queen of Veloria. The only woman in the Universe with the key to my heart..."

Michel Thorne smiled his broad smile, warm and genuine, not missing a beat, "I am pleased to meet you, *Your Highness...* you are married to a remarkable man."

"Thank you Mr. Thorne," she smiled brightly, "I am well aware of that. And I am certain, to have remained friends for as long as you have, you must be equally remarkable." She leaned closer, almost whispering, "May I ask a favor of you, Mr. Thorne..? Might I have a few moments of privacy with my husband?"

Michel's smile never faded as he rose from his chair, "Of course, you may have as many as you wish. I am sure you have quite a bit to talk about..." He patted Jack on the shoulder, leaning in, *"You did good, buddy,"* he whispered in his ear. He straightened up, clearing his throat, "I suddenly feel the need to call Rosa... tell her how much I miss her..."

■ ■ ■

There were a few moments of silence where they just stared at each other, smiles and tears mixed. "The Admiralty has you listed as lost or dead," she said quietly. "They notified us about four weeks ago."

438

"The reports of my demise have been greatly exaggerated," he smiled weakly.

"Your ship is missing in action. It disappeared nearly eight weeks ago and there's been no contact or trace of it since."

Steele's eyes clouded over with tears, and his voice choked, *"Fritz,"* he whispered. "Have they even searched?"

"The Admiral wouldn't tell me, something about protecting operational security. I am so sorry," she told him, wanting to reach out and touch him. "Will you search for him?"

"I'm not really in a position to do that right now."

"I miss you so much it hurts," she squeaked, her voice cracking. "I didn't want to believe I'd lost you... but then when you visited us..."

"Visited..?"

She explained the ghostly apparition of him that had appeared in Colton's room, then again, at a later date, to her alone. "You said, '*If you can hear me, I love you'.*" His face went blank; *did he remember that? Is that even possible? Had he been dead at some point?*

"Where are you, Jack?"

He shook it off, "We're in Madrassas headed to Nihlquist. Michel has a delivery to ArmaCore..."

"I'll send a ship for you..."

"No, no," he waved emphatically, "we're in *dark* territory. I don't want you risking any assets out here. And I definitely don't want *you* out here." He caught her change in expression, "Don't give me that look, *Missy*," he scolded, "I know damn well you'd be on any ship you sent."

"How long?" She put her hands together like she was praying, touching her lips with the tips of her fingers, "Before you're home?"

A number flashed in Jack's mind, followed by a star chart showing each and every system, gate and connection. "Twelve systems," he blurted, not understanding how he knew. Calculations he didn't understand or control, rolled through his mind, "Thirty-three days, thirteen hours..."

"Did you just figure that out in your head?" she interrupted, looking at him with suspicion.

"I must have seen it somewhere," he said slowly, not believing it himself.

"Because I know you, husband, calculus is not your one of your strengths..."

He dismissed it, "I don't know - It doesn't matter. God is bringing me home - to *my Queen...*"

439

*"**True Atheism:** The belief that nothing existed. And nothing was happening. And while nothing existed and nothing was happening, for no reason and without intervention, nothing magically exploded, creating something. Which mysteriously became everything. After nothing exploded for no reason into everything, a bunch of something which was previously nothing, luckily contained all the necessary building blocks for everything, and magically rearranged itself for no reason whatsoever. Without guide or plan, this nothing became something special. Something so magical, so intelligently designed, that it can replicate itself, can reason, is self-aware, can dream, explore, invent, understand, interpret, create, reach into space, yet be stupid enough to reason that everything came from nothing. **Yep, makes perfect sense.**"*

~ *Vice Admiral Jack Steele*

THE END - *FOR NOW...*

Other books in the series...

Book 1 - WINGS of STEELE - Destination Unknown

Book 2 - WINGS of STEELE - Flight of Freedom

Book 3 - WINGS of STEELE - Revenge and Retribution

The work on Book 5 has already begun. If life cooperates without too many obstacles, it will take about a year. No title has yet been chosen. For more information or updates, go to **wingsofsteele.com** *and send me a quick email to be added to my email list. I personally answer all emails, time allowing.*

ABOUT THE AUTHOR

Jeff Burger was born and grew up in Chicago, Illinois, moving to the Gulf Coast of Florida at the age of 28, where he still lives today with his German Shepherd, Jax. Jeff returns to Chicago on a regular basis to visit family and friends.

Originally drawn to law enforcement like his father and uncle, Jeff's extremely creative nature drove him toward a rewarding career in photography, illustration, design, marketing and advertising.

Jeff's choice in career and life in Florida have offered some truly unique experiences which he continues to enjoy. A certified NRA Instructor, Jeff has worked with civilians, Military Personnel and Law Enforcement Officers from many agencies. This has afforded him the opportunity to regularly handle and become proficient with firearms of all types, new and vintage, from all over the world.

An affinity for aircraft and flying have provided many opportunities to fly with talented civilian and military pilots in a wide selection of fixed wing and rotary aircraft. While Jeff finds jets to be supremely exciting, nothing beats the sublime sound or primal feeling of a piston-driven Rolls Royce Merlin V12 in a vintage P51 Mustang.

For more information about the author, additional Wings of Steele content, events, future novels, or to join my mailing list, please visit:

www.wingsofsteele.com

Made in the
USA
Columbia, SC